Killing Ground
A Novel of Africa

Phil Bowie

PRAISE FOR PHIL BOWIE NOVELS:

DEATHSMAN

"Bowie churns out impressive action sequences . . . escalates the narrative by piling on subplots. The North Carolina setting is top notch. Energetic and diverting."
—**Kirkus**

"John Hardin's adventures keep us turning pages. Enjoy." —**"Book Beat"**

KLLRS

"Good, solid, fast-paced adventure fiction from a guy who knows how to write it."
—**Stephen Coonts**, *NY Times* best-selling author

"An engaging action-packed tale. The story line is fast paced but also contains deep characterizations. Thriller fans will appreciate this entertaining tale."
—Reviewer **Harriett Klausner**

"Our enjoyment of *KLLRS* derives from good writing."
—**Rob Neufeld**, *Asheville Citizen-Times*

DIAMONDBACK

"A beautifully written high-octane thriller."
—**Ridley Pearson**, *NY Times* best-selling author

"An exciting suspense thriller with a touch of romance."
—Reviewer **Harriet Klausner**

"A combustible mystery with twists galore."
—***Romantic Times***

GUNS

"Enjoyed it very much. Fast. Engaging. A fine debut."
—**Lee Child**, #1 *NY Times* best-selling author

"Absolutely first rate. Outstanding read."
—Publisher **Helen Rosburg**

"Bowie did the homework to distinguish his *History-of-Violence*-style plot."
—***Publishers Weekly***

"A fine debut novel from a gifted writer."
—New Bern ***Sun Journal***

"Bowie, an instrument-rated pilot, breathes life into smart, cocksure Sam Bass, a man with a mysterious past."
—***Plane and Pilot*** magazine

"Bowie truly has a great plot."
—**Tammy Adams** at *Novelspot*

"Bowie is a skilled writer. I wouldn't have guessed this was his first novel."
—**Clayton Bye** at *gottawritenetwork.com*

"*GUNS* is an admirable debut. A good read."
—**Ken Wilkins** in "Book Beat"

GUNS **earned Honorable Mention at the London Book Festival**

This book is for Naomi

Also in memory of my parents, Erol and Edith, who taught me so much by word and example.

Copyright © 2019 by Phil Bowie
Published by Proud Eagle Publishing 2019

All rights reserved. No part of this book may be reproduced or transmitted in any form or by any electronic means, including photocopying, recording, or by any information storage and retrieval system, without written permission of the author, except where permitted by law.
This is a work of fiction. Names, characters, places, and incidents are the product of the author's imagination or are used fictionally. Any resemblance to actual events, locales, organizations, or persons, living or dead, is entirely coincidental.

Killing Ground

One

The female elephant was alert to potential danger from the huge cloud mass roiling high over the bush with its billowing turbulence obscuring the sun and splintering its light into golden spears. There were no bright tree-like flashes from it yet, but she had lived 63 years and had seen many such storms lash the land with lumps of ice and searing light. She knew the hot breeze that had risen at her back was nourishing the monster somehow. The base of it was turning darker and she was trying to discern which way the mass would choose to move.

The storm, or something else tugging at her instincts, was making her uneasy.

She was the acknowledged matriarch whose wisdom and rule were unquestioned, and she always stood ready to guide the 11 other elephants, including two of her daughters, out of danger. No adult males were with the herd; they were off foraging in pairs or alone because none of the females was in estrus, so the welfare of this elephant family was largely up to her.

In deep bass frequencies, she mildly cautioned the others to be ready to move and to keep the year-old male baby close.

The old cow was on her sixth and final set of molars, the previous five sets having been ground away over the decades in the ceaseless need to feed her four-ton body some 300 pounds of foliage, bark, twigs, and fruit every day. Her wrinkled gray skin hung on her as though it was a size too large. Her benign long-lashed eyes, naturally nearsighted as with all elephants, were somewhat dimmed by age, but she was still a savvy and formidable beast, quite able to command and counsel and protect her herd.

Because of the bumbling vulnerable baby, which had a penchant for straying off in curious happy pursuit of a waddling armadillo or a darting lizard or a fluttering egret, the matriarch was more attuned than usual to any potential threats, but there were only a few dusky white-striped antelope grazing at a respectful distance. They were long legged, long necked, and regal, with large conical ears, and the males carried their elegant corkscrew horns proudly. Constantly attentive to their surroundings, their abrupt bounding flight would serve as early warning to the elephants of any lurking predators, but they were displaying no unrest. The only other creatures evident were small skittery fire finches burning like licks of flame in the acacia foliage and in the nearby thorn bushes.

The matriarch's abiding fear was of lions. Her huge heat-dissipating ears were shaped like mirror images of the African continent. The right one was badly tattered along the outer edge and had a long narrow wedge of flesh missing. It was permanent evidence, suffered many years ago, of what lions could do when they attacked out of the tall grass in concerted ambush—swift and silent and deadly—and she was determined not to let them split the young one away from the herd with their clever diversions. It was a danger that always lurked in the shadows of her mind even though there had been no evidence of lions for days.

The herd kept on feeding. The matriarch and her eight-years-younger and smaller sister had found this stand of seven acacia trees a quarter mile from the edge of the forest. Their leafy domes 20 feet above were heavily decorated with delicious protein-rich seed pods. The sister cows had head-butted the stout rough trunks repeatedly, shaking loose many of the pods in a bountiful clattering downpour, and the herd was feasting, picking up the delicacies with their trunks, the ends shaped like two blunt opposed plucking fingers, and thrusting them past their heavy triangular lips. Rumbling with pleasure.

There was the first dull crack and grumble from within the angry cloud mass and a thickening gray veil of rain began trailing from it. But the rain was still some way off so there was little immediate lightning danger, and in fact the cooling showers on the fringe of the storm might bring welcome refreshment to the herd.

The matriarch slowed her feeding and studied the thunderstorm myopically. She noticed that the wind at her back had died away. As the rain descended from the dark belly of the cell in a torrent, it dashed a current of air downward as well, which spread out along the ground in all directions for miles, and it was not long before she felt that cool outflow coming from exactly the opposite direction than the hot breeze that had been blowing only minutes before.

She effortlessly uncoiled her heavy trunk with its thousands of intricately braided muscles, forming it into an S shape with the tip poised high over her head, tasting this new breeze with a sense of smell four times more sophisticated than that of a bloodhound.

Mingled with the pleasant fresh scent of the rain, she detected a trace mixture of rank offensive odors that sent an electric prickle of alarm through her great body and she emitted a warning. All the other elephants, except for the baby, instantly froze in place.

To flee might only call attention to the herd, and the young one would have a difficult time keeping up. Yet staying here in the partially concealing tree shadows might mean the danger would soon overwhelm them if it could not be driven off. She had to decide.

There were nine of them on horseback, each leading a pack animal. Each rider carried a worn and battered AK-47 with two magazines, rolled in beige plastic tarps and lashed behind their saddles. They were grouped just below the crest of the last rise in burning sunlight, their lathered mounts blowing in the heat, the thunderstorm cell churning high behind them. Their scout, Umar, had just returned to report the exact location of the herd. They had approached the elephants from downwind all morning through rough hilly bush riven with dry washes and sun-heated rock ledges, and they would retreat by the same route so the drivers of any vehicles would find it impossible to pursue them. But they were many miles from any kind of opposition here in the wilds of eastern Uganda near the Kenyan border, so pursuit was unlikely.

Their swarthy leader was Muhammadu Raza, born in West Africa, now a wanted outlaw plundering from his hideout deep in the foothills of the snow-capped Mountains of the Moon.

He prowled throughout several turbulent central African nations with a band recruited from the dregs of three different tribes. He was tall and gaunt, with ears that stuck straight out from his shaved head, a prominent beak of a nose, deep creases that ran down the sides of his long face from his cheekbones to his jaw line, his mouth a severe and lipless horizontal line. But it was his eyes that people never forgot. Close-set under an overhanging brow, they glittered like onyx, and when he fixed his glare on another man there was no mistaking the coiled violence that lay within.

He spoke to the men in the common Bantu Swahili because it was the one language understood by all of them, although, like many people in a dozen African countries, including Uganda, Tanzania, and Kenya, where he often roamed, he also spoke English, a legacy from past British influence. "We leave the pack horses here," he said. "You, Negash, will stay to guard them. We will approach slowly at first. Umar tells us it is good killing ground. They do not see well, remember, but the accursed wind has just now shifted, and they may easily have caught our scent, so if they run, we will whip the horses into full gallop on my order."

He pointed at two of the bare-chested sweating men, their skin like oiled ebony, features devoid of emotion. "You and you, go to the left and head them off before they can seek shelter in the forest. Do not let them get into the trees. Dawud and Yusuf, you will go to the right to half-circle them. The rest of you follow along with me in a line abreast. Remember to aim for the legs to hold them in place. Do not blaze away like crazy men. Cartridges are too costly to waste. Use single fire or short low bursts only, and only when you are close enough not to miss. Any man who damages the ivory will pay in a most painful loss of flesh from his back under my lash, I promise this. Stop them all and then move in close to finish them."

They unpacked their rifles, checking the actions and clacking the curved 30-round magazines into place, charging the first rounds into the chambers, clicking levers to safe, jamming the extra magazines under their belts, their horses now nervously side-stepping and snorting, sensing this would be the noisy violent time again.

They rode over the rise strung out in a ragged line, Raza in the center, the flankers on either end of the line beginning to head off to half-circle the small herd that was motionless in a close group under a thin stand of acacia trees.

The matriarch saw the indistinct line of movement atop the rise and saw the antelope cease their grazing and come to tense alert.

She roused the herd and got them moving slowly out from under the trees, following one of the faint elephant trails on a line that afforded easy walking and would carry them away from the threat at an angle and eventually closer to the forest where they could disperse somewhat and shoulder in amid the dense foliage for cover if necessary. There were several moments of confusion while the baby's mother and aunt tried to corral him with their trunks and get him going in the right direction underfoot with the rest of the herd.

The antelope stood uneasily, big ears swiveling and seeking, staring at the approaching riders. On some signal, they all suddenly broke and bounded gracefully away.

Raza urged his horse into a canter and the others slapped their horses' rumps with the tails of the reins to keep up.

The foul mix of scents was now strong to the old cow and her anxiety increased. These were bad odors she remembered from a place of many bloody elephant deaths she had happened across several seasons ago. She urged the lumbering herd to go faster, the baby running clumsily now, stumbling on grass tussocks and trying to avoid the clomping log-sized legs of the adults, its head bobbing and small trunk flailing. The matriarch hung back protectively at the rear of the procession, turning her great bony head repeatedly to judge the approach of the man creatures, which were now spreading out in a broader line.

Raza shouted an order and the men drove their sweat-sheened chuffing mounts to full gallop.

The old cow heard the increased pounding of the horses' hooves and felt it in the sensitive pads of her feet, and she came to a stop. Urging the other elephants to keep on as fast as they could, she wheeled around to face the threat. She waited until the line drew closer, swaying her head and trunk from side to side, her huge heart thudding faster as she sucked in gales of air with each breath.

She chose her target. A mounted rider closer than the others.

Raza saw the aged cow single him out and pulled his horse to a skidding halt on its haunches when he was only 200 feet from the beast, dropping the reins and slinging his leg over the pommel and vaulting to the ground with the rifle held high in his right hand, thinking, *she is the lead cow. Take her down and the others will be thrown into confusion.*

To the elephant, the dust cloud scuffed up by the horse seemed to amplify the threat and she committed. With her trunk curled under and her ears extended wide to either side of her head and the tops rolled back and rippling, increasing her apparent size to intimidate her enemy, she launched into full charge. There were harsh snapping sounds coming from off to her left and one of the elephants screamed.

Raza lost a moment in terrible fascination at the sight of this enraged beast charging down on him, thundering so hard he could feel the earth tremble, trumpeting a deafening blast of metallic sound. On a remote fringe of his mind he noticed something unusual about the old cow's tusks.

He raised his AK, flicked the selector to full auto, took careful low aim, and tapped the trigger with the pad of his forefinger, traversing rapidly from left to right as the recoil of half a dozen 7.62 mm bullets moving at almost half a mile per second lifted the muzzle. He saw at least three pinkish puffs of dust from leg hits.

For the stunned matriarch it was as though she had run into an invisible blade suspended at knee height. One of the jacketed slugs fractured her lower right leg, another passed cleanly through the flesh, and a third tore tumbling through the inside of her left leg higher up. Her forelegs collapsed and her tusks furrowed the earth, her trunk bending back between her legs painfully, her ears shuddering like gray sails that had lost the wind.

Raza left the dazed old elephant propped awkwardly on her knees and ran around her to take aim at another beast as it fled. He tapped out another carefully aimed short burst. Saw a finger of blood jet out. Watched its rear legs go loose and drag it to a halt, shrieking. Then he saw one of the men, still mounted, try to spray an elephant from the saddle, and he swore under his breath. *Wasting cartridges. Risking the ivory. Idiot.* The man's horse had dodged an ant mound at the last instant and the ragged burst flew too high, impacting along the elephant's side below its humped spine, and it bellowed its sudden pain and extreme fright and flicked its trunk frantically backward, trying to ward off the burning bullet hits as though they were monstrous insect bites. The man finally dismounted and emptied the magazine of his AK at the beast in a long angry chattering burst, raking it from neck to rump. It was the baby's mother and when she staggered and went down in a welter of dust the youngster was pinned by its hindquarters under her shoulder.

The matriarch heard the squealing of the baby through all the chaos of harsh snapping noises and whinnying horses and bellowing elephants, and she struggled up to stand on three legs, calling to the baby's mother. The sounds she heard in response told her the mother was badly hurt. The cow swung her head to maintain precarious balance and tried to hop clumsily on her bleeding left foreleg, attempting in vain to cover the impossible distance to the trapped baby. But she could not move more than a few yards.

The shooting went on until she knew that none of the elephants could any longer flee and it was hopeless. She stood unsteadily on three legs, raised her great head and trunk high, and trumpeted her revulsion and outrage at the man creatures.

The men were moving among the downed elephants now, still firing but in random single shots. She saw some of the man creatures lay aside their fire sticks and take up long knives and long-handled tools that had been strapped to their horses. They started swinging the blades into the warm flesh, working to free the tusks. Some of the elephants were still breathing and struggling weakly as the man creatures hacked at their faces.

The young one wailed in terror.

The matriarch still stood, head drooping, feeling pain she had never thought possible suffused by a depthless loss that was even worse. The harsh odors of unwashed man creatures and urinating horses and pools of elephant blood were strong.

One of the men swore loudly and used a single angry ax stroke to silence the annoying tuskless baby.

She saw the man creature she had earlier tried to attack walk up and lift the fire stick again, and she was filled with renewed hatred. She had guided her herds faithfully for decades and defended them against every hazard and threat, but against these reeking man creatures with their painful spitting fire sticks she had no defense at all.

The man fired and she felt another line of sharp hot burstings, this time across her belly and shoulder. She swayed and lost her footing and crashed to the ground and lay on her side, her rear legs weakly trying to find purchase. Breathing raggedly. Knowing she was torn and broken.

She had a terrible thirst. The pain was like several separate red-hot stones deep inside her, but the overriding grief at the loss of her herd family was a spear piercing her soul.

There was a searing crack of nearly simultaneous lightning and thunder and it began to rain fat drops that mercifully cooled her.

She heard a whirring-slapping sound, and with a supreme effort lifted her head slightly, rolling her wide left eye toward the new noise. Through her vast desolation she saw a violently thrashing machine that she knew must carry still more man creatures and her hatred flamed even hotter as her huge heart slowed to random thumps and her limbs spasmed and her sight began to haze.

Raza swung around to see the small helicopter approaching low and fast out of what little clear bright sky remained. The rain beaded on his bald head and made him squint.

The dark cloud mass was moving like an immense shroud across the killing ground.

Two

Ezekiel Blades, in a denim shirt, jeans, and tooled custom boots, was seated erect in a straight-backed padded leather chair on the supplicant's side of an expansive walnut desk in one of the glassy Spartan offices five stories down from the vertiginous summit of the ChemCorp building in Charlotte, North Carolina. His elbows were resting on the chair arms and his hands were laced loosely in front of his silver eagle belt buckle. The desk's owner, in a vested brown suit, was leaning back in his much larger leather executive chair. Round face fringed at the temples with gray. Round glasses. Round belly. Head cocked. One eyebrow lifted. The trace of a warm smile. Teddy Morton, executive VP in charge of personnel and human relations.

"So what you're telling me with all that nice rhetoric," Zeke said, "is I'm fired, as of right now." He felt like reaching across the desk, grabbing Morton's red silk tie with his right hand, and pulling the man forward to meet his left fist, watching the smile dissolve into an O and the eyes roll up white. But he backed down the beast inside and let nothing show on his own face. Controlling a ferocious temper was something he'd always had to wrestle with. It had gotten him kicked off the high school lacrosse team on the reservation all those years ago, when—after a swaggering muscular star player on an opposing team had repeatedly taunted him, cleverly and secretly tripped him, and finally surreptitiously and painfully smacked him on a kidney with the stick and walked away smirking—he'd felt the rage ignite, slung his own stick aside, overtook the boy in two long strides, and broke his arm. He had since read all the books on anger management and tried his best to channel and control his personal demon through years of Shōrin-ryū karate, eventually earning a third-dan black belt in that discipline without seriously damaging any opponents in contact matches, although a few had limped away colorfully bruised.

"Well, I wouldn't phrase it that way," Morton said. "Let's think of this as an amicable separation. We've been pleased with your services. Well pleased. It's been a mutually beneficial association, you'll have to agree. No complaints in your file other than two memos about the need to wear appropriate uniformed attire while flying. We *are* authorizing a full month's separation pay along with your accumulated paid vacation and sick leave. I'll be happy to provide a letter of personal recommendation, as well. You should have no trouble finding a position elsewhere. I believe I can speak for all of us in saying we'll miss you."

"And we're experiencing this friendly separation because?"

Morton looked at the ceiling. "Well, that really falls into the realm of privileged company information, but I *did* recruit you for our corporate family, what . . ." He lifted a sheet of paper on his desk and noted a date. ". . . just over four years ago now. So, I *do* feel a certain personal, ah, connection. Let's just say that one of our long-time board members has a niece who recently received her commercial pilot's license and is about to complete her Cessna Citation type rating. But you did not hear that from me." He winked, his smile lines crinkling almost audibly.

The demon was smoldering. He took a slow deep breath and said, "Tell her to remember she's in command when she settles her butt into that left seat."

"I'm sorry. I don't follow."

"In the past three months I've had to abort one flight and divert another because of bad weather. In both instances two of our corporate executive family members were agitated. On the latest occasion, strenuously so. They missed an important meeting or something. We exchanged a few heated words. I'm sure this wouldn't have anything to do with my separation from the fold, but I hope your new pilot will stand her righteous ground, because there'll come a time it will not be just her license at stake but maybe also the hides of important corporate family members."

Morton said, "Ah. Yes. I'm sure." He glanced at his watch and stood, smiling full force.

Meeting over.

Zeke got up and shook the offered round hand. Said, "Hey, it's sure been nice, Ted. You keep the ChemCorp family happy, hear? I'll see you."

Emerging on the ground floor from the whisper-quiet elevator into about an acre of awe-inspiring lobby, he saw himself in several of the artfully arrayed mirrors. Inch over six feet. Six-two in his boots. Lean. Long black hair pulled into a braid that hung down his back. Face like a beat-up hawk, as his best friend on the Great Smokies Cherokee Reservation, who also belonged to the Waya, or Wolf, clan had said—a blending of features inherited from his Cherokee mother and white father. High cheekbones and dark complexion from her. Lean build and luminous gray-blue eyes from him. His parents had compromised in naming him Waya Ezekiel Blades, which he used in full only for signing legal documents. His nose was distinctive in that it had been broken twice, once in a lacrosse game and once during a full-contact sparring match in a regional trophy contest. It now had a noticeable tilt westward. He had won the trophy.

That had been some years ago. In two months, he'd be 38. Damned near middle aged.

His boot heels rapped out a tocking cadence on the polished marble, echoing in the cavernous space. Nobody seemed to pay him any attention.

Outside, Zeke took a last look up at the imposing building that might have been designed to house a few thousand efficient stainless-steel androids. It was doing a precise job of coldly reflecting a sky strewn with drifting fair-weather cumulus clouds.

He wasn't feeling missed.

He thought about calling his copilot, Ed Wallup, a grizzled Vietnam chopper vet content these days to ride in the right seat until his pension could start, but Zeke knew Ed would find out about the termination soon enough and would take it philosophically and only somewhat regretfully. They'd been professional partners while flying, but they weren't close friends.

He found his unwashed black pickup truck in the multi-story garage next door and drove away looking for a decent restaurant where he could enjoy a leisurely lunch to commemorate the ostensibly amicable separation. Later he'd decide whether to hit the gym to beat and kick out some of the frustration on the heavy bag or go for a long punishing run in the public park near his apartment.

Maybe both.

It wasn't like he didn't have the time.

In fact, it was early fall, his favorite time of year. The trees were beginning to dress for the season in the highest elevations of the Carolina Smokies. New

England should be in full autumn glory. His parents were both gone. His white father had grown up in the Berkshires village of Williamsburg in western Massachusetts. He'd never been there, and this was as good a time as any to drive up there and explore his father's boyhood home country. A week or ten days would be soon enough to begin serious job hunting.

Three

It was mid-afternoon, and the lowering sun was an angry smear in a milky hot sky. Muhammadu Raza waited with Dawud by a bend in a disused dirt road not far from the dilapidated town of Nabilatuk, Uganda. Most of his other men and all the horses were concealed nearby in a stand of scraggly trees and brush. They had arrived 30 minutes ago and now he could see the single plume of dust stirred up by the truck drawing closer. Any other vehicles along this disused path in either direction would show similar plumes and there were none.

Raza wore an expensive engraved reproduction of the famous Colt Model 1911 .45 caliber semi-automatic pistol in a belt holster, a prized gift from his charismatic younger brother. He pulled it out, racked the slide to chamber a fat hollow-point round and cock it, set the safety, and slid it back into the holster, leaving the flap loose. Dawud stood at his side, cradling a loaded new and well-cared-for AK-47 casually. A trained former Kenyan military officer summarily discharged because of excessive zeal involving innocent civilians during an operation, he was an excellent marksman with the AK and with other much more sophisticated long guns. He was the only man in the gang Raza really trusted. In exchange for that trust, he gave Dawud a slightly larger share than the others, granted him the title of sergeant, and awarded him second choice, after himself, of the young women whenever they had occasion to visit one of the poor villages off in the bush in search of food and drink. Or just for sport.

The battered gray box truck appeared around the bend and rattled to a stop. It had a tall covered body and bore no markings other than yellow Ugandan plates with red lettering. Two men got out, each armed with a holstered pistol. The driver was Salvious Philemon. A large man in his thirties and black as night, with furtive eyes. He was dressed in a straw hat, sweat-stained khaki shirt with epaulets, threadbare shorts, and scuffed boots. His helper and bodyguard was a scarred brawler named Idi Wambuzi, who was holding a sub-machine gun casually.

Philemon and Raza exchanged nods.

Raza, ignoring Wambuzi, said in English, "I have much fine ivory, so you'd better have much money in U.S. dollars."

Smiling and holding his palms wide, Philemon said, "Have I ever not rewarded you handsomely? Now where is this supposedly excellent ivory? Show me."

Raza said, "But first I must ask you, Philemon, to open up the back."

Philemon shook his head, still smiling. He unlocked the truck loading doors and swung them wide. Swept a hand at the partial cargo of sacked maize, and said, "You are becoming increasingly suspicious and fearful as you advance in age my friend."

Raza waved a hand and the two men who had been training their rifles on the truck in the event it should contain ambushers rose into view from their positions in the tall grass on either side of the road, though they remained alert.

Raza gestured at Dawud, who jogged back to bring the others. They came out of the trees walking and leading the loaded pack horses. The ivory was wrapped in the beige tarps that also concealed the guns. Working quickly, they unpacked the tusks and laid them out on the ground behind the truck in neat rows, many of them still with clinging strings of red flesh. The men had pulled and discarded the thick conical central nerves from all of them.

Philemon weighed each one with a scale hung on the rear lip of the truck bed, Raza watching closely. He and Philemon each kept a separate tally on small pads. Idi stood off to one side, his eyes alert, still holding the sub-machine gun not quite casually.

The 11 elephants had yielded 712 kilos by Raza's count, or 690 kilos by Philemon's count. They argued and settled on 704 kilos, or 1,548 pounds. Raza knew he was being cheated by at least ten kilos and probably more because the scale was almost certainly rigged some unnoticeable amount in Philemon's favor, but Raza did not want to linger for a new tally, which Philemon full-well realized, of course.

Raza and Philemon climbed up into the truck cab, out of sight and sound from the rest of the men, and Philemon began the haggling. "These tusks are from eleven elephants, yet they weigh so pitifully little. Several have cracked tips and several more bear marks from the bullets and axes of your men. You should feel shame for bringing me this ivory. For such inferior quality I can pay forty-five U.S. dollars per kilo, and that only because I am a generous man."

"No," Raza said. "There are but a few scratches. Only two with cracked tips. No bullet gouges at all. You have noticed with drooling greed those first two tusks you weighed. They are from the old herd mother and are as close as you will ever find to a perfectly matched pair. They boast an uncommon whiteness and texture. They alone are worth a fortune, and you know this. You will pay sixty-two U.S. for each kilo I have brought you at great risk or my men will load this fine ivory back onto our horses and take it only a short distance to a wise man who will pay us most fairly. What will it be?"

They argued back and forth heatedly as the day grew 15 minutes longer before settling on 58 USD per kilo, which both men knew was within a dollar of the prevailing bush price, anyway. Both men also knew they needed each other equally for future transactions.

When they emerged a few minutes later, Raza was carrying a battered leather case containing $40,830 for the 22 tusks. He regretted only that he had not held back the special pair of tusks for more money in a deal with another smuggler he knew. They had been of almost glowing hue and of nearly perfect proportion, with graceful curve and even taper. With every elephant, one tusk is usually dominant. As virtually every human has a dominant hand, so that tusk is used more than the other and is thus commonly more worn and sometimes damaged. But the old mother's tusks had been near identical in size and shape and weight. They would be prized as a pair to the far-off carvers and collectors. But it was increasingly risky to hold illegal ivory, and that had prompted him to sell now while he had the chance. The other smuggler was some distance away to the north and a notorious haggler. He took a last lingering look at that special pair.

Philemon had of course noted those tusks right away, and now that the deal was done, he instructed two of Raza's men to wrap them together in dampened burlap.

About 40 percent of the truck cargo space was loaded with bags of maize. Raza stood back beside Philemon and they watched impassively as the other men removed most of the maize bags, loaded the ivory, and covered it all around with a thick layer of the musky bags, finally closing the doors and securing them with a strong padlock.

Raza and Philemon exchanged curt nods, each secretly more or less satisfied.

After the truck had done a sloppy roaring K-turn on the rutted track and lumbered off the way it had come, leaving a haze of fine dust in the air, Raza and his men faded into the trees and rode off through the bush.

By the time they had traveled to their rough temporary camp amid sparse trees, the sky was banded with burning ropes of cloud and dusk was beginning to darken into night.

Raza ordered a cooking fire to be built and he told the men they would be paid their shares but first they would dine on *chickwanga*—cassava cooked in banana leaves—and palm wine.

After the meal and liberal swigs of the wine, with Dawud standing at his side, Raza lined up the men and paid each a share of the money left over after he had kept back $35,000 for himself. When he came to the man who had so recklessly expended rounds just to clumsily kill one elephant, he withheld a portion of that share and berated the man loudly. "You fired like a crazy man against my orders. You risked damaging the ivory or killing one of the other men. You are lucky I do not choose to make an example of you with the lash." The man refused to meet Raza's lethal stare and accepted his reduced share with contrition.

Later, after much more wine drinking, as the men were lounging around the fire laughing at crude jokes about this one's legendary prowess with women—although seldom with willing ones—or another man's poor horsemanship, or that one's inability to prevent money from flowing through his fingers like water, one of the men swayed out from behind a bush, his eyes sheened with drink. He stuffed himself back into his filthy khaki shorts, zipped up his fly with some difficulty, and walked boldly up to Raza, who was sitting on the ground with his elbows on his knees, gazing into the flames.

The man said in a loud voice, "I think you have been cheating us. You need to pay us bigger shares."

The chatter and laughter ceased.

In the hush, Dawud calmly picked up the rifle that was propped against a tree and stood up beside Raza, who had not moved, his gaze still fixed on the fire, elbows on his knees, long hands dangling. He said, "You have already taken more than your share of wine, Metuba. Go sit down."

"No, we put our lives at risk, yet we do not share equally in the dollars. We are being cheated. This must not be so any longer. *No.*" He shook his head drunkenly.

Still not looking at Metuba, Raza let his gaze roam the faces of the other men. He saw sullen challenge in several of them. That, he could not allow. He sighed, stood, and brushed dust from his jeans with his hands. He pulled the .45 from its holster and shot Metuba in the neck. He watched without expression as the man's hands flew up like claws, trying in vain to staunch the sudden rush of blood from the severe wound. He flopped down hard on his back in the dirt, choking and jerking violently for long seconds, and then his eyes rolled white and his hands fell away. The breath rasped out of him as he twitched. His right leg jumped with a final spasm and he went still.

The rest of the men were silent. Staring at the body. None looked at Raza.

Raza safetied and holstered the pistol. In a firm controlled voice, while glaring around at each of them in turn, he said, "I give you far more in a single easy harvesting than you could otherwise earn in a year. I give you food and drink and soft young women and boys. I give you guns and cartridges and horses. I protect you from the murderous rangers. I find the biggest elephants for you. I know the best buyers. I have many powerful friends in high places who demand payments to shield us. You know all these things." He placed his hands on his hips, and shouted, "WITHOUT ME YOU ARE NOTHING."

He let the silence linger for a moment, and then pointed down. "This one forgot all of that. Look at him. His blood is soaking into the dirt. He will never again be rewarded with any share at all. There are hundreds who would gladly take his place without complaint. Hundreds."

His eyes glittered blackly in the sparking firelight, and he said, "Even now I know where there is a rich herd. We are going to go and harvest it. If you want to share in that you will follow me without question. If not, you can slink away into the bush on foot and go back to the starving village you came from while the rest of us dream fine dreams. Now, drag this one away for the scavengers to feast on. We leave at first light."

* * *

Philemon and his man Idi took turns driving the dusty nondescript privately rented truck through the night, trending steadily southwestward on bad dirt roads through small squalid towns and villages, skirting the city of Kampala by a safe margin. They saw few other vehicles and nobody challenged them or even took much interest. By dawn they had covered the 320 miles to Goma on the western shore of Lake Victoria, just north of the Tanzania border, where they had rented the truck. There, from a derelict dock outside of town, they loaded the ivory onto a rotting wooden fishing trawler, which would take it and them south into Tanzania. They would offload the ivory at Mwanza, well west of Serengeti National Park, and they would drive farther south in another closed truck—rented from a farmer who asked no questions—crossing the Ugalla River near Kitunda, west of the capital city of Dodoma, and they would stop for two days to pick up more ivory and highly valuable black rhino horns from another poaching gang.

They had three more scheduled pickups in various remote places over several days. Finally they would turn the truck toward the east and the port of Dar es Salaam, where the tusks and horns would linger briefly in a back-street warehouse and then be secreted in one of the thousands upon thousands of shipping containers constantly moving through the sprawling port docks with security that was often indifferent or corrupt.

From there the load would voyage by ship to China, where the comparatively modest 700-plus kilo ivory hoard from the 11 elephants that Raza and his men had killed would alone be worth roughly $1.5 million. As the great herds all over Africa dwindled and the ivory became more scarce and risky to take, so the black-market prices rose dramatically, adding yet greater incentive for those who hunted it and smuggled it and eased the journey to market and for those who ultimately hugely profited at the end of that chain.

Back in Africa most of Muhammadu Raza's lion's share of the prize, and of others like it, would be turned over to his handsome younger brother, who had split away from al-Qaeda and renamed himself Abdul Ahad, slave of Allah, and who was pulling together a small fanatically loyal force to be known henceforth as al-Isra after a magical night journey of the Prophet. The money would help finance this new holy arm of jihad against the infidels.

Four

Zeke Blades was sitting on the sofa in his modest apartment in a Charlotte suburb, a cold Coors sweating a sticky ring onto the glass-topped end table, his laptop on his knees, sending a half-dozen résumés out to various corporations.

He'd spent eight days roaming the Berkshires, immersing himself in the culture and spectacular fall scenery there, imagining his father, Walter Blades, as a boy and a teen attending a small hill town school, picking shade tobacco in the Connecticut River valley at age 14, riding the back roads on a bicycle, fishing for trout in the clear mountain streams, going on chilly hay rides with cider and apple bobbing back at a neighbor's barn, roaming the woods with his border collie at his heels. It must have been a fine upbringing.

His father had been in his mid-20s when he'd gone south to take a lumbering job in western North Carolina, where he'd met a shy Cherokee woman named Awanita Highpine, a lucky happening for Zeke because out of their union he'd been born. More than once Zeke had marveled at the one-in-a-million chain of events that had woven together in perfect synchronicity over many decades to produce himself, the winner of a lottery with odds so long and convoluted as to verge on the impossible. Yet here he was. Every person alive on the planet was, in fact, the winner of their own unique personal life lottery with similar long odds. He wondered how many appreciated that.

For Zeke, the interlude in the Berkshires had been both enjoyable and enlightening.

His smart phone on the end table beside the couch emitted an eagle's shriek.

He set the laptop aside and said hello without looking at the number.

She said, "Hello, Wolf Blades. I'd know your voice anywhere, even after these three years. I'm glad you didn't change your number. How are you?"

"Kate," he said neutrally, although he felt a surprisingly warm flush. "Why the hell would you be calling me?"

"Oh, let's don't start off that way. Like they say, it takes two to make or break a relationship. We had great fun while it lasted, didn't we? I hope we've both moved on."

She sounded nervous.

He said, "Both of us didn't skip off into the bushes with that lipstick salesman."

"Roger was only selling cosmetics and therapeutic preparations for a while to get back on his feet after his business partner in their pest control venture drank them into bankruptcy. But that's all behind us now. He's a top performer in an award-winning dealership right here in Hickory. We've got big plans. Where are you living, by the way?"

"Still here in Charlotte. Same apartment. A new couch. You sound on edge. Is something wrong?"

Katherine Stone—or whoever she was now if she'd gone and actually married the salesman, whose name he chose not to remember—was the 12-years-younger sister of his former flight instructor, Ben Stone, who, beginning well more than a decade ago, had encouraged and lectured and verbally whipped him all the way from starry-eyed airport-haunting wannabe through his private, instrument, multi-engine, and commercial ratings and then on to type certificates in sleek Leer, Citation, and King Air business planes. He owed much to Ben Stone, and there were few people on the planet he admired and respected more. At some point in his intensive training, which he'd paid for by bartending in two high-end saloons while living ultra-frugally one social class higher than a hopeless derelict, he had met Ben's stunning brunette sister, felt an immediate and overwhelming stirring in his loins, and proceeded to make a total fool of himself over her.

"Why did you call me, Kate?"

"Why can't I just've called to reminisce a little with a nice person who once meant so much to me? Somebody I find myself still occasionally having warm and cozy memories about. Do you remember when you flew us out to Ocracoke Island on the Outer Banks in that bumpy little Cessna? The walk on that deserted beach in the salty wind under that practically full moon? The musty second-floor room in that creaky old inn with the bay window overlooking Silver Lake Harbor?"

How the devil could I forget? You were silhouetted in the blue moonlight streaming in that window . . . He cleared his throat. Said, "Not particularly. What is it you want, Kate? I have paperwork to do here."

The phone went quiet.

After a long moment, he said, "Kate? You there?"

Then, in a subdued voice threaded with deep concern, she said, "Oh, Wolf. It's Ben. He seems to have gone missing and I didn't know who else to call."

* * *

The shadows were lengthening in the piney Hickory duplex development where Katherine and her new man were renting an apartment. She and Roger Baxter sat on their couch holding hands.

Zeke sat opposite them in an overstuffed chair. He thought the engagement ring Katherine wore on her left hand was too big to be a real diamond. But the anxiety in her eyes was genuine.

She said, "I called because you and Ben were very close during your training and I thought you might be able to help."

Zeke said, "What was he doing in Africa?"

"He was flying an absolutely ancient round-nosed high-wing plane with two oversized front tires and a tiny tail wheel. Something ridiculously called a Beaver. Somewhere I have a picture he sent."

A de Havilland Beaver, he thought. *Old taildragger with a radial engine. Still a good short takeoff and landing bush plane.*

Katherine said, "He's been flying food and medicines out of Dodoma—that's the capital of Tanzania—to remote villages and clinics. Doing some emergency medevacs. Landing on rough dirt roads sometimes. Working for a nonprofit organization called Global Health Resources under a three-year contract."

"He loves what he's been doing, we know that," Roger said.

"One day a week and a half ago he didn't show up at the Dodoma airport for a scheduled flight," Katherine said. "Nobody's seen him or heard from him since. We've talked by phone with the people he was working for, several branches of the Tanzanian police, the U.S. embassy, everybody else over there we could think of. Nobody has been any real help at all. It's as though he just vanished."

Zeke said nothing. Ben had gone missing at about the same time he'd been fired from ChemCorp. He told himself, *Ben's a tough, smart old bird. Must have had some good reason for not reporting in.*

Roger said, "We were hoping you might go there and ask around. You know, find out who his friends were, who he talked with at work and at the airport. Somebody must know *something*. I can't get away from the dealership right now and I don't know anything about flying, anyway. And Africa's just too dangerous a place for Katy."

She said, "We thought you might have vacation time coming, a week or two, and you could sort of poke around over there and see what you can learn. You know all about flying. But more important, you know Ben."

"We don't expect you to do it all at your own expense," Roger said with sincerity. "We've got some money saved up. We'd want to cover your airfare, at least. We'd insist on that."

Zeke's estimation of Roger clicked up a few notches. The man seemed real even if he was too damned pretty by half. He blew out a breath and stared out the window, watching two squirrels performing a frenetic spiral up a fissured pine trunk. A mad chase. It looked like they were doing it purely for the hell of it.

He had many mental pictures of Ben stored away. Stern, strict, uncompromising instructor. Burly stoic presence. Quiet man who commanded respect. Steel-strong friend. It had been far too long since he'd been in touch with the man to whom he owed so much.

He looked back at them and said, "I'll give it maybe ten days. See what I can find out. I'll cover my own expenses." He stood up and accepted a small spiral pad from Katherine that contained her notes about Ben, his mailing address and phone and contacts with the relief agency and others, and he let her brush his cheek with a kiss.

Roger followed him outside to his pickup and said, "We really appreciate this. Look, I know you must feel like I horned in on your relationship with Katy, and for that I apologize. But she's happy. We're happy. You can see that. I promise I'll take good care of her."

They shook hands stiffly and Zeke gave a parting wave as he drove away.

On the drive back to Charlotte, he thought, *Okay, what do we know about Africa? Really big continent. Couple million square miles bigger than all North America, if we remember our geography right.* He knew there were about four dozen assorted countries, quite a few of those shaky. Sandy Sahara nations like Egypt and Libya and Tunisia and Algeria at the top of the continent were strung out along the southern shore of the Mediterranean. Impressive animals roamed all over the place between there and Cape Town, South Africa. Vast rain forests with big artfully decorated snakes. Exotic flora and fauna. Long rivers like the Congo containing lots of teeth. Beautiful diverse countryside. Snow-topped Mount Kilimanjaro. The Leakey family had dug up some millions-of-years-old humanoid fossils in the Great Rift Valley.

And then he thought, *Places with unpronounceable names. Bloody tribalism that periodically wipes out hundreds of thousands in genocides with guns and clubs and machetes.* Real tall guys with long spears. Real short guys with frog-poison darts and blow guns. Suicidal terrorist cells. AIDS, dengue fever, Ebola, malaria. Widespread poverty, even starvation. Life expectancies a dozen years behind the rest of the world. Entrenched government corruption. Crime so prevalent it was like a quaint social custom. *Do they still have headhunters? Or is that South America?*

There'll be some simple reason Ben's gone out of touch. It'll probably be a wasted trip.

But he couldn't shake a vague dark sense of foreboding.

Five

Zeke spent the next two days shopping, packing, raiding his savings account for traveler's checks, stopping the mail delivery, notifying his landlord and credit card company, and adding shots for typhoid, hepatitis A, and rabies to the routine immunizations he'd already had for travel as a corporate pilot. He walked out of his doctor's office with prescriptions for Cipro and preventive malaria medicine and stern warnings not to drink unpurified water or eat anything that had even been washed in local raw water, and to use plenty of quality insect repellant and sunscreen.

He checked in with Katherine, who sounded even more distressed and told him there was still no word from or about Ben, so he booked a round-trip flight to Dar es Salaam leaving at four thirty-five the next afternoon, a Monday, with layovers in Frankfurt and in Addis Ababa, Ethiopia, arriving in Tanzania at one forty-five Wednesday morning and returning 15 days later, by which time he figured he should either have found out what had happened to Ben or he likely never would. Total flight time would be 20 hours and 50 minutes, the layovers adding almost five and a half hours to that. He had time for two good workouts at his local dojo. He was working to learn a difficult and strenuous ten-minute kata—a training exercise that was a blend of simulated fighting moves and tightly-controlled poses and balanced flourishes. He was trying to perfect it to his sensei's satisfaction.

Later that day he got a call from a large highly rated west-coast import/export company he'd queried by e-mail.

"Mister Blades, you have an impressive record," a warm female voice said. "I'm Samantha Godwin, VP of personnel. We recently purchased a new King Air and we're interviewing pilots. We'd like to talk with you. Fly you out here at our expense. We'll make the arrangements with a commercial carrier and put you up in one of our executive suites onsite. How does that sound?"

Tempting, he thought. He'd always favored the muscular turboprop King Air. But he said, "I'm sorry. That sounds great, but something's come up. I need to leave the country for the next fifteen days."

"Oh, I see. We do have other applicants in mind, actually. Shall we just leave it that you'll give us a call when you're free, then?"

He thanked the nice voice and hung up, knowing it was unlikely the position would remain open for long.

The next afternoon he left his pickup in the apartment driveway and took a cab to the Charlotte airport, allowing plenty of time for check-in and the TSA routine. He had everything he thought he'd need packed in a single large suitcase.

As the huge plane crossed the coast, heading out on a great-circle route to Europe at seven miles high and 80 percent of the speed of sound, Zeke was staring out the scratched plastic window at the empty Atlantic Ocean, knowing absently the air had to be about 65 below zero, Fahrenheit, just six inches from his nose. He was deep in thought.

With a smile, he recalled a cold blustery afternoon when Ben was in the right seat of a much-abused

Cessna trainer plane with his arms folded like a belligerent square-jawed football coach, wearing an Eagles cap, inscrutable behind his big mirror sunglasses. Zeke was in the left seat, midway through his instrument training, with the hood on so all he could see were the Cessna's controls and dials and his approach plate clipped to the center of the yoke. The engine droning faithfully in the nose and the prop slicing the dense frigid air.

He was gripping that yoke tightly with his left hand, fighting the turbulence, freeing his right hand to operate the throttle, flaps, and instruments. Trying to keep the yaw under reasonable control with the rudder pedals. He was flying a simulated blind approach to Hickory Regional Airport, descending out of a tricky racetrack holding pattern on a heading that would take them to the threshold of Runway 24.

Suddenly Ben erupted with, "What the *dirty devil* are you *doing*?"

"Huh?" was all Zeke could manage. "This damned gusty wind . . ."

"You telling me you're hopping around like a berserk rooster because you can't fly in a little *breeze*? You don't even know where in *hell* you are, do you? You trying to land on Eye Forty?"

"What? No, I . . ." There was suddenly a hollow feeling eating away inside him, and he began to doubt everything. The erratic instruments. His timing. His actual position. Had he set the altimeter correctly earlier? There were hills around. Four tall towers near the airport. Was he really heading for Interstate 40 instead of the runway? He fought the urge to throw off the hood so he could *see*. But he took a breath, checked the approach plate, let the tension leak out of his left arm and hand, resumed his steady instrument scan, and thought, *No. Everything's okay. It's fine. Calm down. You're doing this right.*

In a controlled voice he told Ben, "We're good. Heading two-two nine. We'll intercept the localizer well out from the threshold."

"Maybe," Ben said in a stern voice over the headset. "But your belly turned to jelly for a few seconds there, didn't it? Don't you *ever* forget Ben Stone's famous unwritten law. If something bad is gonna happen it's bound to hit you at the worst possible time, when you've got your hands full and the weather is going down like an elevator with its cables cut and you're bone tired after a long flight and you gotta piss and you're skinny on fuel and it's like somebody spray-painted the windshield black. But that's just when you've most gotta keep your cool. The instruments are all you have so you've gotta trust 'em. Doesn't matter a damn what those little voices are screamin at you inside your head. I remember a time I was trying to land a ratty Seminole on one engine in a blizzard . . ."

Zeke realized what Ben had been doing. The crafty son of a gun had been purposely trying to rattle him at a critical moment in a difficult procedure. It had almost worked. And Ben was still trying to distract him in a different way now, much as some nervous and chatty future passenger might, rambling on in a quiet voice he had to strain to hear. So he tuned out the chatter, called the tower to report eight miles out as ordered, was cleared to land with the option to make it a touch and go, intercepted the localizer beam and banked onto final approach smoothly, not overshooting, and brought the Cessna down the glideslope, feeding in more flaps with only a slight crab into the wind. He saw the marker beacon instrument on the dash blink slowly at the outer marker, then more rapidly at the middle marker, Ben still mumbling away, and he reached his minimum descent altitude, flipped up the hood, saw the runway centerline a bit off to the right, corrected, passed over the rapidly-beeping inner marker, and landed with only slight twin chirps from the main tires. He retracted the flaps, flexed the fingers of his cramped left hand, relaxed with a big grin, and looked over at Ben, expecting praise.

Ben shrugged, face impassive, big arms still folded. He said, "Give her full power. You're cleared for the option, so let's go up and do it all over again, except this time you're gonna . . ."

Zeke had a trove of memories like that involving Ben.

He lit up his iPad and began reading web pages he'd hastily saved earlier about Tanzania. He skimmed an item about Rwanda claiming that over two million U.S. dollars in coltan from its mines, destined for Asia and Europe, had disappeared at the Dar es Salaam port, and it was not the first time such cargos had mysteriously evaporated. Government and port officials were denying any knowledge, saying unscrupulous suppliers or truck drivers must have switched the container cargo to cheap cement bricks before arriving at the port. The truckers were in turn blaming port officials. Coltan, the article said, was the metallic ore columbite-tantalite, vital for making circuits in everything from cell phones to laptops. Found here and there throughout turbulent central Africa, it was in high demand, worth up to 400 USD a kilo to buyers. A coltan miner could produce a kilo, or just over two pounds, a day and make up to $50 a week, whereas the average unskilled worker's pay was $10 a month.

Another article lamented the fact that slash-and-burn agriculture was rapidly deforesting and degrading the Tanzania land, although it did at least account for half the low gross domestic product of $690 per capita.

Some 40 percent of the country's 50 million people lived off the land in Tanzania at well below the basic-needs poverty line and with only minimal and sporadic health care, a lot of that provided by international relief agencies like the one Ben had been flying for.

Crime was commonplace. There were warnings about tourists being robbed at gun or knife point or forced to withdraw cash from ATMs or to arrange cash transfers through Western Union. Some were being kidnapped for ransom. Dar es Salaam visitors were cautioned not to carry much cash and to shun unlicensed taxis and people acting overly friendly. Even the better hotels and the popular upscale beaches like the ones on the offshore island of Zanzibar, and the port city center itself, weren't entirely safe. It was suggested tourists leave their passports and other important documents in their hotel safes and carry photocopies for ID.

The rate of exchange, at least, was great for budget-minded American tourists, with 100 USD equal to about 219,000 Tanzanian shillings, and the dollar was steadily growing stronger. Forty USD would get you a nice city motel room, and ten or less would buy a full top-end meal.

An hour and a half later, somewhere well out over the ceaselessly-heaving Atlantic, rapidly boring deeper into the dark shadow of the planet, he turned the iPad off and slipped it into his backpack, suspecting with an itchy sense of unease that Africa could turn out to be more difficult, frustrating, and dangerous than he'd thought.

He leaned his head into the corner between the seat and the cool plastic cladding, folded his arms, and tried to will himself to sleep, knowing he'd need to be alert when he got there and for unknown days thereafter.

The overhead vent whispered a cool narrow stream at him in the darkened cabin.

Drifting off, he thought, *Where the hell are you, Ben? What's happened to you?*

Six

Zeke gazed at the scattered lights that sprawled in a ragged jumble around Dar es Salaam as the big jet descended over flat terrain and landed at Julius Nyerere International Airport, named after a long-time controversial socialist leader who died in 1999.

The terminal, though not as large or impressive as those in many American cities, was surprisingly modern, with tall clustered umbrella-shaped roof structures built of exposed wooden beams, each supported on a single heavy pillar. The facility appeared to operate in efficient chaos, with a good number of travelers walking purposefully here and there, all wearing the universal air-terminal zombie expressions and towing their wheeled luggage briskly even at one-thirty in the morning. It took him an hour to retrieve his single large suitcase and clear customs, submitting the tourist visa form he'd downloaded and filled out in advance and paying $100 in cash. After a short ride in a dusty and dented but licensed cab he checked into the plain tin-roofed Transit Motel on Nyerere Road, waking a sleepy black woman who greeted him with a shy smile. He paid her $50 cash for two nights in a room that was basic but clean with mosquito netting surrounding an old four-poster bed. He took off his boots and jeans and shirt, stretched out, and laced his fingers on his stomach to get some sleep in the quiet room.

He woke with dawn light coming in the window. Wearing only his briefs, he put himself through a rigorous series of crunches, squats, push-ups, lunges, and exercises involving trying to pull apart a rolled-up towel, working one muscle against another in moves that included all the major groups, following up with a series of stretches. He showered and strapped on his money belt, which also contained his ID and passport, and dressed in jeans, scuffed boots, a western shirt, and a crushable Stetson that would shield his face and neck somewhat from the brutal sun. He took his time over a simple breakfast of excellent strong coffee, eggs, and homemade bread, studying a city map the woman at the desk had given him, marking it up with the places he intended to visit that day.

He decided to put off renting a car and to use cabs instead, mostly because he wanted to walk around the city's heart to get a feel for the place and to get some more exercise because he still felt sluggish and jet-lagged after the long flight. The cab the hotel desk clerk summoned for him was no more or less battered than cabs in New York or Chicago and its bored driver was no more or less reckless, though they drove on the left side of the road here, which he figured had to always be strange and disconcerting at first to any American. To make this even worse, most African nations, like bordering Congo, drove on the right side. So there was a mix of African vehicles, some with steering on the right, some on the left.

He began with the U.S. Embassy, which occupied a 24-acre site on Old Bagamoyo Road in the downtown Msasani section. The large secure and well-landscaped compound was enclosed by a high perimeter wall. The complex had been built after a 1998 al-Qaeda embassy bombing that had killed eleven people.

He showed his passport to the beefy suspicious chief gate guard, who said, "Mister, ah, Waya Ezekiel Blades. Do you have an appointment with somebody on the embassy staff, Mister Blades?" The man pronounced it Weigh-ah. The correct way was Wah-ya, but Zeke said nothing.

"No," Zeke said. "Just flew into town this morning early so I haven't really had a chance. But it's about an American who was working for a relief agency and who's apparently gone missing. I've been asked by his sister back home to see what I can find out. I thought the embassy might be able to help. The sister was in contact with an official here by the name of Nancy Daniels."

The guard stepped back into the shack and picked up a handset while two other well-armed guards watched Zeke impassively.

The big guard emerged and said, "Arms straight out at your sides and feet apart please, sir." He ran a wand over Zeke's extremities and torso. It beeped at his beltline and he lifted his shirt to show the silver eagle buckle. The guard nodded and said, "You understand an appointment is usually mandatory, Mister Blades, but Mister Robert Dodds, an embassy aide, will see you." Pointing inside the compound, the guard directed him to the Chancery Building. "Just sign in with the receptionist. Have a good day."

He was kept waiting for a half hour and then shown into a small conference room. Robert Dodds, a short serious man with wire-rim glasses, ruddy cheeks, and sparse hair entered, shook his hand, and closed the door. They sat on opposite sides of the table, and Dodds listened to Zeke's story, jotting an occasional note on a lined yellow pad.

"Is that all you have?" Dodds said.

"That's all," Zeke said. "Except it's not like Ben to go off on a bender or just not show up for a scheduled flight without calling in with a damned good excuse. He's a solid, experienced, responsible guy."

Zeke watched that register with Dodds, whose face became distant and slightly glazed. Like the expression on a harried bureaucrat trying in vain to whittle down the perpetual line at the DMV.

Dodds said, "I see. It would, of course, be nice if we had a bit more to go on. You say this sister has been in touch with Nancy Daniels in our deputy chief's office?"

"It's what I was told."

"Yes. Well, Nan and I often work together, and I'm sure she'll have started a file on this, but she's out of the office at present for a few vacation days. I'll talk with her when she gets back. We'll certainly look into the matter as best we can, but I have to tell you it doesn't seem we can be of much help. Have you checked in with the Tanzanian Police? The Oysterbay Station is just around the corner. A few minutes' walk." Standard bureaucratic response. Pass the buck.

"My next stop."

"Good, good." Dodds glanced at his watch and stood. "I'll find out what we've learned to date about your friend and make some further inquiries with contacts I have. Please feel free to call or text me or Nancy anytime. We have your phone number and we'll get in touch if we learn anything more at all. Here's my card."

The man seemed well-meaning in a detached sort of way, but Zeke had the distinct feeling whatever inquiry would be made was doomed to falter and fail and be buried under routine paperwork.

The Oysterbay Police Station had khaki-clad officers wearing red berets going about various tasks at a languid pace. Zeke worked his way through the system to a portly coal-black officer of some higher rank dressed in a crisp blue uniform over a white shirt and black tie, seated behind a worn but clean office desk. His name was Salim Jumbe.

Jumbe laced his fingers across an ample belly and said, "So, how may we help you today, Mister . . ."

"Zeke Blades. I'm looking for information about a friend who's gone missing. A pilot named Ben Stone. Works for a charitable organization called Global Health Resources." He told the whole story.

Jumbe listened stoically with one eyebrow raised and the trace of an indulgent smile. He said, "And is this all you have Mister Blades?"

"Afraid so."

"You say the police headquarters in Dodoma has been notified?"

"Yes. Specifically, a sergeant named . . ." He consulted his spiral pocket pad. "Named Pinda."

Jumbe picked up his desk phone and, after some difficulties with connections, was able to raise the station in Dodoma. He waited patiently, eyeing Zeke with what seemed to be mild amusement. "Yes, Sergeant Pinda. Jumbe in Dar. I have a man here, an American named Blades. He inquires about a supposed missing person named Mister Ben Stone. A pilot working for an agency called Global Health Resources, with a small office there at Dodoma airport." He listened with no change in expression for 20 seconds. Said, "Ah, yes. I see. Well thank you for that information Sergeant. Yes, you as well." He hung up the phone, shrugged, and re-laced his fingers over his belly. "Sergeant Pinda has little to offer, I am afraid. He has investigated this matter with all diligence and has found no evidence at all of anything amiss. Are you sure that your friend has not found amenable companionship and decided to have a romantic interlude off somewhere in privacy? Or perhaps he has joined a camping safari into the bush. One of our world-famous wildlife preserves. Your friend may turn up at any time now, and we both can most certainly hope that will be the case, no?"

"So. That's it? That's all you intend to do?"

Jumbe spread his hands and shrugged again. "If you develop further information, be so kind as to let us know." He reached into his top desk drawer and said, "Please accept my card. Call me at any time."

Zeke scratched his name and phone on a notebook page, left it on the desk, and stood.

Jumbe said, "One thing, Mister Blades. Allow me to suggest you should take much care during your stay here. Africa can be unsafe for visitors these days. It is a sad fact."

Zeke added the card to his small collection, nodded, and left.

He walked back past the embassy compound and then along Mwai Kibaki Road, exploring several side streets at random. There were plenty of people everywhere, to the point of clogging some of the streets that were lined with jumbled overflowing shops, but there was less vehicle traffic than you'd encounter in any American city of comparable size, and the cars and trucks were smaller and older on average. There were a lot of bicycles and battered motor scooters and dusty popping and smoking one-cylinder motorcycles. Few wore a helmet. In a shopping center called Mayfair Plaza, opposite a modest hospital, he found a clean-looking eatery called the Safari Grill and had a light lunch outside under palm trees that clattered in a warm breeze, watching the colorfully dressed people going about their affairs in an easy relaxed manner. The day had heated up considerably and he was beginning to regret choosing long jeans.

He took another cab to the headquarters of Global Health Resources, Ben's employers. It was a long low white stucco building with a rusty tin roof on Chato Street near a questionable Chinese restaurant. Inside the rusted steel front door there was a small undecorated and empty waiting room with three metal chairs. An empty reception office was behind a counter with a sliding metal pass-through tray and heavy wire mesh from the countertop to the ceiling. There was a button by the tray. He pressed it and heard a muted buzzing somewhere inside the building. In 30 seconds, he pressed it again, holding it a bit longer. After another half minute he was about to press it yet again when a thin man in denim shorts and a loose white T-shirt, who resembled the late singer David Bowie, entered the reception office, glared through the wire mesh, and said with a British accent, "Yes. What is it?"

"Zeke Blades. I'm here about a man who works for you. Ben Stone?"

The man's features softened. "Oh, I see. Yes, yes. His sister called again yesterday and said to expect you coming round. Mr. Blades, isn't it? Just a minute." He disappeared, and the waiting room door opened. "I'm Walter Iverson. I attempt to run this place against all odds." They shook hands and he said, "This way. We can talk back here. My office. Sorry, but we're damnably busy as usual and we're short-handed, also as usual." He led the way to a cramped, cluttered room with a barred exterior window and several file cabinets. Zeke had to move a stack of folders and publications to the floor so he could take the only seat other than the desk chair, which the thin man flopped into.

Zeke said, "I take it you still haven't heard from Ben?"

"No, we have not. It's a dark mystery. But then, sadly, this is Africa, isn't it."

Zeke had always been amused at the British penchant for seemingly asking questions for which they neither expected nor wanted answers. They were masters of the rhetorical.

"Yes, Africa," Iverson was saying. "Land of many mysteries. We made inquiries, of course. To no avail, I'm afraid. May I ask, by the by, what is your association with Stone?"

An actual question.

"He was my flight instructor. Took me all the way from rookie through instrument and commercial. And he's a friend."

"Yes. Quite. I see."

"What, he just failed to show up one day?"

"Precisely, yes. We had a most important flight scheduled out. Well, they're all important, aren't they. Our de Havilland was fueled and loaded and waiting there at Dodoma. He simply never appeared. No call from him, no message, no hint of anything amiss. At first, we thought it was merely bloody inconsiderate of the man. But quite odd. Especially since he'd been so reliable up to that point. Then as time has gone on we've begun to suspect something off about it. With downright sinister shadings, I'm afraid. There's a lot of unrest in Tanzania and surrounding countries at the moment. Damned Islamic militants marauding again. And tribe against tribe. It's the scourge of Africa, isn't it. Bloody tribalism."

"So you've talked with all his associates and friends? Checked with likely hospitals?"

"Of course. And not a clue. Everybody with GHR is equally mystified. It's as though he just vanished. I daresay it's left us in a bind, as well. We have two very much part-time pilots we can call on when they're rarely not otherwise occupied at much higher rates than we can pay, but Stone's disappearance has put us way behind on all fronts, hasn't it." He cocked his head and his eyes took on an intent new gleam.

"What?" Zeke said.

"It's just that you'll be wanting to speak with the people at Dodoma for yourself, I expect?"

"Yes."

"Then our interests align quite well, I should think. Let me explain. It seems we have a new plane. Well, I say new; it's actually quite vintage. A four-seater Cessna donated two months ago by a kind widow in the UK. Old girl even paid to have it ferried to us, although it's a serious question how we're to find the fuel and maintenance money for it in the budget. It's just now at the rather primitive general aviation facility here in Dar. Gives us a fleet of two, don't you see, although with not even a single pilot to be counted on. The new plane needs to be got to our hangar in Dodoma. As the fates would have it, you're needing to go there as well to inquire after your friend. So, you'll fly our plane over at absolutely no cost to yourself. Gives you a chance to see Tanzy countryside from the air in the bargain. No need to thank me." And he smiled for the first time.

Zeke saw nothing wrong with the arrangement, so he said, "Okay. That's a deal."

"Where are you staying? Do you have a rental vehicle or are you cabbing about?"

"I'm booked through tonight at the Transit Motel out near the airport. No rental ride yet."

"Fine, fine. Elizabeth should be back from her late lunch any moment now. I'll have her run you out to the airport. I'll call ahead to the gen-av terminal, so they'll be expecting you. You'll have a look at the plane, check her oil and whatnot. Make sure she has all her rivets and such. Kick the tires. Assure yourself she's ready to go. Tomorrow Elizabeth will pick you up at your hotel and deliver you to the airport. Shall we say ten-ish? Now if you don't mind I've a long list of tasks waiting. No hope of catching up today by half. If you'll leave your information we shall advise of any developments." He stood.

Zeke said, "Okay, then," He wrote his name and number on a pocket pad page and Iverson took it.

Iverson showed him back out to the small waiting room and said, "Elizabeth will be along shortly to collect you. When you try your best to do good things, as we do here, sometimes the fates cooperate. I'm sure you've found that to be true. Most fortuitous, you popping up just now."

"Sure," Zeke said.

"Ah, just one other small thing, by the way. Tomorrow morning Elizabeth will be bringing along your passengers and their supplies."

"Passengers?"

"Yes, yes. Only a husband and wife. They'll be no trouble at all. None at all. Wonderful couple. I'm sure you'll quite enjoy their company. I do hope we'll meet again, Mister Blades, and I hope you can find our Ben."

Elizabeth turned out to be a happy middle-aged blonde who had an air of brisk efficiency. She kept up an animated cheerful discourse about the wonderful work GHR was doing all over Tanzania as she drove him out to the airport in a venerable Rover so he could inspect the plane, which he discovered was a blue-and-white 1975 Cessna 182 Skylane that was in remarkably good condition, although it only had original-style analog instruments augmented with a simple portable GPS. The tach showed just 600 hours since engine overhaul, so it had a lot of time left before major engine work would be due. It was a good load hauler and relatively forgiving to fly, though he suspected it would need new fat tires and maybe a short-takeoff-and-landing, or STOL, kit for the kind of work that would likely be demanded of it here. It had about a 1,000-mile range, depending on cruise speed and altitude. There were the usual signs of wear, a scratch and ding here and there, a missing cowl fastener, a few rips in the seat fabric, but he could find no serious issues with the Cessna and was looking forward to flying it.

Elizabeth drove him back to his motel, stopping on the way at a restaurant so he could get a take-out meal.

After eating in his room, he went for a long run, watched the local news on the small room TV, and turned in early.

Seven

Philemon and his bodyguard, Idi, were in the back recesses of an outwardly shabby but secure warehouse near the Dar es Salaam docks just after midnight, showing the ivory they had picked up over the past two weeks to the woman they worked for. The load was about to be secreted in the rust-streaked unmarked shipping container that rested nearby on a flatbed trailer. Along with the poached black rhino horns that Philemon had bought on his way south from a source, it would be crated deep inside a load of coffee and tea. The rhino horn was much more valuable by weight than the ivory, more valuable than gold, in fact. To the right buyer in Asia it could bring 60 thousand USD a pound. But ivory was still much favored by this woman.

Her name was Yang Feng Kwok, and her reputation in the underground approached dark legend. She was short and stout, with a round pale and puffy face, a small stern mouth, and a wide flat nose. Black hair cut with bangs in front and chopped off just below her ears on the sides and back. She seldom wore any makeup. Her oval eyes were anthracite beneath arched black brows. She was supervising the weighing, measuring, and documenting of each tusk to avoid being cheated when it was offloaded at the end of its journey. She knew that Philemon was skimming, probably by claiming he'd paid more of her money for the ivory and the horns than he had, and Philemon knew that she knew, but as long as he did not become too greedy, she allowed it, mostly because it was difficult for her to know precise details of the dealings with the gangs out in the bush, although Philemon had for some time suspected that Idi might be informing her as her paid spy. Nobody in the trade was to be completely trusted and anybody who expected to last any time in it had better realize that.

At one point Kwok stopped the men who were doing the meticulous weighing. "Wait. Those two tusks. Who did you get them from, Philemon?"

"That devious killer Raza, ma'am, the one with the insane jihadi brother who is calling himself Abdul Ahad, leader of that ragtag new al-Isra bunch. Are they not beautiful? So perfectly proportioned and nearly identical. So unusual. Taken from an old matriarch. I knew you'd like them. We gave them special care."

She walked over and stroked their cool, silken surfaces. With the merest hint of a smile, which was as much as Philemon had ever seen her display, she said, "Yes. Exceptional." She looked at her lead man and said, "Bind these together with utmost care. Mark each of the root ends with a blue star. They are to be delivered to my personal artist in Guangzhou. I know the perfect buyer for them."

Philemon smiled widely, showing his two gold teeth. He performed a little bow. "I am so glad you're pleased, ma'am."

She walked over to look up at him, fixing him with that steely Asian squint that made him feel she could see all the way inside him to his spine. She said, "Yes, you have done well once again, Philemon. And you will be rewarded accordingly. I rely on you heavily, and I'm sure you can always be trusted. Unlike some we've known who have met unfortunate ends."

"You've been most generous, and you will always have my loyalty, ma'am."

It was not the first time she'd made veiled threats, and he wondered once again if half the stories he'd heard about her ruthlessness with rivals, traitors, and those who'd attempted to cheat her too brazenly were true.

Surely not.

Still, Yang Feng Kwok had risen a long way in the four decades since she'd emerged from the slums of Malaysia to carve out a prominent place for herself not only in the tangled Tanzanian underworld but also in legitimate businesses, some of them largely cash-based—restaurants and bars and a South African casino—and thus all excellent money-laundering machines. To Philemon, it wasn't much of a stretch to imagine her having amassed her fortune by stepping over the cooling bodies of uncounted others. Nobody really seemed to know just how much power she wielded or the true extent of her wealth.

He felt a momentary chill despite the hot humid night.

Eight

Zeke was packed and ready when Elizabeth picked him up in the old Land Rover in the morning. He slid into the front passenger seat on the left side and turned back to look at the older couple. Elizabeth cheerily introduced them as George and Linda Robertson, who smiled and nodded. Both were somewhere in their middle 60s. She was liberally dusted with freckles. He had tinted prescription glasses. Both had on roomy multi-pocket khaki shorts and white shirts with epaulet straps. He wore an Aussie hat with the brim pinned up on one side and she wore a ball cap. They had the leathery, studious, slightly sunburned look of people who spent a lot of time outdoors digging up old bones or hiking the wilderness in search of strange bugs. They were lean and fit. He reached back to shake their hands.

Elizabeth was saying, "George is our very finest volunteer doctor. I don't know how he does it. And Linda is an absolute Nightingale. Lord knows how many poor people out there in the dark countryside owe their lives to these two. Multiple hundreds, certainly."

George said, "Don't let Lizzy turn your head, Mister Blades. I'm just a simple country sawbones from the Tennessee hills."

Linda said, "So, you're the new pilot for GHR?"

"No. I'm just here trying to track down a friend. Ben Stone. I need to get to Dodoma, same as you."

George said. "We know Ben well. He's flown us here and there and medivacked some of our patients back to the hospitals at Dodoma and Dar. Good man. Hell of a pilot. We heard he'd disappeared. No further news there?"

"No," Zeke said. "Nothing I've been able to find. When did you see him last?"

"Our last trip here, seven months ago," Linda said

"Did he seem troubled at all to any of you? Distracted? Could he have had any health problems?"

Elizabeth shrugged and shook her head as she steered the Rover onto the general aviation terminal road.

"Not to me," George said. "We've exchanged letters and texts with him since, but nothing I can think of in his messages would offer a clue. He's seemed upbeat as always. Haven't heard from him for at least a month, though."

Linda said, "You know, I did have a mild suspicion something was . . . occupying him. Perhaps weighing a bit on his mind. No clue what. I hope there's some simple explanation."

Zeke nodded.

He was thinking about the flight. Dodoma, despite being the capital city, harbored fewer than half a million people, whereas Dar es Salaam was home to some four and a half million. The capital was 360 road miles west from the port city and 3,500 feet higher, but only 246 straight-line miles by air, or an hour and a half in the Cessna. Should be no problem.

When Elizabeth pulled up beside the plane, which was roped to tiedown rings buried in the pavement near the terminal, she told Zeke, "It's fueled and loaded for you. Ready to go. See Liana when you get there, and thanks for doing this. It's a big help, really. Please let us know whatever you find out about Ben, and we'll do the same, I promise."

The doctor and his wife stood by while Zeke did a thorough walk-around. The baggage compartment was nearly full of what looked like food and medical supplies. Whoever had loaded it had left a note taped to the pilot's yoke that it totaled 83 pounds. Zeke did a quick calculation. With that load, full fuel, their three large suitcases, which he figured at 50 pounds each, and himself and the medicos, he'd be loaded heavy, but he could keep the center of gravity within limits if he put Linda in back with the three suitcases on the seat and floor beside her and the doctor up front with him. It helped that the airport was not far above sea level and the day had not yet heated up to full intensity, so lift would be good. He would burn off fuel weight in transit.

There were even four quality headsets that came with the plane, and each of them donned one. Zeke cranked it up, opening his side window and the vents to let in the cooling wash from the slapping prop. He called the tower, taxied out, and did a run-up behind the hold line for runway 32. The tower cleared him for takeoff and he swung out onto the centerline, feeding in throttle. The takeoff run was somewhat longer than the 700 feet listed in the manual because of the load, but the brawny Cessna lived up to its legendary reputation as a load hauler and had no trouble lifting them into the burning sky. He leveled off at 2,500 feet and took up a heading for Dodoma, with somewhat cooler air rushing in the vents.

The sky was strewn as far as they could see in any direction with dazzling fair-weather cumulus clouds that cast slow-moving shadows onto the terrain below. A chaos of low-end buildings, most of them rusty tin-roofed shacks, interlaced with dirt roads meandering in no particular pattern, spread around the port city. Urban blight, African style. The jumble thinned out and gave way to bush with low trees scattered here and there, and unevenly geometric crop fields—cassava, agave, sisal, coffee, and tea, George pointing out which field was which. A single narrow paved highway stretched away westward through the dusty reddish landscape.

Over the headset, George said, "It's a puzzle. About Ben, I mean."

"It is that."

The doctor gazed out his side window as the miles scrolled slowly by below, the Cessna bounding gently in the building thermals. He said, "But it is Africa, after all. And it's got more perplexing puzzles and seemingly unsolvable problems than you can count."

"Must be tough trying to administer health care here."

"It's a challenge, for damn sure. We mostly work out of a bush clinic in the Biharamulo District, about three hundred fifty miles northwest of Dodoma, south of Lake Victoria. Way out in the boonies. We're well supported, of course, by the GHR people. It's only a basic facility. Twenty beds for recovering patients. Has a minimal lab with basic diagnostic instruments. A small primitive surgery that would be absolutely illegal anywhere in the U.S. We do have electricity, at least, but it's not always reliable. We have an ancient generator, but limited fuel for it. Linda and I work there whenever we can, in loose rotation with three other volunteer teams from the states and the UK. Sometimes we'll have medical students helping. When the word gets out that we're back again, the people will start lining up from all over, some having traveled many miles on foot. They'll wait patiently for hours. Days, even. Never know what we'll get for cases.

Hernias, goiters, thyroids, tumors. There's always typhoid. Injuries of all kinds. We'll do vaginal hysterectomies, emergency caesarian section deliveries, radical mastectomies, amputations. Many cases are aggravated because the conditions have gone untreated far too long. Too many people don't have adequate nutrition or sanitation and they're a lot worse off than merely poor. Big part of the problem is there are just too many people throughout central Africa, period. I don't mean to be so bleak about it. Working for GHR can feel pretty good at the end of a long and tiring day. We're making a difference. Anyway, that's our story pretty much. What's yours? You fly for an airline back home?"

"Nope. Guess the commercial carriers sounded too boring when I finally got my ticket. Hauling herds between the same two cities every day wasn't appealing. I chose the corporate path. Flying a few VIPs all over the place, mostly so they can make a lot more money because they never seem to have enough. But it's always different and I get to see some nice places."

"So you're taking vacation for this search?"

"Not exactly. I got fired recently to make room for a new pilot with better connections. It's not a problem. Lots of other jobs out there. I only need one."

"Well, we hope you can find Ben."

"Thanks," Zeke said. "Do my best."

Nine

As the land gained elevation under the Cessna and Zeke climbed lazily to compensate, it became wrinkled with rolling hills and then crusted with jagged low mountains. On the other side of the chain, it leveled out into a vast grassy plain dotted with trees and clumps of brush, with increasing signs of habitation as they drew closer to the capital city. There were a few herds of grazing wild animals. A group of elegant giraffes. It seemed strange to spot them outside the confines of some zoo.

Coming in over the outskirts of the city, which was plainly a lot smaller than the port city, there was a steep-sided small mountain that looked to Zeke like a juvenile volcano that had blown its top. He called the airport and they cleared him to land on the single runway. He taxied to the tin-roofed hangar that George said was rented by GHR. He shut it down on the apron. The sliding doors were open, and Zeke saw the unmistakable round nose of the radial-engined yellow de Havilland Beaver inside. It looked like there would be just enough room to squeeze in the Cessna.

As they were climbing out of the plane, a woman emerged from the hangar and walked briskly over to greet them, smiling, dressed in the usual khaki shorts and white shirt. She was not beautiful in any stereotypical sense, but she was certainly striking, and Zeke felt something shift inside him. She was . . .

exotic. Mid-30s. Long raven-black hair pony-tailed. Slender but not too. Light brown silky skin and piercing hazel eyes and he thought, *one black parent, one white*. That plucked a chord because of his own mixed parentage. He realized he was staring and reached to help George extricate the luggage for all three of them. The woman embraced Linda and George and offered her hand to Zeke, saying in a British accent, "You'll be Mister Blades, then. Liana Sekibo. You have an interesting first name. Means wolf in one of your native tongues, I believe."

He'd noticed she wore no rings. And no makeup, which he thought she didn't need, anyway. "Uh . . . yes. Cherokee. North Carolina mountains. Call me Zeke. I'm here to—"

"Of course. Iverson briefed me quite well. Shall we step inside the hangar? Bit cooler in the shade."

Trailing their wheeled suitcases, they followed her into the hangar, where a large black man on a stepladder was polishing the high-winged Beaver. She waved a hand at the man and said, "Zeke, this is Dante, who keeps the plane, excuse me, *planes* now, in flying condition and is helpful in numerous other ways. Dante, this is Zeke, pilot and a friend to our Ben Stone."

Zeke smiled and held up a hand and Dante nodded back.

After some happy catch-up chat with the Robertsons, she turned to Zeke again and said, "George and Linda are staying with friends in the city tonight and will be heading out in the morning. I suggest you inquire round the airport as you wish for the rest of the day, and then you'll stay in the caravan behind the hangar while you're here. Save you a bit of money. It's where Ben Stone himself has been staying, so maybe you'll pick up a clue amongst his belongings.

Tomorrow morning we'll much appreciate it if you'll fly George and Linda out to the Biharamulo clinic in the de Havilland. Saves a long drive, you see."

Zeke snorted and said, "Are all you people with GHR like this?"

"Whatever do you mean? Oh, I do see. Iverson shanghaied you into delivering the Robertsons and the Cessna here and you think I'm doing more of the same, is that it? But surely you see the reasoning. You'll want to speak with the people at the clinic because Ben frequently flew there and one of them might know something. After resting up just a bit, the Robertsons must go to the clinic because word will already have got out and people in frightful need will be waiting. It dovetails perfectly. We also have food and vital medicines that can be hauled quite easily and safely to the clinic in the de Havilland within just a few hours, as opposed to a long and arduous trip by Land Rover." She pronounced it med-sins. "And not all the roads are safe these days, sadly. It seems some extremists are rampaging again. So it's really no contest whatever, is it. I'd say in for a pence, in for a pound, far as you're concerned. So, you'll do it then, Mister Blades?"

"Ah . . . okay. Why not? Sure."

"Splendid." She said, "Dante, please transfer the load from the Cessna to the de Havilland, since Zeke has kindly agreed to wing the Robertsons into the hinterlands, and please also load the consignments for the clinic and for the mission at Urambo as well. Get her fueled for long range and ready to go in the morning, oh eight hundred hours."

Dante nodded and seemed to eye Zeke with uncommon interest.

"Urambo?" Zeke said.

"Oh, just a quick stop, preferably on your way out to the clinic. Bit off the track but it should pose no serious problem provided the weather's as forecast. There are dirt strips at both places that have always suited Ben quite adequately."

After Liana had driven off toward the city in another beat-up elderly white Land Rover with the Robertsons and their luggage aboard, Zeke spent some time examining the Beaver and studying its instruments and controls while the black man was busy loading it. He went through all the seat pockets and glove compartment, discovering nothing that might be a clue to Ben's whereabouts, taking the logs and manual back to the 30-foot camper trailer, which Liana Sekibo had called a caravan, for later study. He wanted to take maximum advantage of the remaining daylight, so he only gave the camper a cursory scan, left his suitcase inside, and then began nosing around the airport, talking with anybody who knew Ben, from the mechanics to the lone tower controller. To a person, everybody spoke well of the man and nobody had any idea why or where he had disappeared.

When he seemed to have exhausted the local people of any useful information, he spent an hour going through the camper thoroughly. What disturbed him more than anything was that too many of Ben's clothes and personal items were still there. If the man had planned on going somewhere for any length of time, he should have taken things like his toothbrush and razor and shaving cream and alarm clock and rain gear with him. He poked through the closets and cupboards and shuffled through receipts, letters, magazines, and personal papers without finding anything that caught his attention. He found a rubber-banded sheaf of sectional charts that together covered all of Tanzania and much of the rest of eastern and central Africa, and he spent some time looking them over. They'd been marked up here and there with cryptic notes, none of which made much sense.

There was a single framed five-by-seven photo on the bedside table of an earlier Ben Stone and his late wife. For whatever reason, they'd had no children. She'd died from a bad heart at 59, and Ben seemed never to have fully recovered from the loss. The two had been college lovers and by all accounts so close that people who knew them could not imagine one without the other. That was somehow evident in the photo, in part maybe in the easy way they seemed to be leaning toward each other slightly and wearing similar smiles.

He put himself through a series of exercises and stretches, trying to shake off the lingering jet lag, managed to take the semblance of a shower in the tiny space allotted for it in the camper, and went for a long walk out along the airport road and for some way into the city, winding up for a meal back at a rustic restaurant in the airport terminal, where he also bought two bottles of Kibo Gold beer and a box of crackers.

The setting sun was torching the whole cloud-streaked sky in a glorious display that was fading toward violet and shades of soft gray by the time he got back to the camper. Large aggressive mosquitoes were whining around his ears as he let himself in, so he applied a coating of repellent in case any of the damned things had slipped inside with him and he settled in at the small dining booth to study the manual and logs for the Beaver.

He had only ever flown in the type once, and then not even as pilot in command but as a passenger. Still, he felt confident he could handle it. He did have some taildragger experience, albeit in an old and much smaller turtle-backed Cessna, so he was aware of the breed's peculiarities at least. The lack of much initial forward view on the takeoff roll because of the raised nose as it sat tilted back on the twin tall main forward gear and the small tail wheel, for example, and the tendency for it to suddenly swap ends during taxiing if the pilot wasn't attentive enough with brakes and rudder.

It was full dark outside, and he was memorizing the Beaver's vital statistics—stall speeds, ground roll for takeoff and landing with the STOL modifications, useful load, fuel burns at various rpm, range, ceiling—when there was a furtive rap on the flimsy door.

He got up and opened it to see the big muscular man who had been polishing the plane earlier.

He said, "Dante, right? What can I do for you? Is there a problem with the Beaver?"

The man looked both ways outside and said, "Dante James. They call me DJ. No, no, the plane is ready to go. No problems. It's a great old bird. I maintain it for GHR, part-time, and help out with chores around their hangar when I can. But I work on the field for other owners, too."

"You're a certified mechanic, then."

"Yeah. Freelance now, though. Got my ticket back in Jersey. You, ah, you mind if I come in?"

"Okay. Sure. Take a seat. You want a beer? It's not much of a refrigerator but it seems to keep things fairly cool."

"Ah . . . yes, that'd be good." Zeke noted he had a New York City area accent.

The big man seemed nervous. He sat in a thinly stuffed chair. Zeke retrieved the two beers, popped the tops, handed one over, and sat sideways in the cramped dining booth so he could look at the man directly. He took a pull on the beer and said, "What is it, Dante?"

"Ben talked about you. Respected you. Said you were one of his best pilot students. A good friend."

"So . . ."

"So I've been thinking I can probably trust you. You gotta give me your word that what we talk about here will stay between us, though. You gonna be okay with that?"

The beer looked lost in his big fist. He had not taken the first swig of it and he seemed uncomfortable holding it. He was bouncing one large leg up and down slightly on its toes, rapidly, unconsciously.

"That depends," Zeke said. "Something you need to realize upfront is I'll do whatever I have to for Ben. If he's in trouble that I can't help him get out of myself, if I need to call in the law, then that's what I'll have to do. All I can say is I'll try my best to keep whatever you tell me in confidence. Keep you out of it if I can. Best I can promise. If you know anything at all that might help me find him, Dante, I'd appreciate hearing it, because I have to say so far I'm stumped. His disappearance makes no sense on any level."

Dante used his free paw to scrape the beads of sweat from his mostly bald head, then wiped it on his grease-stained shorts.

He set the untasted beer aside on an end table and said, "Okay. Okay, then. Look, I may be able to help you find him, but first you gotta let me tell you a true story. You need to understand some things."

Ten

The big man took a breath and seemed to calm down a few rpm. He hunched forward, meshed his meaty fingers, elbows resting on the chair arms, and gazed at a spot on the vinyl camper floor. He said, "Her name was Tyke."

Zeke took a sip of beer and said nothing, letting the man get to it in his own time.

After a moment, he said again, "Her name was Tyke. She was found wandering, dehydrated and half dead, after a culling operation in Chiwewe National Park. That's in Zimbabwe."

"Excuse me, culling operation? That another name for a tribal massacre?"

Dante shook his head, which was beaded again with sweat. He met Zeke's gaze. "Sorry. She was a baby elephant. It's how she got the name Tyke. The rangers in Chiwewe were trying to save some of the elephants. They had a good number of them contained within Chiwewe Park for protection from hunting, see? But the park vegetation could only take so much elephant grazing. So they were faced with letting the numbers get too high for the available food supply, the herds then stripping the countryside, degrading their health, and starving. Or they had to control the numbers by culling."

"You're saying to save some they had to wind up killing some," Zeke said.

"I know. Sounds like screwed-up logic, but there it is. They don't do culling in Africa anymore, though. Anyway, Tyke was the only survivor of a culling. She eventually found her way into ownership by the Barrington Corporation back in the States, based in Florida. They owned the Doyle Circus and two other smaller carny operations. Years ago, before I got my mechanic's ticket, I worked for the Barrington Corporation as an elephant trainer. See, I was taught that to control elephants you had to show them who was master, and you did that by hollering at them and beating them. You ever seen an elephant routine in the circus?"

"Once, some years ago."

"Then you'd have noticed the short heavy stick with the hook on the end that handlers carried. It's called a bull hook. Used to prod and pull the elephants into doing tricks, like standing in a line, each elephant's forelegs up on the back of the elephant in front of it or, you know, an elephant standing on its hind legs and extending its trunk, rearing up, a sexy lady on board. What you didn't know was we used the bull hook to beat them during training, but always with the right hand. To get them working, to make them follow your commands, you'd hit them where it was sensitive, behind the ears or under the chin or on the legs. During the act in the ring, you'd use your left hand to manipulate them with the bull hook. If any one of them got balky, all you usually had to do was shift the stick to your right hand like you were gonna start hitting, and you'd speak in a strong voice, and the elephant would do what you wanted.

"But Tyke, she was different. I spotted it the minute I first saw her. She was thirteen and still green. A little smaller than the average African elephant. Right off it was clear she wouldn't respond as usual to beating. Maybe she had bad memories from the culling that orphaned her, had a deep-down distrust of all humans, I don't know. I still tried to dominate her but not by beatings, just with a strong voice. But I also gave her affection, you know? In the wild they touch each other all the time, so I did the same. Petted her. Let her rub against me. Talked to her like a friend, at least outside the training sessions. And it seemed to be working great. I guess you could say we bonded, you know? It was . . . a good feeling. After a while she was ready to join in some of the acts. She even seemed to like all the lights and the noise and the music sometimes while she was in the ring. It went on like that for almost four years.

"Then in Dayton on the last day of a contract run it was cloudy and windy with thunderstorms around, and she was nervous goin' into the tent. Real edgy. I could sense it. A couple of brainless teenaged kids got rowdy. They threw clods of dirt at her and she spun around before I could stop her and made a short mock charge at the kids. Just a stomp or two. Scared the crap out of 'em, the little bastards. It was nothing, really, but it took me a few minutes to distract her and lead her back out of the tent."

Dante was quiet for a moment, examining his hands, lost in thought. Zeke sipped his beer and waited.

"So okay," Dante said. "One of the little bastard's parents complained. The boss said I couldn't handle Tyke. They took her away from me and gave her to a new trainer who beat her bad. A few months later the Doyle Circus was due to perform in Honolulu. The contract said six elephants, two more than usual, and they decided to include Tyke. I told my boss it was a bad idea because she wasn't acting right at all, but he didn't listen. He just wouldn't listen. They chained them all up by their legs for two weeks in the damned ship's hold. I went along but only as part of the general crew and a back-up handler. I could tell Tyke was hating the whole thing. She was right on the edge. The first night of the Honolulu run when they tried to bring her out with the others she balked as soon as she got inside the tent, so the trainer hit her hard on her back leg, using his right hand. She wheeled on him, and when he raised the bull hook at her again she pushed him down with her head and pinned him there. Big elephant, little human. She crushed the life out of him. I don't think she meant to. She just wanted the hitting to stop, you know? The other elephants were calling to her. She stood there, not letting anybody come close, but not charging anybody, either, swinging her head side to side like they do when they're real upset. I tried to approach her with no bull hook, my hands wide, you know? Talking to her real easy. But she'd just flat had it. She turned and headed out of the tent, brushing aside a guy who was in the way. Didn't injure him, just dumped him on his ass. She made it through the crowd and off the grounds and was running along a city street, not trying to hurt anybody, only trying to get out. Get away. Get free.

"Well, the Doyle manager called the cops and word got out she'd killed the trainer. So, killer elephant, right? Elephant gone rogue, they said. Elephant gone crazy. The cops that showed up started shooting her all over her body with their goddamned pistols and shotguns. She was flinching and trying to brush away the wounds with her trunk, you know? Just running along the street. Some news ghoul got it all on video. She just kept trying to run away and they just kept chasing and shooting her. It went on and on. Some civilian idiot hit her a lot with a light rifle, a goddamned twenty-two or something. They shot her eighty-seven times. *Eighty-seven times*. They shot her *eyes* out, man. Some of the people who saw it were crying. Screaming to just stop the shooting, for God's sake. Finally, Tyke, she kind of collapsed, leaning over against a parked car. Still breathing. Not moving. But they were still shooting her and it took a while for her to die. Later they had to bring in a big backhoe with a chain so they could lift her body onto a flatbed and take her away."

"Damn, man," Zeke said. "I'm sorry."

"Yeah, well I quit that day. Told my boss to go screw himself with a bull hook. Paid my own way home. Some good came out of it. Hawaii banned big animal acts. Finally, the American circuses stopped using elephants at all. I'll burn in hell myself for the way I treated 'em."

Dante went quiet and after a moment Zeke said, "Look, I'm sorry for all that, man, but we were talking about what might have happened with Ben."

"Yeah. I'm getting to that. Few years ago, I got to studying on how elephants all over Africa were bein' killed for their ivory. You know, back in the late seventies there were a million and a half elephants in Africa. Now there are only about four hundred thousand left. Here in just Tanzania the herds are down from over a hundred thousand to less than forty thousand over the past five years. They finally made the ivory trade illegal in some places, but there's still a big legal demand in Laos, Cambodia, Vietnam, Thailand, Taiwan, Burma, Malaysia. They sell it on the black market in China and the Philippines. Rich collectors will pay big money for carved pieces. I mean we're talking hundreds of thousands. It's ironic, man. The less ivory there is, the more it's worth on the black market. So there's more reason to go after it than ever, even considering the high risk. Poachers are driving the herds to extinction. I came here to try and seriously do something about it. Try to square things a little."

"I've heard about that. Elephants. Rhinos. Some of the big cats. I guess a lot of the big animals are under heavy pressure. Sounds like a good cause. Trying to help stop the slaughter."

"Yeah," Dante said. "The thing is, though, I talked Ben into helping, too."

Eleven

"You talked Ben into helping how?" Zeke said.

"You can't tell any of this to anybody, man. I mean, it could be life or death. I'll deny it all. These poachers are bad dudes. They've killed over five hundred park rangers who've tried to stop them over the last ten years. They'll kill *anybody* who crosses them in a heartbeat. There's big money involved. Millions. A lot of it gets funneled into Islamic terrorist groups like al-Shabaab; they've got maybe five thousand men in Somalia, not far north from here, a whole army, and they raid into Kenya, sometimes into Tanzania, bombing and shooting civilians. There's the Lord's Resistance Army in Sudan, another bunch of stone killers. And there's Boko Haram to the west. More evil bastards. All of them profit from poaching, not to mention extortion and kidnapping and theft and every other kind of crime. You can't trust the different governments or the military or the police forces of the countries because they're riddled with corruption, and there's not a lot of enforcement cooperation or information sharing across all the borders."

"Dante, how did you talk Ben into helping?"

The big man looked off to the side, shook his head, took a deep breath, and said, "Okay. There's this organization called the Mambas. They work outside the law. They live off the land, pretty much, and they hunt down poachers. A lot of the members are like me.

I mean, they have some special reason to hate the poachers. I know this one guy, for instance, lost a brother who was a ranger the poachers shot dead. The Mambas are well-trained. Well-equipped. They can cross borders anytime they want. They help the poor people when they can, sometimes even fight for them. They've got friends and informers in a lot of the outlying villages to tell them who and where the poachers are. They needed somebody on the outside to channel secret privately donated funds to them and set up deliveries of supplies and medicines. That's what I do. My job here with GHR is separate, but it's a perfect cover, see?"

"So you got Ben into flying for these vigilantes, these Mambas."

"At first it was just a delivery now and then, you know? Dropping off a small load here or there while he was doing some routine GHR flight in the Beaver."

"But it got to be more than that?"

"Yeah. They somehow got a bird of their own and needed a pilot, so Ben started flying on his days off from GHR, on his own time, mostly doing surveillance stuff."

"You think he went missing during one of these flights?"

"Could be. I don't know."

"When have you talked with them last? These Mambas."

"Day before Ben went missing. No word from them since. Could be a lot of reasons. I've just been waiting for them to get back in touch with me."

"How do you contact these people?"

"Satellite phone, usually. Burner cells, too. But they're supposed to call me unless it's an emergency; that case I'd call them."

"Do it. Set up a meeting for me whenever and wherever you can. But as soon as possible, hear?"

"It's not that easy. I don't know where they are right now. And if you tell anybody and any of their enemies get to them because of it . . ."

"I won't tell anybody, okay? At least not until I know a whole lot more about all this. And then I'll tell you before I make any kind of move. I give you my word on that. Thanks for coming to me, DJ, but I need you to set up that meet. Try to call them tonight. Keep trying every few hours, night and day, until you get them."

Dante looked reluctant but finally said he would try, and he faded into the night.

Zeke sat for 15 minutes, thinking. Ben's cryptic marks on the flight charts now began to make some sense. He grabbed his iPad, got on the airport wireless connection, and did some research on poaching and the various extremist groups.

DJ had been right about the Somali al-Shabaab terrorists. Taking advantage of Kenya's shaky and blatantly corrupt government, al-Shabaab fighters had boldly raided in that country. They had recently ambushed a border police post, killed three Kenyan officers, and stolen a police vehicle. Six months earlier, another al-Shabaab gang had attacked a university in Kenya, dragging students from their dorm rooms and shooting in the head everyone who couldn't quote a particular verse from the Qur'an. In a six-hour siege they had killed 152 students and five security guards. They had gotten away clean. The group had claimed credit for recent bombings, as had other African extremist factions.

To the west, Boko Haram, which had ties to ISIS in Iraq and Syria, had been ravaging Nigeria with fire bombings, shooting attacks on civilians and the military, assassinations, and abductions for ransom, leaving some 20 thousand people dead over the past six years and more than two million refugees from the violence, many fleeing into Chad, Cameroon, and Niger. Boko Haram's avowed goal was to take over the country and establish an Islamic state. Nigerian authorities had claimed a major defeat of the group, but random suicide bombings and attacks were continuing across the region. Splinter groups affiliated with al-Qaeda were also raising havoc here and there.

Poaching of various big animals was ongoing throughout central Africa, but it seemed to be of minor concern to the various governments compared with the armed chaos that was killing, injuring, and displacing so many thousands upon thousands of people.

"What a goddamned mess," he said to himself.

Almost three hours went by and he was beginning to think DJ was not coming back that night, but the big man knocked on the camper door again at quarter to midnight.

"I got through. It's set up. Day after tomorrow. I'll have to let you know the time and place."

Zeke suspected DJ knew exactly where and when but was withholding that information as a precaution.

That was okay. It was the first real lead he'd had, and he'd gladly take it.

He turned in to try for sleep. He'd agreed to make the flight the next day and figured he might as well.

Twelve

Zeke woke at six and put himself through a series of strength exercises and stretches. He grabbed breakfast in the airport cafe and at seven used a land line in the GHR hangar office to call Katherine back in the States, where it would be two in the afternoon. After a minute of complicated routing, the call finally went through, and she answered on the third rig.

He said, "Kate, I'm in Dodoma. Sorry I haven't called before now, but I didn't have anything to report. I may have a line on Ben but it's pretty vague." He didn't want to feed her hopes too much or to worry her.

"What is it?" she said.

"I'm not ready to go into it now, Kate, and it could come to nothing. I'll try to call you back whenever I have some solid news, okay? I just need some more time."

"I trust you, Zeke. But I've been looking up things online about that part of Africa and I don't like what I'm finding out. It's very dangerous there. Please be careful. I'll wait to hear from you, but it won't be easy."

"I know," he said. "I hope to have more to tell you soon. I'm digging into it."

He disconnected and went into the hangar to check on the plane.

The de Havilland Beaver gave him no nasty surprises and he quickly became familiar with the controls and the cockpit layout. The large cabin could seat eight people comfortably including the pilot. The total useful load was over a ton.

With Doctor George once again in the right seat, they took off from Dodoma just after eight, the smooth 450-horsepower radial engine bellowing mightily. Despite the Beaver's hefty size compared to the Cessna, it was reasonably agile and responsive, but still had the solid feel of a real workhorse, and he found himself falling in love with the classic airplane. He could easily understand why it was still so well favored by bush pilots the world over even though production of it had ceased in 1967 and only about 1,600 of them had been built. He set it up for cruising at 140 mph, took up the westerly course for the Urambo Mission, and relaxed to take in the view.

The land was reddish sandy soil sparsely dotted with bushes and trees, fuzzed with brown grass and threaded with braided paths that were probably game trails. The occasional roads they passed over were mostly red dirt. There were a few patches of forest, and there were low mountains visible on the horizon.

Over the headset intercom, George said, "You making any progress with your search for Ben?"

"Not much, but I'm working on it."

"So, what do you think of Africa so far?"

"There's a lot of poverty," Zeke said. "Some pretty primitive infrastructure, especially in the outlying areas. From what I've learned on the Net, it's dangerous here. Sounds like what you two're trying to do out in the boonies could get risky."

George fixed his gaze on the horizon. "Yes. The Bill and Melinda Gates Foundation has spent millions trying to eradicate polio from the planet with an ambitious vaccination campaign. They whittled the cases down to a relative few in Nigeria. They had to create their own map of the country to be sure they got to all the people, and they almost had it licked. If they could have deprived the disease of hosts for two or three years it would have gone extinct. But then Boko Haram went on another rampage, killing doctors and volunteer vaccinators. The vaccination effort was crushed, and now cases are on the rise again. A damned shame. It's a horrible disease. I have a doctor friend who was working in Nigeria. He was kidnapped one night right inside his clinic. They took him away and held him for ransom. He managed to escape but he got wounded in the process. He vowed he'll never come back. It is what it is. A vastly different culture, backward in many ways, with all kinds of stresses constantly trying to tear it apart. Just one of the situations we're forced to accept each time we come here. Like only being able to work with what we have under conditions that are far from ideal. All of us who do this work realize going in we won't be able to save them all. But we can save a lot of them. And if we don't try, who will?"

They flew on in silence until Zeke spotted signs of settlement off in the thin heat haze. As the town of Urambo drew closer he could see it was fair-sized with a maze of dirt streets, low plain buildings with the usual rusty corrugated tin roofs, and no discernable center. The airstrip was also dirt with no facilities or attendant buildings. There was not even a windsock. There was a vintage dusty SUV parked in a clearing just off the end of the strip. Back in Dodoma, Liana had said she would call ahead so somebody would be waiting to pick up the load Zeke was carrying. He flew low alongside the strip and noted a few dips and ruts he'd have to avoid, checked the surrounding vegetation for a clue to wind direction, and brought the Beaver in for a smooth landing. When it settled back onto the small tail wheel, he had to S-turn it back and forth so he could see better around the nose. He shut it down in the clearing close to the SUV.

George was studying the small white-haired black woman who was standing by the front fender. He said, "Something's wrong."

Her name was Yusta, and she'd been crying. George placed his hands on her shoulders and said, "What is it? What's wrong?"

She wiped her eyes with her fingers and sighed. "Oh, Doctor George. They came after midnight. Broke in the back door. Seven of them. We were in bed. They seized Galosi and beat him and made him unlock the cabinets where we kept the drugs. They took it all, and our money and food. And . . . and they took Verena. She is only fourteen, with no parents. She helped us, cooking and cleaning and tending to patients. Galosi, he tried to stop them. They hit him and cut him badly on his arm with a machete."

"My god," George said. "Let's go to the mission. I'll examine him and—"

But she was shaking her head. "No, no. There is no need. Doctor Japhari sewed and bandaged him right away and he is sleeping. People from the town have come with food and tools to fix what was broken. There is nothing you can do. But we do need the food and medicines you have brought. We can only pray for Verena."

They transferred the load from the Beaver to the SUV. Linda and Yusta hugged, and the three of them watched in silence as the old woman drove away.

Airborne again and heading north, ever deeper into the wilds toward the bush clinic, Zeke said, "This is the kind of thing you have to put up with? Trying to help these people and this is how it's repaid?"

"We know," George said. "Believe me, we know. Doctor Japhari isn't a full-fledged physician, but he's had some training and he's remarkably competent. In any case, he's it in Urambo for emergency care. Yusta and Galosi have been married thirty-five years. They've been running that mission for twenty-five. There are good people in the town. They'll help."

"What about the young girl?"

Gazing out the passenger window, George said, "There's a police officer in the town. But I'm afraid it's unlikely the law will find her."

Zeke shook his head. *This is Africa, after all.* It was starting to become a refrain.

The flight north was over increasingly dense and hilly tropical forest. The relatively short strip that had been hacked out of the forest alongside the clinic was rough but usable with the Beaver's big soft tires. The clinic itself was a modest low stucco building about 80 feet long with yet another tin roof. There was a scattering of other smaller buildings nearby. There was what looked like a significant dirt road running only a mile or so north of the area, with power poles marching unevenly alongside it, the source of electricity for the clinic.

The landing was uneventful, if dusty. George and Linda were welcomed with enthusiasm by a contingent of six smiling and joking people. Zeke helped unload the plane and talked briefly with several of the clinic workers, but found out nothing new about Ben.

He had a light lunch with the genial staff and took off after bidding goodbye to the doctor and Linda. As he circled up and away he looked back. The clinic appeared to be highly vulnerable to the kind of attack that had occurred at Urambo, and he silently wished the small team there well.

He unfolded one of Ben's charts on his lap. Dodoma now lay southeast, but he was close to the southern shore of sprawling Lake Victoria, which shimmered away clear to the horizon on his left, and he decided to fly along the ragged shoreline toward Serengeti National Park for a while before turning south. The forest canopy was a vibrant emerald profusion below, reluctantly breaking up into several small islands as it merged with the glittering water. From his earlier hasty research, he knew the lake was the largest body of fresh water in all of Africa, and a partial source of the lengthy Nile that flowed northward to nourish far-off parched Sudan and Egypt.

He spotted an area of agitated water on a narrow finger of the lakeshore and dropped lower to investigate. It was a steady thick line of big deer-like animals bounding through the shallows, hundreds of them, churning the water to a lather. Antelope? Waterbuck? Were they driven by some stealthy predators he couldn't spot? Or were they just exuberantly on their way to a better feeding area following a herd agreement? The sight was primal, stirring some atavistic emotion deep inside him, and he felt privileged.

Three miles beyond, most of a wide curved cobalt-blue bay that sliced into the vibrant forest was painted a solid, dazzling white. He dropped down still more to a thousand feet and the sound of the big radial engine ruffled the vast white acreage and broke it up into thousands upon uncountable thousands of egrets, spreading their wings and separating, taking flight en masse like a single huge lacework organism, fanning out over the main lake. He'd never seen such an expansive convocation of wildlife and he stared at it for long seconds, trying to take it all in, knowing there must be few places left on the planet where you could witness such a stunning spectacle.

He began climbing gently so as not to spook the vast flock further.

So this is Africa, too.
Amazing.

Thirteen

They were seated in the cramped living room of DJ's plain apartment on the northern outskirts of Dodoma. DJ and Zeke had arrived first at dusk in the black man's ancient Jeep. The tall figure dressed in black T-shirt, black ball cap, and camo pants tucked into boots had arrived after dark. He wore a holstered pistol on his belt and a red bandana covering his face. He now sat on the edge of a worn couch with his elbows on his knees, large hands dangling. He appeared to be relaxed, but there was a feral tension in him, and his hard green eyes reminded Zeke of some predator. What skin Zeke could see was fair, and he had the impression the man might be Irish, though he'd detected no accent so far in the few words the man had spoken.

Zeke said, "You look like an outlaw out of some old B movie."

The man did not move a muscle and his eyes betrayed nothing.

Zeke said, "DJ tells me you may know what's happened to Ben Stone. I understand he's been flying for your organization."

The man nodded once. Said nothing.

"DJ has filled me in some," Zeke said. "You and your people hunt poachers. What you do is highly illegal. Even criminal. So I assume you've got enemies on both sides of the fence."

"There are people who'd like to see us dead," the man said, nodding once, his eyes never leaving Zeke's. His voice was rough, abraded. "We limit our trust. We live in the shadows. Nobody knows how many we are, or where we'll strike next. There are rumors we're ruthless. Mythical avengers. Our enemies fear us. Gives us an edge going in."

"What gives you the right, though?"

The man said nothing for a moment. He sat back on the couch and folded his big arms. "Poachers are killing off elephants across Africa. A lot of the money from the trade—millions—gets fed to warlords or extremists who want infidels like you converted or dead. We fight the poachers. Sometimes that requires actions some might view as extreme. We don't care."

Zeke said, "I only know about the whole issue of poaching from what little I've heard and read, but I guess if Ben Stone believed in you guys enough to help you, that's enough for me, because I've always believed in Ben, and I owe the man. Now can we get to whatever you know about his disappearance?" Zeke's demon was stirring.

DJ said, "Look, I know I took a risk setting you two up to meet, but I know Ben respected Zeke here. I think we can trust him."

Zeke said, "I have no reason to betray you to anybody. My only interest is Ben."

The green eyes above the bandana studied Zeke for a long moment. Then the man hooked the cloth down with a finger, revealing a close-cropped brown beard. He said, "I'm Ryan Fitzgerald. I run the Mambas."

"Okay. What can you tell me about Ben?"

"We think he's still alive. We don't know where he's being held."

"Being held?"

"He's been captured."

Fourteen

Ben Stone had been piloting the small teardrop shaped MD500N helicopter on what should have been a simple reconnaissance flight that day, now almost three weeks ago, trying to locate an encampment of poachers based on a tip from some villagers in western Tanzania. The chopper could carry five including the pilot, but the rear three-person bench seat had been removed to make room for more cargo space and an auxiliary fuel tank to give it extended range. Ben's lone passenger sat beside him to his right, a black flint-eyed former park ranger named Abasi Kaino, an intense young man whose best friend had been gunned down by poachers. Abasi had a Canon camera with a built-in electronic stabilizer slung around his neck, and a fully automatic AR-15 assault rifle stashed behind his seat within easy reach.

The chopper design had evolved from a relatively low-cost version originally built for the U.S. Army and had since been used extensively by police and other civilian agencies worldwide. Ben had once flown a version of one for three seasons fighting California wildfires. The design had served as a gunship in Vietnam, El Salvador, and other third-world countries, but this was an unarmed executive model. With the front doors removed, plenty of Plexiglas, and a ceiling of 14,000 feet, it was an excellent platform for efficiently scouting enemy positions and movements. Instead of a tail rotor, this N model had an enclosed fan that fed air out through side slots at the end of the tail boom to counter the torque of the main rotor blades. This made the tail a lot less vulnerable to damage in close-quarters landings, and made the machine quieter, so it was perfect for the Mambas.

They were at 5,000 above the terrain to allow an expansive view of the bush all around. There was a huge thunderstorm cell building up to their right front, billowing to probably 40,000 feet, something he definitely did not want to even get near, when Abasi shot a stiff arm out into the wind and over the headset shouted, "*There.* Something . . . yes, something is happening right there. Dust. Riders. *Elephants.* I see *elephants. It's a kill.* Definitely. Take us down closer. I want video."

Ben marked the GPS position by pressing a button. Probably too far from base to get a radio message out. "Not a good idea, Abasi. That storm cell is too damned close. It could throw hail for miles. We can't risk—"

"It's a *kill.* Going on right now. I want video. Go down and make one quick pass and then we'll head back. Just one pass is all I need. They'll be surprised. Looking up at us. I can get *faces.*"

Ben stared at the towering anvil-topped cell. A dense cylinder of heavy rain was descending from the storm's black belly and a brilliant flash lit the heart of it, the stunning crash of the strike loud even over the sound of the engine and the flailing rotor blades. The storm was beginning to cast its heavy shadow over the area Abasi was pointing out. It would be a close thing. If he was going to do it he needed to go right now. "Okay, then. One pass, and we'll be moving fast. I'll dive in low from the right and we'll curve away to the left, climbing hard. Tighten your harness. Be ready."

The chopper could do over 150 miles per hour and they were approaching that as they clattered down in a steep dive. Ben leveled off at 500 feet, Abasi already intently shooting video. Cool air rich with the smell of ozone flooded in the passenger-side doorway. A sudden momentary rapping of fat raindrops was loud against the Plexiglas, instantly staining Abasi's shorts and shirt dark.

Ben risked quick glimpses below as he monitored the instruments and felt the cyclic, or control stick, in his right hand twitch and judder in the turbulence.

He saw an elephant down on its side but still moving, raising its head weakly. A chaos of men and horses milling around in the dust. Maybe ten or a dozen elephants down. A small herd.

A bald man with a rifle to his shoulder was taking aim at the chopper. Time seemed to slow down.

Before Ben could take any evasive action there was a fast spattering of sharp metallic raps and an immediate faltering of the engine and loss of rpm.

Beside him, Abasi jerked and shouted something unintelligible and fumbled frantically behind the seat for the AR-15.

The cyclic stick in Ben's right hand and the stubby horizontally-mounted collective in his left were both becoming sluggish.

The chopper was heading for the ground. The controls would not respond normally and he could not climb. He managed to slow the descent but the engine was sounding worse by the second. He saw a tree line coming up. If he could set the chopper down near there, he and Abasi could make for cover. Abasi would have the AR-15, and he had his own .45 handgun in a belt holster along with a spare magazine.

He concentrated on coaxing the last bit of life from the machine, looking for a clear spot close to the forest, hoping there would not be a fire.

The chopper faltered about 40 feet above the ground and they swooped down and hit on the skids hard, but it remained upright so the impact was lessened because the seats were mounted on crushable metal boxes that could sustain up to 20 Gs. But the thudding blow was still heavy, and a dust cloud rose around the machine from the swishing rotor blades and the slewed landing.

Ben took a few seconds to suck in a deep breath and assimilate it all, and then he shut down the sick turbine engine. He unbuckled his harness and turned toward Abasi, who was slumped forward against his straps, chin on his chest. Unmoving.

Ben put his hand on the man's back and felt slick warmth. His hand came away bloody. He checked the carotid artery. No pulse.

Abasi was dead.

Ben thought fast. He removed the camera from around Abasi's neck and wedged it out of sight down beneath the central instrument console, then reached behind the seat, grabbed the rifle, and was climbing out of the chopper, intent on making for the forest, when two grinning black bare-chested men appeared close out of the dust cloud with their rifles leveled at him.

He thought about trying to fire first, but he was not ready.

He had no choice. He let the AR-15 fall to the ground and raised his hands.

They tied Ben's hands roughly behind his back and kicked his legs out from under him and he went down hard on his shoulder. More men came to look. Spitting dirt, he struggled up to sit and glare at the circle of them.

The bald man, obviously their leader, plucked the .45 out of Ben's holster, searched him and took his watch and wallet. He removed the money and stuffed it in a pocket and studied the wallet's other contents as the rain began to intensify. He leaned in close and said, "You are Stone. I think I have heard that name. I think maybe you fly for the godless Mambas."

Ben stared up at him. The poachers obviously had their own intelligence sources.

The leader took his cap and sunglasses, tossed them to two of his men, gave a few terse orders in Swahili, and strode away.

One man with a rifle kept a silent watch over him while the lashing rain and the stark lightning and stunning thunder raged around them and finally passed over and away. The other men finished hacking the ivory free and loaded it onto their pack horses.

After the men had ransacked the chopper's rear compartment and taken everything loose of value, their leader, the swarthy bald man with mean black eyes—the one who had shot down the chopper—ordered them to cut saplings and foliage from the forest and cover it. Scavengers and rapid decay in the intense heat would dispose of the elephant flesh soon enough, Ben figured.

And Abasi's flesh, as well.

Black flies were clustering on the elephant blood, and vultures, drawn to the slaughter from miles away by their grim keen senses, were already circling lower. Hyenas, maybe lions, bustling armies of ants, and a hungry host of other insects would follow.

They sat him on a pack horse behind a bundle of tusks wrapped in a beige plastic tarp, and the procession moved away, the now calm and tired horses walking.

Ben was appalled at the bloody carnage of the killing ground, the viciously destroyed faces of the elephants. He counted 12 of them, including a baby.

The killing scene receded behind them, but he could not erase it from his mind. He was dazed by the recent events and the heat and the thirst and the swaying motion of the horse.

Ben reckoned dimly that they had gone about ten miles over rough terrain before stopping at a small squalid village to rest and water themselves and the horses in a feeble stream. The few inhabitants Ben saw were obviously frightened, and they slipped away quietly as ghosts into the surrounding trees. The armed men poked half-heartedly through the thatched huts but found almost nothing worth taking.

The leader of the poachers singled out two of his men and gave them stern instructions that Ben could not overhear. The pair distributed the ivory from their horses and from Ben's horse to other horses but kept their AK-47s. They let Ben have two mouthfuls of warm water from a ladle, which partially revived him, and then they led his horse away, the three of them traveling alone almost due west into the lowering sun.

He had never gotten a radio message off.

Nobody would know what had happened or where he was.

Fifteen

"So, just to be clear, when he went missing Ben was flying this helicopter you people stole," Zeke said.

DJ had served the three of them cold bottled water and cakes of rice bread as Fitzgerald told Zeke what he knew.

"The chopper belonged to a Ugandan warlord," Fitzgerald said, "Used it to drop his enemies to their deaths from high altitudes. His favorite sport. We found it covered up with its blades folded, and we transported it by truck to a private strip out in the bush, owned by a friend. The idea was to sell it, but we found out Stone could fly the thing, had flown a version of it firefighting in California, could even do routine maintenance on it. So we repainted it with a new scheme and a fake number and began using it to spot poachers. The day Ben went missing he was flying one of our men, name of Abasi Kaino. Good soldier. Dedicated. They were trying to locate a gang we got a tip about. Never knew who they were. Only knew their general whereabouts. If Ben and Abasi could have sighted them, we could have tracked them down. Instead, we've heard through a contact that the gang shot down the chopper. Claimed they executed Abasi on the spot. Captured Ben and they're holding him until their demands are met."

"What demands?"

"The Mambas don't contact any law, cease all anti-poaching operations, and come up with three million dollars U.S. in ransom. We've pulled back to our current base camp and put out the word we're standing down, but we don't have that kind of money and no way to get it, so we've been stalling for time, trying to get a line on where the gang is holding Stone. So far nothing."

"How do you even know he's still alive?"

"Our contact got an untraceable e-mailed photo of him eight days ago holding a then-current newspaper."

"So that's it? That's all you know?" Zeke's voice was taking on a sharp edge, but Fitzgerald seemed unaware.

"Yeah. Pretty much. You have any smart ideas, I'll listen."

Zeke looked down at his laced fingers. There weren't too many options. He'd found nothing helpful among Ben's things. He took a deep breath, shrugged his shoulders to release the tension in his neck muscles, and said, "Who is it that's been getting information to you about the gang? Why can't you trace them through that contact?"

"Hobart Wexton, a TV reporter working out of a Dar station," Fitzgerald said. "He's done a few stories about the poaching. We keep in loose touch with him. The gang has contacted him with burner cell phones. According to Wexton they feed him scraps of news time to time when it benefits them. They might expose some government official who's been taking their bribe money but has betrayed them to a rival bunch, for example, so they use Wexton to exact a kind of revenge on the official. But believe me, he has no idea who or where they are at any given time. He's been warned not to break the story of Stone's capture until he gets the gang's permission, or they'll take a machete to Stone and get it on video. Put it out on the Net."

Zeke thought for a few seconds. "Okay. You told me you had at least a rough last-known location for this gang. So, what if we lay out a probable course from here to the center of that vicinity. Do an aerial search ten or fifteen degrees on either side of that line. If we can locate the downed chopper, mark its GPS location, maybe your people can track the gang on the ground from there."

"A long shot. We only have a rough idea. They could have gone down anywhere en route. Stone and Abasi could have spotted the gang and followed for a while in some other direction entirely, from high altitude."

Zeke said, "We have to try. We'll put two other people besides me in the plane with binoculars. You and one of your men with good eyesight, one of you to search on each side of the course. Fly high enough so we'll still see good detail but have a wide field of view. Four to five thousand feet above the ground, I'd say. I assume we know the fuel range of the chopper before Ben would have had to turn around and come back, so that at least gives us a maximum radius out. And we'll have our approximate heading. We may get lucky. We'll keep what we're doing to as few people as possible. You, me, DJ here, your spotter."

"You can get a plane?"

"I think so."

"Soon would be good."

"I'll try to set it up for tomorrow. Starting at first light. How can I reach you?"

"Give me your cell number," Fitzgerald said.

Sixteen

As DJ was driving Zeke back to the airport, he said, "You going to try talking Liana into letting you use one of the planes?" He wore a slight grin.

"Only option. Unless you know how I can rent one."

"Not in Dodoma," DJ said. "Maybe in Dar."

"I'd rather not have any record of what we're doing."

"Understood. But good luck with Liana. She's got a lot of backbone."

"I assume you know where she lives, so take me there."

She was renting a modest furnished cottage on the outskirts of Dodoma. Zeke left DJ to wait in the battered Jeep by the curb. There were still lights on inside when he knocked. Liana opened it against a stout chain, gave him a tentative smile, closed the door to detach the chain, and let him in, saying, "Will that be DJ out there?"

"Yes. He'll wait. Sorry for barging in this late. I only need to speak to you briefly."

She was dressed in a flowing many-hued caftan, and barefoot, her hair drawn back into a ponytail. He followed her into the small living area and they took well-worn seats on opposite sides of a scratched coffee table. An oscillating fan swept at a steady rattling pace in a corner.

She said, "I want to thank you for flying the doctor and his wife out to the clinic."

"I was happy to. They're quite a pair. Competent. Courageous."

"Yes, that attack on the Urambo mission all too well illustrates the dangers they face. But they're often the only medical help many out there in the bush can count on, you see."

"I haven't experienced much of Africa yet, but already it's tough to take in all the serious problems."

"Yes, there are many, and we're left to cope on our own, I'm afraid. The rest of the world largely ignores us, don't they. We're quite literally the Dark Continent. Have you seen one of those satellite composite night images of the globe? Europe and North America and China and Japan and all the major cities are brilliantly glowing, much of the land covered with interwoven skeins of light like strings of jewels, but not the heart of Africa. Not us. We're dark as a witch's cauldron. Six hundred million people in Africa have no electricity. But where are my manners? May I get you a cup of tea? A cold drink?" She was smiling, and there was something going on behind her hazel eyes.

"No, thanks. I have a line on what might have happened to Ben. Can't really tell you more because I'm trying to protect the source, and it may come to nothing, anyway, but I'd like to borrow the Beaver to conduct a search, starting tomorrow early, if possible. Discreetly. I'll pay for the fuel, of course."

She smiled and rose gracefully. Her body was giving hints wherever it brushed against the silken caftan fabric that she had nothing on beneath. It was subtly erotic, though she seemed completely unaware of that. He was trying to keep his imagination firmly leashed.

"Do let me get you a cold bottled water, at the least. You can become dehydrated all too easily in this heat. And I happen to have some excellent pastries."

She busied herself in the little kitchen and came back with a laden tray, which she placed on the coffee table. He cracked open a bottle and took a long drink, realizing he was thirsty after all. The pastries were delicious.

She sat back in her chair, legs crossed at her knees and her slender fingers laced in her lap, her expression now serious.

"So," she said, "you're to fly for the Mambas."

He almost choked on a bite of pastry. Took a swallow of water and said, "You knew what Ben was doing?"

"With my blessing, actually. But I do appreciate your discretion. You've passed that test, haven't you. DJ and I are the only ones in GHR who know, you see. It would be worth our jobs, at the very least, if word should get about. The Mambas have paid for their share of the fuel and other expenses, strictly outside of our ops books, so it really has not cost GHR anything. Ben has been on a volunteer basis for them, of course. Flying much more of late in his free time ever since it turned out they had their own aircraft hidden away all along. A confiscated helicopter. I didn't confide in you right away because we wanted to take your measure a bit. Size you up, as you Yanks say. Then I thought it best you meet their leader, Fitzgerald, first, before I confessed complicity. Yes, you may use the Beaver tomorrow. We have her fueled. You can pay for what petrol we use in the search after you return. Fitzgerald says you'll want an observer in addition to him. That will be me. I can slip away for the day. None will be the wiser, and Ben is a special friend to me, as well. This will be agreeable to you?"

"Ah . . . sure. Arrangements?"

"Taken care of. I've already talked with Fitzgerald. At daybreak, you and I will fly out of Dodoma to a certain remote private strip north of here. I have the coordinates. I'll bring water and food. Fitz will meet us there. One more thing."

"What's that?"

"If you're going to be flying for the Mambas—"

"Whoa, hold on there. This is only a one-time thing. I—"

"Nevertheless," she said. "I think it prudent that we, GHR, that is, hire you on at the same rate Ben was receiving. On a temporary basis, at least. We'll say it's just you filling in until we can locate Ben. Saves uncomfortable questions about this and perhaps other flights. Questions from Iverson or anyone else in the organization. Iverson will surely go along with the arrangement quite readily because he does rather desperately need a pilot. You do see all this?"

"I guess so. On a temporary informal basis then. Okay. Has anyone ever told you that you can be frustratingly persuasive?"

"Yes."

Seventeen

Zeke had hauled the Beaver up to 5,000 feet above the bush and had throttled back to a fuel-conserving speed. He was methodically scanning the terrain in a 45-degree arc ahead. They had refueled and picked up Fitzgerald at the private remote rough dirt strip northwest of Dodoma, about 25 miles from the western border of Serengeti National Park, the same strip Ben had departed from in the confiscated helicopter the day he'd disappeared.

The Mamba leader now sat in the copilot's seat, binoculars in his lap, searching ahead and to the right. Intense. Focused. Liana sat in a left-hand seat behind them with another pair of binoculars hung around her neck, sweeping the terrain to the left through amber sunglasses. All of them wore headsets so they could talk despite the roar of the big radial engine.

The sky was clear but fair-weather cumulus clouds began to materialize at 3,500 feet as the morning heated up, and Zeke was forced to reduce altitude to stay beneath them, which restricted their field of view somewhat. The clouds were casting confusing shadows onto the land but that was only a minor hindrance. At least the air was remaining free of a usual obscuring heat haze.

They droned on at slow cruise, not conversing much, each concentrating hard on the search. Three times Zeke deviated from the course to circle some feature that caught their attention but each time it came to nothing. They passed over red dirt roads, a few meandering streams, patches of forest, and an occasional ragged village with small skirting fields of maize and other crops, people shading their eyes with their hands to look up at them. There was abundant wildlife here and there—thousands of shaggy angular wildebeests dotting the grasslands, precisely-painted zebras grazing in herds, flocks of exotic birds. Zeke could not help but marvel at it, even as he searched intently for anything out of place.

Zeke said over the intercom, "I'm going to start zigzagging so we can cover more visual range on both sides. Look sharp now."

As the morning wore on the sun rose to blanket the terrain in heat, the horizon began to haze and shimmer with it, and some of the benign cumulus began boiling higher, fueled by the rising thermal currents. Zeke thought, *there'll be storms later for sure.*

The plane bounded through turbulence as they flew deeper into the immensity of Africa, and they strained to take in every detail for as far out as they could see.

But there was nothing that caught their attention.

Nothing . . .

From time to time Liana would pass a cold bottle of water up to the men from the cooler she had brought. And when the sun was high she passed them sandwiches. They moved steadily northward between the western reaches of Serengeti National Park on their right and the ragged shore of Lake Victoria on their left

They passed out of Tanzania air space and into western Kenya, and farther on into eastern Uganda.

He tried to increase his own vigilance, making regular sweeping scans. Looking for the slightest anomaly.

Still nothing . . .

He took off his sunglasses and wiped the sweat from his forehead with the back of his wrist, hooked the sunglasses back in place, and caught a weak flash maybe eight or so miles off to the right. He fixed the spot in his mind and abruptly banked that way.

Fitzgerald said, "You see something?"

"Maybe. A reflection. Just a quick flash. Let's have a look."

When they were about three miles off, Fitzgerald said, "It looks . . . Yeah, it's a kill site. I see elephant carcasses."

Liana was on her feet, crouching, staring out the windshield between them. She said, "My god. There must be a dozen or more."

Zeke spotted something else, a curious mound of dead vegetation near the edge of a forested area, not completely concealing metal, Plexiglas, and an unmistakable drooping blade. "Look there," he said, pointing. "That's got to be your chopper, no?"

Fitzgerald studied it as Zeke spiraled lower. "Yeah. Set us down somewhere."

Zeke studied the terrain and pointed to the left. "There's a curving game trail over there, about a mile from the kill site. Narrow, but it looks possible."

He reduced power further and brought the Beaver down to fly parallel to and 200 feet above the sandy track. There was a low ant mound and a slight depression he'd have to dodge, but if he came in just above stall speed it ought to be okay. Judging by the motion of nearby vegetation, the breeze slightly favored an eastern approach, so he aligned that way, gave it full flaps, and set it down gently on the fat bush tires. The plane jounced and skidded mildly while bleeding off speed in the soft sand, but it was a good landing.

They climbed out into the still-building heat and set off for the kill site, each carrying two bottles of water.

The smell got worse as they approached. As they topped a low rise, the full horror of the killing ground was spread out before them. The blood had dried to black patches, and the scavengers had obviously been busy, though only random buzzing black flies and columns of ants remained.

A slow anger built inside Zeke as he took in the scene, and for the first time he began to fully understand what had compelled Fitzgerald and his crew and DJ and Liana and Ben to fight for the elephants.

He fixed his gaze on the mound of dead vegetation off to one side and started walking toward it.

None of them said anything.

Zeke and Fitzgerald pulled away the browned vegetation to reveal the chopper. Liana gasped and turned away, and Fitzgerald said, "Yeah, that was Abasi Kaino, the poor bastard. I brought a military trenching tool. We can use it to put him in a shallow grave. Maybe find some rocks around here to keep the scavengers from doing any more damage to him. I'll go back to the plane and get it."

Zeke just nodded and began to inspect the chopper. There was a line of bullet holes puncturing the belly, intersecting the passenger seat where Kaino's body hung against the belts. It had obviously landed hard. The interior was dusty, the seats were canted unnaturally, the skids had gouged a short track in the dirt, and there was a long crack down low in the Plexiglass. He leaned in and inspected the pilot's side of the chopper and spotted a loop of nylon strap beneath the control console. He fished it out and a digital camera came with it. Ben had obviously hidden it there. He pressed the power button but the battery was dead.

The console had protected it from the weather, so the SD card inside was probably still good.

He very much wanted to see what was on it.

After they had buried Abasi Kaino in a shallow grave, Fitzgerald cast around in the kill zone. There were still faint horse and boot tracks here and there, though obviously rains and overlaid scavenger tracks had erased much of the sign. He said, "You two stay here. Keep to the shade under the plane's wings. I'll see if I can follow their trail for a mile or so. I think it leads northwest. If it's still readable enough, we can go back and get two of my trackers to run it down."

But he was back within an hour, his shirt stained with sweat.

"It's no use," he said, mopping his face with a red kerchief. There's a big exposed rock ledge out there over that rise, covers a wide area. Lost all traces on it, and they could have gone in any direction. I searched all around it, but any sign is long gone. Must've been heavy wind and rain in that area. I don't think even my best tracker could pick up a trail now. It's just been too many days. We knew it was always a long shot."

* * *

They were in Liana's small living room that night. All three of them were tired from the stress, heat, and labor of the long day. She had a camera card reader hooked up to her laptop. The photos were well-exposed and sharp, obviously taken with the zoom lens at telephoto strength. There was a video segment and Liana ran it. They could see faces clearly.

Fitzgerald said, "Hold it. Back up a bit. Freeze it right there." He tapped a big finger on the screen and said, "I know that one. Name's Muhammadu Raza. Leads a pack of killers that do all kinds of havoc, including slaughtering elephants. All over the DRC, Rwanda, Uganda, and Tanzania. We've never been able to run him to ground. I'll put out a quiet word to a few of our informants within fifty or a hundred miles of where the chopper went down, asking for any hints of Raza's whereabouts. Any sightings of mounted riders in the days after Ben went missing. Offer a reward. Maybe we can get a line on which way they went. Again, a long shot. We've got a lot worse concerns, though."

"How so?" Liana said.

"Raza has a radical brother. Goes by Abdul Ahad. Means servant of Allah or some such. He's pulling together his own private army of fanatics. They say he has as many as three hundred men. Trained. Well-armed. Maybe based somewhere in the Mountains of the Moon. The same area Raza's supposed to haunt. Tough country, that. Steep-sided mountains. Thick foothill vegetation that's damned near impenetrable. Hardly a better place in Africa to hide out if it's true. The Mambas would be hopelessly outmatched going up against a wild-eyed force like that, especially on their own ground. That's even assuming we could find them."

Eighteen

For centuries the source of the Nile, the planet's longest river at over 4,100 miles—a mighty artery that vitally nourishes a vast area of northeastern Africa—was shrouded in mystery. The truth is it has no single source. The Blue Nile, which joins the White Nile, is born in Ethiopia, while the White Nile flows from much farther south out of broad Lake Victoria and from clear melt streams that vein the Ruwenzori Mountains to the west of the lake, also known as the legendary Mountains of the Moon, strung out along the border between Uganda and the vast and largely lawless Democratic Republic of the Congo.

This rugged, steep terrain covers a relatively small area, just 75 miles long and 40 miles wide, but it harbors half a dozen peaks over 15,000 feet and one at 16,700 feet, all of which are usually snow-capped, despite being near the equator. There are deep gorges and thick tangled rain forests in the valleys and foothills, giving way to alpine meadows, then glaciers that are gradually receding under climate change, and finally barren windy summits often wrapped in dense cold cloud. The mountains are home to a bewildering array of wildlife, including a profusion of exotic brightly and precisely costumed birds, and mammals as tiny as the one-ounce mouse lemur and as huge as the 400-pound critically endangered mountain gorilla, with an estimated population of only 700 left.

It was also a perfect refuge for the growing menace of al-Isra.

Deep within the foothills of that terrain, Ben Stone was thirsty, hungry, dirty, and bruised, his clothing long since reduced to stinking rags, his boots and belt gone, his sunburned face stubbled with beard. With his hands bound tightly once again behind his back, he was kneeling in the dust, a hard-eyed lean ebony man dressed in black with a checkered black-and-white keffiyeh on his head standing beside him, forcing his chin up with the flat of a machete, making him watch what was about to happen out in the clearing.

Some 80 or 90 armed men formed a loose circle around the perimeter of the clearing, hooting and taunting the naked man in the center who was bound and blindfolded, kneeling and trembling.

Through cracked lips, Ben said to himself, "You poor bastard."

The watchdog cuffed the back of Ben's head, driving his neck painfully against the blunt edge of the cool machete, and said, "Silence, infidel. Give thanks to Allah that you are not the one out there to be judged."

The ring of men parted to allow passage of a tall man in khaki shorts and brilliant white shirt with epaulets wrapped in gold braid, polished boots, and a safari hat with a feather stuck in the band. Their leader, Abdul Ahad. The shirt did not hide the fact he was physically fit and strongly muscled. A sheathed sword hung from his belt. His face and arms were chiseled bronze and his eyes were aloof, half-lidded, and feverishly malicious. He held up a hand and the men instantly fell silent.

Ahad strode, back erect and hands on hips, in a slow and regal manner around the clearing, studying the men. The naked man heard the footfalls and tried to blindly follow their progress, his trembling increasing.

The tall leader finally stopped, faced the kneeling man, and said in English, "Men of al-Isra, Allah has gathered you here today to witness holy punishment of this son of Iblis, the Devil, who would rob his righteous Mujahedeen brethren. He has confessed that he secretly stole and delivered one of our finest pack mounts, together with much food and even some money and precious medicines, to undeserving wretches in his home village. Then he tried to escape, but we ran him to ground. He is a thief. He is a betrayer. He was not a true Mujahid, or he would never have broken the sacred trust that has drawn us as brothers to wage jihad. Each of you has sworn an oath to that holy mission we have been given, a sacred oath that stands above all else on Earth save to most high Allah himself, who commands our hearts, and you have also sworn an oath to me, His slave and your humble leader."

He let the silence build once again as he glared around the circle.

Then he unsheathed his sword with a flourish.

Ben's minder leaned down close to his ear and said in a low voice, "Behold what happens to those who transgress, to infidels who profane Allah, to those who defy al-Isra. This may well soon be your fate, also. Do not try to look away or close your eyes or I will cut you most painfully."

Ben could not look away, transfixed by the surreal horror of the scene.

The metallic slither and ring of the sword as it was freed from the scabbard had galvanized the victim like an electric shock, and he whimpered and drooled and gabbled something unintelligible.

Ahad gazed down at the kneeling figure, raised the sword high, took three long strides, and struck with precision, the blade flashing in the sun.

The blindfolded head sprang free on a geyser of blood and rolled twice in the dirt, and the torso toppled to one side and lay still, leaking.

The men all around the circle erupted with shouts of, "Allah Akbar," and they brandished their weapons and shook their fists and cheered. Ben felt a deep numbing sickness.

Ben's minder hauled him to his feet and shoved him stumbling toward the thatched hut that served as his cell. Inside, the black-clad man first re-chained his right ankle to the hut's stout center post that was buried solidly in the dirt, then cut his hands free.

Ben stood there unsteadily, massaging his wrists and staring his jailer in the eyes, stunned and appalled by what he'd witnessed. "You people are the worst kind of barbarians, hiding inside religion."

The guard said, "You have been lucky that Abdul Ahad has been away for much of the time since you were taken. Now that luck has come to an end. Abdul and I will pluck from your brain every morsel of what you know about those who interfere with our harvesting of the ivory."

Ben glared, trying to project defiance.

The guard nodded, gave him an evil knowing grin, and padlocked the door as he left.

Nineteen

The temporary camp in a sparse stand of trees was seven miles over a rough disused dirt track from the isolated private air strip west of Serengeti National Park. Zeke had flown in that morning and Fitzgerald had picked him up in a worn Jeep.

The men stood in a loose half circle, all dressed neatly in sturdy boots, camo shorts, and short-sleeved camo shirts. All wearing holstered side arms. They looked like an alert and elite ex-military group. A mix of races and ethnicities. All obviously fit. They eyed Zeke with expressions ranging from mild amusement to suspicion.

Zeke looked around and said, "How many are in your group?"

Fitzgerald said, "Sixteen including me."

"That's all?"

"Rumors have our numbers high as fifty or even a hundred," Fitzgerald said. "We don't discourage the talk. Like I said, gives us an edge going in if they think we're stronger than we are. But don't underestimate my people. They all have specialties. We work as a tight team. We can move fast. Stay in the shadows. Hit hard. We're damned good at it. Starting over there on the left. Mike Sabo, Craig Raber, Yusuf Uba, Ian Axelrod, Curt Williamson, Shawn Baron, Bill Salconi, Alonzo Zorzi, Jafari Babak, Ligongo Changa, Ganya Madaki, Aaron Roberts, Dave Dunn, and Wade Tyree.

Men, this is Zeke Blades. Pilot, wild Indian, and a friend of Ben Stone. Came to this collection of hell holes we call Africa, in fact, to find out what's happened to Stone. He's already helped find the chopper. He helped me bury Abasi Kaino. I say we trust him, and I think he knows I'll shoot him if I find out we can't."

Zeke was doing his best to memorize at least their last names and associate them with faces. Sabo was inscrutable behind mirrored aviator sunglasses. Ian Axelrod was a prototypical Irishman, blazing red brush-cut hair, a collection of freckles under what looked like a permanent sunburn, with a wide mustache and weathered smile lines. Babak was slender and blue-black, and reminded him of warrior images he'd seen in *National Geographic.* Tyree was squinting at him skeptically out of a bulldog face. Salconi looked like a Sicilian Mafioso. Zorzi had on a green beret. Williamson was angular and lanky and had a confident, easy smile. Roberts was young and fit and looked eager.

Zeke nodded at the men, turned to Fitzgerald, and said, "They look tough and competent. But that's just fifteen, including you."

Fitzgerald said, "Number sixteen is our secret weapon."

Mike Sabo ambled over, one thumb in his pistol belt. He used the other thumb to push his mirrored glasses up onto the top of his crew-cut head. The others resumed talking among themselves and dispersed throughout the tent camp. Three of them went back to cleaning weapons at a crude table. One of the weapons was a sub-machine gun.

Sabo looked like a leathery retired wrestler who'd been in many battles. He was missing part of his left ear and there was a livid scar alongside his left eye. He seemed to have no neck. His arms were massive and decorated with muddy old tattoos. He wore a faded Aussie hat hanging down his back on a chinstrap, and a large western-style bone-handled revolver. He was glaring steadily at Zeke but talking to Fitzgerald. "I don't like some stranger coming into our camp like this. What do we really know about this guy? Anybody could say he knows Stone. Maybe he works for the poachers. Maybe for the goddamned jihadis. I don't like the look of him."

Zeke started to say something, but Fitzgerald cut him off with the wave of a hand, saying, "Dial it down, Sabo. Liana started vetting him when he first showed up. He checks out. I say we can trust him and last I looked I run this gang."

Sabo spat on the ground by Zeke's feet, turned, and walked away.

Fitzgerald said. "He's got ground glass in his head but there's none better in an all-out firefight. Come into the command tent. Something we need to talk about." He beckoned to one of the men, a tall brown one of indeterminate age Zeke thought was named Changa.

Inside the square canvas tent there was a collapsible table with several maps on it. The three of them stood around it, and Fitzgerald selected one of the maps, placing a thick forefinger on a spot in remote western Kenya, outside the vast Samburu National Reserve. "There's an elephant named Satao. Some say he's the largest left on the planet. Towers over the other males in his herd. Tusks almost seven feet long, nearly touching at the tips and almost dragging the ground. Poachers have tried to kill him several times, but he's always outsmarted them. Lately he's been under the protection of the Samburu rangers, but they're spread thin and have a lot of area to cover. Satao and a few other bulls had been staying pretty much in a known area, but they recently strayed into country that's rugged, hostile, a lot of it dense forest, and they've lost him." Fitzgerald traced an elongated area. All they know is he must be in this region that covers maybe four hundred square miles." He nodded at the tall man. "Changa got a tip from a source in a village in the area. Source close to the poachers. Satao has been sighted about here." He pointed to a hilly region.

"So you've advised the Samburu rangers?"

"No, not this time. Tell him, Changa."

In thickly accented English, the tall man said, "I am told a particular gang is hunting Satao. They are led by Muhammadu Raza, I have been told. I believe this information to be most reliable. It comes from the father of a man who belonged to the gang but was killed by Raza. The father's name is Tinibu. The son's name was Metuba. Tinibu has good reason to see the gang brought down."

"You want to go after this Raza," Zeke said.

Fitzgerald's smile was cold, his green eyes feral. "I want to catch him in a trap. Take him alive. If his brother is holding Stone, and we believe he is, we can trade. Raza for Stone."

Zeke studied the map and thought about it. Said, "But if it all goes sideways and Raza is killed, Ben could get tortured or killed by this fanatical brother. In retaliation."

Fitzgerald nodded, expression deadly serious now. "We'd probably get a video of the beheading. I admit it's a sizeable gamble. We'd need to take Raza alive. We could use your help. Unless you have some better idea."

Despite his grave doubts, Zeke did not. He had a growing sense of dread and a dark awareness of little time left to act if they were going to have any hope of saving Ben. He said, "Okay, then. What do you need me to do?"

Twenty

Fitzgerald said, "Changa's contact, this man Tinibu, has a distant cousin who has sold horses and supplies to Raza. Tinibu can get word to Raza through the cousin, who uses a satellite phone, that Satao and his bulls are ravaging crops in this valley and the few subsistence farmers there are angry." Fitzgerald planted a blunt forefinger on the map. "It's all a lie, although the cousin doesn't know that and will be expecting a payoff from Raza. But the valley is close enough to where Satao was last sighted to be plausible, yet far enough from the nearest authorities to be tempting to Raza. It's isolated. And there are rumors that Raza could be somewhere near Mbulu. If that's so, he's within easy striking distance of our valley on horseback. There are rough heavily forested hills all around the valley. Good elephant killing ground for Raza, but also good ambush country for us. The angry farmers bit adds some believability. It's really a common story, elephants destroying crops. Farmers have been known to hunt or poison them because they threaten their livelihood. Raza will believe he'd be doing the people in this valley a favor by ridding them of the elephants, so they'd be unlikely to inform on him. I don't think we'll have a better opportunity if we're going to do this."

"You're banking on a lot of ifs," Zeke said.

"Sometimes that's all you've got," Fitz said. "We'll have to move fast. Right now, nobody seems to know just where exactly Satao's herd really is. We don't have time to get all our men into ambush positions and I don't want to chance somebody spotting us if we try to go in with vehicles. We shouldn't need that large a force, anyway. I'd like you to fly a team in. How many can the Beaver carry?"

"Eight including me," Zeke said.

"Seven on the team, then, to allow room for Raza. Can you handle a weapon?"

"You have an extra shotgun? I haven't had much target practice with a rifle or handgun."

"We do. Pump twelve gauge and plenty of double-ought buckshot."

"All I need. Don't know how much use I'd be in a gun fight, though. Never shot at anybody. Never been a hunter."

"You shouldn't have to do anything if it all goes to plan. The southern entrance to the valley necks down to about five hundred feet wide. There's a dirt track leading in, but it's rough, with blowdowns and washouts. It's rarely even used by vehicles. Raza will figure this is in his favor, too. We know he likes to use horses on his hunts. We station our men on both sides of the entrance, four on this side, including you and me. Three on the other side. We'll be angled so our fields of fire don't threaten each other. You'll need to get outfitted. A good hat, good boots, canteen, and so on. I'll make a list for you. Your part is only to fly us close. Over this hill to the north there's a dry riverbed that should be smooth enough to land on. We'll have to walk into position. About three miles."

"When do you want to leave?"

"Soon as we've set it all up. The fictional elephants would be likely to stay in the valley for a while because they'd have a lot of forage and there's a small creek for water, but they don't usually ever stay in one place for long. They can do fifty miles a day if they take a mind to. Raza knows all this, of course, so he'll come quickly if he's coming at all. We need to be in position and set up before he and his bunch get there."

* * *

Zeke went back to Dodoma. The next day he flew two easy food and medicine delivery missions for GHR and drove a Land Rover into Dodoma to shop for bush gear. That evening Liana invited him to her house. She served him a dinner of roasted fish and fresh local vegetables. He helped her do the dishes and they sat on her couch sipping wine while he briefed her on what Fitzgerald had planned. She was skeptical, but agreed it was worth the attempt.

Sometime during their conversation, he felt a shift in the atmosphere. Their talk became less formal and more personal.

She said, "So tell me why you got into flying."

"I don't know. I guess it offers a kind of freedom you can't quite get from any other experience. When I've got an airplane under my hands, it's almost like I'm controlling a live thing. I become a part of it. I feel I'm where I belong, you know? How did you wind up in Africa working for GHR?"

"I was a paralegal back in Manchester. Making a fine salary. Shared a comfortable flat with a girlfriend. I had lots of *things*. But my life felt colorless. I wasn't doing anything really *useful*. I saw a documentary on the awful plight of so many people in Africa and things just clicked into place inside me. I wanted to do something about it. There was an advert in the classifieds for this position with GHR and out of the blue I went round and applied. They snapped me up like a trout takes a fly. The elephant part crept in later.

I feel guilty because GHR hasn't a clue about it, have they. It started out as a small thing. Seemed innocent. But I'm in so deep now I may as well keep going."

"Family?"

"My mother was a magazine photographer. Met my father when she was on assignment in South Africa. He was an activist, protesting apartheid. They fell in love, but he was black and she was white and South Africa was no place for them to be a couple without causing violence. He moved to England with her and I was born a year after they married. She continued working in photojournalism and he became a bricklayer. They died in a car crash when I was twelve. I had no siblings. Raised by my maternal grandmother and grandfather, both also gone now. There's nobody left that I'm close to back in Britain. You?"

"A similar story," Zeke said. "Father was white, mother was Cherokee. Lost them both a few years ago. No siblings. We lived on the reservation in western North Carolina. Beautiful country. I loved the woods and the mountains. Nearly everybody I was close to is gone. I guess that's part of why Ben means so much to me."

They were exchanging lingering looks. He was acutely aware of her every gesture, and her subtle perfume was hypnotic. At one point their hands touched as he accepted a fresh wine, and it was electric. But he sensed that neither of them was ready to take this path much further just yet, so before things got out of control, he excused himself and drove the GHR Rover back to his lonely bunk in the camper behind the airport hangar.

The next day he and the plane were ready to go when he got word through DJ that it was on. He flew from Dodoma to the remote private strip where the team was waiting. Within 15 minutes they were loaded and taxiing. The Beaver was heavy because of all the weapons and gear they were carrying, but it had not earned its rugged reputation by being sensitive to such things. He could feel the old plane laboring gamely as they lifted off from the dirt strip, leaving drifting curls of dust in their wake, but the takeoff was otherwise uneventful.

The flight ate further into the afternoon. They were cruising north up the Great Rift Valley, leaving Nairobi well off to the east and crossing the equator, low mountains on both flanks, the GPS inching closer to the location coordinates. According to the plan, Zeke approached the target valley area in a lowering sun at 500 feet above the terrain at reduced rpm to limit the noise, and from the opposite direction the poaching gang would be likely to take.

The dry riverbed worked as a landing strip, although there was a dicey moment as the oversized left tire dug into a patch of soft sand and tried to slew the plane sideways. Zeke corrected with a burst of power and both rudder and aileron deflection, and they bounded to a stop just before the riverbed took an abrupt turn to the right. They all got out and Zeke and Fitzgerald spread a large square of camouflage netting over the plane and staked it down at the corners. It would hide the plane from anybody farther away than a few hundred yards, and from any passing aircraft, though that was unlikely here. The men assembled their gear and strapped on loaded backpacks. In addition to a variety of weaponry they had brought supplies of food and water and first aid items. Zeke was dressed in freshly bought camos and hiking boots, which were not yet broken in but would have to do. He was wearing his Stetson. He had his own backpack and canteen, and he carried in his right hand the borrowed twelve-gauge pump shotgun fitted with an oversized tube magazine under the barrel.

Fitzgerald took a compass reading and they set out through the bush at a fast walk, heading for what appeared to be an impenetrable expanse of forest.

The sky was clouding over and looking very much like rain before long, which was consistent with the forecast Zeke had gotten on his smart phone earlier. The overcast cooled the humid air somewhat.

They threaded their way through the patch of forest and stopped at the edge of a field covered in waist-high grass. Fitzgerald sent the beefy Mike Sabo ahead to scout the area, and 20 minutes later the big man came back at a brisk jog and said, "It's clear all the way to the valley, far as I could tell. No sign of anybody. No recent tracks."

They moved out in a line abreast, separated at intervals of 30 feet, weapons at the ready. As they approached the entrance to the valley the land began to rise and the forest began to thicken up again. Fitzgerald called a halt and the men gathered in a half-circle to receive their orders.

Sabo asked, "So how are we supposed to spot this Raza?"

Fitzgerald passed around a mug shot Liana had printed out from the camera Zeke had salvaged from the crashed helicopter. "This is the one we want. If there's any doubt, he'll be the guy giving the orders. Shouldn't be too hard to pick him out. Remember we need him alive."

He passed around another sheet he'd downloaded from Google Earth, which was an overall view of the valley. He deployed Sabo, Babak, and Tyree to a hill on the other side of the valley entrance that could be seen through the trees. He said, "I want one man up in a tree over there with a comm set. We'll do the same over here. Do the best you can for cover. Spread out, hunker down, and eat something to keep your energy up. Set up watches so you'll all get some rest. Ration your water. We'll be here all night and who knows how long after that. Check in with me every hour, and report if you spot anything at all. If Raza and his gang show up, it'll most likely be at least dawn, but could be any time after that. Raza will likely send a scout ahead quietly so as not to spook the herd he thinks will be here, so be on the lookout for that scout. No contact until we see the whole bunch. Typically, he hits a small herd with a gang of ten men or so. We'll try to isolate Raza and grab him without any drama. Quiet. Quick. If you acquire a target and you're not sure if it's him or one of his men, take cover and call it in. If it all goes to hell and a target starts firing on you, try to shoot to suppress fire, or if you have no other options, to wound. Okay, go."

The three men moved off and Fitzgerald deployed Ian Axelrod and Ganya Madaki on the near side of the valley skillfully, taking full advantage of natural cover. Madaki slung his rifle and nimbly clambered up a tree that was hung with several leafy vines and offered good concealment. He would be relieved in rotation with Axelrod and Fitzgerald himself.

Fitzgerald said, "Zeke, you park your butt over there by that ledge. Eat and drink a little. Get some rest. Likely to be a long night. Let us do any fighting. I'll holler if I need you."

The rain began three hours after dusk, falling in big warm drops out of a blackness that was so complete Zeke could not see his own left hand. He was keeping a grip on the shotgun so he wouldn't lose it. He had no night vision gear like the others did, so he just pulled his hat brim lower, sat hunched inside his light rain jacket with his knees drawn up, leaned back slightly against a tree trunk, and endured. Sometime deep in the night he nodded off.

When he woke up the rain had quit and he was cold in his damp clothes. He realized he could see faint gray forms of trees and bushes in what must have been first light. The forest was indistinct and ghostly with mist all around. He spotted one of the shadowy men about 50 feet to his left, looking insectile and alert wearing night vision goggles aimed through the trees. It was the stoic Ganya Madaki.

He stood up and stretched, relieved himself against a tree, took a drink of water, and munched down an energy bar.

As the faint light became slightly less murky, he saw Fitzgerald descend from the lookout tree and nod at Ian Axelrod, who was waiting quietly by the base of the tree. Axelrod slung his rifle onto his back and climbed, disappearing into the vines.

Fitzgerald lifted his night vision goggles so they rested atop his head and walked over to Zeke. "No sign of anything all night. Nothing but a few night birds. It's quiet. I'm going to grab two hours' sleep." He gave Zeke the portable radio and said, "Monitor this. Wake me if anything happens. A sighting from the lookouts. Sounds that aren't natural. Sudden animal or bird movement. Anything at all." He sat, leaned back against a tree, and pulled his hat down over his eyes.

Twenty-one

They came as the first rays of dawn lanced through the forest.

Fitzgerald awoke instantly when Zeke touched his shoulder. He rubbed his eyes and spoke quietly over the radio with Mike Sabo, who was perched in a tree on the other side of the valley entrance. He gestured for Axelrod, Madaki, and Zeke to gather around, and briefed them in a low voice.

Sabo had reported a string of men on horses moving in through the grass alongside the rough dirt track that meandered along the valley floor. Seven of them, all dressed in a ragtag assortment of shorts, shirts, and hats. They were leading three pack horses in addition to their mounts. The group had stopped, and one man had pointed deeper into the valley and given orders. Sabo was 90 percent sure the leader was Raza. The ordered man dismounted, passed the reins of his horse to one of the others, and ran off on foot through the grass, deeper into the valley, not carrying a weapon, just a canteen. That would be the scout, sent to locate the elephants and report their position. The other six dismounted and led their horses back in among the trees to wait.

Fitzgerald said, "The man who gave the orders is wearing a red bandana instead of a hat, and he has what looks like a .45 in a belt holster. Got to be Raza. He's the only one who's visibly armed, but Sabo said all the riders have canvas bundles tied on behind their saddles that could contain long guns. I think we can assume they do. Most likely AKs."

Squinting through the foliage, Fitzgerald thought for a minute. "Okay, this is good. Let's give that scout ten minutes to get clear. He's not going to come back with anything Raza wants to hear. So we'll take Raza fast, before they all get mounted again. Sabo and his guys can move in close behind them from the left flank and wait. We'll move line abreast, forming an L with Sabo's boys. We'll cut the distance between us and the gang as much as we can while staying in cover. Sabo and his guys'll get them all under their guns, then we'll break out of cover and come in at them fast. Put them on the ground and truss 'em up with flex cuffs. Zeke, I want you hanging back right here. Keep to cover. You don't have any training for this."

"And you need me in one piece to fly us out of here."

"That, too."

Fitzgerald gave the orders to Sabo over the radio.

Zeke watched them slip through the trees, ghosting to the edge of the forest and crouching to wait for Sabo to spring the ambush from the other side. The tension was palpable. He could see it in the way the men moved. Intent, focused, ready to shoot. His own senses were acute, on a knife's edge, and he took two deliberate deep breaths. He stayed put for a minute, then edged a little closer for a better view through the foliage, taking up a position partially hidden by a thorn bush. He leaned the loaded and safetied shotgun against the base of a tree. He had a pair of binoculars that were normally kept in the Beaver, and he scanned the other side of the valley, but could not spot any of Fitzgerald's men. *They're damned good at this*, he thought. The small group of poachers showed no sign of suspicion.

Nothing happened for five minutes.

Zeke saw one of the poachers spot something back in the trees and begin shouting and pointing, as three others began fumbling at the packs lashed behind their saddles, but then all of them hesitated and put up their hands as Sabo and his men materialized out of the forest aiming their rifles and shouting commands.

Fitzgerald gave a signal and led his two men out of the trees in a fan at a quiet ground-eating lope, their rifles held at port, closing the distance to the other side of the valley fast.

Then it all went to hell.

Sabo had failed to see earlier that one of the poachers in addition to their leader was armed and ready.

Dawud, Raza's trusted sergeant, had his AK slid into a loose sling hung from his saddle. In a fluid move he dropped on the far side of his horse, drawing the rifle out at the same time. He went prone under the horse's belly and sprayed a vicious accurate burst at Sabo and his men, narrowly missing Sabo but hitting Axelrod, who flung an arm to the side, dropped his rifle, and went down backwards. Dawud swung up into his saddle and prodded his horse into a gallop, carrying him hunched low into the trees. Sabo, Babak, and Tyree had all dropped prone and begun firing short bursts high to avoid hitting Raza, who had his .45 out and was firing at Fitzgerald's men with his right hand while trying to grab the saddle pommel on his startled, pivoting horse with his left. All the surprised horses were side-stepping and rearing, ready to run, but two of Raza's men managed to tear open the bundles behind their saddles, jam magazines into their AKs, and fire. They were un-aimed wild bursts and the slugs flew over the heads of Fitzgerald's men.

Fitzgerald had a clear line on one of the armed and shooting poachers. He stopped, took aim, and cut the man down with two fast shots. That galvanized the horses and the rest of Raza's men. Three of them darted for the trees on foot and somebody downed one of them with a single shot between the shoulder blades.

From his position, Zeke could see Raza run in a crouch, using his frightened horse as a shield, and slip away through the trees, heading back toward the rough valley entrance track. He was trying to control his agitated horse enough to mount it. In seconds he could be galloping away.

Without thinking, Zeke grabbed the shotgun and headed off to intercept the man at an angle, bursting into the clearing with the shotgun held at port and his legs pumping, his hat hanging down his back by the chinstrap around his neck. He heard a chaos of shouts and shooting and whinnying horses off to his left, behind the trees from his point of view, but he kept going full out, only catching glimpses of Raza through the foliage. Raza's horse was still trying to rear and run, but Raza had one of the reins and was bending the animal around in a circle as it pawed and bucked, scuffling up a cloud of dust. The horse calmed somewhat but instead of mounting, Raza tore at the pack behind the saddle and pulled an AK free. He had his left foot in a stirrup and was mounting when Zeke stopped within 100 feet, took aim with the shotgun, and hollered, "STOP RIGHT THERE. I CAN CUT YOU IN HALF. DROP THE GUN AND YOU'LL LIVE."

Raza, mounted now, spun his horse to glare back at him and Zeke was frozen for a moment by the sheer malevolence in the man.

Raza leveled the AK in his right hand. Zeke was reluctant to fire even a warning shot over Raza's head because he didn't know what the spread of the shotgun pellets would be at this range and didn't want to risk killing him.

As Raza fired an un-aimed one-handed burst from his still-skittish horse, Zeke hunched and dropped to his knees, seeing dust spout up close in front of him from two bullet hits. Just then Sabo burst through the brush, took in the scene, aimed, and fired once at Raza, kicking him out of the saddle to land hard on his shoulder blades, his rifle flying free, the panicked horse bolting off through the bush.

Zeke stood, thinking, *no, no, no . . .*

The two of them met up a few feet from where Raza lay. There was a bleeding wound in his side, just above his belt line. He was scrabbling awkwardly with his right hand at his holstered pistol, his black eyes defiant. Sabo reached down, pawed Raza's hand away, got the pistol, and stuffed it under his own belt.

Zeke said, "How bad is he hit?"

"Well he's not dead. No thanks to you."

"You're the one who shot him."

Sabo said. "I had no choice. He'd of chopped you up in another two seconds. I was aiming for his shoulder to disrupt his aim but his horse reared a little just as I squeezed. Fitz said he ordered you to stay back. What the fuck were you doing here?"

The demon living inside Zeke stirred. He clamped down on it and said evenly, "I saw he was getting away. Nobody else seemed to notice. I was trying to stop him."

There were no more shots from the other side of the trees. Zeke figured the Mambas must have taken control of the surviving poachers.

Sabo studied Zeke with something that may have approached grudging respect. He took a breath and said, "I knew you were trouble when I laid eyes on you, damn it. Watch him. He's still got teeth. We'll have to field dress that wound and get him out of here. For Stone's sake you better hope he lives."

Sabo walked off to get Fitzgerald.

Twenty-two

The Mambas were gathered loosely around Raza, three of them facing outward, scanning the area, guns at the ready. Fitzgerald had dusted the entrance and exit wounds with disinfectant and used QuickClot gauze to bind the wound and stop the bleeding. They'd cuffed his hands in front of him and strapped his ankles together.

Fitzgerald drew the group aside out of Raza's hearing and said, "Here's the situation. We lost Ian. It looks like a round nicked his heart. It was quick. Two poachers are dead. Two others are cuffed. There's no sign of the scout. He and another one are in the wind, probably long gone by now. Here's what we'll do. Zeke and Sabo, you cut two saplings and make a litter for Raza. Get him to the plane, load him up, and get ready to fly. We'll bury Ian and the two poachers here as best we can. Shallow graves will have to do. We'll take all their weapons and run the horses off; some of the local people will corral them before long. Just before we leave we'll take cell photos of the other two poachers and then cut them loose with a strong warning. We'll tell them we're only one arm of the terrible Mambas, with eyes and ears everywhere. If we ever hear of them poaching again, we'll hunt them down, cut off their dicks, put a curse on 'em, and hang 'em. Then we'll have to get medical help for Raza, and that's a problem. We can't take him anywhere public.

He's a wanted man, for one thing. We need him fixed up but under wraps."

"I know where to take him," Zeke said.

It was midafternoon before they were ready to go. The Beaver's cabin was cramped with Raza laid out on the makeshift litter, which rested across two reclined seats. Raza had passed out, but the wound was no longer bleeding. His breathing was shallow, but his pulse was still good. Sabo was tending to him.

As Fitzgerald settled into the copilot's seat Zeke said over the headsets, "Sorry about Axelrod."

"It's a war," Fitzgerald said. "In a war there are casualties. He was a good man. We honor him by winning the war. Where are you planning to take Raza?"

"A bush clinic. South of Lake Victoria. I know the couple running it. Doctor and his wife from the States. I'm sure they'll help. But we need to blindfold him. I don't want to put the medical team at any more risk than necessary."

Fitzgerald nodded, looked in the back of the plane, and told Sabo to apply the blindfold when they got near their destination. "Raza isn't looking good. He's in and out. Shallow breathing. How long to this clinic?"

"Two hours if I push it. But there's another problem. Our tanks will be low when we get there. It's just a dirt strip and there's no fuel available, so we'll have to figure a way to get some."

"My men can bring some jerry cans by vehicle. When we're in the air I'll call to get that organized. You just get Raza there alive."

There were towering magnificent but threatening thunderheads clustered around and above Lake Victoria, and Zeke threaded his way through them, the plane occasionally bucking in turbulence, which caused Fitzgerald to look back with concern several times at the wounded poacher. At times Zeke was forced to go on instruments in the misty canyons between the storms.

They finally broke into the clear south of the lake, and the rest of the flight to the clinic was uneventful, although all the way Zeke was watching the fuel gauges creep lower.

Zeke used Fitzgerald's satellite phone to call the clinic when they were 15 miles out. Linda answered and said George was just finishing up a hernia operation.

"I have a situation, Linda," Zeke said. "I'm carrying some friends in the Beaver, and I've got a man aboard with a gunshot wound to the hip. He needs treatment, but this has got to be discreet. We can't have anybody knowing about it. We're only a few minutes out."

Her tone immediately became serious. "Oh. I see. Well . . . okay then. I think we can do that. Yes. Somebody will meet you. I'll tell George. We'll get the operating room ready."

When they landed in swirling red dust a large black man was standing at the end of the strip. Zeke swung the plane around, shut down the bellowing radial engine, and climbed out. The big man walked up, eyeing the others with suspicion as they got out of the plane, purposely without any of their weapons or gear so as not to attract undue attention. The big man nodded at Zeke and said, "I am Funga. Miz Linda Robertson tell me to help."

Zeke and Fitzgerald got Raza out, while the other men stayed near the plane, squatting or sitting in the shade of trees alongside the strip. Zeke took the trailing end of the crude litter, Fitzgerald the front end. There was a line of six people with various ailments waiting on half-log benches in front of the low building, but

Funga led the way around back, where Linda was standing in a doorway.

She smiled at Zeke, then frowned when she saw the litter patient. "Why is this man blindfolded?"

"I don't want him knowing where he's being treated. For your own safety. Make sure nobody tells him or uses any names around him. Once you get him sedated, you can remove it."

She checked Raza over quickly, taking his pulse, listening to his chest with a stethoscope, and lifting an edge of the bandage to look at the wound. She looked at Funga and said, "Take him right to the operating room." She nodded at Zeke and said, "You'd best wait with your friends. I'll let you know how it goes."

They waited an hour and a half, the men restless but uncomplaining, until Linda came out in her blue scrubs, a white bonnet, and a mask hanging around her neck and said to Zeke, "Okay, he's patched up and stable. He'll need bed rest and should have some rehab, but there should be few long-term effects. Who is he?"

"He's a wanted poacher, a bad man, a brother to a jihadi leader who's holding Ben Stone. These men captured him to trade for Ben. Having him here poses a danger for you and George, for the whole clinic. I'm sorry about that, but we didn't have a lot of options. We couldn't take him to a public hospital. You can understand why."

She thought for a moment, staring off at the trees. "But you'll have to keep him somewhere, and he shouldn't be moved for at least a few days."

Fitzgerald was standing nearby, monitoring the conversation. "A suggestion. You could take care of the patients waiting. Then later tonight, when nobody is around, I could set up two of my men here, dressed like volunteers. They'd be carrying their concealed weapons, with better firepower stashed close by. The rest of us could fly out at first light, after my men bring in fuel. As a cover story you could let it be known you're just treating a ranger who had an accident. A broken leg or something. Flights in and out of here, especially with the Beaver, are unremarkable. You just need an explanation to account for the rest of us. So maybe we're the patient's fellow rangers. Don't have to specify which park we're from. That should be enough to squash any rumors."

Linda said, "And you are?"

"Sorry," Zeke said. "This is Fitzgerald, leader of these men. They're . . . sort of a private security team. Ben was doing some surveillance flying for them when he got taken by the jihadis."

"It's . . . a lot to take in all at once." Linda said. She thought for a moment. "We have limited staff space, but your men could bunk in one room, with one always watching the victim. Okay, we could put up your men. They could even be of some real help around here. Yes, that could work. If it's for Ben Stone, I'm sure George will agree."

"There's one more thing we need," Fitzgerald said.

Zeke and he looked at each other, thinking the same thing.

Zeke said, "We need proof we have him."

"A photo," Fitzgerald said. "Cell phone will do, date stamped. Is our patient conscious?"

"He will be soon," Linda said.

Twenty-three

Dawn light was filtering in through holes in the thatched roof of the hut that was Ben Stone's prison. He sat with his back to the center pole in a miasma of his own body odor. He was yet again replaying the horrific beheading he'd witnessed and wondering if that would be his own fate when his minder came in and unrolled a mat near the entrance. The man was dressed, as usual, in baggy black pants and a loose black shirt. Black-and-white checked keffiyeh. Sandals. A sash served as a belt for his ever-present sheathed machete.

"I'm not going to pray to your god," Ben said, "if that's what the mat's for."

"Allah has no ear for infidels," the man said. "You will have the privilege of basking in the light of our leader, who is an honored truth teller, a revered servant of Allah. Get on your knees."

Ben smoothed his short beard with one hand, folded his arms, crossed his outstretched legs, which made the eight-foot leg chain rattle, and stared out through the hut entrance at the insects cavorting in the haze of cooking smoke and powdery red dust motes scuffed up by men moving about in the clearing.

The minder unsheathed his machete and placed the tip of it at Ben's throat. "Kneel."

Ben looked at him and said, "If your great leader wants to talk with me, he won't take it kindly if you've cut my throat before he gets the chance." A trickle of sweat crept into the corner of his right eye, but he did not allow himself to blink.

Flies buzzed in the silence.

The tall figure of Abdul Ahad in a flowing white robe and traditional red-checked keffiyeh bent to enter the hut and said in English, "Let him be, Faraji, and leave us." The man sheathed the machete, bowed, and left. Ahad sat cross-legged on the mat, back erect, long-fingered hands on his knees, penetrating dark eyes fixed on Ben's face.

After a quiet moment, Ahad smiled a mirthless smile and said, "By now you must be having second thoughts about meddling in the affairs of Africa."

Ben, still with his arms folded, stared back. "Not at all. I came here to help Africans. You speak excellent English."

"I studied for a time in your country, at UCLA Berkeley. My father once had money you see. He lost his life and everything else when you Americans brutally invaded Iraq and laid waste in what you so innocently call the Second Persian Gulf War."

"Sorry to hear that. But I had nothing to do with any of that. Why are you holding me?"

"You came here to help, you say. As though you have some right. You Americans are so self-assured, so arrogant in your three hundred and twenty millions, yet with all your excess riches and your vast military might, you are but weak and frivolous infidels, addicted to your technology, to your Hollywood and sport celebrities, to your drugs and drink and toys. Ultimately doomed to a hell of your own making."

Ben said, "We don't brainwash young people into becoming suicide bombers or treat women like anonymous disposable slaves or behead hostages."

"No, you would never have the courage to punish blasphemers and evil-doers up close by the pure sword.

You kill indiscriminately and without emotion from great distances with your missiles and drones and smart bombs, never having to hear the screams or see up close the torn bodies, the warm spilled blood of all those innocent civilians you've killed in so many places all over the world. Europe and Japan and Korea and Vietnam and Kuwait and Afghanistan and yes, Iraq. How many thousands upon thousands have died simply because they were in your way? How many more are still dying?"

"I can tell you we'll keep on fighting and killing your kind. And in the end we'll win."

"As you won in Vietnam? You cannot destroy us as you could not destroy them. Faith is stronger than your guns or bombs. We have the one true God Allah on our side. We have the holy teachings and dictates of the Quran. We have the prophets and all the righteous people."

"You use terror under many different names, and you even fight among yourselves."

"Sadly that is sometimes true. But one day we will unite all jihadis around the world and you will not stand against us. The blessed attacks on New York and Washington humiliated all of America, and it will be done again and again, Allah willing."

"Yeah, well, good luck with that. The man who ordered those attacks is dead. Along with dozens of other terrorist leaders."

"Our martyrs live on in heaven."

"Sure they do. Why are we having this discussion? What do you want from me? I've told you all I know, and that's damned little. I don't know how to locate the Mambas and wouldn't tell you if I did. They move around constantly, never stay in one place for long. They always contacted me through third parties. I only flew some surveillance sorties for their anti-poaching operations. That's it."

"You have not told us all you know. I am sure of that. I could have Faraji practice his unique skills on you. Soon you would offer up your first-born son or your best friend for just thirty minutes free from the pain. In the end you would beg to be killed. None has withstood his creative efforts."

"Maybe I could be the first, then," Ben said. "It would be something to strive for. But you've been keeping me alive and relatively undamaged for a reason. I figure you must be hoping to trade me for something. That's the way a coward bargains. What is it you want?"

Ahad stood and glared down at Ben. "You are merely a pawn. I will admit to that. You are a hostage to certain demands we have made. But our patience is not endless. If our demands are not met, and met soon, within three days in fact, you will have ample opportunity over many long days to test your resolve against Faraji's skills. He is eager to acquaint you with such depths of pain as you cannot begin to imagine. And then, infidel, when you are broken and castrated and blinded, when you beg for an end to it, you will feel the hot kiss of my sword on your neck. Prepare for that moment in your dreams."

Twenty-four

"How bad was it?" Liana Sekibo said. It was evening the day after the Mambas had taken Raza. Zeke had flown in at mid-morning and had crashed in the camper.

They were in her living room seated two feet apart on the couch. She had made salads and sandwiches. They had eaten their fill from plates on the coffee table and were sharing a bottle of red wine.

"It went well at first. It could hardly have been planned better. But then one of the poachers fired and suddenly it became . . . chaotic. Fitzgerald lost a man named Ian Axelrod, and two poachers died."

She shook her head. "Such a shame. I didn't know Axelrod. They've all been so magnificent. It's such a dangerous business, isn't it. But there's a strong chance now of getting Ben Stone back?"

"I'd say so. Yes."

She was quiet for a minute. "We may have another problem," she said.

Zeke looked at her.

"It's Walter Iverson, I'm afraid. I believe he suspects something. Of a sudden he's been showing an uncommon interest in our operations here in Dodoma. Asking a lot of questions about the flight logs and Ben and you. He wants to come for an inspection of everything next week and he's requested to see our books. The books and logs should stand up to fairly close scrutiny. But he can be meticulous and dogged. If there are any discrepancies, I know he'll dig deeper and it could get quite dicey, I'm afraid. If he discovers what we've been doing on GHR time I don't know what will happen."

"This is coming at a bad time," Zeke said. "We may need to use the Beaver to make the hostage swap within the next few days. Can you come up with a plausible excuse to satisfy Iverson?"

"I'll have to think of something. Could be an emergency medevac from out in the bush."

She went quiet. Took another sip of wine, placed the empty glass precisely in the center of a woven reed coaster next to his on the coffee table and said, "What is he like?"

He knew she meant Muhammadu Raza.

Zeke said, "Tall and powerfully built, but lean. Quick. Agile. Shaved head. You don't forget his eyes. They're coal black. He seemed . . ."

"Evil?"

Zeke nodded. "At least that. Yes."

"Puts me in mind of a documentary I saw some time past, called 'Shake Hands With the Devil.' About the nineties slaughter in Rwanda, and the Canadian UN General Roméo Dallaire, who was powerless to stop it. Though he did manage to save a pitifully few hundreds. He remarked on the devilish eyes of those who killed some eight hundred thousand before it was done, in the most brutal ways imaginable."

Again she went quiet for a moment. She leaned forward to pick up the wine bottle and poured some into each of their glasses. She placed the bottle on the table and turned sideways to face him.

"I was quite worried about you," she said.

Something in the atmosphere had shifted. He studied her and his hand reached out of its own volition and rested easily on her waist.

She moved close and they kissed, tentatively at first but then with building heat. She pressed her breasts against him and he ran his palm over her back. When they pulled apart they were both breathing hard. She shook her hair back, stood, and tugged him up.

She said, "Come with me." And led him down a short hall to her bedroom.

She flicked on the ceiling fan, set to a lazy beat. They undressed each other with some haste. He had the easier task because, as he had been suspecting, she was wearing nothing but panties underneath her caftan. She couldn't get his boots off and he had to help, but she managed the rest well enough.

They stood close and he brushed his knuckles across her flat belly, feeling her quiver. She explored his face lightly with her fingertips. They kissed again and then moved to the bed. It was feverish and tender and fresh and wonderfully familiar all at once, and as they found each other's deepest rhythms it took them both to a far place high above all the cruelty and violence and despair and senseless death of Africa.

At one point she was poised above him on her elbows, and they were both willing themselves to be still, holding back time itself. She wore a serious expression, her forehead creased.

She said, "There is something fierce about you."

"I'm a Cherokee Indian. So I'm supposed to be fierce."

"No," she said, shaking her head a little. I mean it. There is something implacable, something . . . steely, maybe even dangerous, down deep at your core."

He started to speak, then stopped. He felt revealed. Exposed.

She stared into his eyes. Her brow furrowed. Searching. She seemed to find whatever it was she was seeking, and she smiled in a way he knew he would not soon forget.

When it was done, she lay with one elegant leg over his thighs and her head on his chest, her hair like smoke against his skin, her long-fingered hand stroking his rib cage lightly.

"That was simply lovely," she said just above a whisper. "You'll stay the night then?"

He cleared his throat.

"Couldn't get rid of me with a cricket bat," he said. "Not a better place I can think to be."

Twenty-five

A persistent muffled chiming summoned them up out of a pleasant haze, still entwined. Soft dawn light was filtering in through the bedroom curtains. Zeke detached himself from her and the tangled bedding, found his jeans on the floor, and fumbled in a pocket for the burner phone Fitzgerald had given him when they'd parted back at the Mambas' strip. He stood and mumbled, "Hello?"

"We got the message to al-Isra through an intermediary," Fitzgerald said. "No response yet, but I need to know you can fly us on short notice to pick up our subject and then to whatever exchange site we settle on. We may not have a lot of notice. There'll be Sabo and Babak and me and the two men now guarding the clinic. I figure we should only load four plus you and me this time to leave room for equipment and our subject on a litter. Total of seven souls. You good to go?"

"Sounds reasonable. Ah . . . how do you know we can trust these people? They could draw us into a trap." Liana was fully awake and sitting up on the bed, making no attempt to cover herself, and on some primitive level he liked that. Her face showed concern.

Fitzgerald said. "We don't. We'll just have to be damned careful, but I need to know you'll be ready to move."

Zeke looked at her as he said, "I think we'll be able to have the Beaver fueled for long range and ready whenever you say, but I'll need to check with Liana."

She nodded.

"Do that right away," Fitzgerald said. "If I don't hear from you within the next two hours, I'll assume we're good to go." And he broke the connection.

They dressed and worked together in her small kitchen to assemble a breakfast of coffee, eggs, bacon, and grilled thick bread slathered with homemade jam, both of which she'd bought the day before in a local market. They ate like they'd just been released from a prison camp. They did the dishes and sat across from each other at the worn kitchen table with second cups of strong coffee.

"Any regrets in the brassy light of day?" she said.

"I have none at all."

She smiled. "Nor do I, but this changes things a bit, doesn't it?"

"How so?"

"Headlines could read 'Global Health Resources Lovers Accused of Taking Part in Highly Illegal Military-style Anti-poaching Operations Across Several African Borders.' Iverson would have a litter of kittens, fire me as publicly as possible, and probably sue the knickers off the pair of us."

"That would be kind of a long headline," he said. "But I guess it wouldn't look too good on either of our résumés."

"Too late to stop either activity now, I suppose. At least for the foreseeable future we'll have to pursue both endeavors with some vigor. I see no alternative."

Zeke nodded. "I would thoroughly agree, yes."

"That's settled, then. Now we need to get to the hangar quick as you like and see to the Beaver. I also need to account for your recent non-GHR flights as best

I can and look over the books and logs with considerable care one last time before Iverson comes to town with his six-pistols strapped on."

Twenty-six

The call on the burner cell came from Fitzgerald wo tense days later at dawn. It woke Zeke, who had spent the night in the camper behind the hangar. "It's on," Fitzgerald said. "One o'clock today. Need you to pick up me and Babak and Sabo in the Beaver, then collect our subject and our men at the clinic, Dunn and Salconi, then fly to the exchange site."

"Damned short notice," Zeke said. Where's the site?"

"The exchange plan is smart on their part. Gives us minimal time to set up anything there in advance. Also, it's a smart location. They gave us GPS coordinates. Puts it in far western Tanzania, near the shore of Lake Tanganyika and just south of the Burundi border. A long way from any kind of effective Tanzanian law, and it gives them the extra options of slipping over the border into Burundi after the exchange or crossing the lake into the Congo jungle. Either one would help frustrate any pursuit. Also, it's probably not far from wherever their base is, if it's somewhere in the Mountains of the Moon. But it's also not bad for us. Google Earth shows it's rough country, low rugged hills, lots of ravines with meandering streams, sparsely populated. The location is a straight length of dirt road that doesn't look much used. There's also what looks like a relatively flat grassy area, covers maybe a dozen acres, within two miles or so, that could serve for landing if the road itself won't work." Fitzgerald rattled off the numbers and Zeke copied them onto a small spiral pad.

He grabbed a chart out of his flight bag and unfolded it. The narrow lake ran along the Great Rift Valley for over 400 miles, the longest lake in the world, and he knew from earlier research it was one of the deepest at nearly 5,000 feet. But it was narrow, less than 50 miles wide near the exchange site, easy enough to cross with a fast boat. Or, Burundi was a small nation but heavily populated. Members of al-Isra could slip across the border by bribing the guards and just melt into the dense population.

Zeke said, "Looks like there's probably enough scrub vegetation all over that area so they could set up an ambush."

"Having the plane gives us a big advantage, though."

"Understood," Zeke said. "We can overfly the area at a safe altitude before landing to look for a trap."

"Yes. They'll be wary of an ambush, too. Not even Stone knows how many men we have. And they can't be certain we haven't alerted the law. Logic tells me they'll want to get out of there fast after the exchange. Fight another day. How soon can you get airborne?"

"Fifteen minutes." He gave Fitzgerald an ETA at the rough bush strip the Mambas had been using and broke the connection. He gave Liana a quick call to tell her the news and turned aside her request to go along. "Sorry," he said. "I don't want to chance you getting hurt. Anyway, we'll be loaded pretty heavy."

"Alright, but please take care," she said. "And bring Ben Stone back to us."

Once airborne he called the Biharamulo clinic and talked to George Robertson.

"Doc, can you have our special patient ready to go this morning? I'm on my way in the Beaver. I'll also be picking up your two visitors."

"He's stable and on the mend, but I have to say it's not the best idea to be moving him just yet."

"Can't be helped, Doctor. And we'll need to blindfold him again to take him outside. Don't want him seeing the building or your sign. I don't want his friends coming back on you, or maybe trying to use you to get to the Mambas."

"Okay, then. I'll load him up with antibiotic and anti-inflammatory and give you a supply of meds to take with you. I'll have him ready. Truth be told, we'll be glad to be rid of him. Nasty character. Reminds me of a bush viper."

* * *

Ben Stone had not been able to snatch any sleep during the long night trussed up and lying on the hard, dirty floor of a rattling van as it jounced along on bad roads. He was bound at the ankles and his wrists were taped together in front of him, so he was at least able to cradle his head on both hands if he was on his side. Some light was flickering in through the windshield, reflected by the headlights and from the occasional brake lights of the Rover leading the way close in front of the van. From the engine sounds he knew there was at least one more vehicle following behind the van. He got some muscle relief by rolling onto one side, then onto his back, then onto his other side. Then onto his back again.

He lost track of time. He thought of other things, as he had since he'd been taken. Good times spent with his late wife. An aerial tour they had flown to the western national parks. The vast steamy cauldron of

Yellowstone. Hiking in cool Yosemite and hot red Zion and among the tall Ponderosas of the Tonto Forest in Arizona. A magical night under what seemed a million visible stars in the Tetons. His sister Kate's prom night and her bittersweet high school graduation. Some of the aviation students he'd taught and befriended over the years. Some memorable planes and outstanding flights.

His minder, Faraji, sat on a bench alongside one wall, all in black except for his checked keffiyeh, a new-looking AK-47 resting upright between his knees, butt on the floor. Three men sat on the opposite side of the van, holding rifles across their laps. The van smelled of gun oil and stale sweat and unwashed flesh.

At one point, while Ben was on his back, Faraji yawned, stretched his arms, rolled his shoulders, and kicked Ben on the thigh hard enough to bruise. Ben grunted but did not cry out.

"Are you not curious about your future, dog? What do you think tomorrow will bring? Will you be let loose in the desert to crawl without water and soon curl up under the sun like fried meat? Will you be cast from a cliff into a river to try breathing water? Is it our leader's plan to cut off your ugly head in a village square and mount it on a pole as a token persuading other infidels to forsake false gods and come groveling to mighty Allah? Answer me, you dog. What demons prowl in your dreams this night?"

"Roast in hell," Ben said.

Faraji laughed. The other men dutifully joined in.

And the night ground on.

Twenty-seven

Zeke, the five Mambas, and a glaring Raza stretched out on a makeshift litter with his hands and ankles bound, were over the desolate coordinates in the Beaver a half hour early. He dropped down to five hundred feet and banked into a slow circle. He and the Mambas scrutinized the whole area.

The hostage-takers had gotten there even earlier. There were three vehicles parked in a row a quarter mile from the exchange coordinates, a rusted pickup, a battered van, and a tail-end vintage SUV. All the vehicles were coated with red dust. As the Beaver passed overhead, several men got out, shaded their eyes, and watched the plane. There were rifles evident, but slung or carried casually, none aimed their way. Zeke circled five more times in a widening spiral. Seated beside him and craning to see past Zeke, Fitzgerald said, "It looks clear. There's not a lot of ambush cover nearby. We'll have to chance it. You agree?"

"Yes. The road looks okay. I'm going to land on it into the wind, facing toward their caravan," Zeke said, "but about five hundred feet from them I'll swing it around facing away from them. That's so the plane will be exposed to any fire at least some distance from them and going away. I'll set the brakes and leave the engine idling. It'll be a downwind takeoff but there's not a lot of breeze, so no problem."

Fitzgerald looked back at his men and shouted over the rumble of the engine, which was at reduced power. "Okay, be ready. Salconi, Dunn, soon as we get out, you move seventy-five feet out to each side of the plane. Dunn right, Salconi left. Your job is to protect it and lay down covering fire for us if we need to beat it back for a quick takeoff. Sabo and I'll take the litter. Babak with us. But we don't move out until we see Ben standing by one of those vehicles. Zeke, I want you staying close to the plane, well out of Dunn's and Salconi's lines of fire. Take your shotgun. Keep your neck on a swivel. Use your binoculars to do a slow scan. If you see anything suspicious, holler out. If it goes sideways you can at least make some noise with the shotgun. Just don't hit any of us. If it looks okay, we'll put the litter down two hundred feet from their vehicles, crossways in the center of the road. It'll serve as at least a temporary roadblock. We'll watch them while they walk Ben to us. Then we'll get the hell out fast. Assuming Ben's mobile, Sabo, Babak, and I'll be walking backwards to cover all of us. That's when everybody needs to be most alert. Okay, let's do it."

The men charged their weapons as Zeke banked the Beaver to bring it onto a final approach, dropped flaps to descend quickly, and set it down to bound along on the rough road. He braked hard and swung it around a hundred and eighty degrees, pointing away from the vehicles. As soon as the plane stopped, the men climbed out fast to take up their positions, rifles at port arms but ready to aim and fire. Fitzgerald and Sabo pulled the litter out through the cargo door none too gently and set it on the ground. As Zeke clambered out with the binoculars slung around his neck and the shotgun in his right hand, he looked down at Raza in the shadow of the wing. The man was glaring back at him with those black eyes. It was hard to hear him over the blustery slapping of the idling prop, but Zeke thought he said, "You will see me again."

Zeke spotted a burly man standing beside the van, hands bound and wearing what looked like rags. He had a short scruffy black beard, but it was Ben Stone, and Zeke felt a smile spreading inside him. Fitzgerald recognized Ben, too, and he and Sabo picked up the litter and began a slow walk to a point midway between the plane and the vehicles, Babak covering. They set down the litter in the road and Fitzgerald beckoned for them to send Ben. Then he and Sabo stood ten feet apart facing the vehicles and unslung their rifles but held them at port arms, unthreatening but ready to fire.

Zeke walked out past the tail, brought up the binoculars with his left hand and scanned both sides of the road and off behind the vehicles. There was a rise in the road beyond the vehicles, so he could see no farther in that direction. He saw nothing all around but ragged thin vegetation and sparse grass moving slightly in a sluggish breeze. The sun had a fierce bite and the air was oppressively humid, making Zeke sweat like a racehorse since he'd gotten out of the plane. He tightened his slippery hold on the shotgun.

Two men, each gripping an elbow, began walking Ben toward the plane.

Ben looked thinned and unsteady, but at least he was shuffling along on his own power. He was squinting in the harsh sunlight. Zeke did another quick scan all around. Still nothing threatening, and when he looked back at Ben, the man was grinning widely and looking right at him. Zeke smiled back and nodded but kept up his area scan.

The two men turned Ben over to Sabo, who began guiding him back toward the plane as Fitzgerald and Babak waited a moment and then walked backwards, ready to give covering fire. Ben obviously could not move faster than an old-man's shuffle in the heat, though he was trying. He was still grinning broadly through his scraggly beard. The jihadis picked up the litter and jogged back toward the van. They moved quickly to get Raza inside. The other men returned to the vehicles, clambering in, slamming doors, the tail-end SUV already reversing to drive away

Fitzgerald and Babak were still backing toward the plane.

Twenty-eight

After the brief firefight back in the valley where they had been lured in search of the legendary great bull elephant, Dawud had escaped into the trees, but had dismounted beyond a low rise, tethered his horse firmly to a sapling, and crept back to witness what would become of Raza. He had seen his leader down and bleeding, but the infidels who had attacked them were tending the wound. He had no idea who these men were. They did not dress like rangers, but more like a military group. Well-armed, fit, and alert. Then it struck him. These must be the terrible Mambas. He felt a faint prickling of fear, but quickly suppressed it. He had shot one of them down easily enough, and that thought raised his spirits. But he dared not attack them now. Their weapons were superior to what he was carrying, and he'd just witnessed their disciplined skill. If he attacked, he would surely be killed, and that would not help Raza. He stole away into the trees.

Raza had earlier confided in him that his brother, who was now called Abdul Ahad, commanded a strong army of faithful jihadis encamped in the foothills of Mount Speke in Uganda's Rwenzori Range, known also in many legends as the Mountains of the Moon. It was supposed to be some sixty miles from where Raza's own camp was established.

Over the rest of that day and the next two days Dawud rode deep into that remote region, and finally contacted Ahad's holy army. They welcomed him into their fold, but he would only tell his full story to the leader himself, so he was escorted into Ahad's tent where he bowed to the tall man and told his tale. Before he and Ahad had finished talking hours later, Dawud knew the Mambas wanted a hostage exchange, and Ahad knew Dawud's personal history, including his interesting stint in the military as an expert rifleman and sniper, and his staunch loyalty to Raza. The knowledge would prove most useful.

* * *

Ben made it to within 30 feet of the idling Beaver's tail. He looked at Zeke and said in a cracked voice, "Wolf Blades. Never been so happy to—" There was a sound like a meaty slap and his chest erupted inexplicably with a jet of blood. Zeke was stunned and stopped breathing. The report from a distant rifle somewhere near the rise in the road followed fractionally later. The expression on Ben's face morphed from a broad grin to bewildered wide-eyed surprise in an instant, then twisted into a grimace of agony. Zeke slung the shotgun and ran to Ben as he staggered, groaning. He grabbed an arm and helped Sabo prop up the big man. Ben's legs went limp and they struggled to drag him to the plane.

Fitzgerald, Babak, Salconi, and Dunn were edging toward the plane, firing sweeps of suppressive fire in the direction the vehicles had taken, although they were now out of sight over the rise. In his peripheral vision Zeke saw a neat hole appear in the fuselage and heard a sharp report from the hidden sniper rifle.

He and Sabo managed to load Ben into the plane. Sabo piled in next, and when Zeke scrambled into the left seat, the other men each fired one last burst, then clambered aboard, and Zeke got the plane moving before they had the rear door closed. He firewalled the throttle and the Beaver lumbered over the rough track, slewing and bounding in the ruts and jarring them, Zeke's feet dancing on the rudder pedals. As soon as the plane had minimal flying speed he hauled back on the yoke and they staggered into the air, the stall warning horn blaring. He kept it low, only a few feet above the ground, to build flying speed while they were still in ground effect. A hole appeared in the windshield as if by magic, and a vibration immediately developed in the engine beat. *Prop's been hit*, Zeke thought, as he made a turn toward the east, still with maximum throttle. He glanced rearward out the side window and saw that the vehicles had stopped just beyond the rise and men were strung out along the rise, some prone and some now standing and firing, but the range was rapidly increasing as the Beaver flew away, decreasing the likelihood of any more hits.

It had been a clever ambush after all. They'd hidden a sniper somewhere, camouflaged and invisible when Zeke had circled the area to scout it before landing. The sniper had obviously first targeted Ben and had then tried to disable the plane so the other jihadis could wipe them all out. Luckily, Zeke had swung the plane away from the sniper's line of fire after he'd landed, at least somewhat protecting the engine behind the bulk of the plane. He felt no changes in the controls, and the engine beat was still strong, despite the steady vibration from the bullet that must have nicked or holed a prop blade, unbalancing it. But there was no way of knowing whether a fuel line had taken a hit. All he could do was get as far away as possible to the east while the plane was still flyable. He trimmed for a maximum rate of climb to gain as much altitude as he could, which would provide a longer gliding distance and more landing options if the engine should quit.

He glanced back to see Fitzgerald working intently over Ben, who was stretched out on the two reclined seats that had held Raza's litter, eyes closed and breathing raggedly. Nobody else seemed to have been hit.

"How is he?" Zeke shouted over the engine noise and the wind whistling through the windshield bullet hole.

Fitzgerald just shook his head irritably and kept working to staunch the frothy blood bubbling up from the through-and-through chest wound.

Again, their best bet would be to get Ben to the Biharamulo clinic. It was the closest medical help now. Zeke shouted his intentions, and Fitzgerald shouted back, "Yes, do it. Fast as you can."

He had established a course to the clinic and was leveling the plane out at nine thousand feet when Fitzgerald shouted, "God*damn*it. Forget it, Zeke. Take us to our strip."

Zeke looked back to see Fitzgerald sitting in his seat defeated, his hands bloody. He took off his cap, wiped his forehead with his arm, looked at Zeke, and shook his head. "I'm sorry. He's gone."

It took a moment to register. Ben was dead. The demon stirred inside him with a molten anger. Then he was suffused with a deep sadness he knew would linger a long, long time.

* * *

Zeke and Fitzgerald sat at a table back at the Mamba camp late that evening over coffee laced with whiskey.

"I have to call his sister back in the States," Zeke said.

"What are you going to tell her?" Fitzgerald said.

"I can't tell her the truth. I don't see any way to bring in the law without jeopardizing your operations. And there's no point. We have no real proof who killed him."

"I agree. So we make up a story."

Zeke thought. "We could say he was flying a freelance aerial photo job in the helicopter, looking for particular geologic formations, nothing to do with GHR. He was doing it for you because your usual pilot wasn't available. You're a wealthy businessman, working anonymously behind several front companies. You wanted to survey a wide area for possible mining operations. For mining Coltan, maybe. Ben was alone in the copter at the time. There was a malfunction. It crashed. He died. It was only today the crash site was found. We could embellish it with just enough detail so it's plausible. It also has to fly with Walter Iverson in Dar, and other members of GHR in the field and up the line."

"I agree," Fitzgerald said. "Okay, so I'm rich but reclusive, don't want people knowing my business. That'll work. I can release a vague news item to one or two media outlets. Hobart Wexton at TV-Three will cooperate. The body was burned badly in the crash, we'll say, and then decomposed. Cremation is the best option. You can get permission to do that from the sister. We can set it up so there aren't any questions. Only a matter of a few bribes to sort out the minimal legalities."

"Yes. Then I can take his ashes back to his sister. Be some consolation for her."

* * *

It was two days later, and Liana was sitting at her desk in a small office at the back of the Dodoma hangar. Zeke was sitting in a straight chair opposite, his arms folded.

"It's just terrible," she said. "Ben was such a good man. We'll miss him awfully."

"Yes," Zeke said. "I owe pretty much whatever I am to him."

"He would be proud, I think."

"Sorry about the plane."

Zeke had flown it back to Dodoma and DJ had helped him back it up tight to the far rear corner of the hangar where nobody would be able to walk around it and see the bullet holes. DJ had removed and hidden the holed windshield panel, and his maintenance records would show it had developed a crack and needed to be replaced. He'd thrown a tarp over the prop and had taped another tarp over the cabin. To anybody curious, he would offer the excuse of wanting to protect the paint while he cleaned the engine with a powerful degreaser.

Zeke said, "Did Iverson buy the story of Ben's death?"

"He seemed to. He'll be here in four days for his inspection."

"And how about the Beaver maintenance?" Zeke said.

"DJ is keeping it uncowled and ostensibly protected for degreasing. I've told Iverson it just needs a new windshield panel and a magneto part, which is on back order. Gives DJ time to fix things properly."

"So your books will pass his inspection?"

"Yes, I think so, but he's asked a lot of questions about the flight schedule. He still seems vaguely suspicious. I think he senses something off. I suppose it's just as well you won't be working with the Mambas anymore. When are you going back to the States with Ben's ashes?"

"In three days," Zeke said.

"I'll call Iverson straightaway and let him know," she said.

They sat in silence and she studied him as she tapped the eraser end of a pencil on her desktop.

She said, "Will you be coming back?"

He brought his hands down to grip his knees, met her gaze, and said, "I don't know."

"The . . . episode between us," she said. "That was merely a dalliance, then?" Her voice was neutral, her expression unreadable.

He was quiet for some heartbeats. The ceiling fan made a sonorous buzzing noise like a large insect. She tapped the pencil.

"Sorry, Liana," he said. "I just don't know."

Twenty-nine

The simple metal urn rested starkly on the coffee table. Katherine Stone sat in the middle of her flowered sofa and cried quietly. A folded death certificate that Fitzgerald had secured lay on the table beside the urn. The photo of Ben and his wife that Zeke had found in the camper behind the Dodoma hangar was on top of the document. A suitcase that Zeke had packed with Ben's personal effects stood upright beside the table. Roger was on his way back from the car dealership.

Zeke sat across from her in the same overstuffed chair he'd occupied when she and Roger had charged him with finding Ben. He looked out the same window. Three small brown birds were fluttering around a feeder hung from a steel pole. It was cold and bleak outside.

I found him, Zeke thought. *And then I lost him.* He looked at her and said, "I'm damned sorry, Kate."

She wiped at her eyes with a tissue. "Do you think he suffered?"

He shook his head. "No. It must have been quick. I mean, judging from the damage to the helicopter." The lie was becoming easier to tell. He wanted to believe it himself.

She stared at the urn. It was such a meager remnant of the man.

Neither of them spoke for several moments.

"He wasn't flying for GHR at the time," Zeke said, "and he wasn't a contracted employee of the man who owned the chopper. He was only filling in for a pilot friend, so I'm afraid there was no business insurance to cover—"

She waved a hand in a quick little dismissive gesture. "That's not a concern. He had a policy that will cover final expenses, with a generous gift to me. He told me about it before he left for Africa. I'm his only heir, you know. I want to repay you for all your expenses in finding him. You did the best you could." She looked at the urn again with an expression that cracked his heart. "And you brought him back to me. There's a plot for him next to mother's in the Statesville Cemetery. There's already a stone. I . . . I need to see about a service. He had many friends, but I didn't know them all. Maybe you could help me make a list?"

"I can't accept any money, Kate. This was just something I wanted to do. Something I had to do. I'll make a list of people and e-mail it to you. Let me know the date and time, and if you need anything else at all, please call."

He heard a car crunch to a stop on the gravel driveway outside. That would be Roger.

Kate was crying softly again, the heels of her hands against her forehead.

He got up and let himself out.

He stopped outside long enough to shake Roger's hand with some sincerity and say, "I'm sorry. Take care of her, okay?"

Roger had a stricken look. He nodded and said, "Thank you. She at least has some closure now. The not knowing was ripping her up. Really, thank you, Zeke," and he went inside.

Zeke got in his dusty pickup and drove away, the wooded development receding in his rear-view mirror.

Late that afternoon he went running for an hour in a public park and put himself through a punishing workout at his old gym. He included a complex series of katas. He took a hot steam bath and a cold plunge in the pool and walked out feeling physically reborn but restless and sad inside, the anger safely pushed back in his consciousness but still smoldering like a nugget of charcoal.

Back at his stuffy apartment he got out his address book and began calling people who'd known Ben. One man, a pilot named Stu Green, said, "Ben was one of a kind, for sure, man. A lot of us owe him. A stupid accident in Africa, huh? Damned sorry he's gone. Text me the time and place, and I'll try my best to make it to the service."

"Will do," Zeke said.

"Listen, I heard about you getting canned by ChemCorp. You signed on anywhere else yet?"

"No. I've been, ah, looking around."

"You remember Jay Figueroa?"

"Sure. Great pilot."

"Well, he's been flying a Citation for an outfit based in Raleigh called Max Builders. They specialize in big construction projects all over the place. Stadiums. Dams. Bridges. The States, Europe, and the Far East. Jay's given his notice, going to partner in a new California flight school. He's just started looking for a replacement pilot. Says the pay and benefits are exceptional. We had a few together the day before yesterday in a Raleigh tavern. Your name came up. It'd be a hell of an opportunity. I'd jump on it myself but I'm under a tight contract where I'm at. Why don't you give Jay a buzz?"

"Sure, sounds good. I have his number. Thanks, Stu."

His apartment felt Spartan and somehow alien. It was depressing. There was no food fit to eat, so he went to a local supermarket to buy some basics and a modest supply of groceries. He made himself a supper of salad, pan-fried chicken, and vegetables. Grabbed a chilled long-necked beer and sat on the couch, the TV on some cop show but with the sound muted. He called Jay Figueroa, who took the news of Ben's passing somberly. Zeke told the practiced lie even more smoothly, keeping things vague and terse enough so as not to stimulate too many questions. They talked about times they'd each shared with Ben over the years, and Figueroa said, "Of course I'll be at the services."

"It'll be good of you to come."

"Been a while since I've seen you," Figueroa said. "How you doing?"

Zeke said, "Matter of fact, I'm between jobs. Stu Green says you're looking for a Citation pilot to replace yourself. Says you've got some damn fool notion about starting a flight school in California. I'm available if you're interested."

"I know, I know. It's a risk, but I think we can make a school work. Got to try. Hey, hell yes, Zeke. You'd be perfect for the slot. The owner is Bill Black, a big brash guy who started out working with his hands and built an honest multi-million-dollar business. No pretentions. No bull about spiffy uniforms for pilots or political protocols. He's a hard charger, so you'd have to argue him out of flying when the weather's going to hell, but what's new about that, right? He'll eventually listen, though, and otherwise he's easy to get along with. I know you'd like him. When could you come to Raleigh to talk it over?"

They set up a meeting in a week. Zeke figured the service for Ben would be over by then.

* * *

The small stone church in Statesville with its skirt of graves, one of which was allotted for Ben Stone's ashes, was on a hill with a narrow winding drive, which was thickly lined with vehicles for what seemed like a mile that afternoon. The church was filled and overflowing for the service, so they'd set up speakers to reach the outside crowd. Zeke recognized many people there, nodded to some of them, shook a few hands, and exchanged the usual hollow solemn words. There were pilots, of course, FBO operators, mechanics, ATC people. The day was brassy, with an unseasonably mild gentle breeze and a cerulean sky decorated with fanciful fair-weather cumulus clouds. The kind of day that tempted a pilot to go up and fool around just for the pure hell of it.

An organist played a few of the old hymns. "The Old Rugged Cross," "My God and I," and "Beyond the Sunset." Zeke hung back in the dappled shadows under an oak tree and thought his own private thoughts about Ben Stone. Afterward there was a brief graveside ceremony. Kate knelt on a patch of artificial turf and placed the simple urn in a concrete cask that would be sunk two feet down into the soil. The cemetery people would install the cask lid and seal it and fill in the hole. Zeke waited until most of the people had left and walked over to stand in front of the stone. He saw that it had been freshly engraved with the year of death. The rising wind was making the tall nearby pines whisper to each other in a language indecipherable to humans.

He said a silent goodbye to his mental image of Ben as he'd looked the day he'd handed Zeke his instrument rating those years ago. He tried to push back the memory of the big man's stricken expression the moment the bullet had torn through him. It was a memory he alone had among all the mourners and it filled him with guilt.

He drove back to Charlotte, ran five miles, and put himself through another punishing workout in the gym. He spent an hour trying to master the subtle moves of yet another new kata. He showered back at his apartment and walked two miles to a bar where he got mildly drunk on shots and beers.

None of it helped quell the turmoil in his head.

Thirty

"You've got a competent résumé," Bill Black said, smiling. "And good people say you're okay. Jay Figueroa for one. None better in my book. Damned sorry to lose him. We had you checked out. Didn't turn up any felonies or excessive extracurricular foolishness." He was a large leathery man with permanent smile lines and thinning hair who made Zeke think of dusty bulldozers and dump trucks, big roaring machines that got big jobs done. They were in a spacious corner office of Max Builders in a low glassy Raleigh building, morning sunlight lancing in through the meticulous landscaping outside the window wall. Black was sitting back in his oversized chair behind his cluttered desk, hands laced behind his head, his biceps about to split his short-sleeved shirt. Zeke sat in one of the leather chairs arranged in a curve in front of the desk. There were large photos of completed jobs arrayed on the walls. A model of a stadium sprawled on a table in the corner, with sponge-tree landscaping, thin stylized generic people on the walkways, and miniature cars scattered in the parking lots.

Black said, "I assume you've at least done a Net search on us. We're a privately held company. No board of directors telling us what to do. Got several large interesting projects under way. We're solid and growing at a controlled conservative rate. You been over the contract we e-mailed you?"

"Yes. The terms are generous. Benefits are great. Couldn't find a thing worth objecting to, even the smallest print set in Lawyer font."

"I think it pays off to treat our people right. What's the braid all about?"

"It's a Cherokee thing. I stop short of war paint, though."

"Probably wise," Black said. "Okay, you want the job, you got it."

"Fine," Zeke said.

Black grinned. "Just see Joanie outside for the necessary paperwork. You can start officially next Monday. Meanwhile, if you want to look over our birds, talk to Jay. He'll give you the tour. Got our own hangar over at Raleigh-Durham. Your co-pilot's a bright kid named Brent Cichy."

They both stood and shook hands across the clutter of important-looking documents and drawings on the desk.

Figueroa and copilot Brent met him at the hangar. They proudly showed him the company Citation and the Cessna Caravan they used for shorter hops, and which Bill Black himself occasionally flew. The hangar was cleaner than a rare 100-percent-health-rated restaurant, with a spotless gloss-painted concrete floor. There was a mechanic's area along one wall with every item precisely placed on an expanse of pegboard and in bright red rolling toolboxes. There was even an alcove with comfortable seating, a computer on a desk for weather information, a snack-filled refrigerator, and a pod coffee brewer. The planes themselves were flawless. They had black tails with sweeping stylized MB logos on the vertical stabilizers. It was a class operation, top to bottom.

The three pilots enjoyed a convivial dinner on the company tab at a high-end Raleigh steak house and swapped scary flying stories illustrated with the requisite hand aeronautical motions. The way pilots had talked to each other for generations.

Zeke drove back to Charlotte late that evening and turned in, thinking he'd have to get a new apartment in Raleigh to avoid a long commute.

The next day dawned gray with a low indistinct overcast. He ate a simple breakfast of oatmeal, toast, coffee, and fruit, and worked out in his living room for an hour. He went out for a long walk in a misty cool rain that gave everything a surreal effect, hands stuffed in the pockets of a light windbreaker that was soaked through in under a mile, along with the T-shirt beneath it. The rain became more persistent. His running shoes began making soggy sounds. There was almost nobody else out in the park and the few people on the city streets were either using umbrellas or hurrying along with shoulders pulled in as though they'd somehow get less wet if they cringed. A woman came the other way holding her oversized purse above her head. A man in a suit walked briskly past trying to shield himself with a limp newspaper.

Zeke had always liked walking or running in the rain or snow up in the mountains on some woods trail.

He lost track of how long or how far he walked.

Back at his apartment he tossed the wet clothes into the washing machine, showered and shaved, and sat at his minimal dining table with coffee and an English muffin with raw honey, and went through accumulated mail, most of which he discarded, and did routine paperwork. Paid some bills. Balanced his checkbook. Looked over his investment statement from the bank. He was doing okay. He had an annuity, a managed stock fund, some bonds, a money market account for liquidity, and a checking account, all through the same bank. Excluding the checking, he had a total of

$189,732. The decade-old pickup truck was free and clear, as was his apartment furniture.

He'd spent thousands on the African trip, and he'd had only his severance and low GHR pay and modest investment dividends since his abrupt parting with ChemCorp, so the generous salary about to start flowing in from Max Builders would be welcome. If the opportunity had not come along, he would soon have been eating into his savings to pay bills. The company benefits package covered him for everything except the common cold and allowed ample paid vacation and sick days. There was even a contract provision for profit sharing, for Pete's sake. Black promised to be an exceptional boss. The planes were rigorously maintained right down to the onboard monogrammed cloth napkin supply. The flights within the States and over to Europe and the Far East promised to be frequent and interesting.

The job was everything he could have hoped for. It was what he'd long wanted.

So why am I not happy? he thought.

Thirty-one

He was sitting with his elbows on his knees on her top porch step, dressed in jean shorts, an Eagles T-shirt, boots, and his Aussie bush hat when Liana Sekibo parked the GHR Land Rover in her dirt driveway, shut the engine off, and looked at him through the windshield. They stayed that way for a few heartbeats. Then she got out and walked over and stood looking down at him.

He couldn't read anything from her neutral expression. He said, "Hi, Liana."

She placed her elegant fists on her hips and said, "Did you forget something?"

"I did what I could, what I had to do for Ben. And for his sister. Then I had a job lined up that was the answer to a pilot's prayer. A stable company. Good money. A fast jet. Lots of travel to exotic places. Got hired, in fact."

"So what happened?"

"Unfinished business over here." He felt his demon lurking. Watching. Approving. Muhammadu Raza was still alive. Still poaching. Still helping fund the jihadis. On some deeply private level he had resolved to put an end to that if he could. To avenge Ben's death, whatever it took.

"You know what I think?"

"What?"

"I think in the end you couldn't stand that Ben Stone was murdered," she said, "so you came back to put things right if you can."

"Maybe so," he said. "And there's also . . ."

"Also what?" she said.

"There's also you."

She smiled and it was like the clouds unveiling the sunshine. If he'd had any doubts, they shredded away on the warm breeze.

She said, "Is that Wrangler at the curb a rental? Is this to be another short-term visit to darkest Africa?"

"Nope. I bought it in Dar. It's ten years old and somewhat beat up, but I figure it's got a lot of miles left to go. Quit the new job face to face with the owner, big nice guy named Bill Black. Sold everything in the States and set up a wire transfer thing between my bank and a bank in Dar. I'm here for however long it takes. But I'll need a job. You happen to need a pilot?"

"As a matter of fact, we do. The pay is fantastic so long as you just express it in Tanzy shillings. We're privileged to have nostalgic and romantic old-fashioned prop machines. The destinations are perhaps not the most exotic, but they can be dangerous and thus quite exciting, and DJ is a fair certified mechanic who hardly ever misplaces the more important motor parts. The cozy bachelor caravan is still out behind the hangar and it's free except for minimal utilities. And . . ."

"And what?"

"And I think I have enough chicken and leftover veggies and wine to create a rather delectable dinner for two right now."

"Okay," he said. "I'll take the job. But don't you need to check with Iverson first?"

"I'm sure he'll be thrilled to welcome an authentic Native American to the team. Enhances diversity, you see. Besides, he's not been able to find anybody else reliable."

* * *

They were relaxing on her couch, sharing the last two inches of wine in the bottle. The meal had indeed been delectable. She'd washed the dishes and he'd dried. They were facing each other, each with an arm on the back of the couch.

"So what would be your plan of action?" She said.

"You mean with the Mambas."

"Yes. Last week Fitz was asking what had become of you."

"I don't know. I'll fly for them if we can work that out. Ben was obviously serious about this poaching thing, so I'd like to take over for him. But I'd like to do more."

"How do you mean?"

"This guy Raza and others like him, they're only the original suppliers of the raw ivory. They must sell to a wholesaler or to some middle people who can move it to the markets in China or other countries where it's still in significant demand. There must be a whole hidden network. Smugglers, carvers, retail marketers, and the rich buyers, finally."

"Yes, I should think so."

"Well, maybe somebody ought to work on that end of it. Find a few strings to pull. See what can be dragged out of the shadows. One of the strings might even be attached to Raza."

"That could be exceedingly dangerous."

"I'll be careful."

She smiled and said, "And what about us?"

"I think it would be good for us to get to know each other much better."

"Righto," she said. "I really know very little about you outside the flying."

"What can I tell you?"

She took a sip of wine. "I don't know. Well, for example," she said, "can you dance?"

"Hell yes," he said. "I can even do the tapioca."

"I believe that's a pudding."

"Not the way I do it."

"I see," she said. "What other skills do you have?"

"If you're not otherwise occupied for the rest of the evening, I could demonstrate."

"Oh, yes," she said. "I think you must."

Thirty-two

"I will teach you everything I know," Wu Lee said in Mandarin, "about the art of carving ivory."

"I am eager to learn, sir," his 15-year-old apprentice, Chao Wang, said dutifully.

They were seated side-by-side at a workbench with a large surface. Two nearly identical tusks rested near the back of the bench in well-used wooden stands that held their graceful curves recumbent like moon crescents, their big roots a bit higher than their slender end tips. In front of the tusks the old man had spread out a roll of paper and anchored the ends with four small iron discs. His white hair had thinned over the decades and his back was permanently bent from his meticulous work at the ancient trade. His hands, though still steady, were slowly deforming now under the cruel scourge of arthritis, and he wore thick round glasses, but he remained one of the finest carvers in Guangdong Province or anywhere else in China. Chao Wang was his favorite nephew. The boy sat up straighter on the stool to get a better view of the precise full-size pencil sketch on the paper. He had known his uncle had been an ivory carver all his life, but had been led to believe the old man no longer practiced what had become, at least ostensibly, an illegal art. Today was the first time he'd been allowed into the secluded workshop.

"What do you see in this drawing, boy?" Wu Lee said.

"I see two dragon boats, sir. They look almost the same."

"Ah, but they are not," Wu Lee said. "When you gaze into a mirror, what do you see?"

"I see myself, sir."

The old man shook his head. "No, you do not. Your right eye is now your left eye. Your right ear becomes a left ear. You see a mirror image of yourself. So it is with these dragon boats that you and I will coax very carefully from those exceptionally fine tusks. They are a near perfect matched pair from a single beast. Each carving will be a precise mirror image of the other, and they will race each other into the ages."

The boy studied the tusks. A small blue star had been inked on each of their bases. Though he'd displayed uncommon artistic abilities in his schooling, it was difficult for him to imagine how the incredibly intricate designs on the paper could be perfectly cut into the ivory. *What if you make a mistake*, he thought. *What if the knife slips?*

"What do you know of the dragon boat legend?" Wu Lee said.

"I know there are several. It is confusing."

"The one I believe to be true is about the loyal poet Qu Yuan, who was chief advisor to the state of Chu. He lived over two thousand years ago during the Warring States Period, yet his poems are still much read and recited today. Slandered by his enemies, he was exiled, and when the Qin State conquered the capital of Chu, he drowned himself in the Miluo River in Huan Province on the fifth day of the fifth lunar month. Sad local people paddled boats out onto the river, beating drums and slapping the water with their paddles to chase away evil spirits, and they threw rice lumps into the water to keep fish from eating Qu Yuan's missing body. Down through the centuries, each year on the fifth day of the fifth lunar month, we celebrate the Dragon Boat Festival across China, with ceremonies and dragon boat races and the eating of the rice dumplings you know as zongzi. The festival is held to help preserve our most important traditions of virtue, loyalty, and honor."

"So these carvings are to be in honor of Qu Yuan."

Wu Lee smiled and nodded. "You could say as much, yes. Although they will also be for a famous and powerful client, as symbols of his business empire. He has approved this design.

"You will observe me closely and listen at first. I will allow you to execute small details and later you will be involved more and more in the skills. In time you will become a fine carver, much respected and sought after and well paid by those who appreciate your work. But we must keep what we are doing most strictly secret, because in these times not everyone understands. You can tell no one. Will you obey this, Chao Wang?"

"Yes, sir," Chao said. "I will."

"Good. Then let us begin."

Chao Wang felt a thrill run through him to be part of such an artistic triumph, although on some fringe of his mind he was bothered by the secrecy.

And he thought also about what the great beast must have been like that had yielded the twin tusks. About how and where it had probably lived and how it might have died. Perhaps somewhere in faraway Africa of old age.

Or perhaps not.

But he pushed those thoughts back and studied the drawings in more detail. The tusk roots would become the mirrored scaly dragon heads, nostrils flared, mouths open wide, teeth bared, long tongues curled, eyes bulging and fierce. The uplifted tusk tips were to become the serpentine tails. The dragons' bodies would be the graceful twin curves of the hulls. Sixteen paddlers for each boat, in conical coolie hats and loin cloths, would sit in two tandem groups, four pairs to each group to make eight paddlers per group, the luckiest number in the Chinese culture. Their paddles would dig the imaginary water powerfully, muscular arms straining. Behind the paddlers in each boat would be a standing drummer with sticks raised, again in mirror image. A banner would stream from a staff in precise mirror image above each boat.

They will be magnificent, the boy thought.

He paid rapt attention to his uncle as the old man rearranged the workbench and laid out the scalpel-sharp instruments that would miraculously transform the tusks under the guidance of his gnarled hands.

Thirty-three

Zeke, Liana, Dante, and Ryan Fitzgerald were sitting in a loose circle on the worn furniture in Dante's living area, sweating. They all had jelly glasses of iced tea. An unevenly buzzing ceiling fan was stirring the humid air listlessly.

"What's been happening on the front lines?" Zeke said to Fitzgerald.

He made a so-so motion with his free hand. "We captured three poachers, father and two of his sons, in the act of chopping the tusks out of a young bull just outside Serengeti Park. We got them under our guns without a shot fired, trussed them up, and made an anonymous call to the rangers. We got gone before they arrived. That's just the way I like to see an operation go. Had a brief skirmish with a ragged bunch of maybe seven or eight amateurs south of Kamwenge near the Katonga River in western Uganda. They high tailed it. No casualties on either side, but we put a scare into them, at least. That'll last until they get another chance at an elephant or a rhino. There's just too much money in it, too much temptation, especially if you can't get a job and your family is slowly starving. A single pair of tusks or a rhino horn can make a whole small gang very rich by bush standards. Ahad's bunch, al-Isra, took credit for a bombing in a Uganda market square that killed twelve and wounded thirty-one. Rumors have them planning a major operation. We've been chasing Raza, trying to get a solid line on him or brother Ahad, but it's not easy. People are afraid to talk. They're more likely to inform on *us* to the damned jihadis, in fact. You in if we need a pilot?"

"I am," Zeke said, "provided we can work that out. I don't like putting Liana and DJ at risk of losing their jobs, maybe even of prosecution. Be better if you had your own plane so we could leave GHR out of it altogether."

"Don't worry about me," DJ said. "You all know my story, why I'm here."

"I don't know how long we can keep Iverson in the dark about us using GHR planes," Liana said, "but I'm with you all the way round the bend. Iverson has been having vague suspicions, though for the moment he seems satisfied. We'll simply have to be more cautious and clever about it, won't we."

"DJ, you did a nice job fixing up the Beaver," Zeke said.

"Wasn't cheap. Had to order a new prop. My log says the old one was wore down out of specs along the leading edges, which happens, 'specially in bush conditions. Prop blows up dirt and gravel, grinds away at the aluminum over time. Good excuse for the replacement. Patching the bullet holes and touching up was easy enough, but the repairs'll show from inside the skin, maybe during a pre-buy inspection for the next owner. Long as I'm the legal mechanic, though, nobody else is ever gonna know."

This was a departure from the way they'd operated before. Zeke, mostly, but Liana and DJ with their own funds, as well, had been covering the fuel costs of the Mambas flights. The costs of the latest repairs were being borne by GHR and that bothered Zeke. He promised himself to reimburse the organization for that.

"So, what's next on the docket?" Liana said.

"We'll keep bird-dogging al-Isra," Fitzgerald said. "Use our informants. Go after any poachers we can flush out of the bushes."

"And build up the terribly fearsome reputation of the Mambas in the process," Liana said.

Fitzgerald grinned and said, "Absolutely."

"Not long after we met," Zeke said to Fitzgerald, "you mentioned some reporter who was targeting the poaching, guy named Wexton, I think."

"Hobart Wexton," Fitzgerald said. "He works for Africa Now TV-Three, out of Dar. An investigative journalist, he calls himself."

"He any good?"

"*He* damned sure thinks he is. Knows a lot about the ivory trade. We've used him when we want to plant some item in the news to mislead poachers or entice them to try for what appears to be an unguarded herd. We've had mixed results. Be warned he's egotistical, arrogant, abrasive."

"I'd like to talk with him, anyway. See what he knows. Maybe there's a way to attack some other part of the poaching network. The wholesale buyers. The smugglers. Some of the others involved up the line. Break the chain well enough, demand should drop, and it ought to cut into the poachers' income, blunt their incentive."

"We've thought about that, and good luck. It's a tangle of political corruption, payoffs, law enforcement apathy if not outright collusion, canny smugglers with lots of resources. Entrenched people with big money in the middle and at the top. Lots of rumors and circumstantial suspicions. A real basket of snakes."

"Still like to give it a try."

"Hell, have at it. Hobart could be a good place to start, I guess. Before you do, though, let me brief you about him a little more. And I'm telling you upfront you may want to bring a sidearm with you."

"Why's that?" Zeke said.

"Because," Fitzgerald said. "I'm betting inside of the first fifteen minutes with him you're gonna want to shoot the bastard."

Thirty-four

The next morning Liana told him it would be at least another day or two before she could clear everything with Iverson, organize the necessary hiring paperwork, and set up a GHR flight schedule for him, so he drove his Wrangler from Dodoma to Dar es Salaam along the narrow paved main road, dodging the occasional pothole that was deep enough to break a wheel. It took him six hours to cover the 246 miles, stopping once for a break and a light lunch that Liana had packed for him. He planned to spend the night, pick up a few items in the shops that Liana wanted, try to talk with Wexton, and look in on Iverson briefly before heading back the next day.

In mid-afternoon, he found the offices of Africa Now TV3 on the outskirts of the city under an array of antennas in a long low flat-roofed stucco building with the logo painted large near the entrance. There were half a dozen other vehicles in the parking lot.

The receptionist in the modest lobby was a plus-size black woman with a glorious oversized Afro, rings on most of her long-nailed fingers and makeup that may have been applied with a putty knife. Zeke stood patiently in front of her desk as she finished typing a paragraph on her computer keyboard. He figured she probably doubled as a secretary. Down a hall on Zeke's left, a tall white man in a slick blue suit and a red tie was standing in front of a smaller man who had a headset hung around his neck. The tall man was gesturing angrily and hollering something about camera angles and timing. The smaller man looked slightly bored. He was enduring the tirade in stoic silence.

The name plate on the receptionist's desk said Asha Onwuatuegwu. She looked up at him and said, "Yes. Help you?"

"I'm looking for Hobart Wexton."

"That would be the screamer down the hall. You are?"

"Call me Zeke. I understand Mister Wexton is an investigative reporter. I'd like to discuss a story with him."

"Okay. Good luck, Zeke. Feel free. He should be finishing up his fit anytime now."

"Thank you, Miz . . ."

She pronounced her last name.

"Thanks, Miz Asha."

She smiled and said, "That braided ponytail is sexy," and went back to typing. He wondered how she managed to do that with those talon-like iridescent white nails without committing a typo in every other word.

Zeke walked along the hall and stood with his Aussie hat in his hand ten feet away from the men, who both ignored him.

Hobart had a long, manicured forefinger poised an inch from the smaller man's nose. "If you *ever again* leave me sitting there *live on camera* for that long after I've finished speaking, I'll have you *castrated*, you got that, idiot?"

The smaller man raised a placating palm, said, "Sure, got it, Mister Wexton, won't happen again," and walked away shaking his head.

Hobart pivoted with his hands on his hips and said, "And who the fuck are you?"

They were about the same height. Wexton was handsome. Evenly tanned, but maybe not by the sun. Ice-blue eyes that could be contacts. White too-even teeth, again probably not natural. A precisely trimmed wave of thick black hair that did look natural. Zeke felt like a buzzard confronting a peacock.

"I'm Zeke. Like to talk with you about an exclusive story that could become very big. International, even. I've heard you're the man who can handle it. Is there somewhere private we can sit?" He forced what he hoped was a nice smile.

Wexton kept his hands on his hips, but he cocked his head and squinted in reappraisal. He nodded a bit, looked at his watch, and said, "I've got ten minutes. You'd better not be wasting them."

Zeke followed him down the hall to a small conference room with used paper cups on the table along with what looked like a dusting of powdered sugar. A coffee machine sat on a shelf with a half-empty pot on the warmer and a stack of paper cups beside it. Wexton took the seat at the head of the table. Zeke closed the door, took the chair closest to the man, and placed his hat in a clean spot on the table.

Wexton said, "Okay, what have you got? It better be good."

Zeke said quietly, "I've recently joined a group known in certain circles as the Mambas. Been doing some flying for them. You've talked with their leader, Fitzgerald. I need to know everything you do about poaching. Facts. Rumors. Conjecture. Names."

Wexton went pale under his tan. He abruptly stood up and pointed at the door. "Out. Get out. Now. This discussion is over."

Zeke looked up at him and said calmly, "I'm a black belt. Before you take a step I can temporarily but painfully disable you. You might yell some, but the people around here are used to your outbursts and won't pay much attention. I'd rather not hurt you unless you force me to. Sit down, Hobart." He felt like a not-very-good amateur stage actor.

Wexton stared at him, took a breath, and sat.

"I know you've been digging into poaching for some time," Zeke said, "trying to put together a comprehensive documentary that could sell in major markets. I know Fitzgerald has, ah . . . cautioned you not to divulge what you know about him or his organization. So far, you've even cooperated with him to some extent, sharing a tidbit of information here or there when you think it may be in your eventual best interests, story-wise. I figure there's a lot you haven't shared. So I'll make you a side deal. Tell me what you know and I'll do what I can to see that you get any big story that comes out of this first. Nobody but Fitzgerald and his most trusted people will know where I got the information."

"How . . . how do I know I can trust *you*?"

"You can check with Fitzgerald." Zeke took out the burner and punched up Fitzgerald's number. "Call him, he'll vouch. Besides, I'm a Cherokee Indian. We keep our word."

Wexton took the phone and hit dial. It rang a few times and was answered. He spoke. Listened for fifteen seconds and ended the call. Nodded and took a breath.

Wexton had lost most of his bluster. He spoke in a lowered voice. "You have no idea of the dangers. The poachers and the people up the line are ruthless. Well-connected. I may already be on some . . . elimination list."

"I understand. But you shine a bright enough spotlight on the whole mess and they'll scurry for cover like roaches. Sometime not far down the road I figure you'll have enough of it to go public in a big way. That will be your best protection all around. We can help. In fact, do you have a card and a pen?"

Wexton produced both. Zeke wrote his name and the burner cell number on the back of it and handed it back. He said, "You can reach me anytime at that number. You need help, call."

Wexton looked at it and put it in his shirt pocket.

Zeke said, "If this whole thing is broadcast, there won't be any need for the poachers to target you to keep you quiet because it will all be exposed, anyway. There'll be too much heat on them to risk making any stupid moves that would only increase that heat. And it will be a story that will make your career. It'll get worldwide interest. You'll be in demand for a top slot at one of the big stations in Europe or the States. The Mambas can fade out of it and you'll get all the glory." He believed at least 25 percent of what he was saying.

Wexton looked out the one dirty window in the room, thinking.

Zeke kept quiet and let him.

After a minute, Wexton pulled another card from inside his jacket and said, "I really don't have much time. I go back on for the news in less than a half hour. Meet me at this restaurant at six. Don't be late. I detest tardiness." He printed an address on the back of the card. He got up and walked out, and Zeke left through the reception area with a nod to Asha on the way.

Zeke was on time at the Karambezi Café, which was perched on the lip of a cliff near the tip of the upscale Msasani Peninsula overlooking the Indian Ocean. Wexton had made reservations for a table out on the deck up close to the wall in a corner. The other diners were clustered along the outside tables with a marginally better vantage for the spectacular view. Wexton was wearing a plain blue ball cap and amber glasses that mostly hid his eyes. Zeke joined him and they ordered drinks. A martini for Wexton and a tall draft beer for Zeke. There was a warm breeze off the ocean and the surf was breaking below on the rocks at the base of the cliff. Pleasant white noise. It was a good place to talk without being overheard.

The man was dressed casually in a blue blazer with white buttons over a white sport shirt, again making Zeke feel vaguely shabby. Sitting back sideways to the table, gazing around through the dark glasses at the lesser beings on the deck, he looked every bit the aloof incognito celebrity.

Wexton said, "Fitzgerald did speak well of you. Do he and I have an arrangement? You might say that. We've exchanged information from time to time. I've planted small news items for him. We observe mutual respect and discretion. Am I interested in deepening that relationship? Hardly. I do not wish to become involved in any illegalities. Am I interested in exposing the poaching trade in east Africa? Of course. What journalist of stature would not? It is barbaric. It is absolutely decimating the noble herds. In some cases, the money from it even funds terrorism. I would be pleased to play a major role in putting a stop to it."

And would you be pleased to do a documentary that would, incidentally, bring you measures of wealth and fame? Zeke thought. *Of course you would.*

A pert shapely waitress delivered drinks and smiles and went over the specials briskly. They both ordered the seafood special.

"I think you're exactly the right person to do the job," Zeke said. "I'd really appreciate anything you can tell me that will help me to help you reach your goal."

"Do I have a detailed picture of the entire trade? No, of course not. But I *have* found out enough, through diligent research and exclusive confidential informants, to learn a great deal and to surmise even more. The story begins, of course, out there in the savage bush..."

With only minimal sycophantic prodding along the way, Wexton opened up. Having two martinis before the meal even arrived and having a third one with the food certainly helped. Zeke took notes on a spiral pocket pad while sipping his way through his single beer. The seafood was excellent, as was dessert.

Wexton ordered yet another martini. He was being careful with his enunciation and seemed to be talking as much to himself as to Zeke.

An hour and a half later Zeke had to pay the whole check because Wexton was too drunk to handle his share of the task. Zeke helped support him as they left the restaurant. Out in the lot he said, "Did you drive here? You need to let me take you home."

"No. Came in... uh... cab."

Zeke called one for him, made sure he had enough cash on him to pay the fare, and waited with him on a bench until it got there. Wexton left with an irritated wave of dismissal, and Zeke left with a pad-full of notes.

Thirty-five

Zeke had gotten back from Dar late the previous night and had crashed in the camper.

Liana rapped on the flimsy door just before dawn, bearing two aromatic hot coffees and a bag of warm biscuits and sweet rolls, which they shared at the small dining table while he woke up all the way. He was learning it would be most wise to get as much done as possible early each day before the heat built up in the afternoon.

She waited while he took a fast shower, and then walked with him to her cramped but neat office in a corner of the hangar. She sat behind the worn desk, her elegant hands relaxed on the chair arms. He sat in a straight chair tipped back against the wall, with the pointed tips of his western boots just touching the concrete floor, his fingers laced in his lap. The office door was open, as were the big sliding hangar doors, and ruddy dawn sunlight was flooding in, painting the waiting Beaver and the smaller Cessna nicely. She was wearing a crisp white sleeveless blouse over loose blue shorts. Her glossy hair was pulled back in a ponytail. Her hazel eyes were luminous and feral in the side light from the low sun. Her silken bronze skin was in primitive contrast to the bright blouse. He thought she looked uniquely exotic and beautiful.

"How was Iverson when you met with him?" she said.

"He was busy as a British bee in Buckingham's gardens," he said. "Gave me a warm enough welcome, though. We went over some GHR regulations and other stuff. I tried to pay attention. Signed in the tagged spots. I went shopping for the things on your list after that."

"A British bee in Buckingham?" she said.

"Thought that one up on the drive back."

She smiled. "And what did you learn from Hobart Wexton?"

"A lot, I think. It's hard to separate the facts from conjecture and suspicions, but he gave me what I think is a good grasp of the business, along with a few names. I have some threads I can pull on."

"Most carefully, I hope."

"Absolutely. The trade is pretty much as Fitzgerald described it. A big basket of snakes. Poisonous snakes. By the way, you told me why you came to work for GHR, but you haven't explained in any depth why you got involved in this risky side crusade."

She turned her head and squinted into the increasing sunlight and thought for a moment. Nodded once to herself, then looked at him and smiled again. "You've a flight scheduled today to the Biharamulo clinic with supplies. The Cessna is already loaded and topped up, thanks be to DJ. I shall go with you. We'll pick up a takeaway lunch over at the terminal, then while you wipe the windscreen and do your walkaround inspection I'll make a phone call, and we'll take off as soon as you like. We'll stop off for a bit on the way back. I've something to show you."

After they landed at the clinic, George and Linda greeted them by the strip with smiles and hugs. There was a ragged line of patients with various wounds and afflictions waiting stoically on the crude outside benches in the dappled shade of the trees.

Linda's smile faded, and she said, "We were so sorry to hear about Ben. How did it happen? Surely not a flying accident, like the news said. You told us he was a captive."

"Not an accident, no," Zeke said. "You ought to know the truth, but we can't let it get out. We had an exchange arranged, using the man you fixed up, but they set a trap. They shot Ben."

George grew intensely serious and looked Zeke in the eyes. "You intend to track them down. You and this independent anti-poaching group."

"Yes," Zeke said.

"Good luck, then. Ben was a fine man. Anything we can do, you let us know."

Zeke and Liana helped unload, then they climbed back into the Cessna and Zeke said, "Okay, where to?"

"Head southeast, please. I'll give you course corrections as we go. We can top up the tanks at Maswa. They have a fuel truck at the strip there and we have an arrangement with them."

They flew near the south shore of Lake Victoria, stopped briefly at Maswa, and pushed on into the thickening heat haze over part of the vast Serengeti Plain, over small Lake Eyasi and the sweeping East Rift Valley to a crude red-dirt strip north of the town of Babati. Farther off to the north in the haze they could see the ghostly conical bulk of Mount Meru, nearly 15,000 feet high. Somewhere off to the right of it, as Zeke knew by his chart, hidden now by haze and cloud buildups, legendary snow-dusted Kilimanjaro rose even higher to over 19,000 feet. Zeke checked the trees below for wind direction, landed easily, swung the Cessna off onto a grassy patch, and shut it down.

A diminutive grinning black man wearing khaki shorts and matching shirt with epaulets, scuffed boots, and a floppy hat with a soiled chin string met them with a rusty topless Jeep that looked like a relic left over from the Second World War.

Liana and Zeke got into the back and the man twisted around to say, "It is very very good to see you again, Miss Sekibo."

"Zeke," she said. "This is Ranger Jabari Mutemba. He refuses to call me Liana. He is a hopeless rascal."

Jabari Mutemba giggled, shook hands, and said, "Mister Zeke." He started the Jeep, ground it into gear, and drove them much too fast along a dirt track for several miles to a turn with a faded sign beside it that said 'Meru Foothills National Park.' A mile farther on he pulled up beside a cement-block building that sported an antenna and a flagpole flying a tattered Tanzanian flag, green and blue with a diagonal black yellow-edged band. He left the engine idling.

An enormous smiling very black woman in a flowing bright red caftan stood in the doorway cradling a naked baby. Zeke started to get out but Liana said, "No you stay with Jabari. He'll take things from here."

She got out, walked over, and held her arms out. The woman proudly offered the baby and Liana held up the child to admire it, cooed something Zeke couldn't hear, and held him tucked on one arm in that easy instinctual way women have. The solemn baby had part of a chubby fist stuck in his mouth. Jabari said, "That is my wife, Winnie, and our son, Ibada." Both women waved. Zeke smiled and waved back, and Jabari lurched the Jeep off much too fast again along an even worse track that wound through tall grass and sparse trees. There was muddy rainwater in some of the potholes and Jabari splashed and rattled through them with gleeful abandon.

Near a clearing with an expanse of thick vegetation beyond, Jabari stopped the Jeep and let the engine idle. With his forearms on the top of the steering wheel, he uttered a long ululation and called, "Miss Mary. Where you be today, my beauty? Come to your very good friend Jabari, Miss Mary. Come to me, my beauty." Again the ululation.

Nothing happened for a time. A mild breeze scented with wildflowers was rippling the grass lazily. Birds were debating some avian issue in the trees.

There was motion behind the vegetation. A patch of the woodland became denser, and a weaving prehistoric shape snaked out of the trees ten feet off the ground. It was followed by a big bony head and large floppy ears and a huge fissured gray body. Through a thin place in the grass Zeke caught a glimpse of a miniature but tuskless version of the big beast, wary, hanging back. The big version moved a few more feet and stopped, the trunk raised, sampling the air.

Jabari was grinning widely. "Stay here please, Mister Zeke," he said. He shut off the sputtering Jeep, got out, and approached the elephant with his arms spread wide. He walked up to her and pressed his hands and the side of his head against the leathery hide near the big shoulder. The elephant moved its ears back, one of them almost completely hiding Jabari, as though enfolding him, then he was revealed by a careful motion of the huge head.

Jabari stood back from the elephant a few feet and beckoned. "Okay, Mister Zeke, please come to meet our Mary. She is most curious about you. I have told her you are a good man because Miss Sekibo say you be. Slowly now, please. Come."

Zeke climbed out and walked cautiously up to her with his arms spread wide, as Jabari had done. She shook her huge head once and met him with the tip of her trunk. He stopped eight feet from her and stood still. The trunk tip was pink inside. The dexterous lips were like two curled fingers. The tip moved over him lightly, brushing him from his hat to his knees, pausing at his pockets. It blew a gusty warm breath at him and was retracted. He edged closer. Looked up at her great eye. From a distance, her eyes had looked indolent, indifferent, like those of a very old being, set in a nest of wrinkles, heavily lidded, heavily lashed, like the eye of a milk cow, except this iris was golden and beautiful. But up close, there was something deeper in this stoic eye. An unusual awareness. A *knowing*. An atavistic wisdom from an ancient age of patient evolution. A serenity blended with a restrained and frightening potential for violence.

She could take my head off with a swipe of her trunk on a whim, he thought. *Or gore me with a tusk or knock me down and stomp me flat, and I would be powerless to stop her.*

As though sensing his thoughts, Jabari quietly said, "Yes, she is a most wild elephant, but she will not harm you while you be with me, Mister Zeke. I believe she like you, even. Come, put your ear to her side."

Moving with caution, Zeke tipped his hat back to hang on its chinstrap around his neck, placed his spread hands against her massive rib cage, and rested the side of his head against the warm skin that felt like wrinkled leather, but very much alive. She had a pleasant musty, woodsy scent. He could hear the great heart thudding a steady slow beat. And something else. A mild rumbling at such a low frequency it was barely audible.

"It mean she is content," Jabari said.

Zeke stepped back and saw the baby between the mother's tree-trunk legs. It was still wary, but curious. He started to reach out to it but then thought, *probably not a great idea*, and stepped back ten feet.

The baby edged out, also testing the air with its small trunk. The mother curled her trunk around the baby protectively, but then swung her trunk aside and just stood quietly. The baby stayed put, its small trunk timidly exploring the breeze in imitation of its mother.

She's so damned big, Zeke thought. He said, "Yes. You have a magnificent baby, Mary."

"She is proud. Like my Winnie. But we have not yet named Mary's baby. It is a female." He rubbed and patted the great elephant's trunk and with a ponderous grace she urged the baby to move ahead of her, back into the cool shade of the trees.

Zeke watched them until they were completely hidden. He felt awed. Privileged. He said, "She is . . . impressive. You've got a special bond with her. It was good to see. Maybe you could call the baby Tyke."

"What does it mean?"

"It means small one. It's the name of a brave elephant who was killed." He spelled it out. "Do you know Dante James who works for Miz Sekibo?"

"I do, yes."

"One day ask him to tell you about Tyke."

"I will, yes. Tyke. I like it."

Back at the small combination house and ranger station, Winnie gave Zeke a smothering hug and insisted on feeding them biscuits and tea. While Winnie unashamedly fed the now-diapered baby at her exposed breast, Jabari told the story of how a poacher had wounded Mary three years ago and the rangers had found her hiding alone in a thicket. "We dart her," he said, "and we tend her wound, and she stay near me and Winnie, and she get well. One day she is gone. We did not see her for long, long time. Then she come here with her baby. She knows it be okay safe here for her baby."

Jabari drove them bucketing back to the red-dirt strip, where they saw an armadillo waddling slowly away through the sparse grass in stark contrast to their recent wild ride. Jabari gave both Liana and Zeke a hug and shook Zeke's hand vigorously.

"How many rangers are there in the park?" Zeke said.

"We are six, Mister Zeke," Jabari said.

"What will you do if the poachers come back?"

Jabari Matumba grew serious, his etched smile lines relaxing. "I have my old rifle. It has a long reach. I will use it."

An old rifle against automatic weapons in the hands of hardened killers was only a notch above hopeless, but Zeke said nothing.

In the plane heading back to Dodoma in the lowering sunlight, dodging their way through a sky thick with spectacular six-mile-high thunderheads pulsing with lightning and sailing on slanted rain veils, Zeke said over the headsets, "Okay. I get it."

"Mary is quite something, is she not?" Liana said.

Zeke nodded. "And so are you."

They landed in deep twilight, the powerful lights of the Cessna turning a sudden rain into bright needles as they taxied. They got soaked pushing the plane back into the hangar and sliding the big doors closed. Liana's blouse was as good as transparent, and she was not wearing a bra. *She's . . . prominent*, Zeke thought. *Must be the cool rain*.

They walked side by side through the rain to the GHR Land Rover.

"We could pick up Chinese on the way." Zeke said. "Ah . . . I could go in and get it."

"That will do nicely," she said.

"I see no reason for taking turns showering at your place," he said.

"Nor do I," she said.

Thirty-six

"There's been another bad kill," Fitzgerald said.

The four of them were meeting again three days later in DJ's place at dusk. DJ had brewed tea and they each had a cup. He'd put out a bowl of fruit on the scratched coffee table.

"How many?" Liana said.

"Nineteen," Fitzgerald said. "Four days ago at dawn, best we can figure. Near Shinyanga. About three hundred miles northwest of Dodoma. Ninety miles southeast of the lake. They attacked on horseback. Bush rumor has it they were Raza's bunch. I drove out to the site yesterday with Sabo, Tyree, and Babak, and the kill fits that bastard's style. Rake them across the legs with short well-aimed AK bursts to put them down. Hack the tusks free with axes and machetes. Babak is our best tracker and he's very good, but heavy rains had washed out the trail. We reached out to our contacts, but we couldn't pick up a whiff of them. They're safely in the wind again."

"Couldn't you do an aerial search for the gang?" DJ said. "We're pretty certain they've got a base in the Mountains of the Moon, right?"

"Sure, but that's a vast, rugged area," Fitzgerald said. "Thousands of square miles. Heavy forest. If they're only half smart at concealment, we could fly right over them and never know it."

"Tricky weather around those high mountains, too," Zeke said. "Likely a microclimate, even, considering those extreme, abrupt changes in elevation. Lots of fog. Cloud cover much of the time. Rains like waterfalls. It would be a hell of a long shot at best, and we can't give it anything like the air hours it would take to do a thorough grid search, anyway, not with the GHR planes. Even if we found them, by the time you could get your men in there on the ground they could have moved their camp fifty miles."

They were all quiet for a moment.

"But I do have an idea," Zeke said. "Maybe it wouldn't lead us to that particular gang, but it might trap some poachers, and better yet, even a few people in the network, like the wholesalers and smugglers."

Fitzgerald raised an eyebrow. "And that idea would be?"

"Can you get a tusk?"

"Sure. We've got a hidden stash confiscated from poachers. We've been planning on burning it in a bonfire someplace public one of these days. Make it a media thing, with anonymous calls ahead of time. Wexton will help by giving it good coverage. We'll let it be known on the bush network the Mambas are behind it. It'll call public attention to the fight, and maybe even intimidate a few poachers. Why?"

"Suppose we imbed a GPS tracker in one? It would have to be cleverly done. Dig out a big enough pocket to hold the tracker and a long-life battery. Then cover the pocket somehow, distress the area or stain it so it looks natural. Feed it into the network and track it on laptops. Once we get a good fix along some road, I could fly the Cessna over high enough so I don't attract attention. Use a camera with a long lens to identify the vehicle. Get a license number."

"You could perhaps coordinate with teams on the ground," Liana said.

"Sure," Zeke said. "If there's no cell service the teams could use hand-held aviation band radios. We could choose a frequency that isn't used by any airport in the region so nobody would be likely to listen in."

"You'd have to feed a *pair* of tusks into the network," DJ said. "Your seller could maybe pose as a one-timer who doctored a watermelon and poisoned an elephant to keep it off his crops, then figured there was no sense letting the tusks go to waste."

"Sure, good thinking," Zeke said.

"Wait for the buyer to start moving with the tusks," Fitzgerald said. "Then we track the load to see where it winds up. The teams on the ground should only keep in real loose contact so the transporters don't get suspicious. Sure, it's worth a try. But I wish we could come up with a scheme that would help us snare Raza."

"It may be easier than you think to reach Raza," Zeke said. "I had a long talk with Hobart Wexton, remember."

"I tried talking with him, too, but I never got very far. Arrogant idiot. I had the feeling he knew a hell of a lot more than he was letting on."

"He likes his booze," Zeke said. "We had a meal, he got drunk, and he told me much more than I think he meant to. There are a lot of poachers out there, and they come and go, but the ivory gets bought up by only a few wholesale buyers who have ready cash, and then smuggled to one of the major ports—for East Africa that's most likely either Mombasa or Dar—and shipped out in containers to retailers in Asia. If we could get a rigged tusk to an important wholesale buyer and track it through to a shipper, we might not only rip up a major operation, but the buyer would be almost certain to know Raza and how to get in touch. We apply some pressure to get the information and then we could set a trap for Raza. Wexton gave me the name Salvious Philemon. Ever hear of him?"

"No," Fitzgerald said.

"Apparently he's thought to be a big wholesale buyer throughout Tanzania."

"So let's go after him with your idea."

"Only thing is, I don't know anybody who could rig the tusk," Zeke said. "You?"

"No," Fitzgerald said. "Liana?"

She shook her head.

DJ finished his tea, set the cup down, and said, "I think I might know a guy."

Thirty-seven

"How do you know this guy?" Zeke said.

They were in Zeke's Jeep well after dark, driving through the sleepy unevenly lighted outskirts of Dodoma.

"Take the next right," DJ said. "We play music together. In a small combo. Name is Juan Armando Rodriguez. He's on the keyboard. We call him Fingers. There's six of us including our singer, a girl named Moody. I'm the drummer. Some soft rock, other stuff like Santana, Buffett, Madonna, Joplin, Tina, Seger. It's a good wide mix. So we can play about anywhere. We do local clubs on weekends. Here and sometimes in Dar. You play together, you get close. I trust him. Okay, here we are. That place there, the one looks like a two-car garage with a shack attached."

There was a sign in the patchy yard saying "Juan Armando's Fix-it Shop Appliances Furniture Small Motors Repaired No Job To Big Or To Small"

Zeke pulled into the gravel driveway of the modest place behind a dusty capped Ford pickup. Rodriguez met them at the door. The living room had a sagging couch, a matching chair, a worn rug, and a nice Korg electronic keyboard in the corner beside a filing cabinet that probably held music. There was a faint scent of marijuana. They sat at the scarred kitchen table and Rodriguez got each of them a beer. He was a wiry

Latino with a neatly trimmed mustache, long sideburns, and an easy smile.

DJ said, "Fingers, this is Zeke. Zeke, Fingers. He's got a whole shop setup out there in his garage. Band saw, drill press, sander, grinder, lathe, hand tools, all that. He knows woodwork, metal work, electronics, computers. Lot smarter than he looks. We got a job for you, my man. But nobody can know about it. I mean nobody. You gonna be good with that, Fingers?"

"You serious?"

"Deadly," DJ said. "But it's for a good cause."

"Well, maybe then, I guess. What's the job?"

Zeke gave him a highly condensed and edited version.

Fingers listened to it and sat there with his eyebrows raised. "Wait a minute. You mean you got an elephant tusk out there in your Jeep? You know that's illegal, right? You gotta realize you could do time for it. And you want *me* to rig it for you?"

"We know," DJ said. "And yes. So, will you do it? I figure you can, easy enough."

"Well, sure, I *can*." He studied his beer bottle, thinking. "A tusk is hollow near the big end, where the nerve was, right?"

"Right," DJ said.

More thinking. "Okay, then. That's where I'd run the antenna, bond it up tight to the inside surface. What you want is a tracker that uses both GPS with the satellites and GSM off the cell tower network, best you could do. GPS'll work good if your tusk is hand-carried, or maybe in a pickup bed under a tarp, anyplace it can read the sky. The GSM chip will take over if the tusk is inside a semi or a car or even in a building. Few months back I set up a system for a guy wanted to track shipments around east Africa. It was spotty. Cell coverage near Dar or here in Dodoma is pretty good, and along the main roads, also good up around Mombasa, southern Kenya, most of Uganda and Rwanda and Burundi. But if you get in the middle of Tanzania, or down south, anywhere way out there in the bush, it ain't gonna work worth a damn, you realize that."

"We figure sooner or later the tusk will be headed for a port, a city where cell service is good. We'll take the chance we can track it well enough."

More thinking. "There's a couple high-end units come with rechargeable lithium batteries. They'll track for weeks before they need a recharge. But say I hide a charge port inside the root, too. I cut a square chunk out of the tusk like eighteen inches up from the base, don't have to be too big, the units are small. I fasten the unit in place. Cover it up with a fitted piece of plastic. Work it over with hand files. Mix up some paint the same shade as the tusk and feather it out with ultrafine sandpaper so it's the same texture and sheen as the tusk. You get ready, you top up the battery through the hidden charge port and you're good to go. Yeah, sure, I *can* do it. But why do I want to risk my ass?"

"As DJ said, it's for a good cause," Zeke said.

Fingers looked at each of them. "You're working, like, undercover for the law?"

"No," DJ said.

"I guess I don't want to know, then," Fingers said.

"No. You don't," Zeke said.

Fingers tapped his fingers in a complicated rhythm on his beer bottle. Thinking some more. "Well I know the story about your circus days, DJ, and I gotta sympathize. You guys must want this rig 'cause you're trying to burn down some poaching operation. And I do fiercely hate those fuckers. So, tell you what. I'll build your rig. My girlfriend will be sleeping over Saturday night, but she don't have a clue what I do out in the shop and don't really care. I'll have to work on it nights, when I got no customers coming in. All I ask, you pay my expenses. That's my DJ discount. Gimme a week. You guys want another beer?"

Thirty minutes later, Zeke and Dante got the tusk, which was wrapped loosely in a blue tarp, and carried it into the workshop.

Fingers Rodriguez walked them out to the Jeep and said, "See you in a week. We'll need to final test the rig and teach you how to use it, so bring a tablet or a laptop. It'll work on a smartphone, too, but you get a better map on a bigger screen."

Zeke dropped DJ off and drove home to the camper. He took off his boots, put his feet up, and scanned the news on his smartphone.

There was a piece about two African men who currently claimed to be Jesus Himself. Bupete Chibwe Chishimba of Kitwe, Zambia, now 46, claimed he'd received his revelation at age 24. He was married with five children and drove a cab when not preaching the end of days. Moses Hlongwane of Eshowe, South Africa, was supposedly anointed in a 1992 dream. To his followers, Moses's wife was known as 'Mother of the Whole World.' He was also touting the end of days.

After a lull of a few years, Somali pirates based in the ancient port of Qandala in Puntland were capturing ships again off the Horn of Africa. There had been ten attacks on ships in the past three months. There were suspicions that proceeds from the piracy were being funneled to ISIS in the Middle East.

A third of Somalia's population faced starvation, mostly because of a lingering extreme regional drought, and three quarters of a million people there were displaced. Across Somalia's southern border, northern Kenya was becoming unstable as a result, and al-

Shabaab was on a rampage, taking advantage of the situation. Women who had to walk miles in hopes of finding food or to carry scarce water back to their villages were being raped on the roadsides.

An election was coming up in two weeks in the diminutive crowded nation of Rwanda, known as 'The Land of a Thousand Hills,' west of Lake Victoria on the remote northwestern border of Tanzania. But there was only one permitted opposition party and they had only been allowed very limited campaigning against the entrenched President Paul Kagame of the ruling Rwandan Patriotic Front. In 1994, Kagame's rebel army had routed the raging Hutus, who had slaughtered many thousands of Tutsi men, women, and children, employing mostly the ubiquitous machetes. Sometimes they had simply swung a Tutsi infant by a leg to bash its head against a concrete wall. Kagami had seized the capital, Kigali, by force and had held power since. He'd won two previous elections with more than 90 percent of the vote. Opposition leaders had been assassinated, jailed, or exiled. Local journalist Robert Mugabe said, "There is no election in Rwanda, there is a coronation declaring Kagame the king." Yet the country was stable, its people were being fed better than in many African countries, and its economy had grown seven percent in the past year.

Tanzania was demanding millions USD in unpaid taxes and penalties from gold and silver mining companies. Lawyers for the companies were protesting indignantly.

Boko Haram had claimed credit for yet another indiscriminate bombing in Nigeria that had killed 18 and maimed 30. UN officials were calling Nigeria a failed state.

An al-Qaeda-linked faction was thought to be smuggling weapons into Africa from Yemen, south across the Gulf of Aden and into Somalia. The intended destination from there was unclear. Months earlier, the U.S. Pentagon had misplaced $300 million in weapons.

In Yemen.

Equatorial Guinea's President Teodoro Obiang Nguema Mbasogo had seized power in a 1979 coup and had ruled the secretive nation ever since. Now his son was under an investigation in France for money laundering.

The son, 50-year-old Teodoro Nguema Obiang Mangue, had recently bought an opulent Parisian mansion on the Champs-Élysées. He owned a large private jet and a fleet of luxury cars, including several Bugatti's and Ferrari's and an Aston Martin. He'd bought the 249-foot yacht *Ebony Shine* second-hand from Russian steel billionaire Viktor Rashnikov. For accounting purposes, the yacht was officially owned by Equatorial Guinea. It had a crew of 24 and its amenities included a swimming pool, a theater, and a sauna. In addition to the Parisian digs, Obiang Junior owned two mansions in South Africa and a $30 million mansion in Malibu. The source of his fortune was allegedly Equatorial Guinea's treasury. The shadowy country had become oil rich over the past few decades, although most of its citizens lived in gnawing poverty.

Teodoro Obiang's lawyers were emphatically asserting that their client had industriously amassed his fortune legally from business interests throughout central Africa and that, in any case, he served as his father's vice president and thus was entitled to diplomatic immunity. Not surprisingly, the lawyers said furthermore he had not been accused of any wrongdoing in his own country, and France had no right to intervene in the affairs of a sovereign African nation.

The article went on to say that France was apparently becoming a favorite vacationing and retirement destination for African leaders in general.

Zeke shook his head, put the phone on charge, and turned in.

Once again, he realized there were so many endemic overwhelming concerns in African that eliminating ivory poaching would be near the bottom on any priority list in many of the turbulent nations, if it was listed at all.

A swimming pool on a private boat? he thought as he drifted off.

Thirty-eight

"The weapons are coming in through Somalia," Abdul Ahad told his supreme council of eight, which included his brother, Muhammadu Raza. They were seated in a circle on a fine silk rug in Ahad's tent, which had been pitched under a ring of trees that essentially concealed it from satellite or aircraft view, and had a full fly spread above it for further camouflage. A woman, rendered anonymous and generic in an enveloping black burqa, was silently serving them tea and bread. Outside, dispersed in the forest on the flank of a foothill deep in the Mountains of the Moon, were 80 of Ahad's men, all supremely fit jihadis and loyal unto the gates of heaven, awaiting only Ahad's command. Seventeen of his men were traveling to northern Kenya in a plain box truck and an escorting GMC SUV, carrying the payment for the arms shipment. They would bring the weapons back to the encampment, taking all measures to insure they were not hijacked or followed. They were expected to return in four days.

Ahad smiled. "They are new, still in crates. Our purchase is but a small part of the weapons our friends in Yemen have stockpiled, but it is enough to arm our men well. One hundred American M4 carbines, which are far more accurate than our old and worn AK47 weapons. One hundred excellent Beretta M9 pistols. Twenty thousand rounds of ammunition. Five sixty-millimeter mortars with one hundred rounds. Forty rocket-propelled grenades. There is even one new weapon the Americans call the 'XM25 Counter Defilade Target Engagement System.' How these Americans love the many lies they tell themselves. A target engagement system. As though it is a bow and an arrow and a straw target, and not a most expensive instrument for merciless killing."

"What is this defilade?" Raza said.

"It means a position protected by shielding from sight or bullets."

"What is this weapon like?" Raza said.

"It is like a pregnant rifle with a box on the top," Ahad said. "The Americans must have spent very much money inventing it. It will fire twenty-five-millimeter projectiles from its magazine, one for each pull of the trigger. I am told it has a reach of seven hundred meters. The box on the top has within it an optical sight, a laser sight, a range detector, and a fuse setter. It can sense the heat of an enemy in darkness or in a forest. You do not need to see him. You only need to know his location and the distance to him. He is perhaps hidden behind a wall of bricks or a barricade. You then fire a projectile that will burst in the air and kill him from above or to the side. I am told it will also fire projectiles that will pierce armor and roast anyone cowering behind it. The Yemenis are sending some ammunition to feed this rifle. It will be your personal weapon for the coming battles, my brother."

Raza nodded.

"These new weapons will make us strong," Ahad said, staring around the circle with dark intensity and a raised clenched fist. "We will soon be unstoppable. Invincible. We will be feared throughout Africa. We will be victorious. May our holy deeds and our humble words carry to the eyes and ears of great Allah, be He praised."

"Allah be praised," the other men said in chorus.

"When will we strike?" Faraji said.

"Yes, *when*," another man said with vehement frustration.

"Soon. We must first train our men in the use and care of the new weapons. How to aim them with accuracy. How to strip and clean them. We must have more explosives for the bombs that will spread fear and confusion like a holy flood before we attack. I am negotiating for a quantity from the Somalis. We will strike with the stunning force of a thunderbolt when we are ready. Until that day you must instill Allah's wrath deeply in the men. You must drill them hard to keep them strong. They must have steady eyes and steel spines and not the slightest thread of mercy. We will be a mighty army. The infidels will fall before us like wheat in a great victory for Allah, may He reign supreme. Allahu akbar."

"*Allahu akbar*," the men shouted.

Ahad dismissed all the members of the council except Raza. The woman wrapped in black refreshed their tea, withdrew into a rear corner of the tent, and sank to her knees, sitting chastely on her heels, hands folded in her lap, to await further orders.

"Has your wound healed well brother?" Ahad said.

"It has, with the help of Allah."

"As is always so. You have made the purchase of the new weapons possible with your harvesting of the ivory over these past months. I am grateful."

Raza nodded. "We are brothers. There is nothing we cannot do together."

Ahad smiled. "Do you have all you need? What may I help you with?"

"The cursed infidels known as the Mambas remain an irritant. The elimination of their pilot struck a blow, but they still pursue us like rabid dogs, and as you know they have another pilot, the tall one I described to you with the woman's long twisted hair. My men fear these demons. I must pay more and more of the harvest money to retain their loyalty."

"Perhaps we should arrange a lethal accident for their leader."

"I am told his men are loyal to the death, as are yours. I believe they would only intensify their efforts."

They were silent for a time.

"The solution seems clear," Ahad said. They move from here to there, we are told. But, like us, they must choose places for their camps that are remote. This gives them some protection from discovery, but also makes them vulnerable because they will always be far from any help. We will press our contacts to help us find them and determine their number, which I do not believe can be near the equal of our army. We will let it be known there is a generous reward for such information. Then we will devise a plan and attack them all. We will end them. We will pick them clean of all possessions and bury them naked and erase all signs of the skirmish. They will simply vanish."

"As soon as we have the new weapons and the men become familiar with them," Raza said.

Ahad nodded. "It will be a good training exercise for the men. It will temper them as fire hardens a fine blade. Before we mount the major attack in Uganda."

"I recall something," Raza said, holding up a finger. "There may be a faster way to find the accursed Mambas."

Ahad looked at him. "Yes?"

"We know the infidel Stone was flying their helicopter. But for the hostage exchange, the pilot with the woman's hair was flying a large light plane with a round engine. As it was climbing away, it turned. Dawud saw the number on its tail clearly through the scope on his rifle. He wrote it down."

Ahad smiled. "You chose wisely when you made Dawud your bodyguard."

They drank their tea and each tore a portion of bread from the dense loaf and ate it.

"You know, brother," Ahad said. "You should take yourself a wife. My wives are the source of much pleasure and comfort. I cherish them. Lubena is with child. I pray it will be a son. Do you not want a son?"

"One day," Raza said. "After we have seized Uganda and have established our caliphate."

"Yes. Al-Shabaab has indicated they will then unite with us to take Kenya. The government there is corrupt and unstable. It will crumble. As we enjoy success, other jihadis will clamor to swell our ranks. We will grow to become a holy army. Our power will spread throughout the heart of Africa, and you and I will reign. It will begin soon, my brother, great Allah willing."

Thirty-nine

The meeting was in Liana's living room for a change. They had decided not to draw too much attention to DJ in his own neighborhood. Also, the food was better here. For the past week, Zeke had flown routine missions for GHR, and had done a fast three-mile dawn run each day followed by a rigorous whole-body strength workout. He was perfecting the intricate new kata as well.

The next night, he and DJ would pick up the rigged tusk. DJ had seen it and reported that Fingers had done a masterful job and was completing the final touches. The electronic implant would be undetectable, even under scrutiny. The antenna and charging port were well disguised inside the root cavity and unlikely to be spotted unless somebody shined a bright light in there. Fingers had installed a program on a laptop DJ had brought and had shown him how to use it. Zeke would hide the tusk under the bed in the camper until they could get it to Fitzgerald. Liana had suggested a hiding place in the hangar, but Zeke figured the whole gamble was his idea, so he should take the major risk of getting caught with the ivory.

"Now all we have to do is feed our tusk into the network," Zeke said. "Anybody got a plan?"

"I've been thinking on that," Fitzgerald said. "Try this out. I told you about the three poachers. A father, name of Joshua Limbu, and two of his sons we caught west of Serengeti Park. We turned them over to the law, anonymously. They're being held in a rough jail in Nyambiti. Waiting to be charged by a traveling magistrate, which could take weeks. The keeper of that jail has been known to accept a bribe for looking the other way when an inmate escapes occasionally. We could send Babak in there to talk with Limbu. He can pose as a cousin. He could tell Limbu we'll bribe the jailkeeper to let the sons escape in exchange for the name and contact info for the buyer they were going to use for their tusks. Probably a hundred USD will take care of the bribe. Limbu will have to take the fall—they were poaching, after all, and all three of them aren't getting a free ride from us for that—but the sons get to go back home to care for the rest of the family. Unlikely the law will bother to go after them. Limbu will probably only get three to six months in jail, anyway, and a fine payable to the magistrate, if he has any money. Local law tends to go easy on the little poachers—the occasional farmer whose crops are at risk from elephants, or a father with a starving family. Anyway, Babak could then contact the buyer and feed him a dozen tusks from our stash, our rigged one included. Should be enough ivory to create a greedy stir in the network. And we could start tracking it."

"What if Limbu betrays us to his buyer?" Liana said. "The buyer would perhaps bribe all three of them out in exchange for the information."

"Pretty sure he'll keep his mouth shut," Fitzgerald said, "because Babak will privately feed him a scary tale about us knowing where his family lives, let the guy know he speaks for the Mambas. We've got a fearsome bush reputation, remember, one we embellish every chance we get."

"It sounds good to me," DJ said.

"Me, too," Zeke said. "We'll have to be ready to track on short notice. Liana, the laptop, her good zoom camera, and me in the air in the Cessna until we can identify a transport vehicle for the ground teams to track."

"Make it three two-man teams," Fitzgerald said. "We can spread them out in three directions some distance from the initial contact site, so at least one of them will be in a position to move in closer fast. The other two teams can follow and catch up. Each team can have a smartphone or a tablet to track for themselves. I'll lead one team."

Liana said, "I'm wondering . . ."

"What?" Zeke said.

"Well, perhaps Babak should have a miniature microphone clipped on somewhere when he goes into the jail, wired to a digital recorder in a pocket. He could make sure he works in the names of this father and his sons, their poaching deeds, and the buyer's name so it will all be recorded. And the ground teams can move in, when things look right and they won't be discovered, to take photos of the transport men and their contacts with their cell phones, but perhaps they should have those little dash cams, too, and don't they make some sort of small hand-held umbrella-like device for listening to conversations at a distance? If in the end we're going to turn this over to some serious law enforcement agency, would it not be good to have solid evidence we can turn over as well? None of us can testify in a court. We'll have to let documented evidence speak for us, won't we?"

Fitzgerald looked at Zeke and raised an eyebrow. "You've got a smart lover there."

"What?" Liana said. "We're just, we're only—"

"Come on," Fitzgerald said. "You think it doesn't show? May as well be written in neon on top of your hangar. You're like a couple of airhead teenagers in high heat. I think it's great. How about you, DJ?"

"Hey, I can live with it," he said with a grin.

Zeke thought, *damn, she's blushing*. He cleared his throat and said, "Okay. DJ, you and I need to talk some more with Fingers about electronic gadgets."

Forty

It was eleven o'clock at night. Zeke was driving his Jeep with DJ in the passenger seat. They were heading north on an uneven single-track red dirt road out of Dodoma, high beams and two rectangular spotlights mounted on the roll bar probing the deep empty darkness ahead. The lights were turning the sparse looming tree trunks bone white and bleaching out the chest-high grass on both sides of the narrow road. The grass was undulating in a stiff humid wind.

They were bringing the tracker tusk and an assortment of gadgets to Fitzgerald that Fingers had secured for them from his geeky contacts in Dodoma and Dar over the past week. Three tablets for tracking. Three hand-held VHF radios with aviation bands, three miniature dash cams, and three hand-held remote listening devices that had built-in digital recorders. With ten-inch dishes, headphones, and a range of 300 feet, the listening devices could easily be used covertly through the open side window of a vehicle parked in shadows. Fingers had given them the owner's manuals and a crash course in how to use the items, and they would pass what they knew on to Fitzgerald. They were planning to meet at a remote crossroads about halfway between Dodoma and the latest Mamba bush camp. Zeke had the directions set into his smartphone, which was in a holder on the dash.

Zeke was checking the rearview yet again when DJ handed him a bottle of water from the small cooler at his feet.

He drank a third of the bottle and said, "Headlights behind us. Maybe a mile back. Been there ever since Dodoma, I think. I don't like it. I had a feeling coming out of the city."

"You think it could be the law?" DJ said.

"Let's find out," Zeke said. There was a loaded .45 semi-auto in the glove compartment and the pump shotgun loaded with buckshot and wrapped in a blanket lay on the floor in back. Fitzgerald had insisted they all be armed, even Liana, whenever they were out in the wilds. Although Zeke had gone along with it, this was the first time he thought it might actually be a good idea.

Zeke waited until the road took a gentle curve, with intervening trees making the following headlights flicker. He found a sparse patch of grass, pulled over, and shut off the lights. Instant velvet darkness. DJ handed him a flashlight from the glove compartment and Zeke used it and the backup lights to jounce the Jeep backward in four-wheel drive, plowing a path perpendicular to the road into the grass for 30 feet. He shut off the engine and the flashlight and they waited. Zeke took down another third of the water bottle and heard DJ crack the cap on a bottle and drink. Neither said anything. Insects were loud in the brush, and not far off in the trees birds were complaining raucously about something.

They heard a grinding engine noise coming, made uneven by the rutted road. The noise grew louder and the roadway was lit brighter and brighter in flashes as the oncoming vehicle bounced and slewed along.

Zeke reached back and unwrapped the pump shotgun and rested the butt of it on the floor between the front seats. He kept his right hand on it.

The vehicle got a lot louder and closer and flashed past, going too fast for the rutted road. Zeke caught a glimpse of a black face on the passenger side, staring wide-eyed at the Jeep. The vehicle was a small dented and dirty pickup. Blue or green. There was a man in the bed, riding backwards. It looked like he was carrying a long gun. The pickup slowed, brake lights flaring. It stopped a short distance along the track.

Zeke jumped out carrying the shotgun. He stepped out onto the track and was washed in the glare of a flashlight. He raised the shotgun and fired a blast high enough over the pickup so as not to hit anybody. The flashlight winked out and the pickup roared into motion, bounding away, spraying dirt. Zeke went back and climbed into the Jeep. He said, "What did you see?"

"Three guys in a hammered dark pickup, green, I think. The passenger looked right at us. Surprised. But not, like, scared. They're not any kind of law. More like up to no damned good, is what they seemed like. I think the guy in the back had a rifle."

Zeke didn't say anything. Just cranked up the Jeep and pulled out, pushing it to close the distance to the receding tail lights.

They followed the pickup for another two miles, when it took a turnoff to the right.

Zeke stopped at the intersection, shut off the lights and the engine, and watched and listened in the humid night until the pickup's tail lights were out of sight. He gave it another five minutes, then put the Jeep in gear and went on for another deserted 20 miles and three turns to the meeting with Fitzgerald, who was standing by a Land Rover with Mike Sabo when they got there.

In the glare from the Jeep's lights, Zeke and DJ transferred the ivory and took out each electronic item and explained its functioning to Fitzgerald and Sabo, who paid close attention.

When they had all the items and the owner's manuals loaded into the Rover, Fitzgerald said, "Babak went to Nyambiti jail and had a conversation with Limbu, got his sons sprung, and got the buyer's name and number. Name's Kafil Mongo. And Limbu told him Mongo supposedly works with that guy you mentioned, Salvious Philemon, so looks like we can jack up some of the major players here. Babak even talked Limbu into calling Mongo and vouching for him. Smart move. Babak called Mongo that afternoon and set up a meet for three days from now, nine o'clock at night at a boondocks bar outside Singida, a small town a hundred and twenty miles northwest of Dodoma. Babak's supposed to bring the ivory. We'll charge up our tusk and load it along with eleven more into an old full-sized pickup we've got. The plates are stolen, so no worries there. We'll cover the ivory with sacks of onions. I'll send Ganya Madaki along as a bodyguard. They can pretend they're brothers. Two other men will shadow 'em just in case. If the deal gets done right away, all my men will pull back so they don't arouse any suspicion, and we'll get the tracking teams ready. You better be ready to fly."

"I will be," Zeke said. "Just call me after the deal is done. We'll start monitoring, and when the ivory moves, we'll take off."

"Something bothering you?" Fitzgerald said.

"It's probably nothing," Zeke said. "But coming out here tonight I think we were being followed. A small blue or green pickup with three men in it, at least one of them armed. I thought for a while it could have been connected to the poachers. But they could have been bandits on the prowl, I guess. Or it may just have been vegetable farmers coming home late from the city market. If so, I hope I didn't scare them too badly. I fired the shotgun, aiming high, and they took off."

Fitzgerald nodded. "You see now why I want you armed out in the bush. If they were bandits looking for an easy score, and that's certainly possible, they could have taken everything, including your Jeep. When it looked like it wasn't going to be so easy, they rabbited. Nobody wants to face a man with a twelve-gauge. It's intimidating. Don't be quick to dismiss gut feelings. Sometimes it's your subconscious piecing together glimpses, smells, sounds, sticky notes stashed in your memory files. When it all comes together to put a twist in your gut, you need to pay attention. Sounds like you did the right thing. It was probably just random thugs. But we'll tighten up security, anyway. You be extra careful, too."

Forty-one

The next night at eleven thirty-five, Hobart Wexton came out of the Africa Now TV3 building and walked to his car, an aging silver Audi sedan. He'd just finished a live news broadcast. He was especially pleased about his scathing bit covering the arrest of a motel owner accused of running a brothel. Privately, he thought the unlucky man had simply not come up with the required bribes to stay in operation.

The parking area was dark. The station owner had ignored repeated requests for a security light. Hobart had just keyed the driver's door when a sinuous arm snaked around his neck and he felt a sudden sharp pain over his right kidney. It froze him. He wanted to say something but couldn't.

"You will be quiet," a rough voice said by his ear. "You are feeling the tip of my knife tasting your back. It is very sharp. You will give me your keys. You will sit behind the wheel. I will get in the other side and give you the keys. You will drive. I wish only to question you but if you do not obey me I will kill you. Do you understand?"

Wexton nodded as much as he could, whispered a yes, and held up the keys. The arm released him and the hand took the keys. His back felt warmly wet and he knew he was bleeding. He got into the car and closed the door. Made his shaking hands grip the wheel. Waited. He looked at the man after he'd slid in on the passenger side. *Good*, he thought. *That must be good.* The man was wearing a ball cap and a scarf that allowed only his glittering eyes to show. *He would not hide his face if he intends to kill me.*

Ahad's man, Faraji, was dressed like an infidel in running shoes, loose jeans, and a plain black shirt. He made sure Wexton saw the knife and said, "Drive. To the right out of the lot."

Wexton got the car going and complied.

A half-mile along the road there was a turnout with a small white dented pickup sitting there. "Pull in behind that truck and shut the engine and lights off." Faraji said.

Wexton did. There was pale light coming in from a high half-moon. He took his hands from the wheel but then put them back to stop the trembling, to have something to hang onto.

Faraji said, "You have done news stories about the harvesting of the ivory. You know the group of what you infidels call vigilantes who chase and kill the harvesters. We think you know all about these devils. You will tell me who is the leader of the Mambas and how I can find him. Where their camp is. You will also tell me how many they are."

"Listen," Wexton said. "I don't know these things you want. I have heard of the Mambas, yes, but I have no earthly idea where to find them. You must believe me."

Faraji was silent and motionless. Wexton could see the man's eyes glinting beneath the ball cap visor.

The silence went on.

"Believe me," Wexton said. "I would help you if I could."

More silence. Stillness.

Faraji's left hand snaked out to grip Wexton's thigh, holding it still like a steel vise. The knife in his other hand flashed in the moonlight and Wexton screamed as the tip of it bit into the side of the knee and hit bone and cartilage.

Faraji released his grip on the thigh, pulled the knife back, and went still and silent again.

"Ohgodohgodohgod," Wexton said, holding his knee with both hands. "Oh *god* that hurts. *Fitzgerald.* Ryan Fitzgerald leads the Mambas. I only met him once."

"Describe him," Faraji said.

Wexton did, and said, "We've been in touch, yes, but he has mostly called me from a blocked number. I have no way to reach him right now. I know *nothing* else about him. He can't . . . can't have many men. I know he gets money from some private donor in the U.S. I don't know who or how much. My *knee.* It's *killing* me, and I know my back is bleeding. Please. *Please* don't stick me again. Fitzgerald can only have a small band. I mean, he has to pay them and equip them and feed them and transport them. They have to be highly mobile. How many can he possibly have? I would say . . . it *hurts* . . . I would say he only has maybe twenty or so men, if that, but I don't *know*, for God's sake. Please, that's all I know. You have to believe me. I would tell you more if I knew. Please." He closed his eyes tightly, squeezing out tears. He pulled in his shoulders and rested his forehead on the steering wheel and trembled and sobbed, still gripping his knee tightly.

He felt the car shift and heard the passenger door open and close. He looked up, wiped his eyes with the back of his shaking hand to clear away the tears, and saw the man getting into the passenger side of the white truck. The plate was muddied and unreadable.

He was having trouble taking in enough air and the pain was like a nail embedded in his knee. His hands were slippery with blood. He started the car and drove away, weaving, using his left foot on the accelerator.

It was 15 minutes to the hospital.

Forty-two

Zeke and Liana were in her hangar office with the door open having a takeout lunch. DJ was doing a routine annual inspection on the Beaver. He had all the small access ports on the wings and fuselage removed. The engine was uncowled and the spark plugs were in a rack on the red tool cart for cleaning. He was on a low stepladder using a pressure gauge to check the compression, rotating the prop by hand to locate top dead center on each cylinder. The big hangar doors were open and banging lightly in their tracks. Outside, low dingy cloud billows were thickening in a gusty cool wind out of the south, heavy with the smell of impending rain.

"Must be a front moving in," Zeke said.

The burner phone in his shirt pocket rang. He flipped it open and said, "Zeke."

"It's on," Fitzgerald said. "Buyer took delivery last night. The load sat outside Singida until now. Started moving twenty minutes ago. Program's working fine."

"Where are you?"

"Forty miles south of Kondoa. With Sabo. Looks like we'll be the closest team."

"What's the weather there?"

"Severe clear. Mean-looking clouds building along the horizon farther to the south, though."

"Socking in here, but we can probably still get out. I'll call you from the air on the burner or on VHF."

"Is the whole thing working, then?" Liana said.

"Yup," Zeke said. He snatched up his iPad from the desk and punched in the weather. It was not pretty. Dense green was filling in the screen from the south, with embedded yellow and red amoeba-like shapes that had to be very strong convective storm cells. There were a few shadings of violet, indicating torrential rain. It was all creeping closer by the minute. He said, "We've got to take off right now if we want to get out from under this front."

Liana's phone chimed. "It's Iverson. I need to take it."

Zeke nodded.

She answered cheerfully and listened briefly, her face going solemn. "He needs to speak with you," she said.

Zeke took the phone and said, "Yes." He looked at Liana.

"We've a life or death thing, I'm afraid. Man in Mbulu has been badly burned in a petrol explosion. Needs to be flown to a burn unit. Passable one at the hospital in Dar, but I've been looking at the weather. You should be able to pick him up before this front overtakes you, but you may not be able to get him to Dar. It will be weathered in soon. Nairobi would probably be best, anyway. Better equipped to deal with it, you see. An ambulance can meet you in Babati. Good strip there. They'll send an EMT along with the patient. The Beaver would be best I should think. No one else can reach the patient faster, apparently. How soon can you take off?"

Zeke was quiet. He'd flown over that route before, coming back to Dodoma with Liana on the day he'd met the elephant named Mary.

"Mister Blades?" Iverson said. "Is there some sort of problem?"

"Ah . . . can't use the Beaver. Dante is doing an annual inspection on it and he's got it all opened up. But I can use the Cessna. It's topped up. Just need to make room in it. Stay by the phone so you can coordinate, please. You could start working on getting me cleared into Kenyan air space so I can land there, and alert the people in Nairobi. Rough ETA Nairobi about two and a half hours from right now. I'll call you from the air when I know more."

He hung up and shouted out the office door, "DJ, how fast can you take the passenger seat and the back seat out of the Cessna?"

"What? I don't know. Fifteen, twenty minutes? What's up."

"Do it. Fast as you can. Got a medevac."

"In this weather?" he said, but he grabbed up a handful of tools and hustled to the Cessna.

"What about the tracking?" Liana said.

Zeke cleared a place on the desk by shoving all the items aside with a sweep of his forearm. He pulled a sectional chart out of the filing cabinet and spread it out on the desk. "Here's Babati." He pointed to it on the chart. "Iverson wants me to pick up a burn patient there and take him on to Nairobi." He pulled up the tracking program on his iPad. It was working, but the red dot was intermittent. He found the road on the paper chart. Good. The dot was about 14 miles out of Singida, edging east toward Kondoa. By the time he'd get there it should have traveled another 30 or so miles east. He poked a finger at the place he estimated for an intercept. It was only about 40 miles to the left side of the heading he'd have to fly to Babati, anyway. Plain dumb luck. "With only a slight dogleg in my course, I may be able to do a quick pass over the transport vehicle. Enough to identify it for Fitzgerald, then go on to Babati for the pickup."

"But don't you need me with you?"

"No. Sorry. No room for a litter and a medic and you."

A sudden gust of heavy rain lashed the hangar, sounding like a massive blast of pellets on the metal roof from a giant shotgun. The light outside had grown eerily yellow.

"I don't want you going up in this weather, anyway," he said. "It's even worse than I thought. Just give me your camera." The dogleg in his course would eat only very little extra time, and he could make that up by firewalling the throttle most of the way. Assuming he could get out of here quickly, if at all, with the fast-worsening weather. "DJ," he shouted. "How you doing there?"

"I'm on it, I'm on it." He was inside the plane and his voice was muffled.

Liana handed him the camera bag and said, "They'll close down the airport, you know, if it gets much worse."

"I'll tell 'em it's an emergency. Show me how to work this thing."

Palm trees outside were bending and clattering, and it was growing even darker.

Forty-three

The Dodoma tower reluctantly cleared him to taxi but said, "Be advised there are strong cells approaching from the south and we are about to close the airport."

"This is a medical emergency flight," Zeke said. The Cessna's wings were rocking, and fat random raindrops were pelting the aluminum skin loudly. "I'll be departing to the north, out of the weather."

He did a quick runup and cycled the controls on the taxi run while the plane was partially sheltered from the stiff wind by buildings, and when he reached the hold line for the runway he said, "Ready for takeoff on two-seven."

"Wind one-niner-five at twenty-four, gusts to thirty-one," the tower said. "Do you wish to file IFR?"

It was going to be an almost 90-degree strong and gusting crosswind in rapidly lowering visibility. Far exceeding the Cessna's official tested crosswind capability. Probably the worst conditions for a takeoff in a light plane he'd ever attempted.

"I still have okay visibility," he said. "Like to depart special VFR if that's okay."

The tower hesitated but granted it.

He held the aileron cranked all the way left to keep the heavy gusts from lifting the wing sideways. He had an image of Ben Stone sitting beside him with his big arms folded, gazing out at the roiling mess through his mirrored sunglasses. Saying, "What, you getting all apprehensive just because it's a little breezy? Let's do this."

Zeke smiled, clamped the toe brakes, and pushed the throttle smoothly to the stop. He waited a few heartbeats for the power to build, then released the brakes, easing off on the aileron as the Cessna lurched ahead, gathering precious speed. Then suddenly the plane danced sideways, almost out of control as a powerful crosswind gust hit, blowing him toward the right side of the runway, the tires skipping and chirping. He hauled back on the yoke just before the wind could blow him off the pavement and into the string of landing lights sticking up alongside the runway, and the bellowing Cessna staggered into the air. He immediately crabbed left, full into the wind, and stayed low to take advantage of ground effect.

When he had enough airspeed above a stall, he climbed into the gale, bucking and yawing wildly in the turbulence. It felt less like flying and more like bulling his way up a raging whitewater river. When he had 500 feet under him, he began a cautious wildly turbulent right turn to wrestle it around almost 180 degrees and head north, the wind zipping him back across the runway. His ground speed rose fast with what was now a strong tail wind, but by 700 feet the ragged clouds were blotting out everything outside and he had to go on the instruments, fighting the controls to keep reasonably level. Trying not to overstress the airframe with too-abrupt control movements. A stunning nearby flash and simultaneous detonation of lightning made him flinch involuntarily, and he heard the tower close the airport behind him. He figured he must be on the leading edge of a major cell. He was rapidly pulling away, though. The rain was heavy and steady and loud against the aluminum skin, the prop blast blowing the water straight back along the windshield in hundreds of quick runnels. Some spritzes were making it through the baffled air vents near the top corners of the windshield to mist on him. No hail, thank the sky gods.

"Well that was interesting," he could hear Ben say. "Think you can keep the dirty side down from here on?"

Within ten miles the clouds began to thin, the turbulence lessened, and he increased the throttle to 160 miles per hour, rapidly drinking gas but gradually making up for the coming dogleg course deviation. He also had the benefit of a brisk tailwind. His speed over the ground had to be at least 180, maybe more.

Five miles farther on he broke out into visual conditions with bright sunshine flooding the cockpit, only scattered clouds, and much smoother air. The transformation seemed miraculous. No more rattling, rushing noise from rain, just the smooth powerful drone of the engine. The Cessna had been topped off and it had a range of over 1,000 miles. It was only 400 miles to Nairobi, so he'd be in excellent shape even with the higher fuel consumption.

He pulled Liana's camera bag close by his seat and unzipped the top. It was a high-end Canon with stabilization and a serious optical zoom. Its pictures would be razor sharp. Liana had shown him just enough to get the shots he wanted. "Try not to touch any of the other buttons," she'd said before he'd climbed into the plane. She'd also kissed him hastily and said, "Take care, will you please. I've become quite fond of you."

He got the iPad out of his flight bag and put it on his lap. Fired it up. The dot was clear and steady now, still edging eastward, and it looked like he was on a good course to intercept it.

DJ had removed the keepers from the side windows so they could be swung up and open all the way, floating pinned under the wings by the slipstream. This was so Liana could have shot her camera out the passenger window, or out the pilot's window while sitting on the edge of the rear bench seat and framing over Zeke's shoulder. Now he would have to both fly the plane and do the shooting.

The distance to the dot gradually grew shorter. He scanned out the windows all around from time to time for traffic but saw no other aircraft. He let the plane drift down from 5,500 feet to 3,000 and leveled it there. When he was within ten miles he began looking ahead intently. Then he saw a small feather of dust. A dirt track angling through the bush. He swung left in a wide half-circle until he was aligned parallel with the road, 300 feet to the right of it, still at 3,000 feet above the terrain and flying easterly. The dust feather was now ahead of him and about six miles off. There was no doubt that the feather was the tracker dot. He put down the iPad and pulled the camera up onto his lap, worked the strap around his neck, and turned it on.

The Cessna had no autopilot, so he fine trimmed for pitch and yaw. The south wind outside had evidently dropped, because he was almost dead crosswind and yet the side drift was not too bad. He could easily stay parallel to the road for at least a while and keep the wings level just by working the rudder pedals with his feet, leaving his hands free. He got a good grip on the camera and tested the zoom on the empty road, the stabilization on.

Something was happening with the dust feather. It was resolving into three plumes, drifting left in the breeze. There were three vehicles with maybe an eighth of a mile interval between them, looking like a small loose convoy.

He flew closer, opened the side window, and let it float up. Made a small correction in the pitch trim, then framed the road in the camera and concentrated on getting several fast shots of each vehicle, only dimly registering what they were. A Rover on the tail end. A pickup in the middle. A Jeep with its soft top down in the lead. Two men in it. The important thing was to freeze all the vehicles into the camera's memory. As he passed alongside them, he kept shooting. The Jeep passenger was looking up at the plane but with only mild interest. It was unlikely the man would spot him and the camera in the shadow of the wing. To the men in the vehicles he would appear only as a small plane on a steady non-threatening course. He twisted back in the seat to get as many almost head-on shots as possible of each vehicle.

He smiled. *Got you, you bastards.*

He let the camera hang by its strap and took the yoke. Kept it flying straight and level as the vehicles diminished to specks behind him. Then he began a gradual turn to come around on his original course again. *I'm just another bush plane going who-knows-where.*

He made sure he was on the heading for Babati, scanned once more for any traffic, then kept his right hand on the yoke and looked at the shots he'd taken, scrolling through them on the camera-back screen with his thumb. An old green Rover was the follower. He could make out only the driver behind the windshield in that one. So, likely no passengers, or somebody else would be sitting up front with him. The middle vehicle was a large rust-spotted and primered Ford pickup loaded with grain sacks that probably concealed the ivory. Again he could see only a driver. Then there was the open black Jeep in the lead with the two men. He had a clear shot of only the passenger's face, the driver's face being obscured by a hat not unlike his own Aussie rig. The dust shrouded the rear plates of all the vehicles, but he got two frames with a clear view of the front plate on the Jeep. He memorized the numbers. Turned the camera off and put it away. There was only one flickering bar on the burner cell so he called Fitzgerald on the plane's VHF radio.

Sabo answered and said, "Yeah. Fitz is driving. What've you got?"

Zeke described all three vehicles in caravan order and relayed the Jeep's plate number. "I figure only four men total from what I could see."

"They make you?" Sabo said.

"Ninety-nine percent sure they didn't," Zeke said. I only made one steady pass at three thousand. No reason they should suspect. To them it had to look like I was only following the road to navigate."

"The caravan thing is smart," Sabo said. "Lookouts and blockers front and rear. Good to know about them. Could have spotted us tryin to tail 'em. Okay, we got it from here."

Zeke edged the cruise speed up and pushed on for Babati.

Forty-four

The ambulance was waiting for him when he landed at Babati. He taxied up near it and shut down. He opened the passenger door and said to the nearest EMT, "You going with us?" He was a thin man in his early 30s with severe features, gray eyes, and crew-cut blond hair, dressed in blue scrubs and soft-soled shoes. He was carrying a small suitcase.

He said, "Yes. Bernie Styles."

He offered his hand and Zeke took it.

"Zeke Blades. Load him up. My boss has it all arranged. We're going to Nairobi."

He jogged inside the FBO to use the facilities and file a flight plan to ease the border crossing and landing. By the time he got back out, the plane was loaded. He did a fast walkaround and strapped in. The litter was sitting at an angle on the floor, with the foot of it where the passenger seat would have been. Styles sat behind Zeke on the floor with his back against the fuselage. The patient had his eyes closed and was swathed in bandages. Various tubes and wires protruded from the bandages. Styles had an IV drip going and was monitoring vital signs on a portable unit in his lap.

While Zeke ran through the checklist he said, "What's his name?"

"Hakim Chiza. He was with a work crew, fueling a machine called a bush hog. Somehow there was a gasoline explosion. He's got a wife and four kids, I understand."

"How bad is he?"

"Pretty bad. He's out of it now with a strong sedative. Massive infection is the issue."

"Okay, we're gonna get him help fast as we can."

He did the control checks on the way out to the runway. The tower gave him immediate clearance, and they departed up the eastern edge of the Great Rift Valley. Within 25 miles he could see the immense conical bulk of Kilimanjaro rising high out of the heat haze far away to the right, its summit draped in snow. He still had a mild tail wind from the front that was looming closer behind him out of the south, and they crossed the border in good time and landed without incident. Another ambulance met the plane on the parking apron.

Styles paused outside the plane only long enough to smile and shake Zeke's hand again. "Thanks man. I'll stay with him, hop a ride back later. He makes it, he'll owe a big part of it to you."

They loaded him and sped away with the lights and siren going.

Zeke stood on the apron watching until it was out of sight. *Good luck, Hakim Chiza.*

The job he'd almost settled into in the States would have been plush and lucrative compared to flogging aged bush planes around Africa for well below minimum aviation wage, but he doubted it would ever have produced what he was feeling right now.

He went inside the FBO to see about getting the fuel topped off on his GHR credit card. He sat in the pilot's lounge behind a computer and was checking the weather when the FBO manager looked in around the door jamb. He was an older black man with sparse pure white hair, round glasses, and smile lines.

"You the guy out of Dodoma with the medevac?"

"Yup."

"What you got on the screen there does not look good."

The front was catching up inexorably. It would pass in the night with strong embedded cells, heavy rains, high winds, and possible hail.

"It's the front from hell," Zeke said.

"Tell you what, give me an hour and then we'll go get something to eat. You want, we'll hook up double tie-downs for your Cessna, pray for no hail, and you can bed down on that couch. We'll fix up something for breakfast. You can get out of here tomorrow morning. That sound okay?"

"Long as you let me buy the meals. And maybe a beer or two."

That evening, well-fed and feeling content and sleepy, he was sitting on the scuffed leather couch in the pilot lounge, his hat and the contents from his pockets on the computer desk, the sounds of the raging storm front muted by the concrete-block walls of the FBO and the white noise of the A/C system. He called Liana on his smartphone. The connection was scratchy but usable, and he brought her up to date.

"Good. I'll call Iverson and tell him it's done," she said. "We watched your takeoff in the storm. It looked like a wild and crazy rodeo performance on one of your Indian reservations."

"Do I make fun of your stuffy British culture?"

"Have you heard from Fitzgerald since your intercept?"

"No, but I have faith in him."

"Me, too," she said. "I miss you. When will you be winging home?"

"Soon as the weather gods hold a board meeting and allow me out of here."

A few minutes after he'd ended the call and stretched out his frame as much as possible on the lumpy couch, his burner phone on the desk sounded.

"Don't use my name. We need to talk."

It was Wexton. He sounded nervous.

"Okay. Something wrong?"

"It is vitally important. But not over the phone. And not at work. When can you get here?"

The man was really shaken. There was none of the usual pomposity in his voice, and he seemed to be teetering on an edge.

Zeke thought for a moment. Said, "I can be there tomorrow. Can you come to the airport general aviation terminal at ten?"

"Yes, I'll be in my car in the parking lot. A silver Audi."

The connection went dead.

He got up, turned on the computer, and checked the latest forecast. It would be clear with unlimited visibility, although breezy, by dawn.

It was a while before he could drift off into a fitful sleep on the couch.

Forty-five

It was still dark outside when the burner phone sounded again.

Zeke sat up, looked at his watch, noted groggily that it was five fourteen, stretched to relieve a sore back muscle, and answered.

"We tracked 'em loosely all night," Fitzgerald said. "They took bush roads as much as they could. We stayed way back and they never knew we were there. The program got hinky during the worst of the weather, but it did the job. They wound up in a run-down warehouse behind a chain-link fence a mile from the Dar seaport. Our other two teams are here."

"What now?" Zeke said.

"Pick a few frames you shot from the air and send 'em to me on my smartphone. We've got Babak's recording and photos we took of the vehicles entering the warehouse. It was lit up pretty good with a security light by the gate. We've also got a long-distance snatch of conversation between one of the drivers and a warehouse worker. They don't mention ivory, but they do talk about how many items they're bringing in and about how they weren't followed. I'll hand-print an anonymous statement that covers everything. We'll put it all into a manila envelope and about mid-morning we'll send it by messenger to a guy we know of in the Dar law structure who's got a reputation as a shark, and he's honest. There should be enough in our package to justify a raid on the warehouse before the ivory gets loaded onto a ship. With any luck they can at least nail the warehouse owner, and maybe the chief wholesaler and smuggler. I figure if they're going to do it, they'll do it fast, probably before the day's gone. I'd like to set up and watch. We've got an abandoned building in the neighborhood picked out that has a good view. Do you want in on this?"

"Hell, yes. I'm still in Nairobi but I'm heading your way. HW called and wants to talk. I'm supposed to meet with him at ten."

"HW . . . oh, yeah. What's that all about?"

"Wouldn't say. No idea."

"Okay," Fitzgerald said. "I'll call you soon as we know something."

Zeke used a cable in the camera bag to download the selected pictures into the FBO's courtesy computer and e-mailed them to Fitzgerald, then got himself a much-needed cup of coffee.

As he was taxiing out to the runway, the day was dawning with the special clarity that often results after a violent frontal passage has scrubbed the air clean. Visibility was unlimited, but there was still a brisk steady breeze out of the south, so he'd be plowing into it on the way to Dar. He'd filed a visual flight plan in a phone call to the tower, again to ease the border crossing, and had done a careful walkaround inspection because of the pummeling the tied-down Cessna had taken during the night.

Shortly, he was climbing into a sky that was the luminous cerulean of a backlit Caribbean wave before it breaks, shading to a pure deep cobalt blue above. All the gauges were good, and the prop sliced into the cool dense air powerfully. The familiar euphoria of flight seeped into him. The feeling of guiding an elegant thing that shunned gravity and seemed almost alive.

The unique feeling of freedom that the lone eagles must enjoy as their right. He would never tire of it. He also figured Mother Nature owed it to him after beating him up in the storm front the previous day.

Kilimanjaro was midway along in his three-hour flight to Dar and only slightly off to his right, so he got a good view of it as he passed by. There were scattered geometrical cultivated fields slashed into the dense rain forest at the broad base of the ancient three-cratered volcano. As the rugged flanks ascended, the forest gave way to tundra, and finally, well above the tree line, to barren cold conditions, where rugged ravines that looked like giant claw marks were lined with snow. He was at 9,500 feet above sea level, which put him just over 6,000 feet above the surrounding terrain, yet the broad top of the mountain still towered almost 10,000 feet more above his altitude. It was one of the most spectacular sights he'd ever seen. Astonishing in its majesty. He used Liana's camera to record a dozen frames, figuring one would look nice blown up on her living room wall. He wished she were here to see all this. And he realized the thought of extending their time together, maybe even well into the future, provided of course she was feeling the same way, was beginning to work its way into the recesses of his mind as something perfectly natural and exciting.

Farther along his course, as the terrain became vast savannah carpeted in grass and dotted with tree islands and cut by an occasional red-dirt road, he spotted a group of grazing zebras near a stand of flat-topped trees, and he dropped down low enough to get photos without startling them.

He landed at Dar with an hour to spare before he was to meet Hobart Wexton. He made a call to Liana to update her, grabbed a sandwich and large bottled water in a small airport restaurant, ate the late breakfast at a scarred picnic table under a palm tree, and at ten, walked out into the general aviation parking lot.

The silver Audi was in a far corner off by itself, reflecting the brilliant sunshine. It was idling and the air conditioner was whirring. He slid in on the passenger side.

Wexton was wearing shorts and a loose gray T-shirt and his right knee was bandaged. A cane was propped up between the seats. He looked like the ghost of the man Zeke had met at the upscale waterfront restaurant. Pale and nervous, hair awry, face greasy with sweat despite the cool air.

"What's happened?" Zeke said.

Wexton had both hands on the steering wheel, as though ready to flee at the slightest provocation. He gave Zeke a haunted look, licked his lips, and said, "I was attacked by some thug working for the poachers. I'm risking my life talking to you about this. I shouldn't be doing it. I don't even know why I am."

"Tell me about it," Zeke said in what he hoped was a calming, reassuring voice. "In as much detail as you can remember. Take your time."

Wexton poured it all out with only an occasional prompting question from Zeke.

"I'm sorry you went through that," Zeke said. "It must have been brutal."

"You have no idea."

"So you gave him Fitzgerald's name and description, the fact he gets private financing from the States, and an idea of how many are in the Mambas. Is that about it?"

"Yes, yes. That's all, I swear. I *had* to give him something, didn't I? He was going to kill me. Or stick me with his knife until he was satisfied. I never told him about you."

What Wexton had done was give the poachers several places to start pulling on threads. Fitzgerald himself. His friends and maybe fellow Mambas. A good idea of where to start looking for his source of financing. A logically believable estimate of the relatively few Mambas.

The more he thought about Wexton's story, the more it sounded like Abdul Ahad had probably sent the man with the knife, and not Raza, which made the threat even more dangerous, because Ahad was reputed to be leading a small army, which could overwhelm the Mambas out there in the bush.

It got him thinking about other possible potential threats to the Mambas. Something had been nibbling at the edge of his consciousness for some time. Now he suddenly realized what it was. The simple glaring truth that he himself may have added to the threat by using a GHR plane in the failed hostage swap. The thought made him go cold inside. Had the poachers gotten the Beaver's registration number? It was the old-fashioned small size, not the new foot-tall numbers emblazoned on the sides of the fuselages these days, but only about three inches high and only on the vertical tail stabilizer, which had been edge-on to the poachers where it had sat on the road. But they could have had binoculars and certainly there had been a powerful scope on the sniper rifle that had killed Ben. Maybe one of them had spotted the number as he'd turned the plane away from the road after takeoff, not thinking, only flying mechanically, trying only to *get them all away*, stunned by Ben's ripped chest. *Stupid not to have altered or covered it*, he thought. If they *had* gotten the number and traced it, everybody who worked for GHR, including Liana, was at serious imminent risk. And through them, so were the Mambas. He'd not even thought about it until now. *Dumb.*

He studied Wexton. The man had shown what was, considering, some degree of courage in calling him.

Neither of them said anything.

Wexton was clearly miserable.

"Listen," Zeke said, "it took courage to contact me."

Wexton shot him a hopeful look.

"Yeah. It took guts," Zeke said, "and I appreciate it. There may be a major story going down today. Right here in Dar. Can't tell you more right now, but how would you like to have it first? Exclusive."

"A . . . a major story?"

"Yup, probably international interest. The number you called me on good?"

"Yes." He had a faint spark in his eyes now.

"Okay. How about you line up a videographer, get into your TV duds, gas up this car, whatever you need to do, and stand by. I'll call you the minute the thing starts happening. Should be within the next twenty-four hours."

He smiled and punched Wexton lightly on the arm.

Wexton wiped his face with his hand. Said, "I . . . sure, okay then. Okay. I'll be ready."

He straightened up in his seat. Took a deep breath. Nodded. "Yes. I'll be ready."

Walking back to the FBO, Zeke called Fitzgerald and said, "Where are you?"

"We're at that observing spot I mentioned, all six of us."

"I need to see you as soon as possible."

"This is important?"

"Could be critical," Zeke said. "I'm at the Dar general aviation terminal."

"Stay put," Fitzgerald said. "I'll send Sabo to pick you up. Camo soft-top Jeep."

Forty-six

The Mambas were on the second floor of a derelict cement-block building. It sat on an overgrown lot that had rusted chain-link fencing around it, but there were holes through the fence in several places and the main gates sagged open. There was graffiti all over the outside walls of the first floor. The doors had rusted padlocks, but the hasps had long ago been ripped out. There was more graffiti all over the inside walls. A variety of detritus scattered on the floors was decorated with glinting shards from broken windows. There were gaping holes in the upper-story ceilings.

The six Mambas had parked their three vehicles two blocks away and had walked in. Sabo had brought Zeke from the airport to make it seven. They were gathered near two still-intact but dirty windows on the back side of the building, with a good overall view of the run-down corrugated-metal warehouse a half-block away across a barren lot strewn with trash. It was nested in on three sides with a cluster of other similar buildings, and it was surrounded by eight-foot chain-link fencing in good condition.

Four men sat on the floor with their backs against the wall, arms folded, heads down and dozing after having been up all night. One man with binoculars was keeping a watch on the building and the nearby streets. They were all dressed in civilian clothes, loose T-shirts or sport shirts with the tails out, concealing handguns.

Zeke and Fitzgerald stood apart across the room and spoke in low voices so as not to disturb the men.

"So what's up?" Fitzgerald said. "Something to do with Wexton?"

Zeke told him all he knew.

Fitzgerald paced a few steps back and forth with a hand on the back of his neck. Zeke said nothing, letting him think.

Fitzgerald stopped in front of him and said, "Don't beat yourself up about the Beaver's tail number. None of us thought about it. It's exactly that kind of simple oversight that can take you down, but there's no help for it now. At least we've got some warning. We know for sure they're actively hunting us. And I think you're right. The GHR people could be in danger, and I need to get back to camp to beef up the perimeter watch. Make a better defensive plan."

He walked closer to the men and said, "Okay, guys. Enough slacking. We may have major problems. Up. Get up. I need your attention."

When the men had all roused themselves and were standing, Fitzgerald explained the situation and said, "Zorzi and Changa, you go take up a watch near the GHR headquarters here in Dar. One of you can sleep in the vehicle while the other one keeps an eye out. When they leave work, tail the director, Iverson, and when you can, check on the secretary." He looked at Zeke. "Elizabeth is it?"

Zeke nodded.

"Keep 'em safe, but don't let on you're there. They don't know about Ben's or Zeke's involvement with us, remember. Babak and Dunn, you go to Dodoma and guard Liana and DJ. Let them know you're there and why. Tell 'em to start watching their backs and restricting their movements. I'm going back to the camp. Sabo, you stay here and keep a watch on the warehouse. Zeke, you're with me. I'll drop you at the airport. Rent yourself a vehicle. Something small, inconspicuous. Then come back here and help Sabo keep watch. Anything happens, try to get some pictures. Pick up some food and whatever else you need on the way. We'll leave night vision gear and a listener. And a weapon for you, Zeke. Let me know if a raid goes down and what it looks like. Once we've taken all the precautions we can, we'll sort out what to do next. Any questions?"

There were none, and the four men filtered out of the building furtively at intervals. Sabo started his warehouse watch, and Zeke left with Fitzgerald.

In the Jeep on the way to the airport, Zeke said, "You never really told me why you got involved in all this."

Fitzgerald took a breath. "Five of the men and I were mercenaries, working for an independent security contractor. Something like Blackwater only with a lot fewer scruples. We worked Afghanistan, Iraq, South America. Couple of African countries. The pay was good, but after a while at that kind of thing you tend to lose whatever ideals you started with. It grinds you down. Sometimes it's not all that clear whether you're working for the good guys or the not-so-good guys. And you get almost accustomed to what they like to call collateral damage, for example."

"Civilian casualties."

"Yeah. Happens more than people know. Some gung-ho air-conditioned kid is sitting in a comfy chair at a black-and-white console in Arizona, remotely controlling a Predator seventy-five-hundred miles away in the Middle East, flying high up over the dunes. He spots what he thinks could be a gathering of terrorists. Turbans, long white or black robes. They seem agitated. They're in a known Taliban area, close to some friendly installation or other. They're in a little caravan of dusty old vehicles. Couple of pickups and a Jeep. Kid thinks he sees one of the guys in a pickup carrying an AK. He kicks it up to a superior. Asks for permission to engage. The upper echelon has a look, they debate it, they finally give the order, based at least partly on 'Why take the chance?' Kid sends the message to the drone and watches the detonation. Potential threat eliminated. No sound. No visible blood. Not half as exciting as most fast shoot-'em-up video games in full color with all the sound effects. Arizona kid finishes his shift and goes out for a burger and beer, shoot some pool with his buddies. Turns out the little caravan was only a wedding party. You think that kind of thing makes the news in the States?"

"No," Zeke said.

"I've seen that stuff and worse. You don't want to know the collateral damage a smart bomb can produce. Anyway, the five men and I got into this detail to bodyguard a certain African strongman and his extended family. The guy had a small army behind him, but he didn't trust any of 'em. I knew it was a bad deal going in, but, like I said, the money was extra fine. All in cash, of course. One day he was visiting this village we had just swept. An old man stepped out from behind a tree and took a shot at him with a rusty rifle that I'm surprised even fired. No idea where he came from. The old guy missed, and two of the strongman's military suck-ups shot him full of holes with their sidearms. That wasn't enough for our guy, though. He was enraged. He had his military people drag the village elder out of his hut and force him to his knees. They spread-eagled his wife and daughter in front of him in the dirt, ripped off their clothes. His men lined up, loosening their belts. The strongman had nine guys in his entourage. My men and I conferred briefly. Then we took them all out. The villagers said they'd take care of the bodies. We confiscated the vehicles and some other things from the strongman's estate and left the country that day. Went freelance, you could say. Another guy who's probably as bad or worse has since taken over."

"Could this be the warlord who used to own the private helicopter Ben was flying? The one who liked to toss his enemies out at altitude with no parachute?"

"He had it on a flatbed truck in his back yard with the rotors folded, under a big tarp. One of our guys used to be a truck driver. We told the estate guards the boss wanted us to bring it to him. Nobody in that hellhole dared to question the boss's wishes. Getting across the borders with that truck was interesting, but we managed. Lot of crossings in Africa have no check points, but they're never the easy ones."

"That's quite a story," Zeke said.

"The whole deal changed us, I guess. I have an old school friend back in the States. Made it big in a dot com, and he hates the poaching. He offered to support us on generous terms. It's not like the mercenary thing, but plenty adequate. We've recruited the rest of the men one at a time, and they're all dedicated. Skilled. Competent. For me it was a chance to do something good. To leave something positive behind. You understand?"

"Part of the reason I came back," Zeke said.

Forty-seven

Zeke and Sabo stood in shadow behind the dirty windows looking down on the warehouse. There were two vehicles parked side-by-side with their noses close to the warehouse side wall, a black soft-top Jeep and a green Rover. They looked like the same vehicles Zeke had spotted from the air. The pickup he'd seen in that convoy had probably been carrying the ivory and was likely now inside the warehouse. There was no sign of activity. A gaunt spotted dog pawed through some trash piled up against the base of their derelict building, found nothing, and trotted on. A one-cylinder motorcycle chattered and smoked by below, and then the neighborhood was quiet. The day was shading into dusk.

Sabo said, "I gotta get a few zees. Wake me if you see anything."

Zeke nodded, and Sabo sat with his back against the wall, folded his massive arms, and rested his forehead on them. There was a nylon bag beside him that carried bottled water, some energy bars, a zoom camera, two pairs of night-vision goggles, and two flashlights with red lenses. Zeke had a .45 semi-automatic and an extra magazine in a belt holster on his hip, making a weighty lump under his shirt. He'd never fired a .45. Fitzgerald had showed him where the safety and slide lock were, how to reload it, and how to hold and fire it. He doubted he could hit much with it, if things came to that. His experience with guns was severely limited, but the pistol provided some comfort as the day sank into darkness.

An hour crawled by.

Another hour.

A black Mercedes pulled up to the gate. Zeke grabbed the zoom camera. The driver, a diminutive Asian man, got out and opened it, pulled the car inside, and closed the gate. The car parked close to the main doors and the driver and a woman got out. Zeke shot a dozen frames, catching the woman in glow from the pole-mounted security light as she looked back around the quiet neighborhood. She was Asian, too. The driver opened the standard-sized Judas door that was cut into the larger warehouse door, and they both went in. The door closed behind them. Zeke didn't think it warranted alerting Sabo, so he let the big man sleep.

The area was quiet. Still. Somehow forbidding in the night. There was a thin ground fog forming. Zeke kept his gaze moving over the whole area visible from the window.

He was beginning to think no raid was coming tonight. The software on Sabo's smartphone showed the tracker still inside the warehouse, but he was concerned they might move the ivory soon and there would be no evidence if a raid were to happen then.

He put the night goggles on and did a sweep.

A slow-moving shadow caught his narrowed peripheral vision. A dark van was approaching the warehouse along the quiet street with its lights off. It was followed by another. And another.

Zeke bent down and prodded Sabo's shoulder, and the man instantly came awake and rose to his feet.

"I think the raid is happening," Zeke said.

Sabo donned his night-vision goggles and they both watched a man get out of the lead vehicle with a pair of bolt cutters. He severed the chain and swung the gates wide and the vehicles moved in fast to stop in a fan in front of the main doors. A dozen men got out and took up positions. Three men moved to cover the other three sides of the building. It looked like they were all carrying sub-machine guns. One man swung a cylindrical ram to slam open the Judas door. He stood back and the others rushed in, shouting orders. The man with the ram put it away and took up a position guarding the vehicles.

"They're not half bad," Sabo said. "Must've had some good breach training."

There were shots inside the warehouse, followed by a brief flurry of automatic fire, and then all was still again, but something was happening on the near side of the warehouse, which was in deep shadow. Watching through their goggles, Zeke and Sabo had seen a side door open, revealing only weak light from inside. Two figures emerged and quickly separated, crouching low. One of them was carrying a bundle. The lone guard on that side of the building had no goggles but saw one of the figures and raised his weapon, shouting an order. The figure froze and put up his hands, but the other figure moved in fast from the side and grappled with the guard. The figure did something swift and brutal and the guard fell and was still.

"Those two are gonna get away," Sabo said. "Keep the goggles and your sidearm. Leave everything else. Let's go. Now. They'll try to go over the fence. We can stop them." He took off across the littered floor at a fast jog, heading for the stairs.

Zeke was only three strides behind him.

They clambered down the stairs two steps at a time and hit the pavement outside at a run.

The figures had thrown what looked like a packing quilt over the barbed wire, clambered over, and had just climbed down the outside of the fence. They looked around, apparently not spotting Zeke and Sabo.

Sabo said, "I got the one on the left. You take the other one down. No shooting if you can help it. Just get him under your gun and hold him." He slid a knife out of a belt scabbard and moved fast toward the bigger and beefier of the figures.

Zeke aimed himself at the figure on the right, remembering to pull his sidearm and hold it down by his side as he ran, index finger not through the trigger guard but safely laid alongside the slide, as Fitzgerald had instructed.

Only 15 minutes earlier, Salvious Philemon and his big bodyguard, Idi, had been seated at a rough table near the back of the warehouse, drinking beer with the two armed drivers who had accompanied them in the small caravan to bring in the latest load of ivory. Two of the warehouse workers sat with them. The caravan had been an innovation imposed on Philemon. The woman they all worked for, Yang Feng Kwok, had told him it was merely added security for the safety of the cargo and for his own safety, but he wondered if her trust was wearing thin.

"She was supposed to be here over an hour ago," Philemon said to Idi.

One of the drivers said, "She is extremely busy. Be patient. Has she ever failed to pay you?"

"I don't like waiting here," Philemon said.

There were three soft beeps on a horn outside and one of the men said, "Ah, here she is now."

She walked in through the Judas door, followed by the slim man who was her driver and bodyguard, and who had his own fearful reputation despite his size. The driver locked the door. They all stood as she walked over and scanned them with eyes like those of a shark. She said, "Show me the ivory."

She took her time examining the tusks, and finally pronounced them to be of good quality.

They were all standing near the back of the Toyota van when Idi tensed, placed a hand on Philemon's shoulder, and leaned in close to whisper, "We need to go back and get our beer."

Philemon followed and when they reached the empty table Idi lifted his bottle and took a drink.

"What is it?" Philemon said.

"I heard something outside. Maybe a car door being closed. Be ready."

When the Judas door was blasted open by the ram, Idi grabbed Philemon's arm and pulled him around the other side of a shipping container, pointing at the side exit door. They ran for it. There was a light above it and Idi paused to shut off the wall switch, plunging them into deep shadows. He grabbed up a packing quilt from a pile of them and said, "There may be guards outside. We must go out to either side of the door and move with care."

Outside, Philemon went left and Idi went right, both keeping close to the building where the shadows were deepest. A uniformed man with a sub-machine gun shouted a challenge to Philemon and he froze and raised his hands. He heard a violent struggle behind him and turned to see Idi cutting the guard's throat.

Idi looked all around and said, "He was alone. Quickly now."

He threw the quilt up to cover the barbed wire and they scrambled over the fence.

On the other side, Philemon was about to move away when he saw an apparition charging at him out of the night, a bizarre creature with weird bug-eyed features, and he clawed for the gun in his belt holster.

Zeke, his inner demon aroused, saw the man reaching for the holster on his belt and without thinking did a vicious running kick to the man's solar plexus that instantly folded him up and put him down, gun skittering away on the pavement, both hands clutching his chest, writhing in pain and trying to catch his breath.

Zeke jammed his own gun into the side of the man's neck and said, "Be still now." He looked aside to see Sabo confronting a man as large as he was. Sabo had holstered his sidearm and each man held a knife. Neither wanted to draw the attention of the other attackers with a gunshot.

Idi was good, but Sabo was a shade better and was wearing the night goggles, which gave him a clear view of his opponent. Both men feinted, then attacked, but Sabo was quicker. He moved in close, deflected the slash aimed at him by using his forearm to bludgeon the other man's knife arm aside, and buried his own knife in the man's chest. He was dead before he slid off Sabo's blade and crumpled to the ground.

Sabo looked over at Zeke and nodded, then reached down and extracted the laces from the dead man's boots. He went through the man's clothing and came up with a wallet, which he pocketed. He came over and used the boot laces to tie Zeke's captive with his hands behind his back, then said to Zeke, "Give me your undershirt."

Zeke complied, and Sabo ripped the black T-shirt into strips and fashioned a gag and a blindfold for the man.

Zeke said, "What are you doing?"

"This guy could steer us back to the poachers, with a little persuasion. He's a keeper."

Zeke had to agree. He and Sabo stood the man up and moved off. The man still had his head down and his back bent and was moaning with the pain. They had to half carry him. When they got to the entrance of the abandoned building Sabo said, "Go up and get our gear. Make it fast. We need to get out of here."

Removing his goggles, Zeke said, "No. You go. I'll watch him. I have to make a call."

Sabo snorted and shook his still goggled head but darted inside the building.

Hobart Wexton answered on the first ring, "Yes?"

"A raid is going down right now on a warehouse that's holding poached ivory. I'll text you some pictures. Could be a major gang. Big story." He gave Wexton the address and said, "Go for it."

"My cameraman and I are on the way," Wexton said, and there was a smile in his voice.

Zeke transferred several shots from the camera to his smartphone and then sent them on to Wexton.

Forty-eight

Zeke said, "You know someplace we can take him for questioning?" He was driving his compact rental car away from the raid scene through the litter-strewn Dar back streets, which were asleep all around them. The man they'd captured was crammed onto the back seat out of sight, trussed up at his wrists and ankles, gagged, and blindfolded.

"Yeah, I know a place," Sabo said. "Take a right on the next street."

Sabo guided him to a ramshackle bar that sat back from a narrow road on the outskirts of the city. It appeared to be still open, but there were only three beat-up cars in the badly potholed dirt parking lot. A red neon sign above the door said, 'Sadie's Place.'

Sabo said, "Park under that tree over there."

Zeke pulled all the way into the dense shadow cast under the tree by a pole-mounted security light. Sabo slid out and said, "Wait. I'll be back." He walked over and entered the bar. Two minutes later he got back into the car and said, "Place belongs to a friend. Be closing in fifteen minutes. Pull around back."

A hard-looking woman met them at the steel-barred back door. Probably in her mid-40s, she wore tight calf-length jeans, a wide silvery belt, a bright red frilly blouse, and low heels that raised the top of her Dolly Parton hairdo to about five ten. She was wearing a lot of makeup.

Sabo said to her, "Appreciate this."

The woman gave Sabo a hug and said, "You big ol' bear. What're you up to now?"

Sabo smiled and said in a low voice, "Hey, you know. This 'n that. It's good to see you, girl. Sadie Thompson, this here's Zeke Blades. He's an Indian. Apache or something. That's supposed to explain the ponytail. We just need to talk with a guy in private, like I said, Sadie girl. No trouble."

"Not Apache. Cherokee," Zeke said, offering his hand. The woman shook it, studying him with eyes that had seen a lot.

"Okay, sure," she said. "You guys can use the kitchen in my apartment. You make a mess, you clean it up, got that? I'll leave you to it. I got to go close and mop. I'll keep out of the way. I don't want to know what it's about, anyway. Give me a shout when you're finished."

In the kitchen, Sabo went through the man's pockets and came up with a folding knife, some keys, a cell phone, and a wallet, all of which he put on the old ceramic-topped kitchen table along with the wallet he'd taken from the dead man. They sat him at the table, still blindfolded, his bound hands awkwardly behind his back.

They went through the two wallets. The dead man had been Idi Wambuzi, who'd had a Ugandan driver's license. Sabo showed Zeke the driver's license for the man at the table. "Salvious Philemon, a Tanzanian. Don't we know this name?"

"Yes," Zeke said. "We were told he buys ivory all over central Africa. The guy must have a long list of connections." He put his smartphone on voice record and placed it on the table. Said, "Interview with Salvious Philemon," and gave the date.

Sabo smiled and nodded. He whacked the man on his shoulder with his large palm. "That right, Salvi, you a big bad ivory wholesaler?"

"What . . . what did you do to Idi?" the man said.

"Good, you speak English. I did only what he was trying to do to me," Sabo said. "I killed him. My blade through the heart."

The man hung his head and moaned.

"You don't have many choices, Philemon," Zeke said. "Your gang is in custody. They got caught with a stock of illegal ivory tonight. They'll do time. You can help us out, tell us about your operation. Give us names of the poachers you've been buying from. Their contact information. Do a good thing. Clear your conscience. And maybe we'll let you go."

"Or you can keep your mouth shut," Sabo said. "Don't tell us anything. And we turn you over to the law. Or, better yet, there's a former ranger I know. His brother-in-law, guy who was also a ranger, got shot dead by poachers. Made my guy a little crazy, you know? So maybe we turn you over to him. I know he'd be real happy to meet a big man in the ivory trade."

"What's it going to be, Philemon?" Zeke said. "We don't have a lot of time here."

"Who are you?" Philemon said.

"See, now, Salvi you're not thinking clear," Sabo said. "You not knowin who we are is a *good* thing. If we planned on doing you later tonight, leavin you out in the bush as a treat for the hyenas and the wild dogs, would we have given you that blindfold? You got to start *thinking*, Salvi. You don't want to know who we are, believe me. And you *do* want to tell us what we want to know."

Philemon said nothing.

Sabo and Zeke let him fret.

Philemon said, "You must listen to me. I . . . I am only a middleman. I buy from the suppliers and deliver to the person who pays me. That is all. That is everything. I cannot help you. Please to let me go. As you say, I do not know who you are. I am no threat to you. No threat at all."

"How do you contact the poachers?" Zeke said.

"I do not. They call me. I meet them out in the bush. Every time it is a different place. I pay them cash. I bring the items to Dar. I take my pay. That is all, I swear this. I am not a poacher. I do not kill anything. I am only a man in the middle. Doing a job. Please. You must believe me."

Sabo said, "I think you know a poacher calls himself Muhammadu Raza."

He shook his head vigorously. "No. No, I—"

Sabo hit him in the same spot on the same shoulder again, this time with a fist. Hard. Philemon yelped and cringed.

"All right. Yes. Yes, I know him. But he is most dangerous. He has killed many men. He will kill me if he finds out I have talked about him. He will kill you. He has a crazed brother who leads a whole army of jihadis. But that is all I know. I am told they both hide deeply in the Mountains of the Moon. But I do not know how to reach them or where in all those mountains they are. I swear it on my mother's eyes. It is all I know. All I know."

Zeke said, "Who have you been bringing the ivory to?"

"Only to one. She was in the warehouse this night. The police must have her in jail by now. You will know all this soon, anyway. She is Yang Feng Kwok. I worked for her. It was her money I used to buy the items. I was only doing my job. She, too, is a most dangerous person. It is said she has had many killed."

"She won't be doing much from a jail cell," Zeke said.

"We can be reasonable people," Sabo said. "So all we're asking now is for six more names of your best suppliers. Your regular big poachers like Raza. And some idea how to find them. We won't tell anybody where we got the names. Give us those six and everything you know about 'em and maybe you'll live to see tomorrow."

It took more verbal prodding and three more hard punches on the same bruised shoulder, but Philemon finally gave up the six names and Zeke's phone recorded them.

"What do you think?" Zeke asked Sabo.

The big man shrugged. "We've got a lot to work with." He pointed to Philemon's cell phone. "And we got that. Maybe your electronics guy can pull something out of it."

Both of them knew it would be awkward trying to turn Philemon over to the law while remaining anonymous themselves. Except for the phone recording, which would reveal coercion, there was not even any evidence he'd been in the warehouse tonight.

Sabo said, "Okay, Salvi. Here's the only deal you're ever gonna get from us. We have you recorded if we need it. This time we're gonna let you go. Only because we got better things to do. But if we ever get wind of you operating with poachers anywhere in Africa again, we track you down and you die a hard death. We'll break your legs and all your fingers one at a time and castrate you and slice out your tongue and blind you before we let you die real slow. That's a sacred promise. We got the manpower and the meanness to do it, and we'll be watching and listening. You think Raza and this Kwok are dangerous? We're worse. You wanted to know who we are. Out there in the jungle there's a thing called a black mamba. It's invisible in the shadows. It's no bigger around than your forearm but grows up to fourteen feet long. It can live in the trees and drop down on you. It's faster than a man can jog. Strikes like lightning. You mess with it and it gets real aggressive. It's the most dangerous thing in Africa. It's lethal."

Philemon went rigid and seemed to stop breathing for a few seconds. He whispered, "You are the Mambas. Ah, God."

Sabo said, "Be glad you haven't seen our faces. From today on you rob banks or you pimp a few raddled whores or you scam the tourists or you sell used motorbikes, we don't give a damn, but you stay ten kilometers away from any kind of poaching operation. You understand?"

He blew out a breath and bobbed his head. "Yes. Yes. Thank you. I will do as you say. Thank you."

They took him out to the car and left him bound and blindfolded while they went back into the bar. The neon light on the roof was turned off.

Zeke said, "You even had me scared there. Good job."

"Wasn't all *that* far from the truth, but yeah, maybe we scared him straight. If not, sooner or later he'll step on his own dick."

Sadie was sitting on a bar stool, watching them in the mirror. She said, "Well, I didn't hear anything breaking back there. You two want a drink?"

"Sure," Sabo said, but we gotta pass. Things to do."

"Maybe a meal then."

"Food would be good," Zeke said. "We'll pay extra for some sandwiches and coffee to go, and whatever we owe for the use of your kitchen. That be okay?"

"Regular prices for the food," she said. "Sabo can pay me back real soon, ah . . . personally, for the use of my place for what I figure was strictly illegal."

Sabo grinned and placed a large paw gently on her shoulder. He said, "That's a deal, girl." Her features softened and she kissed him on the cheek, leaving a lipstick imprint.

They left 20 minutes later with large cups of hot good coffee and a bag of sandwiches.

Zeke drove two miles out from the city on a disused dirt track they found and stopped by a stand of trees. He did a K turn to head back toward the city. The night sounds of insects and birds were loud. It was humid and silken dark when he turned off the car lights, but the track was still visible in the light of a high crescent moon and a scattering of diamond-bright stars. They cut Philemon's ankles and hands free and left him standing there, still wearing the blindfold, rubbing his wrists with unsteady hands and sweating profusely.

Sabo said, "This is the luckiest day you'll ever live, Salvi. You stay here and wait until you can't hear the car anymore before you take off the blindfold. Walk toward the sky glow. And remember we're out there watching."

Zeke left the lights off until they were around a bend. He said, "You and Sadie have some history, then."

"Yeah," Sabo said. "You could say that."

Forty-nine

The raid was big news on Africa Now TV3. Hobart Wexton was resplendent in a tailored dark blue suit, burgundy shirt, and a white tie, and showed no signs of the anxiety that had shaken him when Zeke and he had met.

Looking sternly and confidently into the camera from his studio desk as a red banner scrolled across the bottom of the screen repeatedly flashing EXCLUSIVE BREAKING NEWS, he said, "In a late-night raid on a warehouse near the Dar es Salaam port facilities, a special task force from Tanzania's National and Transnational Serious Crimes Investigation Unit arrested a woman some are already calling Africa's Ivory Queen. Yang Feng Kwok, sixty-two, along with members of her gang, were apparently preparing to ship a load of illegal ivory and black rhino horn worth millions in U.S. dollars out of the country. TV-Three has obtained exclusive photos and footage of Kwok being arrested."

The screen showed two of Zeke's shots and then a segment of a belligerent Kwok and two men in handcuffs with their heads down being hustled out of the warehouse and put into waiting vans. Another man on a stretcher was taken out and slid into an ambulance with all its lights flashing.

Wexton's image came back. "Two of Kwok's gang members who resisted were killed in the raid and one was wounded but is expected to survive," he said. "One member of the task force was killed. The arrests have already aroused national and international attention. A spokesperson for the United States-based Elephant Action League, Shirley Baker, stated to me by phone just before we went on the air with the story this morning that Yang Feng Kwok was known to them and could be the most important ivory-trafficking mastermind netted to date. She said it is a significant blow to a long thriving and lucrative trade that has seen many thousands of African elephants viciously killed for their tusks over the years. Ms. Baker also said an investigation should be launched into the possibility of collusion with—and payoffs to—government and law enforcement officials who may have facilitated the Ivory Queen's operations. Although Kwok, a Chinese-born immigrant by way of Malaysia, has apparently been under suspicion by authorities for some time, TV-Three has exclusive confidential information that a credible tip concerning poached ivory being on the premises finally prompted last night's warehouse raid.

"Tragically, Tanzania has long been ground zero for ivory poaching. The trade has been condemned and is now illegal in many countries, including most recently even in China, long a top importer of ivory. But both legal and black-market demand throughout much of Asia remains stubbornly high. More in our exclusive coverage of this story after this commercial break." The screen was filled with a frenzied sales pitch for Toyotas at unprecedented sacrificial prices.

Zeke had flown back to Dodoma at dawn, and he and Liana were watching the mid-morning news with coffee and toasted English muffins with marmalade in her living room, he in his briefs and she in a terrycloth robe.

She muted the TV and said, "Do you really think DJ and I need protection?"

He yawned, the long night having made him lethargic. "I don't know, but it's not worth taking a chance, at least until Fitzgerald can sort out what's going on with Raza and his brother. The Mambas have poked a stick in their nest, and you can see on the news every week how crazed the radical Islamists can get, even when they aren't provoked. Fitzgerald figures anyone in contact with the Mambas could be at risk." He had seen no reason to tell her about the attack on Wexton, figuring it would only worry her more.

"The two men Fitz sent were just lurking about," she said, "so I gave them fictitious jobs with us, Dunn in the hangar with DJ, and Babak as a local driver. I thought they'd be less obvious that way, although if you look closely you can see they're carrying pistols. Curiously, they've actually made themselves helpful."

"The jobs are a good idea," Zeke said. He was worried that, with the protective GHR coverage in Dodoma and Dar, Fitzgerald's already meager force was reduced to a total of only ten including Fitzgerald, not nearly enough to stand up to or probably even slow down Ahad's army, but he said nothing.

"One or the other of them is still often parked outside at least part of the night," she said. "It is quite reassuring, I suppose."

She clicked the TV sound back on. Wexton was shown interviewing a member of the raid team outside the warehouse the night before. The news segment went on for a few minutes, but the rest was just minor embellishments on what had already been reported. Wexton concluded the segment by saying TV3 would be presenting a one-hour documentary on African poaching soon.

Way to go, Hobart, Zeke thought. With some luck, the documentary might get picked up by a major network in Europe or the States. And if so it might benefit the cause.

"What do we need to do today?" he said.

"There's nothing much pressing for a change," she said. "It's glorious weather, so why not simply enjoy it? We could go to the beach. A girlfriend works at the Dar Hilton Resort, and thus I have two free passes, good anytime. The ocean is clear as white wine. Palm trees shading the beach. Pure white sand like sugar. A bath house for changing. We could sit at the outside bar and order their excellent seafood. We'll tell Fitzgerald's minders to take the day off. What do you say?"

"Will you wear a bikini?"

"Of course. And you can make do quite well with jeans shorts."

"Talked me into it."

The sky was cerulean and decorated with just the right scattering of vividly contrasting benign cumulus clouds to provide shady intervals from the bright sun. He drove the Jeep with the top off. They presented the passes at the parking lot gate and, carrying their gear and two large bottled waters, they walked through the plush landscaping to the beach, which lived up to her promises, with a brisk onshore breeze that made the palm trees chatter and coaxed the surf into foaming curls of crystalline thunder. The hotel was top end, with its own inconspicuous grounds and beach security people. Zeke had his license and a credit card stowed securely inside the band of his crushable Stetson. They staked out two side-by-side lounges in the shade of an elegantly curved palm with their towels and her beach bag, slathered each other with sunscreen, and ran down the soft sand into the ocean. They swam for an hour, then walked the brilliant sand for two hours, him wearing his Stetson and her wearing a big straw hat with a wide brim that flopped in the breeze. They held hands much of the way.

They used the outdoor showers to wash off the salt and lay on the comfortable lounges in the warm wind to dry. They talked of trivial things for a while and then dozed in the fluttering dappled shade.

He had his fingers laced behind his head and his legs crossed when she nudged his elbow. He came awake feeling thoroughly rested and at peace. She said, "Sorry, but I am positively famished. Let's go over there to the tiki bar and order something most decadent, with drinks that have salty rims, shall we?"

"We shall. But I'll stick with a beer."

They sat on stools at the bar and ordered from the menu. They chatted with an exuberant young Australian honeymooning couple for a time. A four-piece combo set up their gear in one of the open grass-roofed huts and began playing sensual African rhythms with intricate drums threaded in. The food was superb, the female bartender was attentive and friendly, and they lingered over the meal and ordered coffee with dessert.

When the day faded into dusk and the decorative grounds lights came on, they gathered up their things and walked to the parking lot. It had been a good interlude from the stress and violence.

They rode back in the topless Jeep through the lights of the city to her place without speaking. Both of them were relaxed and content. It was by now an assumption that he would spend most nights in her bed, and he was looking forward to it.

They showered together. She undid his ponytail and shampooed his hair, then he did her hair, and they became inordinately involved with rubbing each other's backs and meticulously and teasingly cleaning interesting other areas of each other's anatomy, until they were both breathing heavily and the hot water was becoming cool. Now they were on her couch, putting off moving into her bedroom for further explorations, with their bare feet up on her coffee table, him in a T-shirt and clean shorts and her once again in her terry robe, watching the evening news over hot tea, when Zeke's phone sounded its eagle shriek.

She muted the TV and he answered.

"I want to know right *now* precisely what in the bloody *hell* has been going on," Iverson shouted.

Fifty

"What do you mean, sir?" Zeke said.

"Do *not* play me for a fool any longer, do you understand? I began sensing something amiss in Dodoma some time ago. Yesterday is only the latest in a lengthy list of highly suspicious activities. After you transported that patient to Nairobi, you did not fly back to Dodoma, but instead you flew here to Dar and spent the night, didn't you. The Dar tower told me you flew out for Dodoma at dawn. Had you informed me you were here, there is a shipment of supplies you could have taken back, but you had a nefarious reason for not informing me, didn't you."

Zeke said nothing, letting Iverson get it all out of his system. Hopefully he would then wind down enough to listen to reason.

"You've been playing at your secret game for a long time," Iverson said. "When I was last in Dodoma, I recorded the engine hours on both GHR planes, and I've since cross-checked hours against legitimate missions. Of course, they do not agree, do they. As with yesterday, you have flown many more hours in our planes than the mission record would support. I've only just confirmed this beyond doubt with the takeoff and landing records from an acquaintance in the Dodoma tower. I assume you've been using GHR aircraft to fly private charter missions for your own profit. You can only have done so with the collusion of both Miss Sekibo and Dante James, so I further assume you've shared the profits with them. To my mind they are equally culpable. It is a bloody certainty that you'll be fired, the lot of you, and I am meeting with our attorney in the morning to determine if criminal charges can be brought, as well."

Iverson took a breath and Zeke said, "Mister Iverson, it's not—"

"Tomorrow I shall also set up a conference call with the GHR board of directors to inform them and seek their counsel. You shall not get away with this, Blades. Nossir. You shall *not*."

"*Iverson*," Zeke said. "Listen to me. I can explain everything. Before you do anything, why don't you let me fly the Cessna to Dar first thing in the morning and pick up that load? We need to talk face-to-face about all this. I can be there by—"

"*Bollocks*. You listen to *me* you . . . you *fraud*. You are not to *touch* a GHR aircraft. The Dodoma tower will inform me if you attempt to take off. They will deny clearance and I will immediately call the authorities. Do you hear me? You are to vacate the Dodoma hangar and the caravan you've been inhabiting no later than noon tomorrow. Remove all your belongings. Do *not* remove anything else. And mind, you had better not attempt to leave the country."

"Mister Iverson—" But the connection had gone dead.

He tried to call back. It rang five times and went to voicemail.

He looked at Liana.

"I know," she said. "It was loud enough so I heard most of it. He's livid. He's threatening to sack us all. Whatever will we do?"

Her phone on the end table sounded. She picked it up and looked at the caller ID. "It's him."

Zeke said, "Don't answer. Give him an hour to cool off, then I'll call him back on your phone. He'll think it's you. Maybe I can placate him."

"What can you possibly tell him?"

Zeke knew it had always been dead wrong to use the GHR planes to help the Mambas. Like many wayward paths, it had started out seeming mostly innocent and just temporary. Well-intended actions supported by only weak rationalizations. He shook his head, feeling a heavy mix of guilt and frustration. He said, "I don't know."

* * *

At the jihadi camp in the Mountains of the Moon, Abdul Ahad placed his hand on Raza's shoulder, smiled, and said, "We've found them, brother."

"The accursed Mambas?"

"I gave the task to Faraji. He has never failed me, and he did not this time. He interrogated the newsman who knows their leader, who is called Ryan Fitzgerald, and the newsman said he did not believe they have as many men as the bush rumors say. Faraji then began watching their new pilot, the one with the long hair who we have learned works for an infidel agency called Global Health Resources. He found this man through the number on the plane that carried you to the exchange, but he could discover no link to the Mambas, so he put out word that a reward would be paid to anyone in the villages who could supply the location of the Mamba camp. He was told of activity in a desolate area some one hundred miles to the northwest of Dodoma. Faraji sent out three of his best trackers to find their spoor. These African trackers can read the slightest sign and run all day and night without tiring. We now have the coordinates of their camp. It is unquestionably them. Faraji had a description of their leader. There are fewer than a dozen enemy there. One of my trackers is watching them."

"Still, we should use caution," Raza said.

"I agree, brother. I will take twenty-nine of our best men. The ones who are already somewhat familiar with the new weapons. With such a small force we will be able to move swiftly in two covered trucks and a Jeep without arousing suspicion. We will approach them with all stealth, set our ambush, and destroy them. A quick victory will instill zeal in all our fighters."

"I was about to lead my men to harvest a bountiful herd not two days' ride from here," Raza said, "but I must go with you."

"No, no. The money you bring to our cause is far more important than this insignificant skirmish. Once we make contact, it will be but the work of a few hours to kill and bury them. You lead your men for the ivory. I will erase the Mambas. You have my word. We will stand side-by-side in the battles to come. Go to your harvest with the blessings of Allah."

Fifty-one

Liana was having another cup of tea at her kitchen table and Zeke sat across from her with a bottle of beer.

"He should have wound himself down some by now," Zeke said.

Liana handed him her phone and he poked the speed dial for Iverson.

The GHR leader answered on the second ring, sounding more weary than angry. "Liana, I just cannot believe what I know must have been going on there. I want to think you had no knowledge, but—"

"Mister Iverson, it's Zeke. Before you hang up, please give me three minutes of your time. You need to hear what I have to say."

The phone was silent. After several long seconds, Iverson said, "Three minutes, then."

"You're right. I've been flying missions outside the scope of GHR. That's inexcusable. You have every right to feel betrayed and outraged. I apologize. But it hasn't profited me or your people here in Dodoma. In fact, we've paid for all the fuel I've burned on those missions. We've got receipts to prove it. And it hasn't compromised what we've been doing for GHR. It's been for a good cause. We've been helping fight elephant poaching in Tanzania. I hope you can understand why we've had to limit the number of those who know what we've been doing, for their own good as well as ours. We see our work as worthwhile, if not always in line with the law. Poachers are driving the elephants toward extinction. They're doing it with brutal efficiency. Usually with the help of corrupt officials. You know the statistics. We're trying to help stop them. Sometimes that requires extraordinary means. Before you take any action, I'm asking you to think about it. Please try to understand why we've been doing this, sir. And please don't punish Liana Sekibo and Dante James. They're good people. They care. They work hard for GHR. I'm the one who's flown the missions, and I'll accept whatever consequences that entails. Okay, that's it."

More silence.

He waited for some seconds and said, "Iverson?"

"None of what you've said justifies what you've done, you know. You've not only deceived me, but you've also bloody well betrayed the GHR board and all those good people who've donated to our mission."

"You're right, sir."

More silence.

"Alright. The load that must be delivered is highly important. You have my permission to fly here in the Cessna and pick it up tomorrow morning early. But *only* that, am I clear? I will decide in the next twenty-four hours what must be done." The line went dead.

Zeke looked at Liana and said, "He hung up. Said I could fly the one more load tomorrow. So that's something."

"You were brilliant with him. Whatever happens, DJ and I will be with you, I hope you know that."

"I do. Thanks."

They were both silent for a time, lost in their own thoughts.

Then she took a deep breath and said, "I suppose this was inevitable, really. But there's nothing more either of us can do about it tonight. You know what I think?"

"What?"

"We've unfinished business, haven't we." She gave him a wry smile. "So, I think you should take me to bed."

The next morning, he took off while the ruddy horizontal dawn light was casting long shadows of the hangar, the trees, and the accelerating Cessna onto the dewy runway verge. He made good time in the smooth morning air under a metallic cloudless sky. He called ahead from the air and Iverson was waiting at the FBO in Dar. They transferred the load from the Rover to the plane, working together but not saying much.

Iverson said, "Your destination is the clinic near Rungwa. The shipment includes vital medicines and surgical items. It totals two hundred and ten pounds. Needs to be got there quickly. They'll meet you on that stretch of road you've used before. Mind, you are to return directly to Dodoma thereafter."

He'd been to that clinic several times. It was run by a retired Hungarian couple, a team like George and Linda, except both the wife and husband were volunteer doctors with different specialties, her a surgeon and him a general practitioner. The trip from Dodoma to Dar, then to Rungwa, which was 150 miles southwest of the capital out in the bush, and then back to Dodoma was over 700 miles, so he'd need fuel.

"Understood," Zeke said. I know there's no time to talk right now, but I appreciate you thinking about how we can best resolve the, ah, issues. I left this morning with three-quarter tanks, so I need to top up here. While they're doing that I'll grab a snack and water in the FBO."

"You may do so. We've a fuel account here, as you know. I've not yet decided how best to proceed."

"I'll cooperate with you however I can, and again, I apologize."

He snorted. "Bloody little good that does." He shook his head, got into the Rover, and drove away through the automatic chain-link gates.

While the line man was pumping avgas from the tank truck into the Cessna's wings, he hit the vending machines inside the FBO for two oversized bottles of water and a handful of energy bars and grabbed a free banana and an apple from a fruit bowl in the pilot's lounge.

He was airborne again an hour after he'd landed, with enough fuel now for 1,000 miles.

The flight to the Rungwa clinic was uneventful and he put the Cessna down on the same straight stretch of road he'd used before. There was no cell service in the area, but they had a hand-held aviation band radio at the clinic, and he'd called ahead when he was 30 miles out, so a helper from the clinic was waiting for him on the road. After he landed, she drove the vintage capped Ford pickup up close to the plane. She was a shy, beautiful young Swahili girl named Nadra, wearing a colorful dress, with her glossy raven hair done up in dozens of meticulous small braids, each tipped with a bit of silver. She smiled, shook his hand formally, and said, "We are in great need of these things you've brought. We thank you, sir."

"Call me Zeke."

"Thank you, Mister Zeke."

She helped him transfer the load to the pickup. She cautiously backed up the truck and got it headed the way she'd come. She waved a hand and he climbed back into the plane, took off, set his course for Dodoma, and climbed up through the hot air and a layer of widely scattered cumulus clouds with grey bases floating at 3,500 feet above the terrain.

He had the radio set to the standard frequency that planes flying in Tanzania used to communicate intentions when outside any airport traffic area. Because he wanted to fly in the smoother air above the clouds where there were fewer thermals, he climbed to 7,500 feet above the ground. When he reached cruising altitude, he scanned the sky all around for any other traffic, saw none, and began eating the apple with his right hand while flying with his left, enjoying the solitude and the expansive view. For a time it was almost as though he had the planet to himself.

If he'd been any lower he never would have caught the weak and staticky signal from somebody who was repeating the Cessna's tail number, but getting the last two letters wrong—Romeo Foxtrot instead of Whiskey Sierra—and saying, "This is M leader. Z you there? Come in, Z."

No, not wrong letters. It's a code. R F for Ryan Fitzgerald.

Fitzgerald was trying to keep anybody monitoring the conversation from knowing identities.

Zeke put the apple down on the passenger seat, turned up the volume and said, "Z here. What's up?"

Fitzgerald said, "This's M leader. Switch to—" His voice broke up.

"Say again frequency M leader."

The incoming transmission was fragmented but readable. Fitzgerald repeated the frequency. It was near the top end of the aviation band and little used, so there was much less chance of anyone listening in.

Zeke said, "Roger, switching," and changed the radio's numbers. "What's going on?"

"L said you were flying. An informant just called in. Probable hostiles approaching us. Thirty-five miles out. Our same location as last time. We could use an eye in the sky. Can you get overhead here ASAP?"

Fifty-two

Zeke said, "Wait one," and pulled out his sectional chart. He did a rough calculation, figuring in max cruise speed and, thankfully, a tail wind. "I can be there in forty minutes. Maybe less. Stay on this frequency. Do you want me to call in the law?"

"No," Fitzgerald said. "We've got a plan. Just get here soon as you can."

The only problem was he would not have enough fuel left when he arrived to loiter for very long. *It is what it is*, he thought, and added power, hoping the hostiles would not arrive and attack Fitzgerald and his men before he could lash the Cessna to the Mambas' position and provide whatever help he could.

He heard no more from Fitzgerald, so his imagination was running in overdrive as the Cessna ate up the miles. How strong was the hostile force? How were they armed? If it was al-Isra, would the few Mambas at the camp be overrun within minutes? What was Fitzgerald's plan? Would he be able to stage a retreat?

One good thing was if the hostile force had 35 miles still to cover, that would likely take time in the rugged bush terrain, maybe enough time for him to get there first.

He had his binoculars. With them he could circle high above the scene to allow a good vantage and lessen the chances of being shot down. Maybe by spotting attackers' positions, he could help Fitzgerald at least fight his way clear. But the cumulus clouds were thickening. Would he even have enough visibility to help?

Beyond pushing the engine at max cruise, there was nothing he could do to get there any faster. He drank the rest of his last oversized bottled water to stay hydrated. Finished the apple and ate a banana so he'd stay alert. Kept checking his position on the GPS. Refined his course minutely to save as much time and fuel as possible. Flexed his hands and rolled his shoulders to stay loose.

As he finally drew within 20 miles of the Mambas' camp, he let down to 3,500 feet above the ground, flying through some thin clouds, but he saw the air ahead was relatively clear of clouds and offered good visibility. He slowed down. There didn't seem to be any activity below as he banked into a wide circle. The rough improvised air strip was empty. Back in a thicket of thorn bushes, he recognized four vehicles he knew belonged to the Mambas. Then he spotted three unfamiliar vehicles parked in a loose fan under a thin stand of trees a mile from the camp coordinates, one a sizeable straight truck with a canvas cover over the bed. He saw a trail through the grass that the hostile vehicles had made coming in from the northwest. The only track in the area, very rough and seldom used, began near the dirt air strip and meandered away southward. All the other surrounding flat terrain was tall grass with stands of trees and brush here and there. The Mambas' camp was in one of the treed areas. He glimpsed some camouflage netting that hung above their tents.

He pushed the talk switch on the yoke and said, "I'm here, do you copy?" It was some seconds before he got a reply.

Fitzgerald's voice was strained, and Zeke could hear sporadic firing in the background. "Got you in sight. We came under attack a few minutes ago. What do you see?"

"A straight truck, an SUV, and a Jeep a mile northwest of your camp coordinates, just under a tree line." His vantage changed and he suddenly could see men. He opened the side window and grabbed the binoculars with his left hand, flying with his right. "Got the hostiles," he said. "Hunkered down in the tall grass. Let me . . . okay, they seem to be in an arc to your northwest a quarter mile out. Spaced fifteen, twenty feet apart." They were prone, crawling along. Some of them were looking up at the plane, but none of them seemed to be pointing a weapon at him. At least not yet.

He did a quick count and said, "I see twenty-five men. All dressed in black. Crawling in slowly."

He completed his wide circle and said, "No other hostiles I can see. You're clear everywhere else. No. Wait. You've got five more in a cluster northeast. Looks like they're trying to move around to your east flank."

"Got it," Fitzgerald said. "Helps. But you're too low. Grab some altitude before they target you."

The firing in the background grew in volume before it was chopped off by Fitzgerald releasing his handheld's talk switch.

Zeke was coming around for his second circle, increasing the bank angle, realizing he had been letting down unconsciously to see better, the altimeter reading less than 2,600 feet above the ground now, when he saw several of the prone black-clad men in the tall grass roll onto their backs and lift their weapons toward him, and he immediately twisted out of the bank and did a series of fast jinks, jamming the stick and rudders almost to their stops, first to the right, then to the left, the Cessna doing a wild dance. He heard three sharp blows in rapid succession somewhere on the plane's belly, like somebody had hammered on the aluminum with a drumstick. He poured on the power going away, clawing for more altitude, still doing random jinks, hoping a hit would not hole one of the fuel tanks in the wings. Expecting more hits any second. But none came.

"You okay Z?" Fitzgerald said.

"I'm fine," Zeke said. I'll make a higher pass."

He did a half circle and came back over the scene fast at 4,500 feet. The five men in black he'd spotted on the first orbit were in a group, doing something. His breath caught when he figured out what it was. He thumbed the talk switch mounted on the yoke and shouted, "Hostiles on your east flank, two hundred yards out. Setting up a mortar. You're about to get shelled."

"Copy," Fitzgerald said, and began yelling orders to his pitifully few Mamba defenders.

Zeke flew on for a quarter mile and then threw the Cessna into a steep bank to come around on a reverse course. Just as he levelled out, there was a bright blossom of fire in the Mamba encampment and a tree toppled in slow motion. It was surreal. With the headset on and the engine drumming, blanking out background noise, he had not heard anything going on below. He only knew there was a lot of firing when Fitzgerald had been talking to him in a tense voice and he'd overheard the snapping reports. But he did hear a dull thud now as the sound from the mortar round reached him. A few seconds later there was another blossom near where the first explosion had produced a drifting veil of smoke and dust. Another dull thud. The black-clad men to the northwest were all on their feet now, advancing at a slow walk and firing their rifles from their hips.

He called it in to Fitzgerald, but another voice answered. It was Mike Sabo. When they had parted ways after the warehouse raid, Sabo had been picked up by one of the other Mambas and driven straight to the camp.

In a voice filled with strain, Sabo said, "Okay. Can't hold. We're falling back. Help's on the way." He gave Zeke a new radio frequency and said, "Helo from the southeast. They know you're friendly. Just get clear." There was another explosion and the transmission cut off.

He flew on and there was yet another dirty blossom below, followed by another thud. He caught glimpses of two Mambas running through the trees for their vehicles while another one knelt and fired to cover the retreat. He climbed to 5,500 feet above the fight and went into a close orbit. He felt helpless. All he could do now was watch and hope they could get away.

Fifty-three

Mike Sabo had been crouched behind a tree no more than 40 feet from Fitzgerald, who was behind another tree. They each were exposing themselves briefly to fire at the black-clad figures, who were steadily drawing closer through the chest-high grass. Sabo had the satisfaction of seeing one fall when he fired a burst from his sub-machine gun. Fitzgerald was on the hand-held radio slung on a lanyard around his neck, probably talking with Zeke upstairs. Fitz dropped the radio and shouted, "INCOMING. TAKE COVER."

There was an eye-searing flash-bang that shredded the base of a tree, which began to topple in slow motion. When his vision cleared, Sabo saw that Fitzgerald was down. Not moving. He fired another quick burst, ran to Fitzgerald, and dropped to his knees. He checked the carotid, but it was obvious Fitz was gone. Shrapnel had torn away half his chest.

Sabo swore, grabbed the radio, and gave a last message to Zeke, saying help was on the way, giving him a frequency to monitor, and telling him to get clear. He stood, cupped a palm around his mouth, and shouted, "FALL BACK. GIVE COVER FIRE. FALL BACK."

He saw three Mambas take off through the underbrush. One turned, took a knee, and laid down fire in the direction of the attackers, then he jumped up and ran in a crouch, while one of the others dropped to a knee and gave covering fire. Sabo looked all around but saw no more Mambas. He ran his magazine dry in the direction Zeke had said the mortar rounds were coming from and spun to withdraw alongside the other three, reloading as he went.

Zeke was doing a scan when he saw it. An insectile black thing off to the southeast, rapidly growing larger, coming fast. He trained the binoculars on it. Yes. A helicopter. A good-sized one. As it got closer he saw it was a CH-46, with its distinctive ponderous banana shape and tandem rotors. It was an old troop-carrying assault helicopter that had been used by the U.S. military since the early 1960s with heavy service in Vietnam, but it was still a great workhorse. And this one was also a gun platform. He could see a barrel sticking out of its left-side doorway. The helicopter was low, 4,000 feet below him. It went into a purposeful bank. The door machinegun was winking and smoking, tracers streaming out, dust erupting all among the hostiles. Men were going down. Others were running for their vehicles, but the gunner adjusted his fire and the truck blew up, the other two vehicles quickly being shredded and enveloped in the resultant smoke and dust cloud. Deprived of transport, the attackers had nowhere left to run. Zeke saw several of them stand and fire at the helicopter, but they were immediately cut down.

It was all over in a few minutes. He watched the copter do a final slow searching orbit over the area and then clatter loudly a short distance and set down on the grass beside the strip, blasting up a thin mushroom of dust and making the surrounding vegetation shudder and whip. A dozen armed uniformed men jumped down, spread out, and moved off toward the camp, guns at the ready.

He had the radio set to the frequency Sabo had given him, and he heard, "Cessna. This is the helo. Understand you are friendly. Land now, please. We will talk on the ground."

He said, "Roger that," and began a spiraling descent that would put him on a final approach for the rough strip, glancing at the gauges and noting with a start that his tanks were nearly dry.

He shut down the Cessna at the end of the strip, climbed out, and walked over to a group of men in camo uniforms and blue berets standing beside the chopper.

A slim black man with a pair of pearl-handled semi-automatic pistols strapped on was obviously in charge. He turned, an expression of stern appraisal on his sharp features, and said, "You will be Mister Blades. I am Major Moses Kahama. We are an element attached to the Tanzania National and Transnational Serious Crimes Investigation Unit." He offered his hand and Zeke shook it.

Zeke said, "What were the casualties?"

"My men and the remaining Mambas are doing a search. We will know soon."

The remaining Mambas. "How did you know to . . . intervene here?"

Kahama lifted an eyebrow and cocked his head. Regarding him silently.

Then it hit him. When Zeke had first met the Mambas, something Fitzgerald had said.

"You're the sixteenth."

"Excuse please?" Kahama said.

"There were fifteen Mambas. Fitzgerald said they had a sixteenth. Called you their secret weapon. You've been working with them."

Kahama gave him a steely look. "Such a thing should not be made publicly known," he said.

"Understood," Zeke said. "I'd also prefer that not too many know about my association with them, either."

Kahama nodded and showed the merest brief flicker of a smile. He turned back to his men and began talking with them. Zeke sat in the doorway of the chopper and massaged his neck. The air was oven hot and dust lingered on a mild breeze. One of the uniformed men offered him a bottled water. He accepted it and nodded his thanks.

Twenty minutes later, Sabo, Williamson and two more of Kahama's men walked up to the group, their weapons slung.

Zeke stood and looked at Sabo's dirt-streaked face and bloody hands. "Tell me."

"It's bad," Sabo said. "Fitz was killed. By mortar shrapnel. There's only six of us left. Four of our guys are gone, including Fitz. Six hostiles captured. Three of them wounded and getting field aid now. Their body count is twenty-three. Bunch of unholy bastards from al-Isra. We think one of the bodies is the leader of that whole deal. How many jihadis did you count from the air?"

Zeke thought a moment. "Thirty, but maybe I didn't see them all."

"That means at least one got away. Something real strange, though. They all had brand-new American weapons. Be good to know how they got 'em."

Kahama had heard, and said, "With some firm persuasion, one of the captives will tell us where they bought or stole the weapons. He will also tell us how to find the rest of their devils. And if not, one or two of them will contrive to escape from our clutches, and my trackers will follow them. My trackers are very good."

Fifty-four

"That's horrible," Liana said. "Ryan Fitzgerald was a good man. They all were such good men."

Liana, Zeke, and Dante were in her living room, and Zeke was recounting for them what had happened at the Mamba camp. Zeke checked his watch and said, "Time for the late news on TV Three."

Dante used the remote to find it.

After a series of commercials, Wexton, seated at his desk and looking solemn, said, "We have breaking news again tonight. TV-Three has just learned that an element of the Tanzania National and Transnational Serious Crimes Investigation Unit earlier today engaged members of the known terrorist group al-Isra in northwestern Tanzania. The Investigation Unit suffered two wounded. Twenty-three members of the radical Islamist group were killed and six were captured. The dead include the reputed supreme leader of the movement, Abdul Ahad. Three of those captured were wounded in the action and are being treated under guard at the Dodoma hospital. Three are being held in the Dodoma jail pending charges. A reliable source has told TV-Three that the Investigation Unit is now working with elements of the Ugandan military to rout the remaining members of al-Isra, rumored to be in hiding somewhere deep in the Mountains of the Moon. The terrorist group has been responsible for a series of bombings and has been suspected of planning a major campaign of conquest in the region. We will bring you up to date as we receive new information. You're witnessing all the latest news you can trust on TV-Three."

"Good," Zeke said. "They've managed to spin it to leave the Mambas out of it."

Dante muted the TV, which was showing a paroxysmal commercial selling furniture at one-day giveaway prices.

Liana said, "But how did the Investigation Unit get involved, anyway?"

"I think they've always been involved," Zeke said. "When I first met the Mambas in their camp, Fitzgerald told me there was another secret member, or at least a strong ally. Turns out he's Major Moses Kahama of the Unit. Pretty sure that's the man Fitzgerald talked into making the warehouse raid, too. I think Fitzgerald's plan all along was to eventually draw al-Isra out. Into a trap. But I don't think he meant for it to happen so soon. The jihadis must have discovered the camp on their own. So it was a surprise. Fitz needed me to spot for him until help got there. He must have called in Kahama as soon as he realized the threat, but it took time for Kahama to get organized, and he was late showing up."

"Too late to save the Mambas who died," Dante said.

Liana stood and walked to the window, folded her arms, and looked out into the night. She said, "Fitzgerald died not even knowing the attackers were defeated. That's so sad."

None of them said anything for a time.

Liana turned away from the darkness, used both hands to lift and smooth her hair, took a deep breath, and said, "What will happen now?"

Dante said, "Well, I've got six holes to fix in the Cessna. Three bullets went all the way through the fuselage just behind the cabin. Turned the emergency locater transmitter into junk. I've got a spare from a friend's wrecked plane I can use. Otherwise nothing important got hit. You were damned lucky, Zeke."

Zeke had used enough auto gas from spare jerry cans stored on the Mamba vehicles to let him fly back to Dodoma. The Cessna had not seemed to notice it wasn't avgas. Kahama and his men had set about transporting the wounded to the hospital and the bodies to an improvised morgue in Dodoma. It would take two trips in the helo. The remaining Mambas had stayed behind to bury their own dead in a glade not far from where they had fallen. Sabo had said all the Mambas had agreed to such arrangements in advance. None had any close family left, but notifications and wills would be given to whomever each lost member had designated.

Zeke said, "I'll drive to Dar and sit down with Iverson. Tell him about me flying surveillance for the fighting. If he wants me gone, I'll quit on the spot."

"I'll go with you," Liana said. "He may as well know my part in all this."

"Hell, I'll go, too," Dante said. "Make it a group confession."

"That's it, then," Liana said. "We'll all pack it in if necessary. Let's just hope some good came out of all this, shall we. It sounds like al-Isra is all but finished, at the least. That means something. These lost lives *have* to mean something, don't they?"

The next morning, Zeke drove them to Dar in the Jeep, and they met with Iverson in the waiting area of the GHR offices. The three of them sat on hard metal folding chairs lined along one wall and Iverson sat stiffly across the room, pinning each of them in turn with his flinty eyes, his arms folded across his chest.

"Right, then," he said. "What's this all about? I warn you it had better be enlightening, because I've reached my limit of tolerance."

Zeke said, "I didn't fly back to Dodoma after the delivery yesterday. I flew surveillance for the same people who've been fighting the poachers."

Iverson's neck and face were coloring. He shifted his glare to Liana. "You've known about this all along, then, I take it. The deliberate use of GHR aircraft and facilities to make illegal flights. Ill-conceived, illicit, vigilante activities that have seriously jeopardized everything we've been trying to accomplish here. Bloody well betraying me and every other member of GHR. You're in this as well, James?"

Dante nodded. "Sorry, sir. I kind of talked Zeke into, ah . . . getting involved in the first place."

"Everything you're saying is true, Iverson," Zeke said. "It was wrong, but it's been done and I can't undo it. I'd probably do the same again if given the chance. We've helped damage a major terrorist cell and an allied poaching operation, and from my perspective that was something worth doing. As I've said, we've paid for the extra fuel ourselves. I'll pay what I figure should be my part to cover maintenance, too. If you want, I'll quit today. That will end the problem. Your efforts can continue as planned."

Liana said, "I should think there's no percentage in bringing all this up before the board. You have my deep apologies, and you can have my resignation today as well, if you like."

"Hell, mine too," Dante said. "Sir."

Iverson snorted and shook his head. "Just look at the lot of you. Acting like you've simply been caught out in the act of filching sweets."

He unfolded his arms and gripped his bony knees and some of the heat went out of him.

"Well, I daresay I'm forced to partially agree. The damage has been done and there would seem to be nothing of value to gain by worrying the board. Liana and Dante, you've done admirable jobs for GHR, overall, so I'm inclined to keep you on with the promise you shall not engage in any further skullduggery on your GHR time. Mister Blades, I must demand your resignation. Should your actions ever come to light, it will at least lessen the resultant scandal to state you are no longer a paid member of our organization. You do understand?"

"I do," Zeke said.

Iverson went back to his office and returned with a lined pad. Zeke wrote out a brief resignation letter and dated and signed it. Iverson accepted it with no comment and showed the three of them out. He closed the door behind them. He looked at the resignation and shook his head again. He said to himself, "Truth be told, I do have some empathy for your cause, Mister Blades. But you were damned foolish in the ways you went about it. Bloody damned foolish."

He'd have to find another bush pilot. They were not easy to come by for what relatively little GHR could afford to pay.

Then the glimmer of an idea came to him. Perhaps there was a way . . .

Fifty-five

From the cover of trees on a forested hillside in the Mountains of the Moon, Muhammadu Raza and eight of his poachers looked down on the slaughter being wrought throughout the al-Isra encampment. Their horses, laden with the latest harvest of ivory, were being held by three more men well out of sight behind thick brush over the hill's crest. They had just returned from their recent hunt and had been about to enter the valley when the attack had begun.

He was in a seething rage so all-consuming he could not speak. *How can this be?* he thought. *How did the accursed infidels find us?*

They had seemed to come out of nowhere, appearing low over the forested hills from the east. The three assault helicopters thundered into wide orbits over the valley, pouring down destruction with rockets and heavy machine gun fire, shredding tents and trees and running men. They had caught the encampment completely by surprise. Resistance was sporadic. Not at all organized. Somebody fired an RPG from the ground, but it was hasty and inaccurate, missing one of the helicopters by 20 yards to explode harmlessly against a rock outcrop on the far side of the valley, and the helicopter immediately targeted the area it had come from and engulfed it in withering tracer fire. A shoulder-fired Stinger erupted from elsewhere in the encampment and smoked toward another helicopter, but the machine made an agile evasive maneuver and avoided it in the last moment and swung around to fire its own rocket, which erupted in a greasy red-and-black fireball amid the trees. The firing went on and on, and then one helicopter went into hover 40 feet above a brushy clearing at the foot of the valley and men dressed in camouflage uniforms began dropping to the ground on ropes. At least a dozen of them. They fanned out and moved purposefully uphill, firing from their hips as they went. While the first helicopter gave covering fire, another machine settled into a hover above the clearing to disgorge its own fighters. These were joined by more men from the third helicopter and they all moved off up the side of the valley, obviously planning to attack the flank of the encampment. There had to be at least 50 attackers on the ground now adding their firepower to the terrible destruction that still came from above, though now concentrated on noticeably fewer areas of resistance in the valley.

Through binoculars, Raza saw three of the attackers go down when a hand grenade exploded among them, but it did not slow the attack, and Raza knew it was hopeless. Through binoculars, he saw black-clad al-Isra figures scattering, abandoning the encampment in twos and threes, melting away into the forest, some of them being cut down from behind even as they fled. The small arms firing rose to such a chattering crescendo Raza heard it even over the brain-numbing howl-slapping of the helicopters.

Dawud was at Raza's side, as always. He said loudly over the din, "We should go down and fight."

Raza moved close and said, "No. It will be over soon. Back. We go back. The infidels will kill or capture all in the valley and then send out patrols to hunt down any who escaped. We must go now. Fast and far. Get the men moving." He was doing a last scan with the binoculars. "No, wait. I think . . . yes, there. Where the thickest smoke is drifting up the valley on the wind. It is Faraji and . . . three of our men. Making for the top of the valley. There is a trail there leading away. Go and find him, Dawud. Bring him to where we last camped. Be sure you are not followed. We will meet you there. Go, go."

* * *

When Abdul Ahad had set out with his 29 selected men, intent on destroying the Mambas, he'd left Faraji in charge of the encampment. Faraji had just called the men to mid-day prayers, and they were all facing toward Mecca and kneeling on their mats beneath the trees throughout the area. The prayers had just begun when he'd heard the distinctive juddering roar of heavy helicopters approaching out of the morning glare. He screamed, "IT IS AN ATTACK. WE ARE UNDER ATTACK. TO YOUR WEAPONS. HURRY, HURRY. TAKE TO COVER. BE READY."

He ran through the encampment trying to organize the defenses, shouting for Stingers and RPGs. Within minutes he managed to organize a ragged defense, but it was soon crumbling under horrendous fire coming down from the helicopters like an evil hail. The attackers had too much firepower and were too well trained.

The al-Isra men were still unfamiliar with the new weapons, had been caught completely by surprise, and were in disarray. He saw an RPG rise but it missed one of the helicopters widely, and the return fire from the door-mounted machine gun was merciless, accurate, and devastating.

A Stinger rode an arc of smoke from elsewhere in the camp, but the target helicopter evaded it as though it was nothing and wheeled around to answer with a rocket that erupted with an ear-cracking concussion, toppling trees in a huge white-red blossom. The machine gun fire from all three helicopters ripped down through the trees in a hot torrent, obliterating everything and everybody it touched. The smell of explosives and gunpowder was acrid. Eyewatering. And it was suffused with the coppery odor of blood. Al-Isra blood.

He squinted and saw one of the helicopters hover above a clearing in the lower valley and, while one of the other black machines gave covering fire, men began rapidly sliding down ropes like spiders. Within only moments he heard them firing as they advanced on the encampment. The sheer overwhelming sound of the beating helicopters and so many chattering weapons was disorienting. Several of his men were already retreating uphill, firing back wildly. Ineffectively. How many times in training had he shouted at them to aim low? One of the retreating men went down with a thin scream as he was nearly cut in half by a sub-machine gun burst, bright blood splashing a tree trunk like hurled paint.

Faraji knew the attackers would prevail. There was no doubt. He stopped firing, so he would not draw the attention of the attackers and chose three of the best men he could spot nearby. He drew them together in the shadow of a tree and said, "Do not fire anymore unless you are face-to-face with an infidel. The four of us will withdraw. Now. To the highest place in the valley. Take only your weapons. There is a trail I know of. Follow me."

* * *

On the TV3 news that night, Zeke and Liana learned of the follow-up operation against al-Isra led by the National and Transnational force, and Zeke knew Kahama had made good on his vow.

Fifty-six

"I am sorry, but Abdul Ahad is dead," the ragged al-Isra fighter told Muhammadu Raza. The man was on his knees in the dust by the campfire, dirty and exhausted, his weapon lost and his fighting spirit with it. He disgusted Raza. He was evidently one of only a few men at most who had escaped the skirmish with the Mambas. Maybe the only one. He had contacted Raza on a satellite phone that Ahad had been carrying. Raza had sent Dawud and another man in a stolen Jeep to pick up the man ten miles from the destroyed Mamba camp and bring him here to this temporary camp, still in the Mountains of the Moon, but 40 miles from the ravaged al-Isra camp. There were only Faraji and 30 other men left from Ahad's force, and they only had the personal weapons they had fled with. Raza had ten men including Dawud. From a force of nearly 100, they had been reduced in two battles against the infidels to only a pitiful few and had lost many of the weapons bought at great cost from the Yemenis. Luckily, they had wrapped in plastic, crated, and buried part of their weapons and ammunition stock some distance from the al-Isra encampment, but they would be of no use without men.

Raza was still in a smoldering rage. The kneeling man was named Abdi Mizra.

Raza was pacing in front of Mizra. He said, "How is it that you escaped, and my brother is dead? Explain this to me."

"Please, sir. I was near him when the infidels shot him. I tried but could not help him. All around, our men were being cut down. I only escaped by the grace of Allah."

"Tell me about the battle. Leave nothing out."

"We arrived in the area of the Mamba camp at midday. We left our vehicles some distance away under trees and sent scouts ahead. When we knew their strength and positions, our great leader made a plan and ordered the attack. We were advancing and killing them. We were winning. I do not believe any of them would have long survived. But then the plane came."

Raza stopped pacing and glared down at Mizra. "What plane? Describe it. Was it yellow with a round engine?"

"No, sir, it was small. It was blue and white with sticks supporting the wings. We tried to shoot it down but could not. Everything changed when the plane came. It could see where we were and direct the fire of the few Mamba guns remaining. We began losing men, though I believe we killed their leader with the mortar. Then a big helicopter came over. It looked bent in the middle, with two rotating blades, one at each end. It had a heavy machine gun in the doorway, and it was murderous. We could not fight it. I was near Abdul Ahad. He was shooting up at the helicopter, but he was struck by two bullets from the machine. I ran to where he fell. His stomach was . . . blown out, and . . . and his head. His head was . . . partly gone. I took his satellite phone. Thinking I could call for help, but it was too late. There was no time. I am so sorry, sir. Please forgive me. Our men were scattering, and I ran with them. It was no use to stay. No use. I do not know how many of us got away. Maybe only me."

Faraji had been standing off to the side, listening. He said, "The plane belongs to the same people who own the yellow one."

"What?" Raza said. "You are sure of this?"

"Yes. We found where the yellow plane and also the blue-and-white one are being kept at the Dodoma Airport. All this I reported to Abdul Ahad. Before he made the decision to attack the Mamba camp."

Raza scowled down at Mizra. "My brother was fighting when the godless infidels killed him. You ran like a coward. Get out. Get out of this camp before I take your head."

Mizra bowed deeply and scrambled away into the trees. He did not look back.

Raza told the men around him to leave. He motioned for Dawud and Faraji to stay. Faraji stood quietly, watching through hooded eyes. Dawud squatted by a tree, his rifle slung on his back.

Raza paced. It was all becoming clear. He remembered the pilot, the one with the woman's braided hair who had flown the yellow plane for the hostage exchange. He had sensed a hidden fire in the tall man, not unlike the rage that burned within himself. Abdul had been winning against the Mambas when that pilot had appeared in the blue plane to turn the battle against the al-Isra fighters. The pilot, then, must have called in the evil helicopter that had decimated the al-Isra force, the monster machine that had killed his brother. He reasoned the pilot also must have had something to do with sending the force that had then attacked the al-Isra camp with such telling ferocity. Abdul had done well, after all. The Mambas were as good as destroyed, but it was sour satisfaction. That accursed pilot was still alive. Alive and gloating over the destruction of al-Isra. Laughing at the annihilation of Abdul's dream.

Raza looked at Faraji. "You know where to find this infidel pilot?"

"I do," Faraji said.

Fifty-seven

Zeke sat on a metal straight chair in Iverson's cluttered office in Dar. Iverson was seated behind his desk, elbows on his chair arms, splayed fingertips touching and flexing, reminding Zeke of that childhood mime image kids used to make with their hands. *Know what this is?* they'd say. *It's a spider doing pushups on a mirror.*

Zeke was worried, mostly about Liana and DJ. Had Iverson decided to press charges after all?

Neither of them said anything for a moment. Iverson was still flexing his long bony fingers.

"I have an idea," Iverson said.

"Okay," Zeke said.

"Hear me out before you comment, if you please. My proposal in no way diminishes your culpability in the illegal use of our aircraft. I have neither forgotten nor forgiven that. But let us set all that unpleasantness aside for the moment. The Beaver is bloody expensive enough for GHR to maintain. And, although there are times when the Cessna is decidedly a better mission choice, that aircraft is an additional expense we can ill afford. I propose that you purchase the plane on simple low-interest terms to make the arrangement financially comfortable for you. It was gifted to us, after all, so we have no investment in it. You could set up your own enterprise doing charters, or aerial photography, or tourist sightseeing excursions, perhaps. At times we would charter your services for medevacs or supply deliveries, at a special charitable discount for us, of course. Whatever you choose to do with the plane on your own time would then be entirely your affair, and of no concern to us, you see. No longer our responsibility. You'd not be an employee of GHR, apart from the occasional charter. The caravan Ben Stone and you've been using was another donation to us. We have no use for it now, so that could be part of the purchase arrangement. You'd need to find your own hangar space and a lot for the caravan. I should think three thousand U.S. dollars in the front and perhaps a seven-year payment schedule (he pronounced it *shed-yule*) at a fixed three percent annual interest rate would be acceptable to the board. Purchase price to be somewhat less than what that make and model Cessna fetches on average in the open market. Of course, it would only be ethically proper for me to first contact the aircraft donor, assuring her that the Cessna would be providing long-term financial support to GHR from your payments, and would still be used to benefit our efforts. I believe she will agree. So, then, what say you to all of this?"

Zeke was seeing Iverson in a whole new way. Back in the States, before he became qualified in high-dollar corporate planes and snared by the generous earnings available for flying them, he'd had a brief dream of starting his own business in some small picturesque town in New England or the Appalachians, maybe an FBO that could support itself on flight instruction, fuel sales, maintenance, hangar rentals, and occasional charters and sightseeing jaunts for tourists. That dream had lingered in some dim fold of his mind. Maybe this was a chance to resurrect it.

He grinned and said, "Walter, I think it's a great idea."

Three days later the deal was done. Iverson handled all the paperwork in his usual briskly efficient style, and Zeke signed and initialed in all the proper places. He wrote a down-payment check for 3,000 USD to GHR. They shook hands on the deal.

There was a line of six open T-hangars in a long low building on the other side of the Dodoma airport from the GHR hangar, just off a packed-gravel taxiway, back along a stand of trees. It was covered only by a rusty corrugated steel roof. Three of the spaces were rented out to private light-aircraft owners. The other three were weedy and contained junk aircraft parts and a derelict fuel truck. Zeke made a deal with the airport manager to rent one of the three unused hangars at a reasonable monthly rate, offering to clear it out himself. The deal included permission to park the camper in front of the T-hangar that contained the old fuel truck. He worked another day transferring parts from his hangar to the two others on the far end that were already partly filled with junk, and he pulled up the weeds that had sprouted through the cracked concrete floor.

After a good sweeping the hangar looked, if not great, at least pretty good. It would do until he could afford something better. As he worked, he was repeatedly mock attacked by several upset small brown birds that considered the hangar their own and had built their nests in the rafters, but he figured he could live with them. They were, after all, fellow aviators. DJ agreed to come across the field on his own time to do routine servicing and annual inspections, with Zeke himself assisting to cut the cost.

He used the Jeep to pull the camper over. Set up on its jack stands, it made a minimally comfortable home. There was a disused but still functioning bathroom in the back corner of the T-hangar wherein the old fuel truck rested on concrete blocks, and with a little ingenuity, two skinned knuckles, and some choice cursing, he managed to hook up both cold-water and waste lines for the camper. It would never pass codes back home, but nobody here cared. He had the two small propane tanks mounted on the camper's tongue for cooking. It was far better than most living conditions only a few miles from Dodoma in any direction out in the bush. There was power in the T-hangars, so he wired the camper into that, too.

On a hazy and partly cloudy afternoon when the heat was not so intense as it had been, dressed only in shorts, worn sneakers, and a straw hat, he had washed down the Cessna that now belonged to him—and which had therefore taken on a special proprietary aura—and was rubbing on a coat of wax, thinking about naming her *Angel*. He could paint it in script just ahead of the pilot-side door. *I feel like a kid with a new toy*, he thought. And smiled.

Two hundred feet away, in the shadows of the trees, Faraji watched the infidel pilot. Over the past few days he had followed a maintenance worker from the airport, had struck up a conversation with him in a run-down bar, and had learned about the pilot named Zeke buying the airplane that had belonged to the agency named GHR and setting up his home in the small camping vehicle.

There was a security fence around the airport, but it was not in good repair. Its pipes had rusted and sections of it had collapsed in the littered brush and tall grass near the field. It had been an easy matter for Faraji to work his way close unseen. The pilot had pulled the blue-and-white plane out of the hangar using a tow bar he attached to the front wheel and was now cleaning it with great care. The man was tall and fit, ropy muscles flexing as he worked. Faraji imagined how good it would feel to slide his honed knife into that flat belly and draw it sideways, spilling out the warm entrails. For half an hour he watched unmoving and in utter silence, his eyes glittering, noting every detail of the scene.

Satisfied, he drifted like a dark ghost back through the trees to report what he knew to Raza, who was waiting alone in a rough camp they'd made out in the bush.

Faraji was slightly dismayed that he would not have the privilege of killing the man. That right belonged to Raza, who would surely make the infidel squeal like a pig and beg for mercy before he died.

At least he would be able to watch, great Allah willing.

Fifty-eight

It was two in the morning and a hazy half-moon hung in the sky above the quiet Dodoma airport. The airport beacon swept lazily. White . . . green . . . white.

The terminal was still open but not much was going on there and many of the usual interior and exterior lights had been shut off. The few hangars around the field that had doors were locked and dark.

In the trees above the two men, night birds were calling as Faraji led Raza to the place where he'd spied on the pilot the previous afternoon. They both wore jeans, boots, black T-shirts, and black ball caps. Mosquitoes were needling them, and they brushed at their exposed faces, necks, and forearms with their hands.

Ignoring the insects as they approached the edge of the trees, Raza whispered with intensity, "That must be the devil infidel's vehicle."

"Yes," Faraji whispered back. "It is the one I saw. His Jeep. The plane is pushed back into its space."

There was a light inside the camper.

They kept to the shadows as much as possible as they moved closer. They circled the camper. Each was armed with a holstered handgun, but they did not want to use them here. The main terminal was only 300 yards away and, although it was quiet, there would be a few airport personnel and security guards still on duty. They both drew out knives with six-inch fixed blades, honed to scalpel sharpness. Raza was also carrying a short, hooked pry bar in his other hand.

Raza whispered to Faraji, "There is only the one door, and it will yield quickly to my pry. I will go in first, very fast. If he hears me break through the door he will have little time to come fully awake and defend himself. I will disable him. We will gag and bind him. We will take him away. Then I will take my revenge."

Faraji nodded and stood to one side of the door as Raza quietly inserted the chisel end of the pry bar in the door seam beside the flimsy lock.

The door yielded easily with a low shriek, and Raza flung it open and charged inside. There was a small sitting area, a kitchen with a dim overhead light on, and what had to be a bathroom opposite the kitchen. He could see the bed in the back and he lunged that way, ready to use either the knife to stab or the pry bar to break bone.

The bed was empty.

He spun and clubbed the bathroom door open. Empty.

Faraji tried to calm him by holding up a palm, but Raza was in a rage, smashing at the small cabinets and a kettle on the stove, scattering dishes. Faraji grabbed his arm and spoke sharply. "*Stop*. He is not here."

Raza almost stabbed at Faraji with the knife, but he stopped himself and shook off Faraji's hand. He stood in the cramped space, fuming, his breathing harsh.

"*Listen* to me," Faraji said. "We must make it look like thieves broke in. We must search and take everything of value and then go quickly. Do you understand?"

Raza glared at him for a moment, then he sheathed the knife and nodded.

Fifty-nine

Zeke had been pushing the shining Cessna back into its T-hangar late that afternoon when Liana pulled up in the GHR Rover. She got out, placed her hands on her hips, and looked over the scene. "You've made yourself to home, I see. I can't say much for the neighborhood. But all that trash does certainly make the caravan stand out like a jewel in a junkyard. It's a good thing you waited to polish up the Cessna, or Iverson would have charged you more for it. She looks brand new."

He tied the plane down to the three rusted iron rings buried in the concrete hangar floor, one under each wing and one under the tail. "Try to ignore the humble surroundings," he said. "You're witnessing the birth of Blades Aviation Services. If I can borrow some computer and printer time at your place, I'll make up a flyer and business cards. Then it's fair skies and good fortune just over the horizon."

He stood in front of the plane and mopped his face with a hand towel.

"Congratulations," she said. "We need to celebrate. Fetch a change of clothes and come with me. We'll stop by the market. Then we can cook up a proper meal. I've a fair eye for graphic design, so we'll work up your advert sheet and cards tonight."

She made him British-style fish and chips that evening. After they'd washed and dried the dishes, they were working side-by-side at her computer on the logo and a flyer design for the new business and making some progress, but some simple touching progressed to caressing, which evolved into kissing, and then to partial disrobing, and finally, with her breathing quickened and her complexion nicely flushed, she led him off to bed, where they stayed until dawn light filtered in through the window blinds. He made cinnamon-dusted French toast with scrambled eggs, and they lingered over coffee.

She drove them back to the airport. It had rained during the night and the sky looked brand new and bold, cloudless, with a cool fresh scent of a breeze out of the south. They were both sated, relaxed, and content, communicating only through glances and light touches. Looking forward to the day.

Pulling up in front of his hangar, she frowned and said, "Look there. Isn't something wrong with the caravan's door?"

"Up close, it was obvious the thin aluminum door had been forced. It was bent badly near the locking latch, which was no longer holding it closed. The camper had been ransacked. It looked like everything worth more than a few dollars was missing. A stash of 300 USD in cash, the .45 handgun Fitzgerald had given him, and a box of ammunition for it, all of which he'd hidden in the enclosed frame beneath the bed, were gone. His binoculars and smart phone and meager stock of silverware, a gift from Liana, were also gone. Other items here and there had been taken. The casings had been stripped from his pillows, likely serving as carry sacks for the thief or thieves. Luckily, he'd had his key ring with him, so he still had the keys for the Jeep and the plane. He did a quick walkaround of each and saw no damage.

"I was planning to bolt a steel strap for a heavy padlock to the door," Zeke said, a dull anger forming at his core. "Little late for that."

"I've called airport security," Liana said. "They should be here in a few minutes."

The head of the small airport security force was a hefty Irishman named Sean McElroy. He inspected the damaged door, looked at the chaos inside, and said, "Looks like one or more renegade kids did it. The Lord knows there's enough of them around. I'll need a list of what's missing. Do you have somewhere to stay for a day or two?"

"Yes," Zeke said.

"Okay, then. I suggest you don't touch anything. I'll get the police in here today. Might be some prints they can use. Or maybe there're some clues that could link this to other break-ins in the area."

Zeke got a pocket pad from the glove compartment in the Jeep, made a quick list of the most valuable items missing, and gave him Liana's phone number. But something about the break-in felt off, and he was beginning to wonder if this had been something more than a simple random burglary.

Maybe he'd been targeted.

He went shopping for items he'd need to fix the camper door and lock it more securely, helped Liana around the GHR hangar for a while, and decided to service the Jeep. Two Dodoma policemen came by while he was under the Jeep draining the oil into a pan. They spent an hour looking over the camper, dusting here and there for prints, and questioning him, but he could tell from their remote laconic attitude there would not be much hope of catching the thieves. He finished with the Jeep and straightened up the camper. He went for a five-mile run late that afternoon and put himself through a series of strength exercises, including 100 push-ups and 100 stomach crunches. Fifty squats. Curl reps using half a cement block he'd found in one of the T-hangars.

That evening they cooked chicken and vegetables together and were lingering over wine on her couch when her cell rang.

She frowned and said, "For you."

He put it on speaker and said, "Yes, Zeke Blades."

The caller said nothing for a moment, but they could hear him breathing. Then, "Liana Sekibo is there with you?"

"Yes, she is. Why?"

"Walter Iverson."

"He's not here, but yes, I know him," Zeke said. "Who is this?"

The caller had a heavy accent. Middle Eastern? "Dante James."

Liana spread her hands and raised her eyebrows.

Zeke shook his head and shrugged.

"Hobart Wexton," the accented voice said.

Then it hit Zeke. All those people were in his smart phone contact list. His missing phone. As a backup, he had put all the numbers on his contact list into the smartphone as well as the burner Fitzgerald had given him, and he regretted that now. He had not even protected the phone with a password. *Dumb*. He said, "You're the bastard who stole my phone when you robbed my place. Why are you calling? What do you want?"

The voice said, "Doctor George Robertson."

Zeke's demon was stirring. "You *threatening* these people? Is that it?"

"Mike Sabo," the voice said.

"Okay, enough of this. I'm hanging up now."

"Ryan Fitzgerald," the voice said. "But he is already dead, is he not?"

"What do you want?" Zeke said.

"Tonight. Midnight. No later. Begin at the B One-Twenty-Nine highway in Dodoma. Go north on the Arusha Road. Twenty-one kilometers. There is a long curve. Beyond that curve, take the left-hand track into the bush. If you do not come alone or if you call in the police we will know it, and one of those I have named will die before morning."

The connection was cut off.

Sixty

"Who *was* that?" Liana said.

"I don't know," Zeke said. He thought of that poacher's black eyes when they caught him with the ambush, and the evil that had emanated from the man, even after Sabo had shot him off his horse. "My first thought was Raza, but it wasn't his voice. Maybe he's one of the al-Isra survivors."

"Well you can't simply go alone. He—or they; he did say 'we'—almost surely means to kill you."

"I don't think I have a choice," Zeke said. "There's no time to set up protection for everybody he named. He said midnight. That's less than two hours from now. I have a shotgun in the Jeep. Twenty-one kilometers is what, thirteen miles? Do you know this Arusha Road?"

"It's a dirt track that runs all the way to Arusha, maybe two hundred miles—they call it 'A' town, which is in northeast Tanzy, at the foot of Mount Meru. Long stretches of the road are just empty bush. Remote and rough. Potholes and washouts, so it can be slow going. It's known as unsafe."

"You still have that pistol Fitzgerald gave you. After I'm gone, lock up and turn out the lights. Sit here on the couch with the gun and a flashlight handy. Anybody shows up you don't know, call the law. And you should call as many of the people he threatened as you can reach to warn them. I'll give you the numbers for Wexton and Robertson and Sabo."

"But you don't have a phone."

"I've still got the throwaway in the Jeep. I'll call you before I get out of Dodoma, but there may not be cell service out there in the bush, anyway."

"I don't like this. I *really* don't like this."

"I'll just go have a look. If I don't like what I see, I'll turn around. The Jeep is rugged and quick, and it's got four-wheel-drive. I'll be okay." He thought of a memorable flight in the early years of his training, before he'd earned his instrument rating, when he'd foolishly said much the same thing. The weather report that day had been marginal for visual flight, with a quick-moving storm front angling in. He'd told himself *I'll just go up and have a look. If it's bad I'll turn around.* But after he was airborne the weather had closed in unbelievably fast on him, visibility vanishing completely, until it was like flying through milk, and he'd damned near killed himself before he was able to land. If by pure luck there had not been a hole in the cloud cover precisely when he'd needed one . . .

He said, "I'll leave soon. Get there early. Look over the area. Try to set up to handle whatever this is."

"But what if this man is waiting along the way? With a rifle that has a scope sight. You won't have a chance."

"There'd be no need to go through all this if he wanted to kill me from a distance. I think he wants a confrontation. That will give me some time. And it'll give me some choices."

Forty-five minutes later, at the junction of B-129 and the beginning of Arusha Road, he pulled over onto an uneven graveled patch. Brought the Ithaca pump twelve-gauge shotgun up from the floor in back and loaded it with seven double-ought buckshot shells in the tube magazine. He worked the pump with that ominous *shuck-shuck* sound you always hear in the movies, thus jacking one shell into the chamber, ready to fire. He slid an eighth round into the magazine and clicked the trigger-guard safety on. He propped the gun upright between his seat and the door and stuffed eight more shells into the pockets of his light jacket, four on each side, thinking *if sixteen rounds don't do the job, I'll probably be dead, anyway.* He put the rest of the box of shells into the glove compartment. He wedged a compact LED flashlight into the crack between the cushions on the passenger seat, where he could grab it fast, but until then it would stay put even if the going over the dirt got rough. He'd dressed all in black to cut his visibility as much as possible. The throwaway cell was in his shirt pocket. He'd given Liana the numbers of the other people threatened, had uselessly told her not to worry, and had heard the heavy anxiety in her voice when she'd said, "Just come back to me, please."

He zeroed out the trip odometer, flicked on his high beams, and set out northward on the Arusha Road.

He found out within the first mile that calling it a road was an exaggeration, steering around the worst potholes filled with water from a recent storm. At first there were small homes on each side of the red-dirt track, mostly concrete-block boxes with rusting corrugated steel roofs, trash scattered in many of the dirt yards. A man riding a smoking one-cylinder motorcycle passed him close on the narrow track going the other way, and he came up behind an ancient battered black Toyota pickup and followed it for five minutes before it pulled off into the yard of a house. Otherwise, he had the road to himself. The houses, most of them dark now for the night, thinned out, with increasingly long stretches of empty tangled brush on both sides, until finally there was nothing but bush stretching away into the darkness in every direction. The red dusty track wound on.

When the odometer showed ten miles he slowed down, opened both side windows, and began scanning all around intently. There were no headlights in his rearview mirror, no vehicles had passed him going the other way, and except for some night birds calling, the land was empty of life, eerily still, and full of shadows under a scattering of stars and a fingernail paring of moon above the horizon.

At 12 miles he slowed to a crawl and hunched forward over the steering wheel, listening, scanning. He'd still seen no traffic at all since leaving the outskirts of the city.

Nothing . . .

Nothing . . .

Then, coming around a broad curve he saw the rough narrow turnoff to the left going off into the bush and he stopped. It looked disused, with grass close on both sides and in the middle, only faint traces of wheel tracks remaining. He couldn't tell if any other vehicles had taken it recently. He put the Jeep in first gear and turned onto the track. It meandered aimlessly for a mile, dipping down into old ruts in places, tangled brush scraping the Jeep's sides in other places.

Beyond a low rise there was a broad clearing, and there it was, stark in his headlights.

A dented white pickup. It was parked facing out with its lights off 200 feet away, against a backdrop of a thin stand of trees.

He crept ahead, keeping the pickup nailed in his high beams, and stopped 100 feet away from it. It was aimed directly toward him, but he could not see any faces behind the windshield. It looked empty. There were what looked like the remains of thatched-roof huts around the perimeter of the clearing. A long-abandoned village.

He let the Jeep idle with the headlights on, put the flashlight in his back jeans pocket, took the shotgun, and slipped out the door, leaving it open. He braced the gun on the windowsill, knowing the door did not offer much protection against gunfire, and waited, glancing behind him every few seconds.

Two men came out from behind the pickup. The man in the lead had his hands bound behind his back. It was Hobart Wexton, and he looked badly bruised and utterly cowed, his hair spiked, his face swollen, one eye wide and the other closed down into a purplish slit, his shirt dirty, torn, and stained red in places. The man behind him was holding the tip of an extended machete to the back of Wexton's head. The man with the machete was maybe an inch over six feet, dressed in black jeans, black boots, black T-shirt, and a black ball cap. Lean and fit. His face looked darkly Arabic, and he was smiling. Zeke had never seen him before.

The man forced Wexton to his knees ten feet to the left of the truck, keeping the machete tip against the base of his skull, making him bend over until he was almost looking straight down. Wexton was shaking. Obviously terrified.

A third man stepped out of the trees 50 feet to the right of the truck, holding a semi-automatic in his right hand, aimed at Zeke from the hip. In his left hand he held a flashlight. He aimed it at Zeke and turned it on. It was bright, but not nearly as glaring as the new generation of LED blinders. Its light was yellow and cast in a wide pool. The whole clearing was lit up now.

The man with the flashlight was Raza. Also dressed in black but hatless, his bald head shining like wet coal in the harsh light. Chiseled features smiling. Black eyes glittering.

Zeke kept the shotgun barrel pointing midway between them and risked another scanning glance behind him. No lights in any direction. No other men in sight, either. He took a deep slow breath and adjusted his grip on the shotgun, ready to swing it either way. His index finger hovering over the rigger, not touching it. The night was cool but a trickle of sweat tickled its way down his spine.

His demon was coming alive, breathing fire, emanating a dull red glow at his core.

He said nothing.

Raza said, "Welcome, Mister Blades. The infidel with the hair of a woman. The godless pilot who is responsible for the death of my holy brother. You can see what is happening here. Leave the lights on. Put the long gun back into the vehicle, raise your empty hands, and walk toward me most slowly, or your infidel friend will perhaps feel his head rolling in the dirt the instant before he dies and begins his journey to hell." Raza's smile disappeared, and he said loudly, "*Do as I say, pilot. Do it now.*"

Sixty-one

Hobart Wexton had never been more afraid in his life. His mind was wild with random terrifying thought fragments like fluttering rags swirling in a vortex. There was a shameful warm wetness at his crotch. The garishly lit scene before him was jittery because he could not stop trembling. He was assailed by terrible lingering memories from the past four hours. He remembered the sweaty hand from out of nowhere clamped savagely over his mouth as he was dozing in the recliner in front of his TV. Then there was the brutal beating he could not protect himself from because if he turned his head away from a blow another fist would catch him full in the face. If he raised his hands to protect his head, his ribs and kidneys were punished. If he tried to protect his midsection, they would again attack his face. They had dragged him outside and driven him here, the road so rough that every jolt sent splinters of new bright pain radiating through him. He ached profoundly all over. A gruesome image of his own severed head in the dirt hovered at the back of his mind.

But down deep in his soul there was a faint, insistent spark, and his skittering mind fixed on it. He knew with absolute certainty that both he and Zeke Blades were about to die. Neither of his captors had covered their faces to preserve their identities. Both had treated him as mere garbage. A thing to be abused, used, and then to be disposed of.

When he heard the one called Raza loudly order Zeke to put down his gun and to "*Do it now*," time slowed down for him, a weak resolve from somewhere deep within stole in to displace some of the terror, and the trembling slowed and then stopped as if by magic. It was as though his fear had peaked and broken like a fever and had left an eerie inner calm in its wake. He raised his head to the side enough to see Zeke crouched behind the door of his Jeep. The movement caused the tip of the machete to sting the back of his head again and he felt a fresh rivulet of warm blood run down the side of his face. He shook his head slightly, hoping that Zeke got the message.

Then, summoning a last shred of reserve he'd never known was in him, he toppled to his side in the dirt, turned his head back to look at Faraji, the passing of time weirdly sluggish, drew both his feet back almost to his chest, and drove them with all he had at the surprised evil man's knee, hearing the wet crack as the joint gave the wrong way, making Faraji scream and totter on his remaining working leg.

Through his good eye, Wexton saw fury bloom in Faraji's eyes. Saw him steady himself on his one good leg and lift the machete high, still screaming in a shrill inhuman wail . . .

Wexton closed his eyes and cringed, waiting for the final blow.

Zeke had seen Wexton look at him and give a slight shake of his head. Saw him suddenly collapse onto his side and drive both feet at machete man's knee with surprising speed and force. Zeke heard the break clearly. Saw the man totter and raise his machete high, screaming out his rage.

Then everything happened in a rapid unstoppable sequence. Zeke swung the shotgun left and fired. The buckshot, not dispersing much at the relatively short distance, caught Machete Man full in the chest and blew him back and down hard in a misting of blood, the machete flying free. Given the impetus of the vicious back swing, the blade arced, glinting in the light, to stab down into the dirt upright a dozen feet from Wexton.

A stunned Raza extended the semi-automatic at Zeke and fired. Zeke racked the pump but did not have enough time to swing the shotgun muzzle to the right. Raza's slug caught the shotgun on the side of the receiver and went whining off into the night. The second shot from Raza spanged off the Jeep's hood and holed the windshield as Zeke pulled the trigger, but the gun would not fire, so he dropped it, lunged inside the Jeep, and slammed it into gear, the transmission grinding loudly without the clutch, but the gearing worked. He ducked back out and took cover behind the Jeep as it idled forward.

Raza fired two more shots at the Jeep. Zeke heard the impacts.

Wexton had opened his good eye and, unbelievably, saw Farai down in the shadows, bloody and still, and he felt an exultant flush of triumph. Breathing rapidly, he twisted his head so he could see what was happening. Raza had his flashlight aimed at Zeke and was firing his handgun, but for some reason Zeke would not or could not fire back, although he could see Zeke still moving in a crouch behind the Jeep as it advanced on its own very slowly into the clearing.

Wexton swallowed, his throat dry as sandpaper, his mind alive with a crazed wild anger, and croaked out, "Raza, you . . . goddamned *coward.* You . . . *fucking* elephant killer. I'll tell . . . tell the whole world what an evil, no-good *bastard* you are. You *hear* me? Your fucking jihadi brother is . . . *dead.* *Good riddance.* Your vicious pal here is dead now, too, what . . . you think about *that*? You're *alone* now, you . . ." But his throat was raw, and he couldn't force intelligible words past his bruised lips anymore. He rested his head on the powdery red dirt and concentrated on just breathing.

It was all the distraction Zeke needed. Raza had seen him drop the shotgun and must have figured it was not working. The croaky rant coming out of Wexton had refocused Raza's insane rage, and he stalked across in front of the slow-moving Jeep and advanced on Wexton as the rant went on, pointing the gun down at the irritating infidel.

The Jeep was creeping closer.

Zeke darted out from behind the Jeep low, a fleeting shadow, his feet driving into the dirt, throwing up sprays of it behind him, feeling the flood of adrenaline, the old familiar white heat glowing deep inside, the world narrowed down to a razor sharpness, and he *flew* at Raza, hitting him hard in the midsection with his shoulder, driving the breath out of him, the gun and Raza's flashlight both spinning away, his arms flailing.

Zeke stopped his forward drive and recovered his footing. He got the LED light from his back pocket and lit up Raza, who was squirming on the ground grimacing and gasping.

Zeke took three agile steps back on the balls of his feet and waited. The demon never more watchful and aroused. Tensed and ready.

The LED light, set to wide angle, was rock-steady in his hand. His breathing was controlled. His body coiled.

Gradually Raza got his breath and senses back. It took ten seconds. He glared up into the light, then rose to his feet. He shook himself, shrugging his shoulders. Then his right hand went to the back of his neck as though to rub it and came out with a knife, which he held low, blade up.

While Raza was doing this, Zeke lifted the LED light over his head, shining it down onto himself and Raza, so they both could see each other, on some crazy subconscious level making it a reasonably fair contest, as though it was only another karate match, and Raza now made a raking lunge at Zeke's midsection, but Zeke was ready for it. He danced back and drew in his stomach and bent away from the blade, the sweeping tip missing him by only inches. The demon had never been more alive in him, honing his reflexes to a degree he'd never known, focusing all the frustration and anger of the past months. He had a vivid image of Ben taking that sniper bullet.

The most powerful and dangerous blows a martial arts fighter can deliver are not with the hands or the elbows or a head butt, but with the feet. They are unmatched for velocity and sheer kinetic impact energy. Before Raza had completed the lunge, Zeke unleashed a lightning *kinteki-geri* with his booted left foot—a brutal kick to the groin. It was a move he'd practiced a thousand times in various katas and he delivered it precisely with maximum force, holding nothing back, his bright demon in a cold clear rage, acting swiftly on the pure adrenaline rush. It was a crushing blow. When Raza doubled over from the bolt of incredibly intense pain, Zeke let go with a full-out *mawashi-geri*, or round-house kick with the top of his booted right foot, catching Raza in the face, smashing bone, whipping the head up and back and snapping the neck with the sound of a brittle branch fracturing.

The man was dead before he thudded to the ground like a loose sack of sand.

Zeke made sure Raza was gone and then knelt by Hobart and cut his hands free with his pocket knife, the demon within him slowly fading back into its cave and his breathing slowing.

Wexton managed to stand with some help, rubbing his wrists to get the circulation back into his paled hands. Zeke walked him over to the Jeep, which had butted slowly up against a tree and stalled, one headlight shining.

Zeke got him into the passenger seat and gave him a bottle of water, which he guzzled, moaning with the pleasure of it.

"Just sit here for a few minutes," Zeke said. "I have to clean up the area."

He dragged both bodies back in among the trees and brush, emptied the pistol and threw it, the magazine, the cartridges, and the machete out of the clearing. He knew the scavengers would soon be visiting, which would help blur the evidence. Raza was well known to the law, so he figured the investigation of the deaths would not be too scrupulous, anyway. He found the keys to the white pickup in Machete Man's jeans, handling them only with his handkerchief, and left them in the ignition. With any luck, the pickup would quickly be stolen.

He picked up the damaged shotgun and the spent shell casing and put them in the back of the Jeep. He used his boots to scuff out most of the marks and tracks in the dirt and to cover the spilled blood, played the light over the area one last time, and hoped the Jeep would start and run enough to get them back to Dodoma.

He used the flashlight to inspect the worst of Wexton's wounds.

He said, "You may have a cracked rib or two, but I don't see anything else that some first aid and a few stitches at the Dodoma Clinic and some rest won't fix. If they ask, you can tell them you got mugged. It'll be a while before you'll be presentable to go on the air, though, so I hope you have some vacation coming."

The shallow back-of-the-neck machete cuts were still bleeding, so Zeke got disinfectant powder, a gauze pad, and adhesive tape out of the Jeep's small first aid kit and bandaged them.

The starter ground the engine over several times, sounding weaker and weaker. But then it caught, sputtered as though it would die any second, and finally evened out into a steady beat. He took a breath and drove back out to the Arusha road and headed south on only the one headlight, a humid breeze coming in through the holed windshield, taking it slow in the rough places to ease the ride for his passenger.

Wexton, adjusting his position in the seat with caution because of his injuries, shook his head slowly, and said, "Good god, we're alive. You were . . . amazing. Thank you."

"What are you talking about? You saved us twice. Once by taking out Machete Man's knee and then by distracting Raza. You were really something. We did it together, Hobart."

Wexton snorted and smiled as best he could. "We did, didn't we." And he carefully sat up a little straighter. "Machete Man's name was Faraji, by the way. The same one who attacked me outside the TV Three station. I could tell by his voice. An al-Isra thug. I gathered from their talk that he worked for Abdul Ahad, Raza's brother."

Zeke nodded. "You realize we can't tell anybody what went down back there, right?"

Wexton looked at him out of his good eye and said, "I know. Too bad though. Would have made a hell of a story."

Sixty-two

They were meeting again at her place. Liana, DJ, Sabo, and Zeke.

Zeke had given them a highly condensed and sanitized version of what had happened three nights ago on the Arusha Road. None of them had any questions. DJ had been helping Zeke secretly repair the Jeep, parked behind a shielding tarp hung in the opening of one of the unused T-hangars near Zeke's camper, which now had a heavy lock on the door and reinforced hinges. All the windows had screwed-on heavy wire mesh.

"So, what now?" Liana said.

Sabo took a pull on his Kibo Gold beer, eyed the cookies Liana had set out, wiped his face with one paw, and said, "Even with China supposedly out of the ivory market, there's still a big demand for it across Asia, so the bad boys are still at it. There was another kill yesterday outside Kipembawe, down south near Lake Rukwa. Thirteen shot down with AKs. I say we rebuild the Mambas and go after the bastards."

DJ raised his beer and said, "Hey, you guys know I'm in for the long haul."

Liana and Zeke raised their glasses, both half filled with wine. She smiled and said, "Whatever I can do will have to be during my time off from GHR, but yes. The legend of the Mambas is still alive out there in the bush, I'm sure. It would be a shame to let it die."

Zeke said, "We have those six names of major poachers that Salvious Philemon gave us, so we've got a good place to start. And now that we've got our own air force we'll strike fear into their hearts."

Sabo raised his beer and said, "Okay, then. Here's to saving the tembo. We're probably crazy."

And they all took a drink. Sabo pocketed two cookies.

That night Liana and Zeke lay naked side by side holding hands in her bed, blue moonlight filtering in through the window curtains. The window was open to a gentle night breeze. A cluster of three candles fluttered on the side table. A disc by the late Miriam Makeba was playing on the stereo. Long known as Mama Africa, Makeba was singing her biggest hit, the sensual "Pata Pata," about dancing to primitive South African rhythms all night long. Then she sang the deeply moving "Malaika." It was the last track on the disc.

In the ensuing silence, Liana said, "That's just so utterly beautiful. The emotion and complexity of her music. Like Africa itself."

Zeke nodded, watching the play of candlelight on the shadowed ceiling. "What does *nakupenda malaika* mean?"

"It means I love you, my angel. It's a Tanzanian song. They perform it at many weddings."

"Ah." He was quiet for a moment. "Well, *nakupenda*, Miz Liana Sekibo." He squeezed her hand and she felt the sinewy strength in him.

She turned her head toward him and studied his hawkish profile. She smiled and said, "*Nakupenda*, Mister Waya Ezekiel Blades."

Sixty-three

On a flank of an unnamed peak in the Mountains of the Moon, in a wooded glade, seven men were seated with their legs crossed on the floor of a ragged tent, gathered in a loose half-circle around Dawud. The other survivors of the battle against the infidels were encamped outside the tent.

Dawud said, "I have received word from a contact that Muhammadu Raza has been found dead north of Dodoma. Killed. It is not yet known who has done this deed, but we will find out and those responsible will be punished most severely. But there is something of even more importance. Al-Isra must not be allowed to die. It would be a betrayal of Abdul Ahad and of Muhammadu Raza. It would be a betrayal of great Allah Himself. We must rise from the ashes and emerge stronger than before. We still have some of the weapons that our leader bought from the Yemenis. He wisely hid them in reserve some distance from our last encampment. Rifles and pistols, ammunition, rocket-propelled grenades, and even the fearsome destroyer the Americans call the Counter Defilade Target Engagement System. We will recruit and train until this time we are truly ready for the holy struggle to come. You men are the ones Allah has chosen to stand with me as leaders. I need to know you will be loyal unto the death." He looked around the small group and each man nodded in turn.

"So it will be then," Dawud said. "There is but one God and He is Allah. Allahu Akbar."

"The men raised their fists and shouted back in unison, "*Allahu Akbar.*"

Sixty-four

Guang Fong had made his billions in worldwide container shipping. His company, Fong Lines, was based in the bustling port of T'aipei on the island of Taiwan. His offices were only a half-hour limousine ride from his main residence, which was a quiet, elaborately landscaped ten-acre estate outside the frenetic overcrowded city, where he could relax with his family away from the daily rigors of business. At 74, though his thick shock of hair had gone silvery gray, he was still lean and fit, his brown eyes no less alert and calculating than when he'd cleverly, some might say ruthlessly, built up the small coastal freighter business—begun by his grandfather and expanded by his father—into a thriving global shipping empire over the decades.

He and his wife of 40 years had three daughters. Their youngest offspring and only son was Ju-long. They had been blessed with him late in their lives and Guang knew as a result they had indulged the boy more than they should have. Guang Fong was proud of him, nevertheless.

Ju-long had received passing grades through the finest private schools, though the teachers had often complained politely of certain disturbing disciplinary issues. With the help of private tutors, Ju-long had recently made it through Yale University in the States, although there had been several embarrassing episodes associated with alcohol, vehicle accidents, and a fraternity. There had also been an inconvenient pregnancy that had been somewhat troublesome and costly to resolve. Guang had simply considered these incidents mere youthful indiscretions, indications of a healthy spirit, of a strong will that would only help his son succeed over the years as he would steer the business empire into a bright future. At least this was Guang's fervent hope.

Today Ju-long had become 21. The day had been filled with celebration and laughter. The 200 invited guests, many of them influential in business and political spheres, had enjoyed a sumptuous meal presided over by Guang's private chefs. Waiters dressed in impeccable red-and-white uniforms had circulated to make sure every person was well supplied with beverages and gourmet finger food. An orchestra under a large decorated tent had provided traditional and contemporary music throughout the afternoon and evening. Two long tables had been burdened with a lavish variety of fine gifts. After dark there had been spectacular fireworks.

The guests had finally departed and the walled estate was once again serene, the plantings and walkways softly lighted. Guang and Ju-long were standing alone in Guang's leathery study, enjoying a last glass of wine.

Guang put his arm around the young man's shoulders and said, "Come, my son, I wish to show you something."

Guang led him down a hallway to a secure room at the heart of the mansion. The room was a hushed sanctum, temperature and humidity controlled, lushly carpeted, indirectly and pleasantly lighted, designed as a private museum. It showcased his extensive collection of ivory, which had also begun with his grandfather. There were carved Buddhas, Chinese maiden and mandarin statuettes, and carved depictions of the eight Chinese Immortals in various poses drawn from ancient legend. There were horses and swans and elephants and other animals, all rendered in astonishing lifelike perfection. There were intricate nested spheres and meticulous whole Asian villages and delicate lacy gardens. Several of the creations were hundreds of years old. The larger works were housed in their own niches, each with custom lighting that subtly enhanced their features, creating highlights and shadows on the silken convoluted surfaces.

Ju-long had occasionally visited the room before with his father, but something was different tonight.

In the center of the large room there was a simple oiled bamboo table under muted spotlights. Resting on it were two carved tusks unlike any he'd seen.

"Twin dragon boats," Ju-long said. "Nice."

"Look more closely," Guang said.

Something was different about the boats. Then he saw it. "Huh. They're mirror images."

Guang smiled. "Done recently in secret to my specifications by old Wu Lee himself. I believe he is the finest carver alive. They are flawless. Do you remember the story?"

Ju-long nodded. "Some poet named Yuan, I think. Lived in the Chu State a couple thousand years ago. The time of the Warring States. When Chu was invaded, he drowned himself in some river in Huan on the fifth day of the fifth month. People paddled out onto the river to chase away evil spirits or something. It was the origin of the Dragon Boat Festival. One of the stories you told me as a boy." *This pair must have cost a small fortune*, he thought. *Easily a quarter million USD. Probably more. Maybe even a lot more.*

"Yes," Guang said. "Your name, of course, means powerful dragon. Tomorrow you will begin your work at Fong Lines. You will help me build the company into a true dragon among lesser companies. I have just this month commissioned the construction of the largest container ship in our fleet. She will be the *New Dawn*, first of two that will take full advantage of the Panama Canal expansion. In five years' time, she will be followed by her identical sister ship, *Dawn Light*. Just as these superb carvings will sail the sea of imagination far into the future, so our twin ships will sail the world's seas to bring Fong Lines unprecedented riches and power. You will eventually preside over the company, and I know you will protect and enhance what our family has built. One day you will pass it all down to a fine son of your own."

"So, I guess in a way these dragon boats are a symbol of Fong Lines, maybe even of you and me, is that it?" Ju-long said.

"Exactly. I am most pleased you like them," Guang said. "They are yours to do with as you wish. My gift to you this day."

Ju-long was severely disappointed, but he did not let it show. He had waged a months-long campaign of clever hints intended to suggest the birthday gift of a new Maserati Gran Turismo convertible as a replacement for his two-year-old Corvette. He thought his subtle persuasions had got through his father's fiscal armor. Despite what his father had just said, if he were to sell these carvings so he could buy the Maserati, he would incur the old man's immediate wrath and likely his profound and lasting disapproval.

Though on some level he did appreciate the artistic skill that had been invested in his father's obsessive collection, Ju-long himself had no love of ivory, and he privately regarded Guang's treasured items as nothing more than elaborate and highly expensive decorations. A waste of money.

He knew, however, there were many collectors throughout Asia who did avidly covet carved ivory for deeply embedded traditional and religious reasons, and he knew that, after his father had passed on, the collection could be discreetly converted into tax-free millions on the black market. So he would be patient. As it became ever rarer, the ivory would only grow in value, after all.

Ju-long smiled at the dragon boats, summoned up as much sincerity as he could, and said, "I believe they should rest safely right where they are for now, so both you and I can admire them whenever we wish. They are exquisite. I am honored, father. Thank you." ∎

Author's Note

This novel evolved from my anger at the ongoing African poaching that has brutally cut into the once-great herds across that vast and troubled continent. Much of the fictional narration herein is based on facts drawn from printed and online sources, and from documentaries that included the tragic true story of Tyke, the rebellious circus elephant. Satao was also a real elephant. Some said he was the largest on Earth, and he survived on his wits for 50 years. Poachers killed him on 30 May 2014 and hacked out his exceptional tusks. I wanted to give him a place in the story and thought it fitting that he serve to help set a trap for Muhammadu Raza. I've fictionalized the 2015 arrest in Tanzania of Yang Feng Glan, an ivory-trafficking Chinese gang leader dubbed the Queen of Ivory. In April 2019, after several mysterious delays, a Tanzanian court sentenced her to 15 years for smuggling 860 tusks.

In 2015 the Pentagon did lose track of $500 million in weapons, aircraft, and military equipment in Yemen, and nobody knows how much of that stockpile might have been channeled to jihadis. The media treated it as merely another routine news item. I thought the actual account of this incredible blunder was too much to be believed, so I scaled it back to $300 million in weaponry for this story. Al-Isra is a fictional organization but the other Islamic militant groups mentioned are real and ruthless and they do use funds from poaching to support their terrorism.

Since 2009, poachers have killed 595 African rangers, and in recent years two pilots have died trying to help stop the trade. American Bill Fitzpatrick flew a

Cessna 172 for the Odzala-Kokoua National Park in the Republic of Congo on anti-poaching missions. He went missing during a flight out of Nigeria in June 2014 over the cloud wrapped Bakossi Mountains in Cameroon. Ten months later his remains were found still seated in his crashed Cessna in those rugged wilds. He was 59 and left behind a wife and three children. In January 2016, British pilot Roger Gower was flying a helicopter mission to help track poachers in northern Tanzania when the gang shot him down. He managed to land the crippled chopper but died of his wounds before he could be rescued.

This story is in part dedicated to the memory of those pilots and to all the other brave souls for their anti-poaching efforts and sacrifices.

After I finished the tale, I discovered there actually is an organization called the Black Mambas, a group of three dozen African women who patrol South Africa's Limpopo Province in their neat camouflage uniforms, unarmed, by Jeep and by foot. When they discover poachers or evidence of their activities, they call in trained special forces to chase and seize the criminals. Their efforts are credited with reducing poaching crimes in the areas they patrol by as much as 76 percent, saving hundreds of elephants and rhinos. I decided against changing the name of my anti-poaching vigilantes and to keep the fictional Mambas in the story as a tribute to the courageous real-life version.

I've taken limited license with other aspects of the narrative for the sake of the story. Any mistakes are mine alone.

The poaching of big animals goes on in Africa and other continents, driving several species—elephants, rhinos, gorillas, the big cats—ever closer to extinction. Widespread poaching is but one of the more vicious and obvious pressures on wildlife. According to the

World Wildlife Fund, for numerous preventable reasons global populations of a wide variety of land and sea creatures have fallen overall by 52 percent since 1970. The decline continues. This alarming loss of wildlife is a real and tragic story that should concern us all.

If you care about the plights of the many threatened species that are attempting to exist with us on this fragile planet—which is as much their only home in the vastness of the Universe as it is ours—please donate whatever you can to one of the agencies fighting to stop the decline. A portion of the proceeds from this book will be so donated.

Phil Bowie
New Bern, North Carolina

Check out the four acclaimed novels in Phil's suspense series. Visit him at *www.philbowie.com*

Made in the USA
Middletown, DE
16 November 2019